The Turbulent *Tide*

The TURBULENT Tide

A Historical Novel of the Russian Revolution

Ruth Wildes Schuler

Library of Congress Control Number:		2010914446
ISBN:	Hardcover	978-1-4535-8763-8
	Softcover	978-1-4535-8762-1
	Ebook	978-1-4535-8764-5

This book was printed in the United States of America.

To order additional copies of this book, contact:
Xlibris Corporation
1-888-795-4274
www.Xlibris.com
Orders@Xlibris.com
87129

To

my husband, Charles Albert Schuler,

and in memory of

my father, Wilbur Leighton Wildes
(who taught me his love for history),

and

my mother, Mary Eddie Bryant Wildes

ACKNOWLEDGEMENTS

I would like to thank the following for their proofreading and encouragement.

My husband, Charles Albert Schuler;

my son, Steven Charles Schuler, and his wife, Kathleen;

my daughter, Jeanne Leigh Schuler Farrell;

Eric J. Voorsanger;

my copy editor, Mary Jane Essex;

and in memory, my thanks to my Russian friend Alex Kluskin,

a soldier that guarded the royal children before their execution,

for the rare Russian books that he loaned me.

CAST OF CHARACTERS

Katrina Kazakinova (Katie)----------	Niece of Ivan Kozakov
Ivan Kozakov------------------------	Count of Usadiba Na Holme Retired Army Officer
Mathilde Kozakov--------------------	Second Wife of Ivan Kozakov
Aleksander Ivanovich Kozakov (Alex)—	Son of Ivan Kozakov
Sonya Kozakov ----------------------	Daughter of Ivan Kozakov
Nikolai Sokoloy (Nicki)-------------	Friend of the Kozakov Family
Provovich --------------------------	Driver for Usadiba Na Holme
Peter Sovinsky----------------------	Peasant Farmer on Ivan Kozakov's land
Maria Sovinsky----------------------	Sister of Peter Sovinsky
Old Man Sovinsky -------------------	Peter and Maria's Father
Dmitri Gogol------------------------	Neighbor of the Sovinskys
Cecilia Gogol-----------------------	Daughter of Dmitri Gogol
Tanya Yarmolinskaya-----------------	Niece of Ivan Kozakov's First Wife
Leon Ibragimov ---------------------	School Friend of Aleksander
Janusy Gorecki ---------------------	Polish Jew
Marian Gorecki ---------------------	Janusy Gorecki's sister
Countess Alexis --------------------	Neighbor of Ivan Kozakov
Pavel Tzankvsky---------------------	Army Comrade of Nikolai
Boris-------------------------------	Monk
Yurievich (Yuri)--------------------	Monk
Vladimir----------------------------	Menshevik leader, a former professor
Steni ------------------------------	Old Man in South Eastern Siberia

PART 1

History offers no man an explanation for its unpredictable flow. Its languorous trickling ebb can, at any time, surge forth violently into a tremendous tide that sweeps everything in its path chaotically toward the falls and then nonchalantly resume its even flow without ever noting the smashed and shattered wreckage left behind.

RESTLESSNESS

Though a darkening mist enshrouds us,
Ever onward do we come,
Seeking, searching, ever watching
For we know not what or from.

Where does history try to lead us?
From what perilous trail behind?
Is it merely fate that guides us?
Then what would it have us find?

What is this eternal stirring,
With which we have been blest?
Help us. Grant us mercy.
Give us eternal rest.

CHAPTER 1

1905

The coffins of eight-year-old Katrina Kazakinova's parents stood side by side in the parlor for three days while she watched, frightened and white-faced, from the hall. Flickering candles cast shadowy shades of light upon the parade of her mother's and father's friends who flocked to the house to look inside the plain wooden boxes. Some of them stood stoic and pale, some who were mere strangers to Katie silently made the sign of the cross, while others cried and stumbled from the room with tear-filled eyes to pat her on the head, mumbling, "Poor little Katie."

The funeral took place on a stormy day, with a long procession of mourners winding through the mud under the fierce downpour. A woman in black standing behind Katie beneath an umbrella complained loudly, "It always rains for funerals."

At the last moment, someone had requested a graveside service, but it was too late to put up a canopy, so all the mourners stood fighting against a wind that tried to blow their umbrellas away. A young assistant held an umbrella over the Russian Orthodox priest while he chanted the service, but the censer that the youth held was extinguished by the storm.

When the priest's prayers were finished, Katie's mother and father were lowered into their graves. The gale picked up in intensity. The priest stepped forward and grasped a handful of mud and threw it upon the double coffins side by side in the earth. The other chilled and soaked mourners each picked up a handful of soil. The first few dropped the earth gently on top of the coffins, but as the tempest grew in fury, the remaining grievers hastily slung the mud into the grave and hurried to escape the elements. Others followed one by one. It was only when the rest of the crowd had departed that Katie stood at the edge of the burial pit and wailed her grief into the roaring wind until at last, Nana took her hand and led her away.

After the funeral, circumstances began to change. Creditors stepped forward to confiscate the furniture and the paintings from the wall. Food grew scarcer. The servants left one by one until at last, only old Nana remained. A perpetual sadness haunted Nana's face, and Katie often heard her crying in the night. Katie also cried herself to sleep; she felt lonely, angry, and confused at the collapse of her world. Then late one night, Nana shook her until she was awake and commanded, "Come quickly with me, child."

Katie jumped out of her bed and followed her nurse down the long flight of stairs, through the narrow hall, and into the study. There she came face-to-face with a fearsome man who seemed to reach almost to the ceiling. Beneath his broad nose hung a thick black beard that appeared to fly about wildly in every direction. His gigantic shoulders and menacing scowl made him even more forbidding. He stared silently at Katie for several moments and then in a loud voice pronounced, "She's rather puny!"

The three words shattered the silence of the book-lined room. "Puny and pale as a pallbearer," he reiterated. "How old are you, girl?" he demanded.

"Eight," Katie replied tersely.

"Mmm," he muttered as he studied her thoughtfully. It seemed an eternity to Katie before he spoke again. Finally he boomed, shaking his head as if to affirm his decision, "I'll take her! Now back to bed with you, child," he roared.

Katie flew back upstairs to her bed but woke several times from nightmares in which the gigantic bearded man carried her off into the dark unknown.

The morning after the stranger's visit, Katie sought out her nurse. "Who was that terrible man?" she asked with great apprehension.

"Ivan Kozakov," Nana explained. "He's your mother's brother."

"Why didn't he ever come to see us before?" she questioned.

"Because he didn't approve of your mother marrying your father, who was only a university professor without much money. Your uncle considered that your mother married beneath her class, so he disowned her. But now that they are both gone, he has agreed to take you to live with him."

"I won't go," Katie declared, shaking her head. "He frightens me, and if he didn't like my papa, then I know that I won't like him."

"I wish that you had a choice," the old nurse told her, "but alas, Katie, he is your only living relative. Your mama and papa, being such kind souls, gave away most everything they ever owned. All the unfortunates found your parents' hearts open, and their hands held out to help, and now we are destitute." She sighed and shrugged her bent shoulders. "As for your Uncle Ivan not liking your father, it was due to the one's will being as strong as the other. Your uncle is not one to stand for anyone to cross him. There lay the problem. But your mother loved him deeply, Katie, and she would want you to do the same." "I'll try then, Nana," she promised. "So long as you're with me, I'll be all right."

"Ah, little one," Nana moaned. "That is not to be. Your uncle is kindly giving me a pension, and I am going to live with my sister in the provinces."

"No!" Katie wailed. "Oh, Nana, no!"

"I'm getting old, my pet," she said with tears creeping into her eyes. "My sister is ill and needs my care now."

"He won't let you come," Katie stated knowingly. "That's why you're going away!"

"I have cared for you since the cradle, Katrina Kazakinova," Nana reproved her softly. "You are a big girl now, and you must learn to make the best of things. It will not be so bad. There are two cousins whom you have never met, and you will be raised with them. It will be nice for you to have companions of your own age."

"It will not be the same, Nana, and you know it!"

"Think of what your mama and papa would have wanted, dearest Katie," the old woman said as she reached her gnarled hand inside her dress and pulled out a tiny metal cross on a long thin chain. "This was put around my neck on the day that I was baptized, Katie. I have never taken it off all these years, but I want you to have it now." With that, she unfastened the catch and hung it around Katie's neck. "Wear it and remember me! If you have troubles, pray. God will listen."

On the train ride to her uncle's estate, Usadiba Na Holme, Katie's thoughts kept returning to the events of the recent past. She remembered the last time that she had seen her parents. The night had started out no differently than any other. Her parents were merely going to the opera. She had watched her beautiful mother dress, smelled her perfume, and then her father had come into the room, saying, "I really question the wisdom of going out tonight, darling," he said. "There have been riots in the streets, and many people have been injured. I do not feel it is safe. The rabble is so unpredictable these days that I fear venturing out."

"But I have so been looking forward to seeing this opera for such a long time," her mother had pleaded. "I just cannot bear to miss it. We can keep to the main streets," she reasoned.

"Very well," he said with a sigh, and he came and picked Katie up and tossed her in the air. "See, Katie, I can't deny my beautiful girls anything."

Her mother had scolded him for exciting her so at bedtime, but then they had all laughed. She had kissed them good-bye and then watched them from the window as they had climbed into their carriage. The driver shouted to the horses, cracked his whip in the air, and then they were gone.

"Gone!" Katie sobbed as the Russian landscape flew past her eyes.

"Murdered!" Nana had told her. "Killed by bloody revolutionists."

"What are re-revol-revolutionists?" Katie had asked her.

"Evil black hearts, child!" Nana replied with anguish. "They go around blowing up innocent people like your mama and papa who never hurt anyone. They bring disaster upon the whole world."

Katie could form no picture of these revolutionists who had killed her mother and father; therefore, she felt helpless to understand why her parents were dead.

Now everybody and everything was gone, and she was traveling toward that terrible, fierce man whom she had seen but once.

Provovich, the coachman for Usadiba Na Holme, met her at the station. He had a full head of carrot-colored hair and a serious face filled with hundreds of overlapping freckles. A sleeveless black velvet coat hugged his frail form from the shoulders to the waist, where it then fell in numerous folds like a skirt. Under the coat, he wore a bright green silk shirt, and upon his head was a small round black felt cap with a yellow peacock feather that stood up in the air.

The coachman helped Katie into the open carriage, and as they rolled over the dusty rut-filled roads, she plied him with questions. "What is my Uncle Ivan like?"

"Little miss, I can tell you for sure that Ivan Kozakov is a man used to having his own way."

"What is my aunt Mathilde like?"

"Your uncle does not fancy her as much as he did his first wife. His first wife was a beautiful noble lady. They had a son, but when your uncle was away on army duty, a cholera epidemic struck and took both his wife and his nine-month-old babe. There was no living with him then."

"That was really terrible, Provovich," she exclaimed. "Is that what made him so cross?"

Provovich chuckled. "Ah, he was in a state until he finished his army days, it's true. After a time though, he pulled himself together and took an interest in his estates again. Then he wanted another heir. But to have a son, one must first have a wife.

"Is that when he married my aunt?"

"Aye, but he was no longer a young man, so his prospects were somewhat limited. Countess Mathilde is tall and thin with pale skin and hair like straw. Your uncle told me that she turned out to be a nag, so he has never been too pleased with her."

"That's too bad," Katie commented. "And what are my cousins like?"

"That's not for me to say really, missy. Your cousin Aleksander Ivanovich was born the first year of their marriage, and then two years later, your cousin Sonya came along. Aleksander looks like your aunt—tall, thin, same strawlike hair, and chalky complexion. Miss Sonya is pale too, but she has black hair like your uncle. She's pretty enough."

Katie grew tired of talking and turned to observe the passing landscape. The land was flat, and only small thatched-roofed cottages and cultivated fields intruded upon the vast stretches of Russian earth that lay cracked and broken from years of contrasting extremes in temperature. She saw an old man dozing in the sun, an old woman struggling with a wiggling infant, but apart from that, it was only in the fields that life moved. There, men, women, and children worked side by side under a scorching sun.

"It's not much farther, little miss," Provovich comforted. Katie felt dirty, hungry, and tired. She closed her eyes, and the rocking movement of the open coach soon lulled her to sleep.

It was only when the movement of the coach ceased that Katie opened her eyes again. There she saw, on top of a steep hill, Usadiba Na Holme. It was tremendous in size, with a long flat roof that rose to a peak in the center. Six white columns dominated the front, and a flight of marble steps led up to a vast porch. On each side of the stairs stood large vases with junglelike plants growing out of them and spreading in several different directions. The entire hillside was one massive lawn, broken only by clusters of flowers, attractively grouped at symmetrical intervals. It was breathtaking, and Katie felt her spirits lift for the first time since her parents had been killed.

After having been shown her room, Katie descended the stairs and heard her uncle arguing with someone in the library.

"How dare you bring that child here without even consulting me," a woman shouted.

"This house is mine, woman, in case you have forgotten," Ivan raged.

"I won't have her, do you hear me?" Mathilde screamed, and Katie could hear her stamping her foot in uncontrolled anger. "She's been raised among common city riffraff. Her father was nothing but a teacher. She'll be a bad influence on our Alex and Sonya."

"Any influence that she might have on our children is bound to be for the better," Ivan sneered. "Unfortunately, you have spoiled them and molded them into capricious and self-centered monsters."

"Beast," she screamed, "you have never loved our children."

"That is because they are too much like you!" Ivan scoffed. "Our son is a whining wimp, and our daughter is a vain strutting peahen. I can tell you that it was with considerable apprehension that I went to view my sister's child, but I was both surprised and pleased with what I found. Katrina has the Kozakov spirit. You will not crush this child!"

"I won't have her in this house!" Mathilde reiterated.

"Then pack up and leave yourself," Ivan returned. "This golden-haired girl has raised long-buried hopes. She is my flesh and blood."

"And what are your own children, Ivan Kozakov?"

"I already told you my displeasure with them," he jeered.

"I hate you," Mathilde raved.

"There is no love lost between us," Ivan threw back at her. "She will stay," he announced firmly, "and that is the end of it!" He strode across the floor, and Katie heard Mathilde rush to bar his exit, but he opened the door and shoved her aside roughly.

As he left the room, her high-pitched voice screamed after him. "She is not welcome in this house! She cannot stay! Do you hear me, Ivan?"

Katrina crouched on the stairway, not daring to move. Her aunt's shrill voice rang in her ears as her uncle stalked out of the library, slamming the door behind him. Trembling, she crept down the long flight of stairs and slipped quietly out through the front door. She raced down the green hillside past the flowers, across the fields, and into the nearby woods. Branches tore at her dress, but panting painfully, she fled until her legs could carry her no further. Only then did she throw herself down on the earth in utter exhaustion.

She found herself in a small clearing where thick branches of tall trees blocked out the brilliance of the sun overhead. Close beside her stood a small low-forked tree with a nest of eggs in one of its boughs. A tiny bird perching on one of the limbs gave an indignant screech and flapped away. Unable to control her despair any longer, the tears came, and she buried her face in the damp green moss beneath her.

Everything was gone. Her home. Her world. Everyone was gone. Mama! Papa! Nana! She clutched the cross around her neck, but Nana was so far away. Her chest hurt so badly that she could barely breathe. She cried until her lungs felt as though they were bursting, and then finally, with her emotion spent, she found that she could cry no longer.

The smell of the earth intermingled with pine needles, and the moss felt cold against her wet cheeks. Shaking her head as if to shed her misery, she sat up and angrily dabbed at her eyes with the hem of her now dirty and torn dress.

It was then that she saw him—a solemn dark-haired boy staring at her from the edge of the clearing. He was about twelve years old, with a serious face and a lock of coal black hair hanging down upon his puzzled brow. He approached her uncertainly and then unexpectedly thrust a bouquet of wild flowers into her hands. She looked at him in surprise then hesitantly raised the flowers to her nose and inhaled their fragrance. She smiled, and the boy's tense look disappeared. He sat down on the ground beside her.

"My name's Peter," he said. "Peter Sovinsky." Then as if he were feeling awkward, the boy dug into his pocket and pulled out his handkerchief. "Maybe you'd better wipe your face," he suggested. She took the offered handkerchief and rubbed her eyes and cheeks roughly. When she had finished, he opened the basket that he had been carrying and took out some wild strawberries. He laid some in her lap, and she ate them so quickly that he smiled and gave her more.

"What's your name?" he asked.

"Katrina," she said. "But nearly everyone calls me Katie."

"Katie," he repeated. "That's a nice name."

"My mother got it from an English book that she read once," Katie explained. "The girl in the book was named Kathleen, but they called her Katie for short. My mother decided she would call me that for a nickname."

She smiled, and a glow of warmth crept through her. The bird returned to his skinny tree and gave another screech. She laughed, picked up the flowers again, and buried her nose in the bouquet.

The boy continued to stare at her with fascination.

"I'm glad that you found me, Peter," she said. "Do you come here often?"

"No, but I will now."

Her cheeks flushed with pleasure. "I'll look for you then," she said. Shyly, she reached out and grasped his darkly tanned hand in her own, and though he blushed, he made no effort to remove it. They sat there for a while in the peaceful stillness of the surrounding forest, and once again, life felt tolerable to Katie.

"I have a sister your age, Katie," Peter confided. "Her name is Maria. The next time that I come here, I'll bring her."

"I'd like that," she told him.

The children talked quietly through the afternoon until the shadows lengthened. At last, Peter said, "I have to go now."

"So soon?" she cried.

"I'm afraid so, but I'll come again."

"Tomorrow?"

"No, not so soon," he said, shaking his head. "Most days, my father can't spare me from the fields."

"Then how will I know when you are here?" She thought for a moment and then said, "Maybe next time you can just come to the house," she suggested, "and perhaps we can ride the ponies."

"Ponies?" Peter questioned, and an uneasy frown crossed his face. "Where do you live?"

"Up there on the hill," she said, pointing in the direction of the mansion.

A distressed look flashed into Peter's dark eyes, but he didn't say anything. Finally, Katie asked, "What's wrong, Peter?"

"I didn't know you were one of them," he said. "I've never seen you at the manor before."

"I just came today," she answered. "I'm going to live there with my Uncle Ivan."

Peter's eyes grew even darker, and he looked down, seemingly to search the ground.

Katie suddenly felt frightened and whispered, "What's wrong, Peter?"

"I don't think that I can explain it to you," he said softly. "I didn't notice your dress before because it was torn and dirty, but now I see it is very fine."

"My dress?" she asked, looking down at her white silk garment. "What has my dress to do with anything?"

"It's not just the dress, Katie," he sighed. "Look at me," he demanded, and for the first time, Katie noticed his shabby clothes.

"But I don't care about clothes," she cried out passionately.

"I know," he said. "But they do!"

"They? Who?"

"Those upon the hill. Your aunt, your uncle, and your cousins. They'll not let you come around someone like me."

"But you're my friend," she insisted with pain in her voice. He didn't say anything, and her face clouded with apprehension. "Don't you want to be my friend?"

"It's not what I want, Katie," he said gently. "They just won't let you have anything to do with us peasants, and after you've lived there awhile, you won't even want to."

"That's not true!" she protested. Tears were gathering in the corners of her eyes, and she tried to sniff them back. "Then you won't be my friend?"

"Not won't be, but can't be," he muttered sadly.

She couldn't control her tears any longer, and they started rolling down her cheeks.

"I'm sorry," he said, and he stood, turned, and hurried way.

"Peter. Peter," she called after him, but the clearing was now empty.

CHAPTER 2

1908

Katrina Kazakinova opened her eyes and stared at the high ceiling overhead, and then shivering from the early morning cold, she pulled the covers more tightly around her neck. Her gaze drifted over her elaborately carved bed with its tall posts and then roamed to the upholstered benches on the far side of her room. She yawned and turned over to go back to sleep when she suddenly remembered that today was her eleventh birthday. She threw back the blankets and leaped out into the cold room. "Today will be wonderful," she shouted, "but first, there will be the vicar's birthday benediction to endure."

The vicar and his undercurate arrived immediately after breakfast. The vicar wore a golden brocade robe with a high purple hat that rested on the black flowing locks that hung down his back. After a brief greeting in an enormous bass voice, he lit his silver censer, which gave off a reddish glow through its perforated cover. A pungent blue smoke filled the room immediately. As always, the perfumed incense made Katie's eyes water and her head feel light.

The undercurate lit some small wax candles and handed one to each person in the room. Both men began chanting, the tone of the vicar's deep voice alternating with the high tenor of his assistant. Katie was filled with feverish excitement and was impatient for the benediction to be over.

After the ceremony, they all retired to the table for a second breakfast. As the two religious figures prepared to depart, the vicar reached out as if to shake hands with her uncle. Katie noticed that as always, Ivan pressed money into the vicar's palm.

"Go and fetch your wraps, Katie," her uncle ordered. When she returned, he took her by the hand and led her outside toward the stables. It was a beautiful morning, and the warm rays of the sun were melting the last of the winter's snow into hundreds of little pools of water.

They passed the stables where the stud horses were kept and continued on to the lodge that housed the livestock. There stood a chestnut-colored pony with a shiny coat. The pony held his head erect, and his nostrils quivered with excitement as they approached. Provovich, who had labored the whole morning, grooming and brushing the little stallion, stood by proudly, waiting to see if the child would like her uncle's gift.

Katie gave a scream of delight and ran forward toward the pawing animal. "Oh, Uncle Ivan, let me ride him," she cried out. Provovich lifted her into the wicker saddle that was padded with soft red velvet, and then she was off, racing into the early spring morning.

She galloped over the fields, waving excitedly to the peasants working in them, and on until she spotted Peter, his sister, and his father. "Peter," she called excitedly. "Look at my new pony!" He turned, frowned as always when he saw her, and then looked away. Only his sister smiled and waved back at her.

After a vigorous ride, she returned to her uncle and Provovich, gasping for breath. "He's so wonderful, Uncle Ivan," she cried. "I just love him, and you have made this the most wonderful birthday ever!"

"And what are you going to call him, Katie?" her beaming uncle asked.

"Pride!"

Now it would no longer matter that her cousins belittled her so, she thought. She had her own special friend. She laughed joyously and rubbed the little pony's mane.

Two weeks later, Tanya Yarmolinskaya came to live at Usadiba Na Holme. Katie knew that something out of the ordinary was about to happen because Ivan and Mathilde had been quarreling loudly for days, and Ivan had assuaged his rage by drinking heavily.

It was a stormy day when the carriage pulled up at the bottom of the hill, and Katie was surprised to see a girl of her own age emerge. Provovich lifted her bags down, and the two of them raced up the slope, lashed by the pelting rain. The stranger entered the hallway, and as she removed her wet cloak and hood, a mass of beautiful auburn hair tumbled free and fell halfway down her back. The girl had a broad face with exceptionally large brown eyes, very white skin, and shoulders that were unusually wide. She smiled shyly, and Katie felt an immediate surge of emotion for the newly arrived stranger.

Mathilde, Alex, and Sonya joined them in the entry hall. Ivan took the child's hand and announced, "This is Tanya Yarmolinskaya, a niece of my first wife. Her parents were killed recently when a runaway horse dragged their carriage over a cliff." He introduced each one of them to her, while Mathilde scowled, with her eyebrows drawn together severely.

"Since Tanya has no living relatives," Ivan explained to them, "friends of her family wrote to me as a last hope. I have agreed to take Tanya to live with us, hoping that she will bring us as much happiness as our Katie has these past three years."

"Why don't you just hang out a sign?" Mathilde snarled. "Home for Orphaned Children!"

Tanya's face turned pale. Ivan grimaced and quickly summoned a servant to take the new arrival to her room. He then turned on his wife and snapped. "Mathilde, don't get yourself worked up into another violent state. My decision has been made, and it will stand!"

"This happens to be my home too," she snapped bitterly.

Ivan's expression darkened, and the children quickly retreated to the kitchen. Katie drew close to the kitchen hearth and warmed her hands, glad to have escaped from another unpleasant scene. The windows throughout most of the mansion were kept locked during the cold months, which left the air suffocating and stale. But here in the kitchen, the air was more refreshing because the servants going in and out were constantly opening the doors.

Fifteen-year-old Alex removed a cigarette from his pocket and lit it with an elaborate flourish.

He hasn't changed much in the past three years, Katie thought. *He has grown taller but still has the same pale complexion, watery blue eyes, and long thin nose. His unruly strawlike hair is in a constant state of disarray. His long arms end in bony white hands, and his legs look like slender poles attached to the bottom half of his body. He surely is his mother's son,* Katie concluded.

"Did you finish your lessons?" Katie asked him at last, merely for the sake of conversation while holding her hands closer to the fire.

"God forbid, no," he answered, blowing a smoke ring to the ceiling. "I've better things to do with my time."

"Did you at least go riding today as Father suggested?" Sonya injected. "He claims you're far too lazy and refuse to put yourself out for anything."

"Oh, he is always griping about something," Alex rebutted. "All he ever does is find fault with me."

"I wonder why," Sonya added disdainfully.

"Hey, can we be pleasant today for a change?" Alex requested. "What do you think of our new arrival?" he asked with a grin. "She's a looker, eh?"

Sonya, looking totally bored, made no comment at first, but then sniffed. "I only hope this one isn't a roughneck."

Katie bit her tongue and resisted the impulse to grab her cousin's crow-colored locks. Sonya's beauty had continued to bloom since Katie had arrived at the manor, but her disposition was as unpleasant as her brother's. Sonya spent most of her time arranging her hair and studying the latest fashion in clothes. She could not comprehend her father's pleasure in what she considered Katie's barbaric behavior riding in the wind, rain, and snow. She considered her cousin Katie childish, wild, and coarse.

Katie, with tolerant restraint, held out her hands over the fire in the hearth and let the flickering flames mellow her somber mood. "I think she's nice," she offered, "and I think it's going to be great fun having her here."

"I'm not surprised," Sonya retorted.

"Hear, hear!" Alex laughed. "Let's just hope for my sake that she's not like either of you two beauties."

The door opened, and one of the kitchen maids entered, carrying a large box of eggs from the poultry house. She set them down and put another log on the fire. Yawning, she involuntarily made the sign of a cross before her lips.

"Your peasant behavior repulses me," Sonya snapped scornfully.

"Best to be safe, Ms. Sonya," the servant woman answered. "The holy sign keeps the evil spirits out."

"And there are some who think these empty-headed creatures can be educated," Alex ventured with a sneer. The servant scurried from the room with her head down.

"Stupid peasant," Sonya muttered.

Katie shook her head. "She's not stupid, but you're rude." Then she hurried upstairs to become better acquainted with the beautiful stranger.

Maria Sovinsky trudged wearily home from the fields. She always left earlier than her father and brother, Peter, so that she could get home and start their nighttime meal. Maria bore a strong resemblance to the men in her family, but both her dark curly hair and complexion were a shade lighter, and her features were cast in a more delicate mold.

On the way home each evening, she stopped off to look in on the baby of her neighbor, Dmitri Gogol. The infant's mother had died of fever several months earlier. Since Dmitri had to work his fields, the infant was left alone. Maria found the infant already awake and cooing softly to herself. "Poor Cecilia. Good thing you are so strong or you would never make it," she asserted, as she picked the infant up and patted her gently. "It's a terrible thing that your father drugs you into a day-long sleep by chewing poppy seeds and putting them into your milk every morning. But you know he has to work his fields, Cecilia," she explained. "If he took you with him, a wolf or a snake could get you, or you could get bitten by insects or get badly sunburned. He can't watch over you every minute."

Maria changed the infant's diaper. "It's good to have another girl to talk to, baby, as it's hard being the only woman in a house." The infant stared at Maria's face intently. "Of course, my brother, Peter, helps me whenever he can, but I miss my mother. She died of fever like yours. Peter and I were lucky, though—she taught us how to read and write. On the estate where my mother was raised, the master actually had a school for the children. Can you imagine that? I will teach you to read and write when you get bigger."

Maria sat the infant in a chair and began to feed her a boiled egg and some rye bread softened in milk. "Isn't that good?" she asked. The baby sucked greedily on the food. "Whenever I get some money," Maria continued her monologue, "I always buy things like ribbons for my hair or cloth to make a new dress, but Peter, he just patches up his old clothes and buys books when the peddler comes round to the market place. He reads whenever he can, and he's teaching himself French. He's the smart one in the family. He wants to know as much as those up on the hill, even though he hates them."

Maria looked around Dmitri's hut with distaste. "This place sure looks like a pigpen, Cecilia. You will have to clean it when you are older. I like to keep our place neat and clean. My father and Peter made us a cupboard for our dishes and food and a chest to hold our extra clothes and linens." She warmed some milk and then rocked Cecilia until she finished her bottle. When the baby was finished, Maria laid her back in her bed and set out for home.

Maria stood for a moment in front of their cottage, feeling her usual sense of pride. The roof of the cottage was thatched, with a solitary hole in it, from which the smoke escaped.

Maria entered the well-kept house with its big brick fireplace. A large Bible and a single candle in a beautifully carved holder stood on the cupboard. Against the far wall stood three rough wooden beds with straw mattresses. The fourth bed had been put in the animal shed many years ago when her mother died.

Maria removed some salt cabbage from the cupboard and put it over the fire to stew slowly in a black kettle. She took some black rye bread from the cupboard and placed it on the table, and then went out to their animal shed to get some fresh eggs and milk for the evening meal. A wooden partition divided the shed from their one and only room. They owned a cow, two pigs, and a dozen fowl.

When everything was prepared, Maria glanced out the window and saw her father and brother. At a distance, the two looked very much alike, tall and broad shouldered, and as they drew closer, one could also see the same black unruly hair and sun-baked skin. They entered the hut, kissed Maria, and then washed the dirt from their hands in a basin before sitting down to eat.

Cutting a slice of bread, Peter's father offered some statements enthusiastically. "Prime Minister Stolypin is the first one to let us own our own land, Peter," the old man said. "A man can take pride in what is his, and he can dream of someday buying more land."

"But will you really be able to?" Peter asked, taking another slice of bread. "That's the question, Father. We have never gotten anything except promises."

"But this is fact, Peter. Not a promise! There will be more to come. And soon! Believe me, son," he urged. "The future looks bright."

"I hope you're right," Peter sighed.

Maria got up and went across to the fireplace to fetch the kettle. She served her father and brother another helping of the cabbage, returned the kettle to the fire, and then sat down. "Father," she interrupted with a frown, "I'm really worried about Dmitri's baby. I think Dmitri should consider remarrying."

"This isn't our affair to meddle in," her father admonished.

"But Father, the child is all alone most of the time!" Maria persisted.

"Which isn't our concern, Maria," he said gently. "All of Dmitri's labors are now going into sustaining the child and himself. The cost of the funeral is not long over, and it's still the custom for a bridegroom to pay his father-in-law a small sum of money. I doubt that Dmitiri has any extra cash on hand. When his grief has passed and his pocketbook is fatter, maybe then he'll find the little one a mother."

"Money to bury, and then money to marry," Peter lamented.

"I know," his father agreed. "Not to mention the endless taxes that crush us, but things will get better," the old man said, smiling optimistically.

Maria sighed with resignation as she left the table. She went to the cupboard and withdrew a *lampoda*, which she lit before kneeling to pray.

Peter went outside to tend to the livestock. "Father's hopes and Maria's prayers," he muttered bitterly to the livestock. "How worthless they are!"

CHAPTER 3

1913

Katie and Tanya pressed their noses against the frosted glass and stared out anxiously. A current of excitement flowed between them, for tonight there was to be a banquet and grand ball at Usadiba Na Holme. The wind was driving snowflakes with a violent frenzy, and tiny bits of ice lashed again the windowpane. The world, as far as they could see, lay covered with a soft white blanket.

During previous winters, the family had stayed at their home in the capital, but with so much political tension and talk about war, Ivan had chosen to stay on his estate this year. Driven to distraction with complaints of boredom from Mathilde and the three girls, he finally consented to this week of social events.

By three o'clock in the afternoon, darkness was already stalking the sky. Even though many visitors were already present, Provovich continued bringing in new arrivals in one sleighful after another. Katie and Tanya, close friends for the past five years, now chattered excitedly as each new guest entered. When they could no longer see into the darkness of the late afternoon, they rushed to Tanya's bedroom to inspect the gowns they would wear tonight at the long-awaited ball.

Tanya's exuberant state amused Katie. "You would think there was no one else in the world besides Nikolai Sokoloy," Katie teased.

"Oh, Katie, there isn't for me. Since Alex brought him home from school to visit last year, I haven't been able to think of anyone else. I am so in love with him," she bubbled, wrapping her arms around herself. "And just think, he will be here any minute now!"

"I have to admit that I'm fond of him myself." Katie laughed.

"Do you think Nicki will like my gown?" she questioned. "Be honest, Katie! I so want to look my very best!"

"Nicki will love your gown."

Tanya sighed contentedly. "It's going to be such a lovely night. It would even be nicer though if we didn't have Her Highness Czarina Sonya to contend with. The airs that she puts on."

Katie laughed again. "She is beautiful, Tanya, so it's natural that men flock around her. Our only comfort is that she is older and will probably marry first, leaving all the rest of the handsome young men for us."

"It can't be too soon for me!" Tanya added.

As guests continued to arrive, fragments of conversation filled the hall. "My *shuba* is soaked! Here, please hang it where it will dry."

The girls greeted friends that they had not seen for many months. At last, dinner was announced, and they all went into the huge dining room.

The meal included champagne, cognac, seemingly endless courses of soups, meats, vegetables, and at the end, mousse and other rich desserts. Several times, the revelry was interrupted for one guest or another to make a speech or propose a toast. At last, tea was served, and stirring and sipping sounds were added to the already existing noises.

At the table seated next to Katie, a prince sat in conversation with an elderly count directly opposite him. "There will be war in the near future," he declared.

"It seems that war is inevitable among men," the count admitted sadly. "The same distrust and hatred perpetuates itself generation after generation."

"Still, most Europeans are intelligent people," the prince declared. "It would be madness to involve whole nations in war just because of the fanaticism of some small groups."

"Ah, but passion rules rationality," the count replied, leaning across the table. "Each of us touches the other, and the action of even one man can spark a conflict, which might bring an entire empire into destruction. I cannot see the Austrians turning the other cheek when the Serbs are demanding independence. A single hostile act could precipitate war, and if Austria and the Serbs go to war, they will drag our Russia into it."

"There has to come a day," the prince declared, "when men can settle disagreements by means other than violence."

"Perhaps," the count ventured. "But I see no signs of man moving out of the savagery of the animal kingdom in our lifetime."

Katie turned away from the political discussion and turned to look at Nikolai Sokoloy sitting at the other end of the table. Nicki was one of the most interesting young men that she had ever met. He was twenty-one, strong, and self-assured yet had a gentle disposition. His green eyes, ruddy cheeks, and chestnut-colored hair made him almost irresistible. He was so handsome that she wished that Tanya were not in love with him. She could not bring herself to compete with her best friend for his affection. Right now, Sonya was flirting outrageously with him, but Katie was glad to see that Nicki was ignoring her.

At nine o'clock, the orchestra began playing. The ballroom was immense with wide glass doors and tall white Corinthian columns. Large crystal chandeliers hung from the ceiling at each end of the room, and along the walls were huge marble vases. At the far end of the spacious hall was a gigantic portrait of the first count of Usadiba Na Holme.

The two girls descended the long flight of marble stairs into the ballroom. Katrina wore her golden hair piled high on top of her head. A pale blue dress, trimmed in white fur, enhanced the depth of her azure-colored eyes.

Tanya's cheeks were flushed with expectation as she walked beside Katie in a dark green silk dress, her long auburn locks pulled back and caught up with a green velvet ribbon. Her smooth white skin seemed to mirror the glimmering lights. She was fervent with excitement.

The orchestra was playing, and as the girls entered the ballroom, Nicki Sokoloy immediately captured Tanya and waltzed her away onto the dance floor. Alex gallantly bowed to Katie and led her into her first dance of the evening. The merriment continued with the girls circulating from one youth to another until they were breathless.

Sonya made a late entrance, slowly descending the staircase with her head held erect like a swan. She wore a red brocade gown trimmed with black velvet. Her ebony hair was piled high in an elaborate hairdo with one crest of waves falling atop another upon her fair-skinned forehead. She immediately became the center of attention, and an anxious circle of men rushed to claim her for her first dance. However, Sonya grasped the hand of another woman's fiancé, claiming him as her first partner. The other women in the ballroom whispered their disapproval.

Nicki caught Katie between partners and whisked her out onto the dance floor. "It is almost impossible," he teased with his green eyes twinkling, "to get a dance with the most beautiful girl in the place."

"I bet you say that to every girl you dance with," she scoffed. "Still, I have to admit that I like to hear it."

He grinned and stopped dancing long enough to ask, "Do you suppose that we might slip out of here long enough to catch some fresh air? It's suffocating, and I'm really in need of a cigarette"

Katie laughed, and they slowly maneuvered their way to the edge of the dance floor and slipped out a side door. They walked to the conservatory on the other side of the manor. It was a huge room with two sides glassed in from the floor to the ceiling, and it served as shelter for many of the plants during the long winter months.

The room was cold, and Katie shivered. Nicki removed his jacket and placed it around her exposed shoulders and then lit a cigarette. They stood silently for a while, staring out of the frosted windows into the night. "It's so beautiful," Katie sighed. "And look at that magnificent moon! Shining down and lighting the ghostly world beneath it."

"The majestic touch of nature's brush upon the world." He smiled.

"You see it too," she murmured happily. "It's hard to resist the impulse to go dashing out into it." She turned to him. "Unlike so many others, I never get tired of watching the snowfall."

He grinned at her tenderly. "Yes, it's always beautiful," he agreed. "Like you. Only your beauty is not icy and cold but rather warm like a summer day.

"Oh, there you go again with your compliments."

"Why won't you ever take me seriously, pretty Katie?" he asked, smiling affectionately.

"And have you break my heart?" she teased.

"Only a foolish man would do that," he said.

He lifted one eyebrow quizzically, but Katie turned away from him to watch the drifting snow outside, thinking to herself, *If only Tanya were not in love with you.*

Nicki lit another cigarette to postpone their return to the crowded ballroom, content to watch the moonbeams sifting through Katie's golden hair. Feeling his gaze, she turned her head and smiled.

He finished his cigarette, slowly crushed the burning end, then in a movement so swift that it surprised her, he leaned down and gently kissed her lips. She stood still at first, but after a moment of surprise, she looked at him indignantly.

"Someday when you grow up, Katrina Kazakinova," he said, laying his finger on the tip of her nose, "you are going to consider me seriously. I can wait until then."

She was uncertain how to respond, so after a few moments, she awkwardly suggested, "I think we had better return to the others."

He took her arm, and they walked back to the ballroom, where a tall young cadet immediately captured Katie and whirled her out onto the crowded dance floor.

Over her shoulder, Katie noticed that Nicki was once again dancing with Tanya and gave a sigh of relief. Nicki belonged to Tanya, and she must not let herself forget that. She danced the rest of the evening until she felt faint with exhaustion. In the early hours of the morning, the guests finally drifted off to their rooms.

Tanya joined Katie in her bedroom after the ball, and they relived the excitement of the night all over again.

"Wasn't Nicki splendid?" Tanya bubbled. "I thought him the most handsome man there."

"Without a doubt," Katie agreed.

"And did you notice that he danced with me more than anyone else?"

"Yes," Katie answered with a twinge of guilt. "But I don't blame him," she added. "You really looked stunning."

"Sonya was her own nauseating self, though," Tanya remarked ruefully.

"You have to admit that she looked beautiful."

"Well, I'm not about to tell her so."

"I wish you and Sonya would make more of an effort to get along and stop quarreling for the sake of Uncle Ivan. After all, we do owe everything we have to him."

"I know," Tanya admitted. "You're right." Then she returned to her favorite subject. "Do you think that Nicki will ask me to marry him some day? I don't think I could live if he didn't."

"You would live," Katie said, "but I think your chances are pretty good."

"I hope so," Tanya said, smiling happily. "Katie, would you mind if I slept here tonight? Going back to my room now would be such a dismal letdown."

"By all means, stay!"

Katie followed Tanya to bed but found sleep elusive. She finally got up, lit her *lampoda*, and decided to search for the novel that she had been reading earlier in the week. Concluding that she had left it in Tanya's room, she eased into her slippers and slipped out the door into the darkened hallway. She crept noiselessly toward Tanya's room, aware that her Uncle would be displeased if she woke any of the guests at this late hour.

As she turned the corner, she was startled to see a blur in front of her. Then Sonya opened her door, and the shadow of a man was silhouetted very clearly against the dim flickering light of the bedroom. He slipped inside and closed the door softly, leaving the corridor once again in darkness.

Katie leaned against the wall and fought down a wave of shock. *My God*, she thought. *If Uncle Ivan ever finds out . . .*

The snow was falling heavily, and the thermometer registered well below freezing. In spite of the blizzard, Maria Sovinsky had been sent out to gather logs for the fire.

As she piled them in the shed, the quarreling voices of her father and brother penetrated the walls. She busied herself tending to the animals' needs, chores ordinarily done by Peter, but she was in no hurry to return to their hut tonight. A friend had told her that Dmitri Gogol had asked her father for her hand in marriage. She was shocked at first but had reached the point now where she could consider the proposal rationally. She did not love Dmitri, but on the other hand, she did not hate him. He had no outstanding qualities that she could think of, and this was unfortunate. However, there was his child, Cecilia, whom she loved. Also, Dmitri's farm was next to theirs, so if she did marry him, she would still be close to her father and Peter.

Dmitri was a close friend of her father, so he would look upon the proposal favorably, but Peter would know that she could not be happy with Dmitri. He would be against the marriage because of the age difference. *Still, Father would make the final decision.*

I must be able to accept whatever is decided. I only wish that Peter could also accept the realities of our life. But no, every time a carriage of the aristocracy passes, his face clouds with bitterness. And then there is that girl with the golden hair up on the hill that haunts him so . . .

Inside the hut, old man Sovinsky shouted angrily at Peter. "Maria could do a lot worse than Dmitri Gogol!"

"That is true," Peter granted. "But then she could do a lot better too."

"What is it that you find so terrible about Dmitri?"

"Nothing, Father," Peter replied. "But he's not the right man for our Maria. Dmitri is a muzhik, a common peasant in every sense of the word, while Maria is a sensitive girl, deserving of someone better."

"I hear him, but I don't believe it," his father cried, waving his hands in the air. "It seems to me that you have a mighty high opinion of your sister's worth. Perhaps you have in mind some royal husband, eh? Maria is sixteen and long overdue for a husband. At her age, your mother was married a year already."

"Father, what can you be thinking of?" Peter demanded, pounding his fist on the table. "Maria is still so young, and Dmitri is too old for her."

"You call thirty-four old?"

"No, but it's too old for Maria. She should marry a young man. Besides, it is not fair to tie her down with a child of five on her wedding day."

"Maria is fond of the child. She has helped raise the babe since she was born."

"That is not enough, Father."

The old man exploded. "You seem to forget that I'm the head of this house, Peter. Maria will marry who I say, or she'll get no dowry from me. Maybe you think that she'll get a husband without a dowry? Maybe you think the tax for Maria would mean nothing to this fine gentleman that you have in your imagination. It seems, Peter, that in your eyes, no man is good enough for your sister!"

"That's not true, Father," Peter said, trying to control his temper. "Dmitri is a good friend, but he's backward and unwilling to learn anything new. He drinks too much. He is tightfisted with money. Maria is such a gentle girl. Now that Mother is gone, she is all that we have, Father. You can't just throw her away so lightly."

"Throw her away?" he questioned angrily. "What would happen to her if I should die? I'm just getting her settled. Arranging a husband so she can have a home of her own. That is what fathers are supposed to do for their daughters."

"I know, Father," Peter said softly. "But can't you just give us some time here? Maria has me. I will always look after her if something happens to you. Can't we wait a while and see if someone better comes along? Someone that Maria could be happy with?" The elderly man strode to the hearth and crossed himself and then said a prayer before turning to his son. "All right, Peter," he sighed. "It's against my better judgment. I'm an old man. I wanted to see my daughter secure before I died. However, if this marriage will make both you and Maria unhappy, then there's no point to it." His shoulders slumped. "I'll turn down Dmitri's proposal tomorrow."

CHAPTER 4

SPRING 1914

The late afternoon sun warmed Katie pleasantly as she bounced along in the open carriage, but she was irritated by the slow pace of the ride. *Mounted on Pride, I could be racing over this stretch of land instead of crawling along like a snail.*

She had eaten a light lunch with her eighty-year-old neighbor, Countess Alexis. The countess rarely entertained these days and fatigued easily. Katie sensed this and had begged an early departure.

She felt reluctant to return to the manor so early in the day because no one would be there. Alex was away at school, and Tanya and Sonya had left at dawn on an all-day picnic

On an impulse, Katie shouted to Provovich, "Leave the road and make a drive through the village."

"Your Uncle wouldn't approve of that, miss," he told her.

"Just do as I ask," she insisted.

"I'd do anything to please you, Ms. Katrina," he said with a frown, "but I don't trust the villagers. Feelings are running high these days, and there are stories that the gentry have come to harm in many places. The master would be angry with me if he knew that I exposed you to danger."

Provovich saw Katie's face set in a look of dark determination, and he realized the futility of arguing with her. His young mistress had the same stubborn nature as her uncle, so with trepidation, he turned the carriage to the village.

From a distance, Katie could see a crowd gathered in the square.

"We had better go back, miss," said Provovich, slowing the carriage. But Katie's curiosity was aroused. She climbed up next to him on the driver's seat. As they came nearer, she gave a horrified gasp when she observed that a flogging was about to take place. The victim's arms were bound to a stout pole.

Provovich laid a restraining hand upon Katie's wrist, but she brushed it aside and leaped from the carriage. "No, miss!" Provovich cried out. "You mustn't interfere."

She ignored him and edged her way through the crowd. Just then, the sound of the whip exploded like a thunderbolt in the midst of the tense, silent observers. Though the lash of the *nagika* tore open wounds on the victim's back, no cry escaped from his lips.

"What has he done?" she asked frantically of the woman standing next to her.

The woman's eyes flashed with hatred. "One of you dare ask that?" she replied, spitting in defiance at Katie's feet. Katie turned to some of the others but found the same hostility reflected in their faces.

Provovich frantically pushed through the angry mob until he reached her side. "Please, miss," he whispered, as he tugged anxiously at her arm. "It isn't safe for you here."

"But what did he do?" she demanded urgently.

"He struck one of your uncle's overseers for flogging a small boy with his riding crop," a woman told her. "All the child did was accidentally splash some mud on his horse."

Katie's mouth tightened while Provovich watched her fearfully. The victim moaned slightly and turned his head. In that instant, Katie's composure completely crumbled. "Peter," she whispered hoarsely. "Peter Sovinsky."

Momentarily stunned, her anger suddenly erupted. She sprang forward and grabbed the whip from the overseer's hand. Startled, the big man let go. Katie seized the whip and lashed out at him in fury. The man stared at the young girl in disbelief; then as the pain registered, he bolted. He wanted no dealings with any of Ivan Kozakov's family.

The crowd tensed and waited.

"Your knife, Provovich!" she demanded. "Let me have your knife!" The driver extracted it from his belt and handed it to her, and she clumsily sawed at the ropes that held Peter a prisoner.

As he was released, his body trembled. He turned his dark eyes on Katie and mumbled, "Thank you."

"Let me help you to our carriage," she offered, reaching out toward him.

"No!" he replied.

Katie recoiled. "I only want to help you," she said in an unsure voice.

"You have done that already," he said. "And I am grateful."

"But if you will not accept a ride," she asked, "how will you get home?"

"I'll walk."

"You cannot possibly walk in your condition."

"I can," he said, his jaw tightening.

Katie looked at the bloody welts on his back and started to speak but stopped when she saw the unyielding resolution in his face. "I'm going with you then," she said. "Provovich, take the carriage home."

"I can't let you walk all that way, miss!" Provovich insisted.

"You can't take the carriage through the woods, Provovich," she pointed out. "If you leave it here, the villagers will destroy it, and Uncle Ivan will be furious."

Peter turned from her, staggered slightly, and began to walk. Katie left Provovich and hurried after him. In spite of his wounds, Peter strode through the village so rapidly that she was forced to run to catch up with him.

"You should not walk so fast," she called out to him.

"Can't you keep up with me, countess?" he taunted.

Katie could see his teeth pressing against his lower lip. "I will manage," she responded, somewhat out of breath.

He left the village and started across the fields. The sun was hot, and she could feel the perspiration rolling down her back. By the time they had reached the woods, she was breathing heavily from her efforts to match his long strides. As they entered the forest, Peter set out along a well-worn path. His pace remained steady, and he squared his wounded shoulders. Katie could not help but admire his strength.

"Couldn't we rest for just a moment?" she called out at last, fearful that he would collapse.

He stopped and turned to her. "Are you tired?"

"Very!" she said, noting his tightly clenched lips.

"Have a seat then, countess," he said, waving his hand in a patronizing gesture. Gratefully, she sank down on the soft grass while he eased himself down beside her.

"Why do you dislike me so much, Peter?"

"I never said that I disliked you, countess."

"You don't have to. And why do you call me countess?" she asked. "Have you forgotten my name?"

"No, but right now, I don't feel like engaging in small talk. I hurt like holy hell."

"Oh, Peter, I'm so sorry!" she said with genuine anguish. "You must be in terrible pain, and here I am babbling on. Please forgive me!" She removed a handkerchief from her pocket and gently dabbed at his wounds, but the blood had already hardened. "Is there some water nearby?" she asked.

He nodded. "There is a small stream in the thickets a short distance from here."

"Show me," she urged.

He led her to the brook and sat down by its edge. Katie dipped her handkerchief into the rushing stream and gently sponged his bloody back. The cool water numbed his pain somewhat, and he closed his eyes. Her touch was soft, and the clean, fresh smell of her hair as it brushed his naked shoulder tantalized his senses.

"Does it feel better?" she asked at last.

"Much. Thank you, but we had better be going now, countess."

"Why do you persist in calling me that?" she asked with annoyance. "My name's Katrina."

"I know," he said with a mockery in his eyes. "And Katie to your friends. I was in that category once briefly when we were children. Or don't you remember? I was the knight in shining armor. However, it seems that time has reversed our roles, and it is now the fair princess that rescues the heroic knight. Somehow it doesn't seem quite right."

She smiled. "Still, it is ironic, Peter, that after all this time, we are once again here in the woods. It is almost as if the clock has been turned back to our childhood days and that nothing has changed."

"Everything has changed," he said, letting his eyes wander over her slim body. "And you know it."

"Then you have noticed me after all," she said with a note of triumph in her voice. "All these years whenever I passed you in the fields, you have turned away from me."

"You already had more than your share of admirers," he said sarcastically.

"But never you," she stated. She straightened out her legs and leaned toward him, with the low cut of her dress exposing the swell of her breasts, and he pushed her back abruptly. "What's wrong, Peter?" she asked.

"Under different circumstances, I might find the idea of a little girl playing siren humorous."

A flush of embarrassment crept across Katie's face. "No gentleman would say such a thing."

"But I am not a gentleman, Countess Katrina Kazakinova," he pointed out.

"You are making fun of me again, Peter," she said in a hurt voice. "Since that first day we met, you have rejected me. My every approach to you has been met with either open disdain or that infernal mockery of yours. Why do you rebuff me? What have I ever done to make you dislike me so?"

"It is not personal, Countess Kazakinova," he said. "It is enough that you are one of them."

"But that's not fair," she said angrily. "You haven't the right to put me in a category. I'm a human being just like you."

"You're right, Katie," he said, amused by her irritation. "I agree to a truce." With that, he stood up.

"Why are you in such a hurry?" she asked. "You should rest longer."

"I am merely thinking of you, Katie. Your reputation could be thoroughly blackened. A proper lady spending the afternoon in the bushes with a peasant."

"It would not be the first time that they have talked about me."

"Maybe you're right," he smiled. "But there are other more serious reasons why we should go. We peasants are considered rather primitive, you know." He looked at her sideways. "Aren't you afraid of me, countess?"

Her face deepened in color, but her eyes met his. "I would not be here if I was."

"Touché!" he said.

"And now such a serious look, Peter."

"If I look serious, Katie," he said, stopping to sit beside her again, "it's because I'm trying to decide what it is that you want from me."

She shook her head. "I don't want anything, Peter, other than to be your friend. It is what I have always wanted." Impulsively, she reached over and pushed the dark curls up off his forehead.

In return, he reached out and put his hand around her neck. Slowly he drew her face within a few inches of his own, and his eyes searched hers. "You are so beautiful, Katie," he whispered. "So damnably beautiful and sweet." Then he kissed her mouth very lightly.

Her lips trembled, and she opened her eyes very wide. "I always expected that a kiss from you would be more dramatic than that, Peter," she exclaimed.

"You always expected?" he said, shaking his head, and then he laughed. "Ah, Katie, you're so very young."

"That is what you told me when I was eight years old, Peter Sovinsky!" She grinned. "I rather think that I've gown a little since then."

He hesitated briefly and then suddenly reached out and pulled her within the circle of his arm. Tilting her chin with his other hand, he pressed his mouth down hard over hers.

Katie felt as if there were hammers beating at her temples. *I'm sinking,* she thought. *Sinking.* His lips pressed harder against hers, and his arms enfolded her until her whole body throbbed, and she could feel the same demanding urgency in him. She was afraid, yet she could not tear herself away, and all at once, her lips were returning his kisses, and her body pressed back eagerly against his. It was he who finally broke their embrace.

He leaned back against a tree, momentarily oblivious of his torn back. His breathing was heavy, and his eyes glazed with emotion. "How is it going to be with us, Katie?" he asked.

"I don't know what you mean," she said.

"I mean, do you really care for me?" he asked. "Or . . . or am I just a plaything to while away an idle afternoon? If that is the case, am I the first? Or have you had a long string of them like your cousin, Sonya?"

"What are you talking about?" she demanded with a frown. Then Sonya's face rose before her. *So Sonya had toyed with the peasants too. What would happen if Uncle ever found out?*

But Peter allowed her no further time for thoughts. "Katie, the first day that we met, I told you that we were people of two different worlds."

"Yes, I remember."

"I know the rules of my world, but what are they in yours?"

"I am not sure what you are talking about, Peter."

"We are not little children anymore, Katie," he said. "Kisses are nice, I grant you, but only to a point. Our feelings can't really go anywhere. Under the circumstances, I don't think we should see each other again."

"You mean," she snapped with anger, "that you haven't time to bother with anyone that you cannot tumble in a barn loft at first try."

Peter leaned back. "Perhaps you are not as innocent as I supposed."

"Perhaps I am not!"

He reached out to pull her toward him again, but she tore herself away. "Keep your hands off me!"

"All right," he agreed. "But damn it, I wish you would make up your mind. You've picked a hell of a time to play a love scene, Katie."

Katie's lips trembled. "Don't hurt me this way, Peter. You have always been special to me," she pleaded. Tears crept into her eyes. "Pease. Peter, don't . . ."

A look of remorse crossed his face. "I'm sorry, Katie. I didn't mean to hurt you. You are so young and . . ." Then he shrugged helplessly.

"Sixteen is not really that young, Peter," she said shyly. "Besides, there has never really been another time to play our love scene." She reached up and gently brushed his lips with hers.

Unable to control himself any longer, he leaned down and crushed her mouth savagely in return; Katie could feel the passion throbbing in his body. The same surge of desire filled her own, and she wrapped her arms around his neck. They clung together until Peter withdrew his mouth from hers and buried his lips in her neck. The intensity of his passion frightened her.

"Please stop," she pleaded. "Please stop, I'm afraid."

He pushed her at arm's length, and she lowered her eyes before his searching gaze. "You give me a look of virtue now," he accused. "Yet the fire of your kisses is still on my lips." He shook his head in frustration. "You lead me on then stop me then lead me on again."

"You're not being fair, Peter."

"Not being fair!" he exploded, his eyes black and brooding. "Does this mean that your afternoon of sport is over now?"

"I should slap your face," she told him.

"Go ahead," he barked. "It might make both of us feel better and would brush me off with a proper flourish."

"It seems to me, Peter, that your world is a very narrow and unpleasant one, when all a man wants is a woman's body. It's not very romantic."

"We peasants work long and hard. We don't have the leisure for your kind of romance, with picking up handkerchiefs and muttering meaningless nothings. We have to grab and satisfy our hungers quickly." His eyes were dark and brooding.

"Oh, Peter," she wailed. "I do like you so. I like you a lot! When you kissed me just then, I felt like . . . like . . . well, I never felt like that before. Not ever! I didn't want to stop, yet I felt so frightened. And I'm still frightened." She lowered her eyes again. "Maybe you're right, Peter," she said. "Maybe I am too young."

"All right, Katie," he sighed. "Go home and grow up. Learn the facts of life so that in the future, you'll be equipped to deal with them."

"And when I am grown, Peter Sovinsky," she asked, "what will you want from me then?"

He sighed again, more deeply this time. "What indeed? Everything." And then he poured the words out quickly before he could change his mind. "I want to make love to you physically, of course, but my desires run deeper than that. So deep that they are in the realm of fantasy. Since that day I found you in the woods eight years ago, you have been my golden-haired princess in the ivory tower. I turned away from you in the fields because of envy and jealousy. There you were, always riding a fine horse, accompanied by beautiful women in fine clothes and escorted by tall handsome aristocrats, while in contrast, there was I, a ragged peasant doomed to a life of toiling in the fields by a mere accident of birth."

"Peter—"

"No, Katie," he stopped her. "Let me finish telling you my impossible dream while I have the courage. I've always felt that you were drawn toward me. Not in the same way or degree, of course, that I have been drawn to you. But in my imagination, I have fantasized asking you to marry me even though I have nothing to offer you but love. I have prepared speeches telling you how young and strong and willing to work I am. How even though I have no land of my own, someday, my father's land will be mine, and in the meantime, I could work nights for others and save enough money to buy land of my own. How I could at least earn enough to build an extra room in my father's house for us? Though wild and improbable, I let myself pretend that my love could make up for all the lack of luxuries." He smiled, and there was a hopeful hunger in his face. "But of course, this was all mind play, and my wishes are completely absurd."

Katie could not even look at him. Silence hung between them for several minutes before he spoke again. "I know it was a rather ridiculous idea."

"Oh, Peter, you are so wonderful." She swallowed hard and ran her tongue over her dry lips before she could continue. "You are so handsome and strong and—"

"The coat of whitewash isn't necessary, Katie," he said softly.

"All right," she said with her voice trembling. "But the truth does not sound very pleasant, not even to myself." She stopped and looked into his face. "I don't know what I expected you to answer just now, when I asked what you wanted from me. I guess I just had not thought that far ahead. But the idea of marriage . . ." She stopped a minute, unable to go on.

"But the idea of marriage . . ." he prodded bitterly.

"I have to be honest, Peter," she said. "I can't help comparing the mansion on the hill to a one-room hut. I know what you are thinking," she said, raising her hand to still his voice. "You predicted that I would become spoiled on the very first day that I came here. Well, you were right. They did spoil me, or perhaps it would be more honest to say that I spoiled myself. It would be easy for me to imagine that a life with you would be heavenly, Peter. And I'm sure that it would be some of the time. But not all the time, and not even most of the time. Perhaps it's unfortunate, but I have become used to the best things in life. And even if I could defy Uncle Ivan and all the other obstacles, I could not stand my family's rejection, and they would reject me, Peter. My uncle disowned my mother when he felt that she had married beneath her status. I am attracted to you, Peter, and I always have been, but marriage is something else. The truth is that I don't want a life of slaving in the fields and fixing dinners of cabbage stew. And if we had children, probably half of them would not even survive. I am not made for your kind of life, Peter."

"And I was not born to yours, Katie."

She felt naked before his gaze. "You do understand?"

"Very clearly," he said. "I am the forbidden fruit that tempts, but only momentarily."

"I wish I had more strength of character," she said.

"I wish you did too." His eyes burned into hers.

"I do care for you, Peter," she declared. "But when I make love someday, I want it to be in a soft feather bed with sheets of silk. Not on a bed of straw."

"Do you think the sensations will be any sweeter, Katie?" he asked mockingly.

"Don't be bitter, Peter."

"Bitter?" He laughed scornfully. "Why should I be bitter? It has been an amusing afternoon and should make quite a story at one of your fancy gatherings . . . the dirt farmer muzhik dreaming of sharing his humble hut with the royal countess who saved him from a flogging."

"Don't," she pleaded.

"Ah, Katie, we have both learned something today," he went on relentlessly. "You, that you really like your high little niche in the world. And I, that you are no different from the rest of them. It's really better this way, you know. We both know exactly where we stand now."

She turned her face away.

"Enjoy your fine things while you can, Katie, for there may come a day when someone will take them away from you. There may also come a day when I will share that fine feather bed of yours, but it will be on my own terms."

When Katie dared to look up at last, he had disappeared into the thicket, and she felt utterly desolate. "Peter, I am so sorry . . ." she whispered. Then she laid down her head in the damp grass and cried.

CHAPTER 5

SUMMER 1914

It was a hot and humid day, so Katrina, Tanya, and Nicki had set out early to avoid the heat of the noon sun. Dust rose beneath the pounding hooves of the horses. Sweat soaked through their clothing, and dirt adhered to their perspiring faces. The horses snorted seemingly in protest at the temperature. Nicki called out. "That looks like a perfect spot in that grove of trees up ahead."

They had planned their picnic to escape the oppressive heat of the manor. It was the last day of Nicki's leave from the military academy, and they had grown tired of lounging around the gardens of the manor.

Nicki Sokoloy spent a great deal of time at the Kozakov residence, and though Alex brought other young men home from school, Nicki remained the favorite with both Katie and Tanya.

The three riders reined in their horses and dismounted into the shade of the trees. They spread a blanket and then turned their mounts loose to graze in the lush grass. They unpacked sandwiches, samovar, juice, and small cakes from their picnic basket.

"I cannot believe that Alex and I will be graduating from the Military Academy so soon," Nicki declared.

"Commissioned officers at last," Katie teased.

"For certain," he replied with a grin and a salute.

"I can't stand this heat," Tanya complained.

"It is damnable," Nicki agreed. "I, for one, will be glad when autumn arrives."

"Well, at least the high temperature helped us escape from our lessons," Tanya interjected. "It's the only time Uncle Ivan ever lets us off. I don't mind the music and drawing, and I love the dancing, but the languages and stuffy old lessons in scriptures and church history—believe me, those I can do without!"

Nicki laughed. "How do you expect to capture a rich, handsome husband, my pet, if you remain dull in mind?"

Tanya blushed and lowered her eyes.

Katie changed the subject. "Let's find some wild strawberries to eat." They leaped to their feet and were off with renewed vigor. Their hunt was successful, and after they had eaten their fill, they removed their shoes and stockings and waded in a cool stream until the sun began to lower in the sky. Then they started for home.

As Nicki and the two girls pulled up before the stables, Katrina felt a flash of annoyance that Provovich was not there to greet them. Though there were many grooms on the estate, Provovich always personally took care of Ivan's great black stallion and Katie's horse, Pride. She waited impatiently as Nicki went inside the stable to find a groom. Suddenly, Provovich came from behind the stables and stood before them with his eyes turned downward. His face was drained of color, and his mouth twitched nervously when he tried to speak. "There's bad trouble, missy, and Master Alex wants you to keep the young gentleman away from the house. Master Alex is in the kitchen.'

"What's wrong, Provovich?" Katie asked, but the groom met her question with an evasive silence. In distress, she turned to Tanya. "Do you think that you can keep Nicki away from the house while I find out what the trouble is?"

Tanya nodded, and Katie started for the house, running to the top of the hill without stopping. As she opened the front door, she heard Ivan's voice coming from the library. "Trash! Wanton trash. That is what my daughter is! Cheap wanton trash!"

Katie heard what sounded like a hand striking blows and instantly realized that her uncle had found out about Sonya.

"My own flesh and blood!" he cried out like an enraged animal. "That is how you raised our daughter, Mathilde! No more morals than a common alley cat. Indulging and spoiling her all her life."

"Black-hearted monster!" Mathilde wailed in return. "It is easy for you to lay the blame at another's door, and what kind of a father have you ever been? When did you ever even pretend to care about her! You turned your back on your children the day they were born. Instead you brought that niece of yours here and lavished most of your love on her, and what was left over, you gave to that child who hasn't even a drop of your own blood in her veins!" Her voice rose menacingly. "You cherished the outsiders, and there wasn't enough love left over to give to your own children. Now you are paying the penalty, Ivan Kozakov!" Then she lowered her voice from a shout to a whisper and pleaded in a piteous tone. "Have mercy on her!"

But Ivan's wrath could not be contained. "She will have guidance from here on out," he roared. "If necessary, I will chain her in her room. But she will march the straight and narrow line from this day forward. If it's not too late, I will wipe the dirt out of her, and if it is, then I will bury her in it!"

Katie could hear Sonya's choking sobs behind the library door, and shaking with anguish, she rushed to the kitchen to find her cousin. Alex's normally pale face had now taken on the hue of a dead man, and he was nervously pacing back and forth across the kitchen floor, cracking his knuckles as he went. It came as a surprise to Katie to note that Alex actually cared for his wayward sister. Katie crossed to the fireplace. The combination of fatigue and nervous shock rendered her helpless momentarily, and she leaned her aching head against the cold bricks.

Alex's voice was shaky. It took a moment before he could speak. "You knew about her?'

Katie nodded her head. "For a long time," she whispered, aware for the first time of her own depth of feeling for Sonya. They stood staring at each other in silence, allies for the first time in their lives.

Alex lit a cigarette, puffed nervously for a moment, and then in a pain-filled voice, narrated what had happened. "Father caught her naked with one of the village boys. He beat him senseless and then took his riding crop to Sonya. I have never seen him so angry, Katie, and Mother is sick with horror." He swallowed hard and then pounded the brick fireplace. "Oh god, what do you think he'll do?

"I don't know, Alex."

"You know she can't help it. I mean . . . it's a kind of . . . a kind of sickness." He paused. "It's in her blood . . . wild and unpredictable."

Katie nodded, never able to forget that afternoon in the woods with Peter, when her own Kazakov blood had raced in such a frightening fashion. "I understand perfectly," she said, "but he won't."

It seemed an eternity before the library door creaked open, and they heard the patter of Sonya's feet fleeing up the marble stairs. They waited for a few moments to see if Ivan and Mathilde would follow, but the large door was pulled closed again. When they passed it, they heard only subdued whispers inside.

They found Sonya sitting in the middle of her bed. Her hair was mangled and knotted in a wild state of disarray, and her ash-colored face and nude body were streaked with dried blood and dirt. Alex turned away, sickened by the sight.

Sonya laughed hysterically. "So the jackals have come to devour the carcass of their own," she mocked.

"For God's sake, stop it, Sonya," Alex moaned with anguish.

"What is the matter, dearest brother? Don't let a little thing like this bother you. I am a fallen woman and have no shame or sense of decency."

"Stop it, Sonya!" he shouted, trying to control his pain.

Katie got a basin of cool water and some clean cloths and began sponging the sores on Sonya's white body. Alex walked to the window and stared out. Sonya remained silent while Katie did her job quickly and then brought a silk nightgown and drew it over her cousin's head. Sonya raised her head and looked into Katie's eyes. "He cannot change me!" she said softly. "I hate him. I hate him, and I always will."

Katie knitted her eyebrows together and looked from Sonya to Alex but said nothing.

Alex came over and gave his sister's wrist a reassuring squeeze, and then he and Katie left the room. Outside they leaned against the banister of the huge stairway wearily. "I guess," Katie said, "I had better find Tanya and prepare her."

"You won't tell her everything, Katie?" he pleaded.

"No," she replied. "Only what she will have to know."

They descended the stairs together and found the entry hall deserted. Alex opened the front door, and they stepped out into a cool, refreshing late-afternoon breeze.

They noticed a rider galloping hurriedly toward them from a distance, and when he did not stop at the stables but kept racing up the hill, Alex shouted to his father to come at once.

Ivan and Mathilde rushed from the library, and Tanya and Nicki hurried around the corner of the house. They could see now that it was one of their distant neighbors. Katie immediately felt apprehensive.

The man pulled a tight rein on his stallion and jerked him to an abrupt halt, and then he blurted out his news in breathless excitement. "It has happened! Today the kaiser officially declared war on Russia!"

An icy chill ran up Katie's spine, and she lifted her eyes and stared into the setting sun. The sky was streaked with rays of red and purple, and the blood-colored splotches seemed like an ominous warning, foretelling of disaster and doom. She felt frightened and was seized by a vague sensation that this day's nightmare was only the beginning, that her world was inexorably moving toward some unknown catastrophic destiny.

CHAPTER 6

AUTUMN 1914

Peter Sovinsky had devoured a bowl of kasha porridge upon arising and then packed a lunch before setting out for the day. He wandered about aimlessly most of the morning and now stood looking out over the long stretch of barren fields. The so-recently productive land presently stood lifeless. The last of the crops had been harvested. The fields lay dull and dreary yellow under the midday sun; their bleakness was a startling contrast to the rich, vivid colors of the forests in the distance.

Peter sank down on the warm earth and leaned against a mutilated tree stump. The sense of accomplishment that had come with the harvest had vanished. The autumn freedom from responsibility that he had welcomed in previous years now left him restless and depressed.

He opened his lunch and munched the dry black bread without relish. The milk in his jug was already warm. Pounding hooves drew his attention, and he saw a hunting party on the trail of a frightened hare. His eyes darted over to the riders. Katie was not among them. As always, he felt relief and disappointment at the same time. Savagely, he pushed the stopper back into his milk jug.

Throughout the long summer, all his attempts to turn his thoughts from Katie had failed. Her face tormented him constantly, and he cursed his inability to forget her. *I should have followed through with my decision to take a wife*, he told himself. He recalled his visits to many of the neighboring villages and the inquiries about eligible women. Many had sturdy physiques and pleasant personalities, but always he felt dissatisfied. Inevitably, the comparison of his golden-haired, blue-eyed, smooth-skinned Katie with her soft, delicate form and enchanting voice rose to haunt him. There was no substitute. Finally, he gave up the idea of taking a wife.

Next he tried to bury his longing for her through toil, and he labored to the utmost of his strength and endurance. The endless strain wearied his body and mind. At last, a day came when he felt secure that he was once again the master of his emotions.

Then one afternoon, he had raised his tired, aching body and glanced off in the distance. There outlined against the sunset, he saw her racing on horseback beside a tall young noble. Instantly, his world crumbled. Renewed jealousy cut through him like a sharp knife. Filled with pain and rage, his humiliated pride once more festered with bitterness and frustration. He realized that he could no longer purge himself though hard work. He had to get away.

Friends and neighbors had already swollen the ranks of military volunteers, but he could not reasonably justify his departure before the crops were in. Now a comfortable winter was assured for his father and Maria, and he was free. He would be called to military duty eventually, but to go at once would solve his problem. Maria still had her father's protection and would probably be getting married in the near future. If the war went quickly, he might be home in time to help with the spring planting.

There really was no excuse to justify his staying. After the war, he would be able to better come to grips with his problems. Perhaps they would even seem insignificant.

* * *

Katie climbed into the carriage with Tanya and her Uncle Ivan for an early-afternoon visit to the elderly Countess Alexis. She had anticipated a dull day but was pleasantly surprised when she found that a twenty-year-old grandson of the Countess was on a furlough from the front. He was plain of face but full of humor and zest.

"Would you girls show my grandson, Sergei, the countryside?" the countess requested. Katie and Tanya jumped at the opportunity, and the three of them spent the afternoon exploring every clump of woods within riding distance.

When they returned to the manor, the countess insisted that they stay to dinner.

After they had eaten, an old servant came in and played on his squeaky fiddle. Ivan, Tanya, Katie, and Sergey cavorted around the parlor, and the old Countess laughed until there were tears in her eyes. It was with great difficulty that the three of them managed to take their leave at last.

On the way home, the carriage bumped along slowly, and Katie shivered from the cold night air. She pulled her wrap more securely about her and strained to see out in the passing blackness. Soon, a silvery moon rose to give the empty fields a ghostly glow.

She sighed with relief when they finally reached the manor. Ivan helped her and Tanya from the carriage. Tanya went upstairs to her room immediately. However, after taking off her wrap, Katie sought out Sonya. She found her sitting in the study before the fireplace.

Her uncle had kept Sonya confined to the house and grounds for the past six months. Her once vain cousin with the elaborate hairstyles now wore the simplest frocks with her hair hanging plain and straight. She kept her pale face locked in a mask of apathy, with her large eyes just staring out into space. She shunned the company of her mother and Tanya, avoided her father, and only accepted the company of Alex and Katie when it was thrust upon her.

Katie had tried to intervene with her uncle on Sonya's behalf, but her entreaties had been met only with a violent rebuff. "When you're a parent," he had snapped, "you may render your own punishments. Until then, do not interfere!"

Katie sank down gratefully across from Sonya in an oversized stuffed chair. The fire played on her cousin's face, and Katie thought that this plain Sonya was even more beautiful than the glamorous one of yesterday.

Silence hung between them for a while. At last Sonya broke it with an announcement. "Alex brought a new friend home from school today. His name is Leon Ibragimv. He and Alex are both going to be sent to the front when their leave is over."

"They are all going now," Katie sighed with despair. "Nicki received his orders too. It doesn't seem possible." She shook her head sadly. "This is certainly going to be a long dreary winter. All the young men will be at the front along with Alex. Travel will be impossible, and there is no knowing how many of our young men will return." A second deeper sigh escaped into the silent room.

Riding their horses beneath a harvest moon, Alex turned to his friend Leon. "I heard there's a band of gypsies passing through the villages around here. It would be tremendous fun to join in a night of their festivities. We could use the diversion of some dancing and singing, and some of those gypsy girls are mighty pretty. Perhaps we could find a couple of vacant haystacks," he added with a wink.

Leon grinned, and they urged their horses to a fast pace. They spent a good part of the evening riding around aimlessly, searching for likely spots where a gypsy band might camp, but their efforts met with failure. Alex was annoyed and grew increasingly bad tempered.

Riding past a barn, they heard some laugher inside. Alex pulled the reins of his horse and jumped off. "It looks like we may have found some excitement after all, Leon," Alex announced. "It sounds like a couple of muzhiks making love in here. Let's investigate."

Leon dismounted reluctantly and followed Alex into the old barn. They found two peasants kissing in the hayloft. The girl broke loose and turned in surprise to look down at them.

"Come down here," Alex ordered them. The dark-haired girl drew back with a frightened look.

"Alex, leave them alone," Leon, urged. "Let's get out of here."

"Sir," the boy protested, "this girl is young, and I don't think—"

"Shut your mouth, beggar," Alex roared. "No one asked what you thought. It's time that the likes of you learned a little respect for your betters."

The frightened muzhik descended the ladder without further argument.

"Please, don't go," the girl begged him, but the peasant fled through the open barn door. Alex laughed at his lack of courage and then proceeded to climb up into the hayloft.

"Alex," Leon called again, but his call was blotted out by the girl's cry.

"Please let me go," she demanded as she drew back against the wall. "Oh, you mustn't."

Alex laughed again as he forced the unwilling girl into his arms. "Not every girl of your station can claim the honor of spreading her legs for the heir of Usadiba Na Holme."

"Please," she begged as she struggled frantically. Breaking loose from Alex, she tried to get to the ladder, but Leon saw Alex grab her more tightly. Panic-stricken, the long-haired girl broke away again and tried to jump, but Alex grabbed her by the ankle and dragged her back in the corner. She screamed and fought in terror, but she was no match for his strength. Leon felt a knot in his stomach and went outside.

After a time, Leon saw the girl run out of the barn into the night. Alex came out swaggering, and he removed a flask from his saddlebags. "Cigarette?" he asked Leon.

They both lit up. Alex took a deep drink from a flask and passed it to Leon. Over a period of time, they passed the whiskey back and forth until the flask was empty. By this time, they were both drunk.

Without warning, a man suddenly leaped out of the bushes and punched Leon in the face; he next lifted a big rock and cracked it over his head. Leon was dimly aware of what went on after that, but he was too stunned to do anything.

The peasant seemed like Satan himself. He attacked Alex and pounded him like he was a punching bag. Alex had had too much to drink, and though he tried to defend himself, he was no match for the stranger's strength. The peasant continued to beat him.

"Stop," Alex pleaded. "For God's sakes, please stop!" But the stranger had no mercy. When Alex fell to the ground and was unable to get up again, the antagonist pulled a knife from his belt and slashed Alex's face with it.

"I am branding you for the rapist that you are," he said. "You will carry this scar to your grave, Alex Kozakov, and if you ever touch my sister again, I will kill you! That is a promise, so help me, God!

Then the peasant was gone. When Leon finally regained his senses, he dragged himself over to Alex and found him unconscious. Somehow he managed to throw Alex over his horse and started back to Usadiba Na Holme.

The evening hours had passed quietly between Sonya and Katie until they heard swift-running horses outside, then a scream pierced the silence of the night. In terror, the girls ran down the stairs to see what was happening.

They found Ivan, Mathilde, and Leon hovering over an unconscious Alex. Disbelief registered on his parents' countenance. At the sight of Alex's mutilated face, Sonya gave a shocked cry and fainted. Leon's face seemed frozen in immobility.

Ivan sent one of the servants for a doctor and then ordered the hysterical Mathilde out of the room to get some bandages and hot water. Tanya, who had been sleeping, entered the hallway and stood rooted to the spot. Katie tried to revive Sonya while Ivan examined his son's wounds cautiously and then began to sponge the blood away.

After reviving Sonya, Katie ventured closer to determine the full extent of Alex's injuries. His eyes were blackened, his nose twisted and broken, his face beaten into a pulpy mass, and carved into the upper part of his right cheek was an *R* about two inches long. Katie felt sick to her stomach.

When the doctor arrived, he set Alex's nose, applied medication to his wounded face, and administered a sedative for the pain. Ivan and Leon carried Alex up to his bedroom and left the worried Sonya to watch over him. The rest of the family adjourned to the library. Ivan poured each of them a shot of brandy and turned to Leon with questioning eyes. The youth's face was flushed, and his blackened eye twitched nervously.

"Perhaps, young man," Ivan suggested, "you had better start at the beginning."

Leon nodded and sipped on his drink as his mind raced back to the turmoil of the night's events, from which he was still trembling. He tried quickly to arrange the sordid tale into the least offensive presentation.

When Leon finished narrating the story as delicately as he could, Ivan swore wrathfully, "I am mounting a hunting party to find that scoundrel."

"Don't you think, Uncle Ivan," Katie offered feebly, "that he might have had some justification?"

"When I want your advice, Katrina," he roared, "I'll ask for it. I have told you that before. No one acts against this family. The peasants are just our property."

He turned to Leon. "Come on, young man. You're the only one who knows what this damn renegade looks like. When we catch him, he'll pay for this savagery."

They saddled the horses quickly and galloped off into the darkness. Katie heard the hoofbeats disappear into silence. She went to Alex's room to relieve Sonya of her watch. It was almost morning before Alex opened his swollen eyes.

"Your assailant, Alex?" she asked with dread. "Who was he?'

It was an effort for him to get the words out through his swollen lips. "Sovinsky," he said. "Peter Sovinsky."

CHAPTER 7

OCTOBER 1914

A damp, raw wind blew in from Finland, biting furiously at all those foolish enough to venture out into its icy path. Katrina shivered and drew her *shuba* closer against her body. Then, as if to make her misery more compete, the heavens opened to discharge a deluge of hail that beat upon the roof of the carriage. The horses struggled to pull though the slush. It was only ten in the morning, but already the day was dark as night. There could be no more fitting day for a funeral.

After a long ride, the coach groaned to a halt. Provovich helped Mathilde, Tanya, Sonya, and Katie out onto the muddy ground. Katie looked about for her Uncle Ivan, who had ridden over earlier on horseback. Not seeing him, Katie started up the long walk to the house. Her legs felt stiff after the freezing journey.

The chunks of hail now changed to a dreary drizzle that penetrated her heavy clothing. A chill overtook her, and she hurried ahead of the others, anxious to reach shelter.

The huge hall that she entered was also damp and cold, and Katie surrendered her *shuba* to a servant reluctantly. The smell of death seemed to seep from every corner of the house. The coffin lay open in the huge old-fashioned parlor. Candles burned, and the scent of perfumed incense hung heavily in the air. This was the third and final day that the living could pay their respects to the deceased, and the house was crowded.

Katie moved forward to look upon the countess Alexis for the last time. Silver hair curled around her small delicate face, now white from the touch of death. Her body was clad in a blue brocade gown. A look of tranquil beauty was etched into her countenance. Tears ran down Katie's cheeks, and she made no effort to check them. She leaned over and kissed the old woman's face and then knelt beside her and said a prayer. In the background, a deep voice intoned the Bible while a high voice chanted softly. Overcome by emotional strain, she turned and fled from the room.

She sought solitude in a storage room and released her tears behind a pile of old furniture, cardboard boxes, and empty wooden crates. So many memories floated before her—the countess over her dainty teacups, her stately dignity, and her laugher the day they had danced to the old fiddle. Katie raised her tear-filled eyes and was startled to see a young monk staring somberly at her.

He had black eyes, a long dark beard, and a sympathetic look that drew her toward him. He was of average height but had very broad shoulders. His full black robe had enormous trumpet-shaped sleeves, and he wore a tall brimless hat trimmed with a veil. Two golden stars on his chest denoted the high rank that he held in his monastic order.

He beckoned to her. She approached him and threw herself on her knees. He made the sign of the cross above her head with folded fingers. "Child," he said gently, "we all must learn to bear grief."

"I know," Katie murmured, rising.

"She was a good and saintly woman, who will now reap the rewards of a higher realm. At last she has joined her husband and our Heavenly Father. You must not cry, for she is happy now. There was no kinder woman on earth than my grandmother."

Katie's eyes widened in surprise.

The young monk seemed to read her mind. "My grandmother never approved of my religious vocation. She would rather have had me marry and serve in the church, but golden brocade robes and a well-lined palm were not my idea of dedication to God." Amused by her shocked look, he smiled. His gaunt appearance proclaimed his life of poverty. She took his outstretched hand. Without additional words, they returned to the crowded room for the funeral service.

The vicar in his high purple hat began singing. Blue smoke curled from his censer. Another look at the monk's face fortified Katie for the long service in which the countess's gracious life was praised. When it was over, people rushed to fetch their coats and join the funeral procession.

The journey was dismal, with a heavy downpour and carriages sticking in the mud. At the cemetery, the coffin was lowered into the oozing earth while the mourners stood listening to the final benediction beneath the unwelcome gift of the perverse heavens.

The mourners returned to the house to eat. The heavy atmosphere dissipated. With the exception of the one grandson, there were no relatives present. The other grandsons were at the front. The war made transportation impossible for the countess's other relatives to attend.

In one corner, an oversized prince elaborated on his personal theories of war. "Such a patriotic spirit we have in this country. Everywhere the streets are filled with workers kissing our officers in gratitude. The peasants throughout Russia are mustering to their country's call. It makes me feel so proud."

Katie moved to the other side of the room, nibbling at a fancy dessert without enthusiasm. An old nobleman was bemoaning the war. "If only that stupid young fool had not assassinated the archduke Ferdinand, all this futile destruction could have been avoided.

"I don't agree with you," a young officer cut in impatiently. "All the countries in Europe have been hungrily grabbing up territorial claims. Germany, England, and France are devouring Africa like savage dogs. We are the only country fortunate enough to have a surplus of land. Europe has been sitting on a keg of explosives for some time. This murder was merely the match that lit the barrel. The whole world is hearing the explosion now."

The old noble rubbed his chin before speaking. "When one reaches my age, international quarrels seem at first to be so impersonal, but suddenly, without warning, they are no longer so. The grandsons we love lie dead on foreign soil, our granddaughters are widowed, and their children are left fatherless. Too late, we wake up to the danger." Tears crept into the old man's eyes. "My only grandson has been killed in Germany. My granddaughter's husband is missing, and she is left alone with three small ones. Our world has gone mad!"

The young officer lowered his eyes to the floor before replying, "Yes, the vision of so many corpses lying in the fields can't be erased."

Katie drifted to another section of the room, only to encounter more war talk.

"How can they expect us to win this war with only one supply line?" an officer questioned with a flushed face. "It's imbecilic. The line is always jammed when we need to bring up fresh reserves. Movement of our wounded is paralyzed. When we have to evacuate, our supplies are held back. Without decent transportation, we have to resort to long foot marches when we need troops. By the time our soldiers arrive at their destination, they and their horses are exhausted, and our precious supplies are used up."

An old man intruded in a timid voice. "My grandson writes that men drop in their tracks from sunstroke. He says it's an awful sight to see young men lying with their faces swollen black from the blistering rays of the sun."

"The sun is no longer a problem, old man," another soldier injected. "Mud, rain, and slush have replaced it. Visibility is poor, and travel slow. Typhus and cholera have broken out and run rampant through our ranks. It's hell out there for our troops!"

Katie's spirits sank lower. Alex, Nicki, and most of the young men whom she knew were at the battle lines. She fled into the hall, where she encountered the countess's grandson again. "Isn't there a ray of hope somewhere?" she asked him desperately. "Still we have our czar to guide us,"

"Do not put too strong a faith in Nicholas, little one," he said. "It is the interior of a man that counts, and though our czar is a handsome, striking man, I fear he is weak inside and ruled by his misguided wife."

"You are a strange man," she replied. "You do not seem to respect what others hold in high esteem. What do they call you in your monastery?"

"Boris."

"And what should I call you?"

"The same," he replied. "There are no formalities in my order. Our goal is to help one another. By doing this, we believe that we are serving God and his desire that all mankind be united in brotherhood. Respect must be earned. It is not a God-given right."

Mathilde and Ivan entered the hallway. "We are ready to leave, Katie." Sonya and Tanya joined them, and they all donned their wraps.

The ride home was one of misery. Ivan had sent his horse home with one of the servants so that he could join them in the carriage. Darkness swallowed up the countryside. There was no moon to guide them. Several times they had to stop and get out so that Ivan and Provovich could push the carriage out of the clinging mud. No one felt inclined to talk. The prevailing silence added to the gloom that had hung over the whole day. Katie longed for the crackling fire that awaited them at home.

The vague outline of the village in the distance brought back memories to Katie of the events of two months ago. Alex had recovered from his wounds. Only the disfigurement on his cheek remained a reminder of that night. He and Leon had both received their commissions and had already left for the front.

Peter had not been apprehended, and she worried about what would happen if he should ever return.

When they had climbed out of their carriage at Usadiba Na Holme, Provovich removed his tall driver's hat and approached Ivan.

"It's a bad time to ask you, sir, what with you being shorthanded and all, but I've been feeling that perhaps it's time for me to join the army too.

Ivan smiled tenderly at the small man before him. "You have my blessing, Provovich. You have a real sense of loyalty and will make a good soldier. When do you plan to leave?"

"In the morning, sir, if it suits you," ventured the driver with a look of relief.

"We will miss you," Ivan said. "I hope you'll come back to us after the war. See me in the morning before you leave for your wages. I'll have a package for you."

"Thank you, sir," the servant said, blushing at the unexpected gesture.

One more loss, Katie lamented as she climbed the hill beneath the curtains of rain that had once more begun to fall.

As the family entered the mansion, they were astounded at the sight that greeted them. Nicki stood in the hallway, beaming broadly at their look of surprise. The group encircled him while hurling a barrage of questions at him. Everyone talked at once. He grinned at their excitement.

"How did you get here?" Sonya wanted to know.

"I was sent to deliver some papers to a general in the rear lines. He was so overwhelmed with the good time I made that he granted me a short leave. Unfortunately, it has taken me so long to get here that I will have to leave within the hour if I am to return to my lines on time."

"Oh, Nicki, why did you make such a long exhausting trip if you can't spend any time with us?" moaned Katie. "Whatever possessed you to do such a thing?"

He grinned. "I have my reasons, which I would like to discuss with Ivan now, if you ladies will excuse us for a few minutes." With that, he and Ivan disappeared into the library and closed the door.

"What is he up to?" ventured Sonya.

"I think that it's perfectly obvious," remarked Mathilde. "Come on, Sonya, I don't think we'll be needed here." Mathilde and her daughter went upstairs to their rooms.

"Oh, Tanya, it's so exciting," Katie beamed. "At last the time has come. I bet you anything that he's asking Uncle Ivan for your hand."

"Do you really think so?" Tanya questioned excitedly.

"Of course, silly, what else?"

"Oh, Katie, I'm so happy that I could cry. I love him so much and have for such a long time! It seems like I have been waiting all my life for this moment!"

The girls sat there tensely. Finally, the sound of the library door opening echoed throughout the stillness of the house. Nicki came out and put on his overcoat in silence. He smiled and kissed them both. Ivan descended the hill with Nicki to the stables, and the girls stared out the open door until the two men had disappeared into the darkness.

Again came an interval of waiting. It seemed like hours before they heard Ivan's footsteps on the porch. He removed his outer clothing and then beckoned them into the parlor, where he poured three glasses with whiskey. He handed one to each of them before taking the last for himself. "It seems there is going to be a wedding in the family. That is providing the bride is willing, of course," he announced.

The girls could not control their smiles.

"Yes," he continued. "I consider it a great honor that Nicki should ask for the hand of one of my girls. Will you accept him, Katie?"

Tanya dropped her drink. The glass shattered against the brick fireplace. An appalled silence filled the room.

At last she turned to Katie, and her eyes were filled with pain. "You took him away from me," she said. "I always thought that you were my friend, but all this time you only pretended! I'll never forgive you, Katie. Never!" Rage and loathing twisted her beautiful face into an ugly mask. "I hate you!" she screamed. Then she turned and fled from the room.

The month after Nicki's visit had been a gloomy one. His proposal had been as much of a shock to Katie as it had been to Tanya. She had tried to reason with her friend, but Tanya had locked her heart against her. Katie felt miserable and sought her uncle for advice.

"What can I do, Uncle Ivan?" she pleaded. "Tanya ought to know that I would not marry Nicki when I know how much she loves him."

"That attitude will only condemn the three of you to a life of misery," her uncle pointed out. "Regardless of what Tanya may feel for Nicki, he does not love her! He never has. It has always been you. I have watched him on all his visits here. It was the sight of you walking into the room that made his eyes glow. You and Nicki are alike, Katie. You are the kind of woman he needs. Nicki is venturesome and unpredictable. He needs a woman who is not bound by convention. I love Tanya too, but she came to us as a strange, withdrawn child, and she a grown into a strange, introverted woman. She loves Nicki, but if she were to become his wife, she would strangle him by wanting him to settle into a routine that revolved around nothing but her and their children. Nicki's greatness is his love for life. She would drain it from him. Their marriage would be a mistake, Katie, and its tragedy would be passed on to their children. Think about it carefully."

Her uncle's words rang true to Katie. "In spite of everything that you have said, Uncle Ivan, I still can't marry Nicki. I don't love him!" she insisted.

"Eh, and what do you know of love?" he questioned. "Nothing but what you have read in those trashy novels that I have forbidden you." Katie flushed guiltily. "Now let me tell you a thing or two. You will never meet anyone else like Nicki. He's from one of the best and wealthiest families in Russia. I know only too well that you would not be pleased at having to do without nice things. He is intelligent. Full of energy. You would never find life with him dull. He has one of the best titles, land, good looks, and brains—all this added to the fact that he is hopelessly in love with you. Tell me, what more could you want from a man?"

"I don't love him."

"Nonsense. What is this concept of love you have? Perhaps you are confusing the thrill of a first kiss with a lifetime emotion," Ivan retorted.

Katie felt embarrassed at his piercing look. He seemed to sense everything that she felt. The vision of Peter rose to her mind. Strong, handsome, rugged Peter who had nothing but pride. She could not forget the emotions that he had stirred within her. *I wonder if, given the chance, Nicki could arouse that same kind of passion in me. Everything Uncle Ivan has said is true. Who else can I marry? The other men of my class seem like shadows compared to him. Marriage to Peter Sovinski is an impossibility. Besides, he is gone now and will probably never return.*

"Maybe you're right, Uncle Ivan, but someone else could always come along," she said.

"Don't delude yourself, Katie," he said gently. "The male population of Russia is decreasing rapidly. There is only one Nikolai Sokoloy. Make up your mind to it, and then write and tell him that you have accepted his proposal. That boy needs you. He is alone out there and needs to know that the woman he loves is waiting for him."

"Let me talk to Tanya before I decide," Katie pleaded.

"Do you think it will do any good? It will be no kindness to tell her that she has lost him. She knows that already. I will talk to her, but do not expect too much. It will take time for her to get over this."

Katie thought of Nicki with his laughing eyes, tender smile, and love of life. She remembered all the happy hours that they had spent together, the joys they had shared. *I could have a lifetime of them if I could bring myself to hurt Tanya, but then Tanya is already lost to me. She will not even speak to me. It is not likely she will forgive me any time soon. Uncle Ivan is right.* At last she said, "I'll write to Nicki tonight and tell him that we can be married whenever he wishes."

CHAPTER 8

NOVEMBER 1914

Katie turned away from the window and opened the letter in her hand.

My Dearest Darling

You cannot imagine my joy when I received your letter accepting me as your future husband. All these months, in which I received no word, I was obsessed with doubt. I was afraid that because of your love for Tanya, you might refuse me. I could not help being aware of Tanya's feeling for me, but though I love her dearly, it is more the love for a sister than that of a sweetheart. Now I live for the time when I will be able to come home and hold you in my arms. The thought of you belonging to me at last will give me the courage to bear the hardships now at hand.

The conditions here are extreme. Supplies are inadequate, and our boots are wearing thin. The roads are frozen, and travel is difficult. One blizzard follows another, and we have learned to live as close to the snow and ice as to our own comrades. I can no longer imagine the sensation of a warm sun shining. The wounded freeze to death where they fall before the medics even have a chance to reach them, and frostbite is taking as many casualties as enemy bullets.

It seems that we have been in constant retreat since the Battle of Tannenberg. We either withdraw or fight savagely to hold our present position but never advance. We can only cling to the hope that things will change for the better when spring comes. It will not be so difficult to transport our food and clothing then, and the change of weather is bound to raise our spirits.

> I must close now as I am to lead an exploring party behind the enemy lines and must finish my preparations. Give all the family my love, and tell them that I think of each one fondly. Write to me soon and often, my love. Out here a man has little to live for, except the warmth gathered through the written pages of his loved ones. Take care of yourself. I love you with all of my heart.
>
> Nicki

The letter made her restless and discontented. Feelings of guilt continue to plague her as she saw Tanya's sorrow-filled eyes day after day. In a melancholy mood, she retreated to the desolate conservatory at the end of the house.

Watching the snow flurries through the window, she recalled the night of the winter ball at Usadiba Na Holme. Was it only a year ago? It seemed like a lifetime now. She recalled Nicki's gentle kiss and wondered what it would be like to be his wife. The decision had involved an intense struggle within herself before she could bring herself to accept his proposal. Now she was committed.

Staring out of the conservatory glass, Katie saw it had finally stopped snowing. On impulse, she decided to go for a ride. She rushed to her room and put on her coat and riding boots before setting out for the stables. She saddled Pride, mounted, and rode out into the nipping air. It stung her cheeks and set her blood racing rapidly. She laughed aloud as she raced Pride across the snow-covered countryside.

The woods looked very different this time of year. The trees, once so green, were now naked and forlorn with their pitiful limbs stretched up as if begging for the warmth of spring again. Katie dismounted and pushed her way past the frozen thickets to the stream where she had bathed Peter's wounds. The tiny creek could scarcely be found beneath the many layers of white crystals covering it now. With a small branch, Katie pushed some of the loose snow away until she could see the brook. There were no running ripples now. Just solid ice.

The crackling of a twig behind startled her, and she turned around abruptly. A girl stood there. Only her face was visible among the heavy clothing, but her resemblance was so strong that there could be little doubt. It had to be Peter's sister, Maria.

The two of them stared awkwardly at each other, and it was Maria who finally broke the silence. "You're the one they call, Katrina."

"Yes," Katie answered softly.

Another pause followed, and then Katie spoke. "How are you and your father?"

"We're both fine.

Katie longed to cry out, "And how is Peter?" but she fought her desire.

Marie spoke again. "This is the first time I have ever seen you this close."

"I know."

"You've very pretty."

"Thank you."

"I heard you are going to be married," she said.

"Yes."

"May I congratulate you."

"Thank you again," Katie said. She longed desperately for news of Peter but could not bring herself to ask directly. She waited, hoping that Maria would eventually volunteer it. "Are you and your father managing all right?"

"Oh yes. It's the crop time that's difficult," Maria explained. "During the winter, we just catch up on the chores, mending the house, repairing the furniture, and things like that. We were lucky that Peter attended to everything before he left."

Katie saw her opening and shot the question recklessly. "And where is he now?"

Marie shook her head. "It would be extremely foolish for me to tell you that."

"You think that I would betray him to my uncle?" she asked.

"And why shouldn't you?" Maria questioned. "You're one of them."

Yes, she thought. *I am one of them.* Another stretch of silence hung between them before Katie brought herself to ask. "Is he all right?"

"Why should that matter to you?" Maria asked. Then she paused when she saw the hurt in Katie's eyes. "It really does matter, doesn't it?" Maria replied. "You really do care."

"Yes," she whispered. "I really do."

"Will you give me your word that you will never tell anyone where he is?" she asked. "The rest of your family is worthless as far as I'm concerned, but somehow I feel that I can trust you. If you ever betray him, though, you will pay dearly."

"I know," she said. "The Sovinskys' revenge is swift and merciless."

Maria blushed and looked away.

Katie withdrew Nana's medal that hung around her neck. "I swear by all that is holy that I shall never cause Peter any grief or pain."

"It may be a little too late for that," Maria said in a quiet but accusing tone.

Katie flushed guiltily. "Please tell me, Maria, if he's safe. I promise that I'll never tell anyone."

"He's as safe as any of the young men these days," Maria said at last. "He's in the army."

"Of course, I should have known. Is he at the front?"

"Yes."

Katie nodded and stared again at the frozen stream. Maria finally broke the silence hanging between them. "It's strange that I should find you here. This is the spot where Peter often came when he was worried or troubled." Maria thought for a moment then offered softly, "But perhaps it's not so strange after all. Maybe you have your memories too."

Katie felt the blood rise to her cheeks, but she said nothing. She recalled the emotions that she had felt in Peter's arms that spring morning so long ago. *Will I ever be able to forget them?*

Maria watched the emotion on her face. "If you really care about my brother, why are you marrying someone else?"

"It is too complicated to explain."

"Love isn't really complicated," Maria offered as she searched Katie's eyes with cynicism but then asked, "will your wedding be soon?"

"I don't know," Katie answered. "I suppose that it will be on the first extended leave that Nicki can get, but we have no way of knowing when that will be."

"Do you love this Nicki very much?"

"I think I do, but then I'm not really certain what love is," she answered honestly. "I know that I'm happy when I am with him. He is handsome and strong. He wants the same things out of life that I do, and he loves me very much."

"But he's not Peter," Maria said softly.

Katie could find no reply to that so fixed her eyes on the ground.

The snow started to fall again, and the flakes drifted down, breaking cold against their faces. Maria stood up. "I think we had better head for home before another blizzard hits."

Katie rose slowly. "You have a very long way to go," she said. "May I take you there? Both of us could easily ride my horse." Katie saw the refusal rising to her lips. "Please, Maria, let me!"

"All right," she consented.

Upon returning home, Katie opened the front door and heard Sonya sobbing hysterically. At the sight of Ivan's anguished face, Katie's glanced around and she saw that Tanya's countenance was also drained of color. She spoke to Katie for the first time in many weeks. "Where have you been?" she lashed out. "We couldn't find you anywhere."

"What's wrong?" Katie asked.

"She is dead! Sonya screamed. "Dead! Dead! Dead!"

"Who?"

"Aunt Mathilde!" Tanya rasped.

CHAPTER 9

DECEMBER 1914

Nicki looked out over the snow-covered landscape. The only buildings that he could see were small farmhouses scattered across the white plain. The wretched huts squatted low on the flat earth, with drifts piled halfway to their roofs.

His mission was to set up a line of barbed wire in front of them then, if time permitted, to erect a sturdier barrier to hold off the advancing Germans. He raised his arm, signaling for his men to follow.

Walking was slippery, and it was a continual struggle to maintain an upright position. The wind blew furiously, and huge hunks of sleet stabbed at his face. His beard was a solid mass, and he licked his lips to melt the ice that constantly formed. His stomach contracted in spasms. He and his men had not eaten for two days because their supply train had not arrived. They received a report informing them that the engine had been ruined by bad coal, and the train lay somewhere on a sidetrack with its precious cargo. He raised his arm again and motioned for his men to halt.

The farmhouse in front of them had a large jagged hole exposing almost the whole front wall. Nicki lowered himself to his stomach and edged forward slowly. The men were tense. They could hear nothing except for the pitiful wailing of the wind. Visibility was poor. Nicki proceeded cautiously. Reaching the hut, he crawled around the entire exterior before entering. He felt an immense sense of relief when he found it empty.

The rest of the soldiers crawled closer. Nicki gave them orders. "We've got to install this jagged wire." The combatants fought against the ferocious wind until they had completed their objective.

"Rest a few minutes," he told them. "Then we have to dig a trench in this frozen earth and erect a sturdier barrier to protect us from the enemy." *I am asking them to attempt an almost impossible job*, Nicki thought.

He lowered his own weary body gratefully onto the icy surface and looked back at the desolate huts. The scene was an ordinary one but not entirely lacking in beauty.

"I wonder where all the people have gone," one of the soldiers pondered aloud.

"They are probably all refugees," Nicki replied. "They are a continual curse and a never-ending problem these days. They slow our troops down along the roads and steal from the precious few supplies that our army still possesses."

"But you can't blame them," another soldier interjected. "They are cold and hungry too."

"Of course," Nicki nodded, noticing that several of his men had removed flasks from their rear pockets. He hesitated about reprimanding them. Drinking was the scourge of the Russian army. Still, what other comfort was there from the biting cold and aching hunger? He shifted his eyes from the weather-beaten faces of his men and pretended not to see.

Absentmindedly, he broke flakes of ice from the beard that he had grown to protect his face from the cruelty of this climate. The image of Katie crept into his thoughts. *What would she say if she could see me now?* He grinned at the thought because she had always been outspoken on the subject of beards. She disliked them intensely, with the exception of her Uncle Ivan's. She had explained it to him one day. "I have never seen Uncle Ivan without a beard, so I can't imagine it absent from his face. It gives him such an overwhelming appearance of dignity."

Nicki smiled. His memories of Katie were the only comfort against the pain and misery that he now endured. He looked at his men. Their faces were gaunt and their eyes hollowed of expression. Beneath their cumbersome clothing stood lean tired bodies. *They are sick of this war and have failed to find any honor in it. Fifteen million men have been called up and sent out into these trenches. Many of them will never climb out when this slaughter is over.*

He shouted at his men against the background of the howling storm. Reluctantly, they staggered to their aching feet. With iron mallets, they chipped away at the frozen earth and shoveled snow. But the holes that they hollowed out were pitifully shallow. Their empty stomachs growled, reminding them of their weakness.

"Stop digging now," Nicki ordered. "We need to erect a protective wall of some sort." The soldiers gathered stones from the shattered farmhouse and some broken tree branches, but their progress was slow. It took most of the night to finish the job, but when morning came, they were ready for the enemy.

The enemy came, but instead of the bullets that they had anticipated, clouds of poison gas arose on the horizon.

My god, Nicki thought. *This is not war but a massacre. What insanity!*

Nicki held his breath then buried his face in the snow, seeking to extract enough fresh oxygen to clear his head. He opened his mouth only long enough to shout one word. "Retreat!"

Those who could, did.

One more small defeat added to the endless chain, Nicki thought. *Each one snowballing until our gigantic Russian army is crawling slowly but certainly toward its own backdoor.*

It was a wretched Christmas season at Usadiba Na Holme. Mathilde had been dead for a month. Her heart attack had been a stunning blow to the family, and they still had not fully recovered from the shock. Ivan wore a hollow look of guilt because of the way he had always treated his wife. Sonya retreated more than ever from the world while Tanya, consumed by her own personal anguish, ignored all of them. Katie missed Tanya's companionship and longed for someone to confide in. *I will be glad when Nicki returns and we can get married and escape from this house of grief.*

She talked her uncle into continuing the annual Christmas tradition. "Uncle Ivan, please let the village children have their Christmas tree and party," she begged. "They have so little to look forward to."

"I don't feel up to playing Saint Nicholas this year, Katie."

"I could get one of the grooms to take your place, Uncle Ivan."

"Very well," he agreed with no real interest.

On Christmas morning, Katie put on her warmest clothing to face the subzero weather. She felt excited because this was her first break in the monotonous routine that they had observed since her Aunt Mathilde's death.

Rushing down the stairs, she gathered up all the parcels in the front hall that she had wrapped the night before. With her arms loaded, she raced down the hill to the waiting sleigh.

She laughed at the sight of the stocky groom.

"I know, miss," he said. "I make a ridiculous-looking Saint Nicholas."

"The children will love you!" she assured him.

As they pulled into the village, she could not help but gasp in admiration at the tree so beautifully decorated with ornaments from the manor. She was so glad that her uncle had consented to have the tree in spite of the death in their family. She searched the faces of the children as the sleigh pulled up before the tree. A short time ago, these children had been stocky and rosy-cheeked, but now their young bodies were lean and their complexions pale.

The children wore such looks of anticipation that Katie could not make them wait. She and the groom removed all of the presents from the large sleigh. The boys' gifts were wrapped in green, and the girls' gifts were wrapped in red. The children came forward and accepted their parcels, and Katie smiled at their happiness.

"My daddy is away," one small girl confided to her.

"All of our fathers are away fighting, stupid," an older boy injected.

The younger girl stuck her tongue out at him.

"I got a book!" the first girl exclaimed.

"I got a wooden horse," a small boy announced, "but I wish my daddy could come home for Christmas." Then he started to sob.

"Crybaby," an older boy scolded. "Your daddy can't be here. Our fathers are fighting the war, silly. You want the Germans to come to your home and kill you?"

"No. No," the smaller boy whimpered with tears rolling down his cheeks. "But I miss my daddy so much." The child's mother now started to cry with him.

"Oh please," Katie injected in misery. "You must try and have a happy Christmas. Your fathers would want you to."

"Yes," Saint Nicholas seconded. "Ho! Ho! Ho!" He rubbed his fat stomach and danced a ridiculous little jig, which amused the children.

"Is there anyone here who has been bad this year?" Saint Nicholas asked. Katie smiled at the silence that met his question.

"Well then," Katie demanded, "I think that the rest of you had better come up and get your gifts."

"Do you have a present for me, Saint Nicholas?" asked a tiny boy who pushed forward aggressively.

"Indeed I do," the man in the red suit replied.

"I helped my mommy all year long," the next little girl announced. Katie gave her a hug, and Saint Nicholas gave her one of the red packages.

The children filed up one at a time in line. Some of the smaller children were excited. Others were timid. The older children had no smiles. Their apprehensions about the war rode on their backs like heavy weights. Their pinched faces reflected no joy. The mothers stood in a circle some distance from the children.

"You're pretty, Ms. Katrina," one of the little girls told her.

"You are pretty also," Katie answered, lifting the child high and whirling her in the air.

It was over all too soon. The bleak-faced mothers took their children's hands, and then the young ones and their gifts were gone. The square was deserted again.

"I guess there is nothing else to do but return home," she announced to the groom.

"That's right, miss."

She climbed into the sleigh, but as they were driving out of the village, she heard a cheerful voice shouting, "Merry Christmas!"

She turned to see who had called out the greeting. It was Maria Sovinsky. Katie waved, and when the peasant girl returned her gesture, she felt her spirits soar.

The war that had started so favorably was going badly. German general Paul Von Hindenburg was called out of retirement, and it was like a prophecy of doom. The losses of the Russian army were so enormous now that they no longer bothered to keep a record of their dead.

It was no real consolation that the Germans were forced to recall several much-needed divisions away from their western front.

A commanding officer sent Alex and Leon out with a party of thirty men to try and rescue some comrades trapped behind enemy lines. Cold, hungry, and tired, they preceded with extreme caution.

"I've had no sleep in two days," Alex grumbled. "My eyes are so heavy that it's an effort to keep my head from sagging on my chest."

"Don't expect a medal from me," Leon replied.

"The cold even crawls beneath this wretched excuse for an overcoat," Alex added. "There's no way to keep warm."

Leon laughed. "Brothers are we all, sharing this great military adventure."

"Damn!" Alex snapped.

"What's wrong now?" Leon questioned.

"A sliver of ice just cut my foot through one of the holes in these sad excuses for boots."

"You bitch too much, Alex," Leon reproved.

"Yeah, sure I bitch too much. Know how many rifles they wanted to give us for this mission? Eight! Know what they told me when I protested?"

"Something sarcastic, I'm sure," Leon said with a grin.

"You're a soldier," they said. "If you need more guns, go and get them from the enemy."

"And what is their justification for such idiocy?"

"Our so-called leader told me that our rifle shortage is acute," Alex relied. "He said that half our forces on the front lines have no rifles now. Can you explain that to me?"

"Ah, Alex, this country was bankrupt already from the Russian-Japanese farce previously initiated by our illustrious, dim-witted czar. We entered this war with a million more men than rifles in our arsenals. Our factories are still not producing enough rifles, bullet, cannons, or anything else, and we are not getting them from our allies."

"So why were we dragged into this fiasco?" Alex moaned.

"Because of a pack of crazy nationalistic Serbs that we don't really care a damn about," Leon explained, kicking at a snowbank. "However, they share our great, noble Orthodox religion. So it's our duty to God and the Russian empire to march forth and be slaughtered by the German guns."

"It's sheer folly to send us on this assignment without adequate artillery, Leon," Alex raged. "Surely they could have mustered enough rifles. But no, I was told that they could not risk thirty-two rifles. We might get killed or captured, and the supplies were too low. I told them that with just eight rifles, they could count on us being captured or killed. I refused to budge without a rifle for each of my men. Our leaders are bloody incompetent."

"You want competency?" Leon laughed. "Join the German army. They have the rifles, the machine guns, the cannons, the warm coats and boots, and even polished helmets. It's because of our generals' incompetence that we are retreating farther eastward each day. Before this war is over, we will be lucky if we haven't ended up in Siberia."

"This is a hell of a war," Alex said, spitting into the snow, which had just started to fall again. "Well, it's been hard enough to see in the dark, but now this damn cursed weather will slow our travel even more."

"The fall of the cards," Leon said good-naturedly. "Let's divide our men and plan to rendezvous. We'll have a better chance of slipping through the enemy lines in two smaller groups."

Alex and Leon split their forces and started out in different directions. It took Alex and his men most of the night to reach their objective. He checked his watch. It was four o'clock in the morning. Leon and his men took the longer route. "It will be at least an hour before we can expect them," he told his men and motioned for them to halt.

"You three stand watch," Alex directed. "The rest of you can sleep. God, I could use a cigarette now," he said, licking is lips.

"The risk is too great," one of his men objected. "The Germans might see the glow."

"I know that," Alex snapped as he sat down. He lowered his aching shoulder against a huge snowdrift and laid his rifle across his stomach to protect it from the dampness. He struggled to keep his eyes open, but he finally gave in to the overpowering desire to sleep. He was awakened by one of his men, shaking his shoulder roughly. "It's five o'clock," he reported, "and the others are not here."

"Damn," Alex spat. "I had hoped that they would arrive on time." He roused his sleeping force, and they waited noiselessly in the dark.

The crunching sound of soft snow foretold that someone was approaching. One of the men whispered to Alex, "There are too few of them to be ours. It must be a small German scouting party."

"Maybe," replied Alex, "but hold your fire." They waited quietly.

Finally, he heard Leon give the password, and his disheveled soldiers stumbled into view. Alex was horrified to see that here were only five men with his friend.

"What happened?" he asked.

"Ambush. It's a miracle that any of us escaped," Leon reported, throwing himself down on the cold earth in exhaustion. He raised his eyebrows questioningly. "What do we do now?"

Alex was deeply disturbed. "We only have twenty men besides ourselves. It would be suicide to attempt our original plan." Hesitantly, he suggested. "Maybe we should go back."

"Are you crazy?" Leon snapped. "Eighty of our comrades are trapped in that wooded area over there. Headquarters thought there was a chance of us rescuing those men. That's why we're here. There are only two machine guns and thirty men holding them on this side. A surprise attack from behind might wipe those nests out and release our men."

"But the odds were against us even when we started, Leon," Alex argued. "Now with only twenty men, we don't stand a chance."

"War is always a gamble," Leon pointed out. "However, the player who is willing to bluff and take the biggest risks is often the winner in spite of his cards. As long as there is any chance, old friend, we are stuck with it."

Alex was silent. He was no glory seeker, but if they did not proceed, they would be labeled as cowards. His father would never let him live it down. "All right then," he agreed. "We had better get moving."

They eased forward into the silent darkness. The sun came over the horizon just as they reached their objective. They pulled to a halt and hid themselves in the bushes and behind the trees dotting the landscape. From their position, they could see no sign of the enemy. Alex sent two men out to scout the area. The men returned. "We could locate only one of the machine guns," they reported.

"Damn," Alex snapped.

"They might have pulled the other one out during the night," Leon suggested.

"Maybe," Alex grunted, "but it's more likely that it is well camouflaged."

Alex and Leon each studied the other's face. Both were inexperienced and filled with indecision. "I guess we had better take a chance," Leon ventured.

"Yeah," Alex agreed reluctantly.

They informed their men of the known machine gun's position, and then Leon gave the order to charge. They were halfway to the nest when the other machine gun opened up upon them, and they found themselves trapped between the two. A few of the men continued toward their initial objective of capturing the machine gun nest, but most of them panicked and fled. Alex and Leon dived behind a shallow snowbank. "What should we do now?" asked Alex.

"God only knows," Leon said and then after a moment added, "I guess we had better try to get that other nest."

Alex was frightened. The sound of bullets whined in his ears. His tired body lacked strength and coordination. His lips were dry, and his chest pounded from the frantic beating of his heart. The odor of gunpowder and blood filled the air. He could hear his men screaming in terror and pain. He stumbled over a dead comrade and hastily turned his eyes away. He rushed on, following Leon blindly. They were close now.

Leon shouted excitedly. "We're going to make it, old buddy. We are—" He didn't. A bullet stopped his flow of words, and he fell with an impact upon the new-fallen snow. Alex crawled to him, and Leon tried to speak from the gaping hole in his throat, but only horrifying guttural sounds emerged. A gush of blood exploded from the wound. His eyes rolled around, and a last violent convulsion seized his body. When it had passed, Leon lay still.

Alex looked at him with horror. He shook the lifeless body in disbelief. He raised his head. The sound of bullets bombarded him from every direction and seemed to detonate in his brain. He broke out in a cold sweat and was seized by severe chills. His stomach churned convulsively, and he vomited beside the corpse of his friend.

Alex's eyes darted about. In every direction, it seemed he could see, hear, and smell death. Overwhelming panic surged through him. He looked at Leon's face again.

That could have been me . . . It still might be me!

Suddenly, his terror became so great that he could not endure it. He turned and ran from the battle.

CHAPTER 10

JANUARY 1915

Liquor bottles lay scattered on the table in front of Ivan. Four were empty, and the contents of the fifth were already half-gone. He had been drinking for four days. His clothes were dirty and rumpled. His beard was uncombed. Books were strewn about the floor along with other objects that he had knocked off the table.

Katie entered the room and stood for a moment before speaking to him. "Uncle Ivan, don't you think you have had enough?"

He murmured a slurred comment and then bellowed angrily, "Damn it to hell, are you proposing to tell me what's good for me?"

Katie shrugged. He had been drunk constantly since he had heard the news of Alex's desertion from the army after Leon's death at the front.

"What'd you want?" he snapped. "For me to sing my children's praises to the world? I am the proud father of a daughter who is a slut and a son who is a coward. Long live the proud line of the Kozakovs!" He pulled himself to his feet and flung his empty glass across the room. It shattered, and the explosion brought a brief moment of silence to the room.

"Please, Uncle Ivan. You can't go on this way," she pleaded. "You will kill yourself."

"Who'd care?" he demanded.

"I would," she said, standing on her toes and kissing his cheek.

"You're a good girl, Katie," he said. "A good girl! All girls ought to be as good as you. World would be all right then. Now go way and leave me in my misery."

There was no reasoning with him. She gave up. She had gone only a few steps down the hall when she heard the crash. She rushed back to the room and found him lying on the floor with his head in a pool of blood.

Several days had passed since Ivan's accident when he struck his head on a heavy oak table. Now that he had regained his senses, he spent his time trying to terrorize those caring for him. Katie refused to take his bullying seriously. "You are not going to have anything more to drink for quite a long time," she stated forcefully. "So don't threaten me!"

He growled and then gave up. *That girl has a streak as stubborn and strong as my own,* he allowed. Confined to bed, Ivan had had a lot of time to dwell on his troubles. *It is impossible now for Alex to become the master of Usadiba Na Holme. Even if I can forgive my son someday, he's a deserter, and the rest of the world will not forget. That leaves Sonya and her heirs to inherit my land.* "Christ," he cursed softly. *Even if my daughter ever marries respectably, and I have my doubts about that, she will probably bring no end of scandal to our proud name. I doubt she will ever remain a faithful wife to any man.*

If only it were possible to leave my estates to Katie and Nicolai! Katie has the qualities that I wanted in my own children. And Nicki, how I admire that boy! He has the breeding that Alex has always lacked, but to disinherit my own daughter would bring immediate attention to this house and air all of its ugly secrets. What a blunder my marriage was. If I had not remarried, my title and lands would pass to Katie, and there would be honor in the generations to come.

Sonya entered the room to check on her father's condition, and Ivan let his eyes sweep over her beautiful face and long dark hair. He felt guilty about his harsh treatment of her. *Perhaps we could mend our differences*, he mused. *It might not be too late.*

"Come here, child," he ordered.

She approached him timidly.

"May I have a glass of water?" he asked.

Sonya poured water from a pitcher beside his bed into a glass and handed it to him then crossed to the other side of the room to shut his window. "Is there anything else that you want before I leave?"

She hates me, he thought. *She hates me bitterly. It really is too late!*

Maria trembled with excitement as she looked down at the letter in her hand. It had been two months since she had last received any word from Peter. She missed him so much. The house seemed empty without him. Her father brooded silently with his loss lying open on his weather-beaten face. She had never been talkative, and lacking Peter's stimulation, she had grown silent also. She sighed and tore open the envelope. Peter's bold handwriting leaped out at her.

My Dearest Sister,

I am sorry to have left you without word for so long, but it has been difficult to arrange channels to forward a letter to you. I dare not use the ordinary ones.

I have been promoted since I last wrote. Otherwise, there has been little change in my life. Conditions here are miserable. There is not enough food to go around. What we do have is of inferior quality, and many of the men are suffering from malnutrition. Our clothing is badly worn, but there is none to replace it. My own coat has four holes in it. My boots have worn thin like cardboard. We lack rifles and ammunition and are forced to limit our aggression to absolute successes.

Not a day passes that I do not wonder how you and Father are faring. Is his health good? I hope that the war has not made your life too difficult. I am hungry for news of you both. The soldier who brought this letter will return for a reply in a day. Send me word by him.

The weather here is bad, but I cannot seriously complain, for I know that it is the same at home this time of year.

Resentment is fairly high against the government these days. Our offensive has been completely broken, and the blame must be laid on someone's shoulders.

Desertion has become a major problem. Our army has not found an adequate resolution for dealing with it. In some locations, much to our horror, our troops have begun to openly fraternize with the Germans and Austrians. This is an insane war. Most of our soldiers are uncertain what they are fighting for.

Time is running out, little sister. I must relieve a comrade of sentry duty within the hour, so I will seal this letter and entrust it to a friend who is traveling your way.

Love from your brother,
Peter

Maria read the letter again and again. How she longed to see her brother. She shrugged with resignation and sat down at the table to begin her reply.

At the sound of the church bells in the distance, Boris laid down his pen and stretched his cramped body. All day he had been laboriously copying faded scriptures into a crisp new book. He felt tired in body and mind. He pushed back his stool from the rough wooden table that served as his desk and stood erect. His cell was no different from that of any other monk. It was small, dark, and contained no other furniture than the table, chair, and a straw mattress on the floor.

He felt chilled from the cold creeping beneath his flowing robe. He rubbed his hands to restore better circulation and then made his preparations to go out.

The monastery was spartan but entirely self-sufficient. It was surrounded by small fields and orchards that were cultivated during the spring and summer months, but the fields lay white and frozen now. The livestock that usually grazed on the grounds were securely enclosed in an area with a lean-to during the winter months.

On the way to chapel, Boris passed a holy well. In the summer months, the peasants came from near and far to drink the blessed water, but in winter, it was locked beneath a solid block of ice.

Boris entered the chapel and knelt before the altar. He prayed today, as he did every day, for the thousands of wounded and dead lying in the trenches throughout Europe. *Will there never be an end to this destruction of life?* he questioned. *Within this country, 96 percent of our men answered the call to duty. Slowly their numbers are decreasing. Those that are still alive have become hardened by this war . . . drained of emotion by the deprivation and killing. How can they be brought back into your fold, Lord? How can they be taught goodness and decency again? My work will only be beginning when that of others has ended . . . How insignificant I feel. Will my brothers and I be able to bring about the birth of love again?*

He bowed his head and prayed for strength.

Katrina rode out into the January afternoon. Although a heavy snowfall lay on the ground, the air felt comparatively warm. *I am so bored with life on the hill. I feel I have to escape. Uncle Ivan is feeling better, but his improved condition is not making our lives very pleasant. A strong, capable man all of his life, he finds the role of invalid unbearable. Everyone has suffered for his lack of mobility. I will be glad when he is up and around again.*

She rode toward the village with the faint hope that she might see Maria but was unsuccessful. Feeling disappointed, she began the long ride home. On impulse, she headed into the wooded area where she had first met Peter. The sun slanted through barren tree limbs casting shadows on the recent fallen snow. She urged Pride on in a slow walk and was about to turn when she heard someone weeping in the distance. She dismounted, wrapped Pride's reins around a tree, and proceeded quietly.

"Sonya! What on earth are you doing out here in the woods?" she cried out in surprise. "I didn't see your horse. How did you get here?"

"I walked," her cousin sobbed.

Katie drew closer and sat down beside her. Sonya's face was pale. She seemed to have been disturbed about something for some time now.

"Is there something I can do for you, Sonya?" Katie asked.

"I don't know," Sonya choked between sobs.

"Maybe if you talked about it, it might help."

Sonya struggled with her grief for a few moments longer and then attempted a smile. "It's just been so much at once, Katie. First Mother, and then Alex. I know neither of them were very wonderful people, but they were the only ones besides you that ever cared for me. Father can't stand me."

"Don't say that, Sonya."

"We both know it's true, Katie. He can't stand me, and I hate him! Tanya has always hated me. You are the only one that I have left, and soon you will be marrying Nicki. Then you'll be leaving also. I'll be left to live the rest of my days with two people who hate me." She started crying hysterically. "It might have been different, you see, because he cared. He didn't know about all the others." Her voice became shrill. She was wide-eyed with grief. "He really did care, Katie!"

"Hush, Sonya," Katie soothed.

"You don't understand, Katie," she insisted. "You don't understand."

"I'm trying to, Sonya. If you will only tell me!

"He is dead like Mother," she cried. "Forever gone. Dead!"

"Who, Sonya?"

"Leon," her voice moaned in a tired, thin whisper. "And I'm going to have his child."

Sonya wrung her hands in anguish. "It's obvious that I cannot hide my condition much longer, Katie. Yet I'm terrified of breaking the news to Father. Could you . . . would you consider telling him?"

"I would do anything in the world to help you, Sonya, but the only honest thing is to tell him yourself. You'll have to face him sooner or later."

"I know," Sonya agreed, "but that doesn't make me less frightened. Will you at least come with me?"

"Of course."

Sonya stood up, and Katie reached out and steadied her trembling cousin. "I wish I had your courage, Katie," she sighed. "He already hates me so. How will he feel when he finds out about my baby?"

Katie shared Sonya's apprehension. There was not much consolation that she could offer Sonya, so she said, "Let's just get it over with."

Ivan, who had completely recovered from his accident, did not look up from his newspaper when Sonya and Katie entered the study. "The war is going from bad to worse," he proclaimed.

Katie cleared her throat to gain his attention, and he raised his eyes from the newspaper that he was holding.

Sonya stepped forward. "I want to talk to you, Father. I know that this will be a terrible shock, but I don't know how I can cushion the news. I'm going to have a baby," she announced.

Ivan's face clouded suspiciously. "You were married secretly?'

Sonya lowered her eyes.

"Then you will be married immediately, by god!" he shouted.

"I can't, Father," she said softly. "It's Leon's child, and Leon is dead."

Ivan rose to his feet. His eyes darkened. "I should have known that you would never change!" he roared. "Now my dishonor is complete. A bastard will reign as the future Count of Usadiba Na Holme!"

Sonya backed away from her raging father. Ivan's countenance flushed crimson. Raw hatred flashed in his eyes. "You are worse than a whore. At least they get paid for their favors." He slapped Sonya's face, and the impact of the blow vibrated through the tense room. He grabbed hold of her shoulders and shook her until she started to cry.

"Stop it, Uncle Ivan," Katie screamed. "You are hurting her!"

"And what do you think I have in mind?" he shouted. "Perhaps you think that I ought to kiss her sweet face and tell her, 'Well done, daughter!'" He slapped Sonya brutally again, and she began to sob hysterically.

"Uncle Ivan," Katie pleaded, "you are forgetting her condition."

"Damn her condition to hell!" he roared.

Katie was terrified that her Uncle might seriously injure Sonya. She picked up a large book and struck him on his back. The blow distracted him long enough to allow Sonya to escape from the room. Katie followed her.

That night, Sonya swallowed half the ingredients in their medicine chest. One of the servants found her lying on the floor. Katie pulled her to her feet and induced her to vomit. Afterward, Sonya lay on her bed with her eyes closed.

Oh, Sonya, I remember how you used to swallow ink or chalk so your complexion would appear pale and delicate on special occasions. You were ill several times from your folly, but you looked healthy then compared to now.

The contrast of Sonya's black hair against her pallid complexion was startling. The sheet that covered her showed the ever-so-slight swelling of her child. *She carries her baby well. It is her fifth month, and no one has noticed her condition.* Katie leaned over and kissed her cousin's brow then tiptoed from the room.

She went to Ivan's bedroom, knocked, and entered without waiting for a response. He sat in a chair by his bed, reading a book. He looked up and was startled to see her. She lashed into him before he had a chance to speak.

"All of this is your fault," she shouted. "If she had died, it would have been the same as murder. You're a harsh and ruthless man, Uncle Ivan! You've no forgiveness in you. Did it ever occur to you that you are responsible for what your children have become? Thank God that I was not born into this house, or I might have turned out just like them."

"You dare to talk like this to me?" he asked with his eyes widening.

"It's about time that someone did! You rejected Alex and Sonya in their childhood. They didn't look or act like what you thought a Kozakov ought to, so you withheld your love. You're responsible for the love-starved creature that Sonya has become."

Ivan sat silently with his eyes fixed on Katie's face, shaking his head in protest.

"It was unfortunate that Sonya was not born brilliant or gifted. Perhaps then she could have escaped from her cold and shallow world. All she had, though, was her beauty. She learned to use it to get the attention that she craved. In each man's arms, for a little while, she was his world. It was the only kind of love that she ever knew, but it was better than none."

"Stop it, Katie," Ivan demanded.

"Oh no. You thought that you could change Sonya by imprisonment and brutality," Katie accused. "A lion in captivity may appear tame, but turn him loose and he will revert back to his true form. You can't force character. You molded your daughter into a love-starved creature. Now you want to cast her out and forget what you have wrought."

Ivan's eyes became moist, and his stern face turned ashen.

"And Alex!" she went on relentlessly. "Did you ever try to build his character? Instead of a father to look up to, he was forced to grovel before you. He was pathetic in his attempts to try and impress others by his pursuit of women, drinking, and cruel acts. He could never please you though. So in the end, he ran from a life that he had never learned to face."

Ivan's cheeks tightened. He pushed his hand out toward her, trying to shut off her words. "Stop! You've said enough!" he shouted.

"But we haven't talked about poor Aunt Mathilde yet. You never gave her love either. She was simply a convenience to breed your children. She was merely tolerated. She never had a chance because she couldn't compete with your first wife."

"You're unfair, Katie," he said. "I have been good to you and Tanya."

"Yes, but Tanya was not important. She had no Kozakov blood in her veins. It is not necessary for her to live up to your standards."

"You are an ungrateful girl, Katie," he said. "I have never done anything to hurt you."

"True, but it was only because I happened to be what you thought a Kozakov should be." Katie and Ivan locked eyes.

Minutes passed before Ivan finally asked. "How is she?"

"She's very ill, but she will live."

"You think, then, that I should forgive her and bear her shame?

"You have no other choice," Katie exclaimed. "Mathilde and Alex are gone, and I'll be leaving soon. Sonya is all that you have left. Cast her out, and you will die a lonely old man. It is not likely that she will make an honorable marriage now. That baby of hers, legitimate or not, is the only heir that you will ever have."

"I have you, Katie."

"No, make no mistake about that," she emphasized. "Usadiba Na Holme is not my heritage. I am going to be Nicki's wife. His heritage will be mine. Accept Sonya's baby. Give her child the love that you never gave your own children. Then you will have someone to build for again, a Kozakov heir that you can be proud of. The baby's illegitimate birth will not matter in the end. I think Sonya will be a good mother because for the first time in her life, she will have someone of her own to love. Help her, Uncle Ivan!"

He looked at Katie. Tears were running down his cheeks. "I will try," he said.

He stood up wearily. "I think I will go to her now."

CHAPTER 11

FEBRUARY 1915

Peter broke the brittle branches from the tiny tree with great reluctance. *Another tree that will not bloom in spring . . . War destroys everything in its path, but there is no alternative. Firewood is scarce. The men have to have an occasional fire before which to thaw.* He rubbed his own frozen hands and then picked up the meager pile of faggots that he had gathered. *If we are lucky, we will have enough to cook our dinner tonight. Food is inadequate and tasteless enough without having to eat it cold and raw.*

In the distance, he saw a soldier fleeing across the white wasteland. He pondered whether it was worth the effort to pursue him and decided against it. *I would have to put my precious kindling down. Odds are the man will make his escape anyway. There is no stopping them now. They are deserting by the hundreds, traveling by train, cart, foot, or any means that will take them away from this freezing, starving, miserable line known as the German front. Poor fools don't even know what they are fighting for. Why should they throw away their lives for autocrats and generals? Their thoughts are on the coming spring planting. They want to get home before they lose the whole year.*

Those still here are losing their hatred for the enemy. They have come to think of the Germans as common folks like themselves. They visit across the lines whenever the officers are absent. This friendly feeling for the Germans is another obstacle to a Russian victory. The Germans exploit it by filling our troops with free liquor. Then they photograph our lines and extract information from our men about major Russian operations.

Peter grunted in disgust. *How can we hope to win this goddamn war when we have an army of ignorant, homesick farmers? Even some of our officers have grown lax. One was shot last week as a traitor after he had been seen accepting a cigarette from an enemy officer. The youth of this nation have certainly lost their illusions of war being exciting. They know it now for what it is. Foul and corrupt.*

Peter was glad when he reached the comparative safety of his own trench. He laid the bundle of branches before his men, and it was accepted with appreciation. "You didn't have to do that, Captain," one of them said.

"Hey, we're all in this together," Peter replied. "An officer shouldn't ask his men to do anything that he's not willing to do."

The soldiers sat there silently, content just to be inactive for a short period. They let their thoughts drift where they might. Peter couldn't help musing, *Our great Russian army is not very impressive looking. We're just a lot of tired men in long shabby coats of drab field green, tall fur caps, and unoiled boots. Our sordid appearance in tattered and dirty uniforms does nothing to raise our sunken morale. We are a dismal comparison to the striking appearance of the German army with their neat, well-fitting uniforms and polished steel helmets.*

Peter had risen rapidly through the ranks. His appearance was one that commanded instant respect. He joined in the most dangerous tasks yet performed the most meager and boring duties that had to be carried out for the group's survival. As a result, his men rarely complained about their assigned duties.

Peter sat down with his men but let his thoughts drift across the miles. He centered them on Maria, his father, and Katie. His sister never mentioned Katie when she wrote, and his pride would not let him ask for the news for which he hungered. As he thought about what he would be doing now if he were home, he spotted an officer walking toward the entrenchment. He hoped that it did not mean additional assignments for his men. They were close to exhaustion. This was their first quiet afternoon in weeks. The enemy had pulled back temporarily, leaving only enough men to hold their lines steady. It was a luxury to relax in the prevailing lull even though the firing was liable to resume again at any moment.

Peter and the officer exchanged greetings. "You're a lucky dog, Sovinsky. You're being sent back to the rear with some documents. There's a three-day pass waiting for you. Hope you enjoy yourself. I wouldn't mind trading places with you, but you've earned it. After you've gathered your gear, report for the papers."

Peter was pleased with the unexpected change. *There is not much to do behind the lines, but at least it will give me a chance to catch up on some of the sleep that I've lost this past month. Sometimes there are even a few women serving refreshments of a simple sort to us soldiers. A female face would be a pleasant change after nothing but the bearded countenances of my comrades for so long.* He smiled at the thought. *Perhaps I will get a chance to do some reading, but most of all, it will be good to just relax. It will be wonderful to wake up in the morning without the sound of exploding artillery.*

He said farewell to his comrades, gathered up his equipment, picked up the papers that he was to transfer, and drove to the rear lines where he delivered the documents. Upon dismissal, he reported to the sleeping-quarters area and was assigned a space. He left his gear atop a cot and set out to see what he could find.

He was disappointed that there were no women in the camp area. The only building maintained for pleasure was a teahouse, which now served as a bar. Since there was nothing else to do, he decided that he could use a drink. The small building was in the middle of the camp, and men were pouring in and out of it in large numbers.

The hut was crowded, and a thick haze of smoke hung over the occupants. There were many and varied groups of men sitting around tables. Some were singing. Some were telling jokes that brought forth howls of laughter. Others were quietly getting drunk. Around one table, though, was a large group of men with only one man talking. The others stared at him, seemingly spellbound. Peter ordered a drink and joined the crowd surrounding the speaker.

The man was small in stature and slender. His hair was gray except for a striking streak of black running across the top. Judging from his sitting position, the man seemed to be less than medium height, and his shoulders curved slightly forward in a stoop. A long, thin nose protruded from his sensitive face, and his eyes were set back deeply. The ashen hue of his face gave him an unearthly look in this smoked-clouded room. It was not his appearance, though, but his voice that attracted like a magnet. It was very soft but remarkably resonant, and his audience hung on to each word that he uttered with awe reflected in their eyes.

"I have seen Czar Nicholas, and he's handsome and striking in appearance, but he does not understand his people. The country looks to him for strength and guidance in these troubled times, but how can he help us when he doesn't even know us? He's ignorant of the conditions in his own country. In spite of the pleas of those close to him, he turns a deaf ear. We need a leader who is close to the people, for it is the people who are, in reality, the country!"

Peter nodded. He could not help but agree with the little man.

The soldier standing next to Peter shouted, "You are right, Vladimir."

"Czar Nicholas is concerned only with his own family," Vladimir continued. "Whether you live or die is of no consequence to him. Did you ever ask yourselves how such a state of things came to be? Why are strong men like you ruled by a class of puny degenerate nobles? Just because their fathers dominated your fathers! And you accept this as a way of life. Why? Leaders should be chosen because of worth and capability rather than because of an accident of birth. You are fools!"

"Yes," Peter agreed again. "That's what we are!"

"Each of you have been ground beneath the heel of tyrants," the speaker continued, now raising his voice. "I beg you. Wake up! Band together! Educate yourselves and prepare for leadership. Evaluate your own worth. If you have weak points, strengthen them. If you have bad ones, eliminate them. Are none of you stronger or more intelligent than these aristocrats who have trampled on you? Think about it. Prepare! This country belongs to you. Make your sons the free men that you have never been!"

Vladimir studied the men before him. Most of them seemed to be of the usual mold, honest but common. Only one seemed different. He was no ordinary soldier. This one's dark eyes blazed with unmistakable passion, and his face looked intelligent and self-assured.

"I was once a professor in a large university," Vladimir continued, "but was exiled to Siberia for my so-called extreme and radical views. Since my return, I have dedicated myself to trying to interest you in your own unfortunate plight. I have traveled throughout this country, speaking whenever possible. I am incensed that our Russia is rated as a second-class nation. Russia is one of the largest countries in the world. Yet it has not progressed very far beyond the Middle Ages. I dream of the day when our Russia will be a world power, one that other nations will look up to rather than down upon. We have to educate our people first though. They have to want something better than what they have now. The nobles will never educate the masses. It would make their own position too precarious. Someone has to do it. I need to find leaders within your ranks. Men who see the truth and are willing to do something when the time comes."

Peter spoke out, choosing his words carefully. "This idea of education is all well and good, but it is useless without organization. Hundreds of singularly prepared men will accomplish little spread out across this vast nation. To be an effective force, they must be bound together under the proper leadership."

Vladimir smiled when he heard Peter speak. "We will organize while we study!" Vladimir assured him. "When we are properly qualified and large in number, there will be no question as to us taking what rightfully belongs to us."

The older and younger man locked eyes across the table. They understood each other instinctively. An invisible bond was immediately formed.

"I think, my friend, that we want the same things," Vladimir said with a smile.

"Yes, the abolition of injustice against the common man who is constantly crushed by a crumbling aristocracy," Peter said. "And the building of a new world, where men are judged by their individual worth rather than an accident of birth."

As the other men drifted off, Vladimir stood up and asked Peter, "Would you like to come to my room and have a drink? My carriage is outside and will take us to the nearby town where I am staying."

Peter accepted, and the two men left the teahouse together.

Katie sat in the parlor and watched the sunlight dance through the windows between the heavy wine-colored drapes. She glanced down at the written pages in her hands, and the words jumped out in a challenge.

> My Dearest Katie,
>
> At last I have been promised the leave that I have been hoping for so desperately. In three months' time, I will be home. I will only have two weeks, so make all the wedding preparations beforehand. None of our precious time must be wasted. The longing in me has become unendurable. My only consolation is the knowledge that in May, you will become my wife.
>
> Love,
> Nicki

A definite date! Katie tried to keep herself from trembling, but she felt frightened. *Everything will be different now. Nicki will no longer be just the friend to ride across the countryside with. No longer Tanya's love. He is going to be my husband. I will lie in his arms . . . in his bed . . . every night . . . for the rest of my life. I will bear his children.* A sense of panic rose within her. "Oh, dear God! Have I made the right decision?"

She stood up and walked to the window. The world outside suddenly seemed different. She pressed her shaking hands against the glass in an effort to push away her uncertainties, but her apprehension mounted.

"I just wish that it were not so soon," she murmured.

CHAPTER 12

MAY 1915

Due to the priority of troop shipments and supplies, Nicki's relatives had been unsuccessful in making the necessary transportation arrangements to attend the wedding. Katie felt relieved that she would not have the burden of meeting Nicki's relatives at such a strenuous time.

They had not invited many people because of Sonya's condition. She was now in the eighth month of her pregnancy. Tanya had gone to stay with friends until the actual wedding day as she did not want to bring any awkwardness to the occasion.

At the sound of his bold knock, Katrina, Ivan, and Sonya rose to their feet simultaneously and rushed to the entrance hall. A servant was already helping Nicki remove his coat and hat. Katie studied him anxiously. Physically he was the same except for a slight weight loss, but there was another change. She tried to pinpoint it exactly. She saw that his green eyes no longer danced with laughter and that tiny lines pulled at the corners of them. His face was taut, and his lips pressed more tightly together than before. No easy grin played on his mouth now, and he looked very fatigued.

Throughout dinner, Ivan plied Nicki with questions pertaining to every aspect of military life. Nicki answered him patiently, but his eyes continually sought Katie's across the table. After dinner, Ivan suggested that they retire to the library to have a drink.

Ivan sat in his enormous red leather chair while Sonya sat on the rug, leaning her dark head against her father's knee. Katie smiled at the picture. *They have become very close these past few months. It is touching to see my big gruff uncle finally devoting himself to his delicate daughter. Sonya's body is so swollen with her child now, and both of them are waiting anxiously for the baby's arrival. The baby has become a symbol now of a more rewarding life to come.*

"Well, Nicki," Ivan's deep voice boomed, "tell me how things are going at the front. Where are the lines? What is new?"

Nicki smiled tolerantly. "The weather is the only improvement in our war conditions. It is beautiful! You have never lived until you have seen Poland in the spring. It is like a fairyland, but it will not be so for long. As we retreat, we leave nothing but piles of rubble, and slowly, foot by foot, we are being forced to draw back from Poland."

"Why?" Ivan demanded.

"The main reason is the lack of munitions," Nicki explained. "We just do not have enough, while our enemy seems to have an inexhaustible supply. We are heavily rationed and limited in all our movements. On top of that, our losses have been catastrophic. Besides the deaths, we have had an endless stream of men deserting and others taken prisoner. Many of them happily so, I'm afraid. They're thankful to escape the constant cold and hunger surrounding us."

"Young men today lack the spirit that we used to have," Ivan commented, shaking his head. Lack of ammunition would have merely stimulated us to make more daring plans."

"Yes," Nicki agreed. "Our soldiers do seem to have lost their spirit, but the living conditions are so intolerable. There is practically no sanitation. Besides being cold, hungry, and under constant threat of death, we are pestered with lice, fevers, and plagues. The men just don't care anymore. It's a constant battle just to stay alive under such godforsaken conditions. Can you blame them? They are farmers and factory workers, not professional soldiers. They don't even know what they are fighting for. They don't understand concepts like colonizing and politics."

"Do you think that there is any chance that we will win the war, Nicki?" Sonya asked.

"There's always a chance. We have the manpower, but it is the inadequacy of supplies that is ruining us. Our soldiers must often wait until one of their comrades is dead or wounded before they can acquire a rifle. In contrast, our enemy has heavy artillery concentrated along the whole front. Foot soldiers, many without any weapons, are scarcely a match for cannons and tanks."

"It sounds pretty hopeless to me," sighed Sonya.

Ivan opened his mouth to continue, but Nicki had become impatient. He was tired of war talk. "Ivan, I think that Katie and I want to spend some time together now."

Nicki's directness startled Ivan, and he stared at him for a few seconds with a surprised look upon his face. Sonya's body tensed but relaxed when her father broke into a roaring laugh. "Forgive an old man's whimsy," he said. "At my age, it is easy to forget the hot blood rushing in the veins of youth."

Katie's face flushed with embarrassment.

"Go ahead, you two," Ivan smiled affectionately. "Get out of here."

Eagerly, Nicki grabbed Katie's arm and pulled her from the room. "Where can we go to be alone?" he demanded. "What about the conservatory?"

"It's too cold there, Nicki," she said. "But we can go into the study."

As soon as they entered, Nicki closed the door behind them and turned the key in the lock. "That's not necessary, Nicki," gasped Katie.

"I want to be sure that no one is going to disturb us for a while," he said. Then he crossed the room in a couple of steps and grasped Katie in his arms. He lifted her chin with one hand and stared down into her eyes. "You are so damn beautiful!" he said before pressing his mouth on hers.

She found his lips warm and demanding, and his body pressed urgently against hers. She tried to pull away, but he only held her more securely with his lips pressing harder, demanding a response to his ardor. His hand fumbled with the buttons on her dress until he had opened it to the waist. He grasped one of her soft breasts through her thin undergarments, and his breath was hot on her face. She pulled back from his violent embrace, edged away, clutching her dress tightly around her neck.

Nicki watched her, silent and unmoved. It took her a minute to regain her composure. "You are acting like a wild animal," she accused as she buttoned up her dress.

His eyes darkened, but he forced his voice to remain calm. "You used to be a little girl, Katie, but now you are a beautiful woman, and I am a man! I have been out in the trenches for a long time, and I want you!"

Katie bit her lip and lowered her eyes. Nicki waited with a look of impatience on his face while the seconds ticked by. "You're not the same man that I knew before, Nicki," she whispered. "You're different now!"

"Of course I'm different!" he said. "How can any man go into battle and come out without being different. War hardens men. We live with death. We are lulled to sleep by exploding cannons, and we've had to learn to look away from the cruelties around us. We tighten our belts when friends are blown to pieces before our eyes. When you live like that, you long for only one thing. Life! You fight blindly to maintain it. You can't afford the luxury of mercy. Giving a dying enemy a sip of water could cost you your life, for he's likely to stab you in the guts as you bend over him. If you stop to retrieve a fallen comrade, your head may be blown off. So you have to stop feeling. To love a comrade means pain when he's gone, and most of them go sooner or later! So what do you expect of me? You want sweet talk and gentle kisses? All right. I will give them to you later, but not now! I'm starved, Katie. Starved for your love. I want to make sure that you are really mine."

"Oh, Nicki," she pleaded.

"You do love me, don't you?" he asked. His eyes locked with hers, and she could not look away. "You don't answer. Your eyes have always been a mirror of your emotions, Katie, and they have given you away." His eyes darkened more, and he frowned. "Is there someone else?"

"No, Nicki. There's no one else."

"Then what is it?" he asked.

She shrugged with confusion. "Don't press me so hard, Nicki," she said softly.

"I'm not really sure how I feel. I'm not even sure what love is. I know that I've always cared for you and liked being with you, but I am not prepared for the change in our relationship," she stammered. "I know that I should have been. I'm afraid that in this house, we've been left on our own to acquire the necessary knowledge and experiences of life," she explained. "Someone else once told me that I needed to grow up, but I'm afraid that I haven't." She blushed. "I'm confused. I can't promise you anything, Nicki. Under the circumstances, maybe it would be best to postpone our wedding for a while."

Pain replaced the passion in Nicki's eyes. "No, Katie!" he said forcefully. "If you don't love me, I'll just have to learn to live with that fact, but I still want you. I want you in any way that I can have you. If you do not love me now, then I can only hope that someday you will." His voice turned soft and husky with emotion. "What about it, Katie? You will go through with the wedding?"

Katie looked into his rugged, honest face and knew that she could not refuse him. Most women spent a lifetime looking for such a man, and he loved her. "Oh, Nicki, please forgive me," she cried softly.

She pressed her soft lips against his and let herself be captured in the warmth of his embrace. He was gentle now. He smothered her with kisses, and she felt content. But then his ardor began to rise once again, and his body became more demanding. His lips pressed harder, and as she felt the strength of his renewed passion, she made no attempt to push him away this time, but as his hands unfastened her buttons again, she pleaded. "No, Nicki."

"Why not, Katie? We are going to be married in a couple of days. What difference can it make?" he asked. "I want you so desperately that it hurts!" He pressed his hot face against her soft breasts.

Do I have the right to refuse him? Katie asked herself. *He loves me, and we are going to be married.* She stroked his hair tenderly and then lifted his face so that her eyes looked directly into his. "Nicki, if you want me tonight, I don't really think that I can refuse you, but I will not feel right about it. It will not be the same, the way that I dreamed about it. Not here, and I know afterward that I would not be able to look Uncle Ivan in the face. He always senses my guilt. Can't we wait just a few days longer until it's right and there's no shame involved?"

Nicki looked into Katie's face and then nodded reluctantly. "You are right, of course, darling. I have been acting very selfishly. Can you forgive a fool who just loves you too much to be reasonable?"

Katie smiled warmly and answered him with a gentle kiss.

CHAPTER 13

MAY 1915

Since meeting Vladimir, Peter had indoctrinated most of the men that he had come in contact with, a relatively easy task since his men worshiped him. His sincere face and blazing eyes were enough to swing these tired, war-weary men over to his convictions, for Peter held out a shining dream. Who were they to say nay to such a promise?

Vladimir was able to travel farther and had a greater degree of freedom than Peter, but both worked feverishly and met whenever possible. Peter continually pondered their circumstances. *Our war conditions grow worse. Our soldiers' morale sinks lower all the time, making them easy recruits for our new philosophy. Our enemies have taken a million of the czar's troops prisoners. The wounded and the dead are too numerous to count anymore. I wonder if Russia can ever recover from this tremendous drain of men and materials. What have our losses really accomplished? How can it possibly mean a better world in the end?*

Exhausting their theme of politics one day, Peter and his older friend leaned back against a gigantic tree, each puffing on a cigarette. "What is your opinion of the church, Vladimir?" Peter asked.

"Well, it is an escape like many things."

"You don't believe in God, then?"

"I very definitely believe there is an all powerful force," Vladimir hastened to explain. "In fact, I feel that it is guiding us in our present mission. However, I do not believe that the costumed men of the church are God's sole representatives or that he can be reached only through them. Many of these brightly robed ones are hypocritical parasites with ever-outward-stretched palms."

"Yet they serve as a comfort to many," Peter countered, thinking of his sister.

"Yes," Vladimir conceded. "The church provides the love and security missing from the daily lives of the masses."

Peter frowned. He seldom found himself in disagreement with his new friend, but he felt some confusion now. "You don't think, then, that religion is beneficial to mankind?"

"My dear Peter, as I told you, it is an escape! There are many forms of them," he pointed out. "There is the bottle. Books. Then others might lose themselves in the ecstasy of music or poetry, and the addict comes to live with the needle as his marriage partner. Each neurotic finds his own individual hatch to slip through. Each one, though, is running from something. We also find the world objectionable, but we do not accept it and pray that the next world will make up for all the miseries that we are suffering in this one. It is better to try to right the existing wrongs. That is the difference between an escapist and a realist."

Peter ground his cigarette out in the dirt. "Of course, you are right as usual, Vladimir."

Boris paced restlessly across his tiny cell, finding himself unable to concentrate on the demanding task of copying the old manuscripts on his table. He stopped and took a sip of wine. *It is useless to struggle anymore*, he decided. *I will go to the chapel. The solitude there usually restores my sagging spirits.*

He stepped out into the morning sun. The cherry trees were in bloom, and their fragrant scent filled the air. The small fields surrounding the monastery had already been plowed and planted. On the hillside, fellow members of his order were picking wild mushrooms and berries. Their black robes blew in the breeze and stood out vividly against the lush green of the hills.

Other monks labored in the fields while some of his brothers were tending to the gardens of turnips and carrots close by. A scene of complete serenity lay before his eyes. It was only the booming of the church bell that detracted from the universal quiet of the hour.

Boris strode down the dusty unpaved street past the grazing livestock and entered the tiny chapel. There were no seats. One either stood or knelt to God here.

Boris observed some of the peasants slipping coppers into the collection box to purchase tapers. The burning candles threw flickering shadows on the wall.

He knelt before the altar and lost himself in prayer. A feeling of ecstasy swept over him. He completely lost track of the passage of time until the gong of the dinner bell brought him back to reality.

The patrol had been a long and tiring one. Peter was exhausted and thankful that the Russian lines were almost in sight. He was tired and dirty. The sweat running down his body made his clothes stick to his wet skin. *God, how I long for a bath to cleanse this filth and get rid of these vermin crawling over me.*

Suddenly, Peter and his men were startled by artillery fire. Peter shouted to his men and pointed. "Scatter, and form up in the woods over there."

He threw himself down and crawled along the hot earth. The smell of the black soil brought a rush of memories, but he crushed them instantly. *I have to think of the here and now. Our rifles are no matches for their cannon. We need to get out of here as fast as we can.*

He had almost reached the safety of a wooded section when a blast from one of the cannons crashed ahead of him. Before he could get out of the way, one of the trees came tumbling down on top of him. It lay across his back and pinned him to the ground. He tried moving his limbs, and they seemed to be all right, but he was trapped.

He heard vehicles coming close. *I can think of only three possibilities that await me. Firstly, I might be run over by their approaching vehicles. Secondly, I might be taken prisoner. Lastly, if undiscovered, I might be left here to starve.* His mouth felt dry and numbness crept over him. Then he heard leaves rustling. Someone was approaching. He tried to dislodge his rifle, but it was also held fast under the tree. He was helpless.

A stranger approached until he stood directly over Peter. Straight black hair fell over the man's forehead. He ran his eyes over Peter's uniform and seemed to be satisfied with what he saw. "Don't be frightened! I'm a Polish army officer working with the underground," he said in Russian. "I'll have you free from here in no time." He seized a large tree limb from the ground. Using it as a lever, he raised the tree enough to let Peter ease his body and rifle free. "Are you all right?" he asked.

"I think so," Peter stood to test his limbs.

"Come with me!" the stranger commanded.

Peter followed his rescuer into the underbrush. They had scarcely concealed themselves when an armored vehicle appeared at the spot they had just vacated. They held their breath and waited. Moments later, the vehicle turned and rumbled off in the direction from which it had come.

"We're safe now," the youth whispered.

"Thanks!" Peter said gratefully.

The thin youth smiled, and Peter felt an instantaneous liking for him. "If they had caught you out there in those civilian clothes," Peter pointed out, "it probably would have meant your life. Is there any way that I can repay you?"

"Yes, you can take me to your commander," he said. "I have some valuable information to pass on."

Peter hesitated for only a moment. *I'm seldom wrong in my judgment of character*, he told himself. *I instinctively trust this man.* "All right," he agreed, "but first I must gather my men."

Peter looked up from the bunk that he had been assigned and was surprised to see his recent liberator coming toward him. "I'm through already, and I thought, if you could get off for a while, we might have a few drinks together before I return across the lines."

"I would like that, and I'll check right now. By the way, my name is Sovinsky. Peter Sovinsky." He extended his hand, and the Pole grasped it in a firm friendly shake.

"I am called Janusy Gorecki," he replied.

Peter checked with his commanding officer, and finding that he had the evening free, he returned to the waiting youth. The Pole was sitting on Peter's bunk when he returned. He held out a white envelope to him as he approached. "Someone left this letter for you while you were gone."

Peter snatched the envelope eagerly and tore it open. It had been six weeks since he had heard from Maria. He scanned the contents with an eager hunger.

Dearest Brother,

It was so wonderful to receive your last letter. It is pure repetition to tell you again how much we miss you, but we do. We do and so very much.

Father is feeling ever so much better. During the winter, he suffered a lot from his rheumatism. With you gone and so much time on his hands, he brooded until he had worked himself into a dreadful state of depression. Since the arrival of spring, though, he has become his old self. We have plowed and planted the fields already, and I am pleased to tell you that we managed to do it quite well. Now that Father is feeling better, he is full of energy and zeal. The cottage is in good condition and survived the winter without any problems. There are no major repairs that need tending to at the moment.

I hesitate to tell you this news as I suspect it will sadden you. You will find it out eventually though, so perhaps it is better for you to hear it from me. Katrina Kazakinova and Nikolai Sokoloy are to be married tomorrow. By the time you get this letter, she will be his wife. I am so sorry, Peter.

I will close now as I must prepare Father's dinner, and I want to get this letter on its way. Write us again soon.

All my Love,
Maria

Peter crushed the letter in his hands. His mouth tightened, and he clenched his fists.

"I take it that you have received bad news."

"You take it right!" Peter answered. "But then, when does one ever get good news in these times?"

"Is there anything that I can do, Peter?" he asked.

"Yes," he said. "I'm going to get stinking drunk, and you can join me if you'd like."

"Do you think that's a good solution?" Janusy asked.

"For me, it is the only one right now," Peter answered. "I have a friend who would call me an escapist, but there are times in every man's life when he has to escape, especially when his dream has been shattered. I'm going to drink until I can't stand on my feet, and then I'm going to drink some more. I'm so sick of this goddamned war with all its filth and death. I've been at the front for so long that I feel like a celibate monk. It's time that I did something about that too. What do you say, comrade? Do you care to join me?"

"What are we waiting for?" Janusy grinned.

The day before Katie and Nicki's wedding was to take place Nicki received a letter demanding his immediate return home.

"My father has died," he told Katie. "I am now the head of the Sokoloy estates. My mother and sister are awaiting my return for the funeral. Our wedding is out of the question under the circumstances."

"Oh, Nicki," she said. "I'm so sorry!"

"Again, Katie, I'm forced to leave before we are legally united. I'm cursed. My father's death, the postponement of our marriage, and the grim prospect of returning to the dismal front fill me with bitterness. Damn the cruelties of this world!" he cursed.

Upon departing, Nicki held Katie close to him in desperation. "I have to brace myself once more to face a long spell of misery and sheer endurance before we can be together again."

JUNE 1915

Sonya's time had come. She lay in her bed trembling with pain, her face white and moist with perspiration. She twisted her damp hair nervously in her fingers and moaned.

"Where in damnation is that old woman?" Ivan thundered for the fifth time.

Katie and Tanya had water boiling over the fire, and everything was laid out ready for the coming birth. They waited now for the midwife to arrive. She was a shriveled old crone, but she had delivered every Kozakov born in Usadiba Na Holme for the last four generations.

She arrived finally, scrubbed her gnarled hands, and set to work with Katie and Tanya's assistance. Sonya's labor was a long and painful one. They poured whiskey into her, trying to ease her discomfort.

Ivan paced up and down the hall outside the bedroom door. His face was clouded with concern. Nothing seemed to calm him. Unable to stand it any longer, he burst into the room.

"What do you want now?" the midwife bellowed.

"How is she?" asked Ivan. Then looking sheepish, he retreated toward the door.

"Fine as can be expected with so many people bothering her," the old woman growled.

"I expect that you'll be discreet about this birth," Ivan questioned.

"And now, it's discreet he wants me to be, as if I blabbed the dark secrets of this family to the world. Do you think this is the only skeleton in this family's closet?"

Ivan stared at her. "What do you mean?"

"With all of them long dead now, I don't suppose it matters if you know," she said. "I delivered your grandmother's firstborn when your grandfather had been away in the war for a year. I found a home where the unfortunate little tyke was welcome. Your uncle, without benefit of the Kozakov name, climbed to a very high place. If this babe turns out even half as fine as him, you'll have much to be proud of. So let's have no more of this 'being discreet' talk."

Katie thought of the majestic portrait of her great-grandmother in the parlor. So that austere-looking woman also had the hot flowing Kozakov blood. How many of them were so cursed? Would she too weaken someday if she met another Peter to stir that passion now lying dormant within her? It was a frightening thought.

Ivan retreated to the other side of the door. After what seemed an eternity, Katie appeared before him, beaming.

"It is a boy, Uncle Ivan. It's a boy!"

CHAPTER 14

SEPTEMBER 1915

Vladimir looked out over the dirty small Lithuanian village. *It is just like dozens of others that I have recently visited. Every corner appears dismal and insignificant. Nothing about it seems capable of lifting a man's spirit. Little wonder these soldiers turn to alcohol as an escape. So be it! What better breeding ground to spread my ideology?*

He decided that the café was the best place to start his night's work. Inside he found a crowd of unshaven, unwashed soldiers lolling around or bent over tiny tables, laughing and shouting in boisterous tones. A waiter ran from one table to another, trying to keep the men supplied with drinks. He was rewarded with kicks and blows when he failed. An unkempt female with matted hair wailed in a high, off-key voice in the back of the café. She slouched forward, leaning heavily on a battered old piano. Her mournful tones elicited no response from her audience except for a few soldiers who called out suggestive remarks, but she seemed oblivious to them.

Vladimir turned his attention to the men. *What a foul-looking lot! They look like the scum of society! Can these specimens really be the basis of our revolution?* He sighed and then strode to the center of the room.

He started talking, easing into his eloquent oration, and he immediately captured an audience. Soon, more of the troops gathered around him. His passion rose, and he forgot his sordid listeners. He was expounding his dream, holding out hope, offering the possibility that they might build a new Russia.

The men listened and nodded their heads in agreement when he told them that they were fools to die for men who cared nothing about them.

"You must build a society in which you count. One where you are as important as any other individual." He had the attention of every man in the haze-filled room now. Not a sound rivaled his inspiring message. His voice rose to a feverish pitch. "Answer the call! Sons of Russia, arise!"

He continued talking until his throat grew raw. When he stopped, his listeners drew close to ask their questions. He vainly searched the sea of faces before him for another Peter.

Tomorrow he would speak elsewhere.

Peter looked back at the blazing city of Warsaw. Flames seemed to dance and leap, oblivious of the havoc that they rendered. The sky mirrored the brilliance of the flames below, casting a bloody hue over the earth. Collapsing buildings covered the landscape. Raging fires spread destruction everywhere. The surrounding fields ignited, destroying months of backbreaking labor by the farmers. The crops burned to the ground, leaving the earth charred and barren. Peter looked at the landscape ahead, unwilling to dwell on the chaos of war.

The long retreat from Poland had begun. The Russian offensive was completely broken. Peter's thoughts were black. *There is nowhere to go but home. Day after day, we march eastward. The men are tired and discouraged. The Russian Army has no goal now, and the Germans press persistently upon our dragging heels.*

Eventually, they reached the imperial hunting grounds in western Russia. There were no paths or trails through the tangled growth. Little light penetrated the thick foliage. It was damp and cold, and they were hampered by the continual flow of refugees. They were more aware of them at night, for then the black forest sprang to life with hundreds of flickering campfires burning.

Peter and his troops sat around their own crackling fire, absorbing what warmth they could. Among the trees, the eyes of wild animals shone brilliantly.

"Wild Buffalo," one of the soldiers assured another.

"So you say, but it could be anything," a second injected. "It makes my flesh crawl."

"This place is like the bowels of the earth," yet another commented.

Peter ignored their complaints. *As long as they are united in sharing their common miseries, they will not desert.* He laid his head on the soft moss-covered earth and closed his eyes. *Tonight I can sleep easy.*

"Listen to me, son!" the old man implored passionately, his face filled with anguish. "You are a Jew!"

Janusy Gorecki stood patiently before his father. "That's true, Father, but I am also a Pole."

"You are the only one of my sons to survive this war. This is not your fight. Quit before you share your brothers' fates."

"This is my fight, Father," he said. "Poland is our country!"

"Ah, and when have we Jews ever been anything but second-class citizens here? Answer me that if you can."

"I can't," Janusy sighed. "Yet I can't toss away my birthright because of this deplorable injustice."

"Birthright?" cried his father. "Yours is a longer and a more reaching birthright than Poland."

Janusy's face tensed, but he remained silent.

"I have saved all these years, Janusy, so that someday my sons and I might go to the Holy Land of our forefathers. Now that I have the money, I am too old to go. My bones cannot stand transplanting at this late age. But you? You could go and work on that soil of our ancestors. I don't want you crushed beneath the weight of the prejudice here. It will return as always when this war is over."

"Prejudice? Every time we're criticized, you cry prejudice, Father. The word has become an epithet behind which all of us hide."

"They have turned you against your own kind," the old man shouted now with tears in his eyes. Janusy reached out and put his arms around the frail old man. He had been born to his father in his middle years, the last of twelve children. Now only he and two of his sisters remained. He was a Jew; he was a Pole. But both were intertwined and had become one and the same thing.

"I speak Polish, and I feel Polish, Father," he explained patiently.

"And I have given enough to Poland," he shouted. "All my sons except for you! Flee from this country that keeps you in a ghetto. There's no future for you here!"

"That is where we made our error, wrapping ourselves in garments of religious superiority. We're different because we have made ourselves different. I am proud of my ancestry." Janusy shook his head stubbornly. "I can't wear this laurel of righteousness that you are trying to fasten on to me. I am no rabbi. Stronger than that ancient tie is the bond I feel for all men. I believe in it, and unless something happens to shatter my faith in brotherhood, I can't leave Poland."

"Then consider this carefully, Janusy. Poland has no future. You stay only to see her die. Germans? Russians? Whoever the victor, we will be the spoils."

Janusy's face clouded. "If after all I have done, I find that Poland cannot be saved . . . if . . . then . . . Maybe someday . . ." His voice trailed off, and they stood silently, a generation and a world apart.

Little Leon sucked greedily at his mother's breast, unaware of the adoring adults surrounding him. The baby had a constant attentive audience. Katie and Tanya seldom left Sonya's side. The three-month-old infant was the hub of all activity in their house. He was a wondrous plaything and a novelty in a house that had grown heavy with boredom and stagnation.

There was none who revered him more than his grandfather Ivan, for baby Leon was a small incarnation of the older man, with the same mass of ruffled black hair and bold features. The baby was large, with exceptionally broad shoulders, and looked exactly like a Kozakov. Katie couldn't help but muse on the irony of fate. If Alex had looked like this baby, perhaps his relationship with his father might have been different. Instead, Alex had physically favored Mathilde, and Ivan had never found any of himself in his son. Now, a generation late, came the child that he should have had, and Ivan idolized the infant. The transformation in him was astounding. Tenderness had replaced his former harsh manner toward his daughter. She and her child were now the center of his universe.

The Russian army began the long march northward. They marched from one village to another, each lying peacefully in the sun, untouched yet by the horrors of war. Cows munched on tender shoots of grass in their pastures, far from the thunder of guns. Trees drooped with their heavy burden of fruit. Crops stood tall in the fields, waiting to be harvested. Nikolai took a deep breath. *I wonder if the ravaged part of Poland will ever look like this again.*

At last the army reached the outskirts of a city. The soldiers hastened to make their camp before nightfall. It was exciting to see such a stream of life again. After dark, the lights flashed on, one after another, filling street after street with their bright paths. A theater's blinking red and green bulbs stood out in a dazzling brilliance among the sea of white luminaries.

When their temporary camp was pitched, some passes were issued for short leaves. Nikolai received four days. His first action was to hasten to a hotel, rent a room, and indulge in a luxurious hot bath. Refreshed, he crept into the soft clean bed and slept for sixteen hours. When he awoke, he shaved, bathed again, dressed, and went to the theater. For a brief interval, he managed to forget the war. He let his thoughts drift back to his boyhood.

When he came back out on to the streets, his nostalgic illusions disappeared. The blur of countless military uniforms brought him back to reality.

He spent his leave sleeping, eating, walking the lighted-paved streets, and taking advantage of whatever amusements that he could find. After four days, he returned to the rough campsite on the fringe of the city. It was here that he received the shattering news that the czar himself had taken command of the Russian army from the grand duke Michael. A wave of protest ran rampant through the camp. A sea of angry voices decried the change with contempt.

After mess, Nicki and several of the young officers joined a group of enlisted men gathered around a bonfire conversing loudly.

"We've enough graft and corruption already with the czar in the administrative end of things," one officer claimed heatedly. "Now he's going to get the military in a state of confusion as well."

"No sense in griping," a young boy chimed. "From what I can see, the military is already in a state of confusion. What do we ever do but retreat?"

"But that weak idiot isn't going to change our situation for the better," put in an old veteran. "He couldn't even run a platoon efficiently, never mind an army!"

A sulky-faced soldier sneered with contempt. "You don't think he plans to run it, do you? He'll just turn us over to the enemy. Everyone knows who the power in court is these days."

"Yeah, I've heard the czar's completely dominated by that German wife of his," the old veteran added, "while she in turn is run by that foul, fish-faced Rasputin. Everyone knows he's a German agent."

"I don't know if he is a German agent or not," remarked another. "But for sure, he's a vile and filthy character."

"Right," said an older soldier, who had sat silently until now. "I saw Rasputin once, and I have never seen an uglier man."

"There's no doubt that Rasputin is from the bottom most rung of humanity," one of the younger officers said reluctantly. "It has been reported that his obscene behavior has caused any number of scandals at court."

"Yes, I've heard gossip that he's insulted some of the well-bred ladies," another added.

"The talk I've heard claims he has a vicious temper and frequently smashes anything that he can lay his hands on."

"He sounds like a crazy son of a bitch to me," another in their ranks stipulated.

"Why is the czarina drawn to such a foul, drunken bastard?" asked the sulky one.

"It is rumored that he has saved the little czarevitch's life many times," one youth offered. "They say Rasputin has a hypnotic power over the child."

"Over the czarina too, I'd lay a bet," another added.

Nicki mused on the tragedy of the royal family. The czarina had borne four daughters and had almost given up all hope of bearing a son. When at last she was delivered of one, he became the center of her world. Though supposedly a state secret, rumors ran riot that the boy was a victim of the dreaded disease, hemophilia, that had cursed the males of the Czarina's family for generations. If true, the long-desired heir to the throne of Russia might never live to see manhood. It was whispered that the boy had been at death's door many times, only to have Rasputin call him back to life. No one knew what his magical powers over the child were. The czarina was convinced that he had been sent by God to protect her child's life. She was completely in his power. It was widely assumed that she dominated her husband, Nicholas; thus, many felt that Rasputin was, in reality, the power behind the throne. Everyone feared him.

Morning brought Nikolai and his men the news that the Germans were closing in and would reach the city by nightfall. The command to move on was given, and again they were trekking eastward. The warm sun blazed down on green and fertile fields, and in spite of everything, Nikolai felt that it was good to be alive.

Too soon the roads became cluttered with refugees. Carts were stacked high with possessions. Peasants trudged along wearily on foot, dragging their children behind them. Pets and livestock on ropes hampered the army's progress. One ragged old man carried a thin duck under one arm and a huge monstrosity of a clock under the other.

At first, Nikolai tried to order the refugees off the road gently so that the troops could pass, but they refused to cooperate. He ended by forcing them aside under some shots of rifle fire. The people shuffled bitterly to the shoulder of the road.

"Poor devils," Nikolai muttered. "Running, but they don't know where. In the end, they will still meet up with the Germans."

The troops marched for three days. Then word came to them that the enemy was now ahead of them as well as behind. Curses ran through the ranks. To engage in combat now would be a disaster. They were low on food and crucially short of ammunition. Orders were given by the high command for the troops to swing directly westward.

It was to no avail. They came face to face with the enemy at the base of a large hill. There was no time to dig trenches or to string wire. Both sides scampered for whatever refuge was available—rocks, trees, shallow holes, or mounds of dirt. There was no alternative but to fight. The air ignited with sparks of rifle fire. The crackle of bullets surrounded them.

Several hours later, more pursuing war parties caught up and joined ranks with the Germans already assembled. The rattling sound of machine gun fire tore through the air, and rifle fire was now discharged more rapidly. Each of the Russians' precious bullets had to count. They were surrounded on three sides with their backs to the hill. *If only* we *could reach the top*, Nicki reasoned, *we might have a chance.*

It was late afternoon, and the sun shone directly in their eyes, making it exceedingly difficult to see their targets. They were greatly outnumbered and knew that they were caught in a hopeless situation. There was little chance of escape; all they could do was pray for a miracle. *What a futile sacrifice of life*, Nikolai reflected bitterly. *There is no glory or honor involved here. We are merely prey caught in a trap with men falling in every direction. Death surrounds us. We are a stockpile of corpses. Such is war! We are all nothing but puppets.*

Night fell, and quiet prevailed temporarily. Only occasionally did a rifle bark in the stillness. Some of the exhausted soldiers momentarily closed their strained eyes to rest them. The urge to sleep was overpowering.

Feeling hopelessly inadequate, Nikolai and the other officers surveyed their position. The casualties were heavy. There was very little food or ammunition left. Both would be depleted by morning. Tomorrow the only alternatives would be to surrender or be totally annihilated. They had to escape while it was still dark. They were blocked on three sides and would have to expose themselves if they went up over the hill. The officers discussed the situation, and since there was no alternative solution, they gave the order to their men to proceed to the top of the hill as quietly as possible.

They were halfway up the hill when the Germans opened fire. Nicki heard the bullets whizzing about him then felt the impact as one smashed into his arm. He felt a hot flash of pain shoot through him. He bit his lips savagely and shook his head to clear the fog that had begun to engulf him. He felt himself beginning to lose consciousness and fought to stay upright. *If I go down, I will never get up again.* So he struggled on until at last, he reached the top of the ridge.

When Nikolai awoke, he felt as if flames were licking at his flesh. Everything was blurred. He tried to open his eyes, but he could not focus them properly, then suddenly, the fire went out, and he was caught in the grip of icy chills. When his mind broke free from the imprisoning haze, he realized that he was lying on a straw mat in a room with many other wounded soldiers. At the end of the long dormitory stood a priest who was blessing one after another of the injured and dying men.

He felt the fire return and spread until everything retreated into a mist. The piercing pain returned. He alternated between convulsive chills and hot, gnawing flashes. His throat was dry and burning, yet saliva ran unchecked from the corners of his mouth. Someone was pressing upon his arm, and the pain was unbearable. Then a voice far away said, "We will have to amputate."

Now someone was screaming, "No! No! No!" Nikolai was filled with rage. The voice was hysterical and shrill, and it hurt his ears.

"Don't cut off my arm!" the voice screamed. "Oh god, please don't cut off my arm!"

CHAPTER 15

DECEMBER 1915

The Russian front was quiet now. The war had reached a point of stagnation. The trenches ran close to each other, yet there was very little rifle fire from either side. The men were tired of fighting. They sat in their entrenchments, their minds mainly occupied with thoughts of food, for they resented the scant portions allotted to them.

The weather was subzero, and the wind stung with an ugly, pinching fury. The soldiers held their frozen hands over tiny cookstoves and inhaled the fragrant aroma of the roasting potatoes within.

Neither the Russians nor the Germans felt any motivation to attack. Occasionally, the Germans would swoop out of their icy holes, rushing on to the surprised Russians in order to capture a prisoner from whom they might extract some piece of needed information. Other than these occasional raids, the war remained at a standstill. The two sides became friendly with each other and engaged in long amicable conversations. They even exchanged supplies on occasion.

A rifle spit a bullet into the silent night. The wolves howled, and snow started to fall heavily. Peter felt unbearably chilled. He wrestled between his need for sleep and his need for companionship. Loneliness proved to be the more urgent of the two desires, and he sought out a group of his comrades. They were sitting around a huge fire, rubbing their cold limbs, and sipping from a bottle being passed from one to another. The men greeted Peter as he joined them and offered him the communal flask. A swallow of the hard liquor flamed temporary warmth within.

The conversation as usual centered on the war. War, women, and food! What else was there for the bone-weary soldiers to discuss?

"The whole mess can be laid at the czar's feet," the first speaker contended.

"He's always lacked character and has the backbone of a jellyfish," offered one private. "They say he does nothing now but drink because the responsibility is too much for him."

"I don't believe that," another said. "Nicholas has never been known to drink."

"The blame has to be laid on the czarina," another offered. "Everybody knows that she makes Nicholas jump to her tune. She's a German first and always. God have pity on us being locked under her thumb. We've never had a chance."

A former university history professor, now an officer, sitting on the edge of the group spoke out for the first time. "All this gossip of individual characteristics is really insignificant. What it all really boils down to is that this is a war of democracy versus autocracy. Not surprisingly, our inept czar managed to line himself up in the wrong camp. France and England are composed of armies of the people, all free men! Germany, Austria, and Turkey are ruled by dominating monarchs. If we were to win this war, Russia would be the only remaining autocracy. The czarina is not a stupid woman. She can't fail to see the facts and their significance. If France and England overthrow her brothers and friends, then her own fate is sealed. If all the other people in the world are free, wouldn't it be logical that the people of Russia would want to be the same? The Russian royal house can't stand alone."

The men were silent for a few moments.

"I never thought of it that way," admitted one of the soldiers.

"I wager that the German bitch has been supplying crucial information to her brothers since the beginning of the war," a young soldier with a scraggly beard interposed. "They probably know our plans before our own officers do. What a hell of a war! If they shot that rotten trio running this country, we might still have a chance," he said, spitting bitterly into the fire.

"I don't believe that the czarina is a German spy," a soft-spoken man added. "I'm sure she loves this country. However, it is rumored that she does share the battle charts with the evil monk and that he takes them back to his flat and leaves them lying around. If that's true, a whole German spy corps could tramp through and study them."

"Well, I, for one, would not mind changing sides," an old soldier muttered. "What have our great allies done for us? No supplies. No aid of any kind since the beginning of the war. When they needed us, we bravely charged to draw the German troops off of their necks. Now tell me, have they ever done the same for us? I think we'd be smart to make our own peace with the Germans and Austrians and let the rest of them go to hell. Our allies consistently let us down. No help in combat, no food, and they haven't even given us guns. I don't see where we owe them a damn thing. All we've done is throw Russia down the drain."

"The British aren't that bad," spoke another youth. "But well, a Frenchman is a Frenchman, and when has one ever thought of anyone but himself? So what do you expect?"

"Let them go to hell," said the original speaker vindictively. "All I want is for this stinking war to end so that I can go home. A year and a half of my life is gone, and for what purpose? Can any of you tell me?"

"Stop griping," growled Peter. "None of us are any better off than you! At least you still have your life and limbs, which is more than many have." The group fell into a shamed silence. Nothing could be heard except the sound of the wolves in the forest.

Suddenly, a German shouted across the lines. "Hey, comrades, want some cigarettes? We got fresh supplies today."

"Hell of a war," muttered Peter. *How ironic! The enemy sharing their goods with us, while the first lady of Russia travels across the country with drawn blinds so that she doesn't have to look upon the common people. Someday it will be different though. Someday all men will be brothers. Vladimir, myself, and others will make it happen.* Peter stood up. The men could see the fatigue in his face. "Each of us has his own personal thoughts and solution to this bloody mess that we are in, but the one thing that must remain a certainty is that the losses we have suffered must not be in vain! A new and better Russia must emerge from this in the end so that we can someday live as free men."

"Amen," echoed one soldier. Silence prevailed as Peter trudged back to his bedroll.

Boris knelt in the quiet chapel. He had been transferred recently from his scholarly labors on the monastery's historical books to the task of instructing new entrants into their order. He found his new job rewarding.

After breakfast, he came to offer his morning devotions, and when he had finished his prayers, he remained on his knees, absorbing the tranquil atmosphere of his surroundings. The tiny chapel was open to the public from early in the morning until the supper hour. A number of the local peasants were now in the church. He turned his eyes on a tall, thin girl approaching the Virgin Mother image.

She lit a candle and knelt before the statue. "Mother of Jesus, please listen. I pray for you to bless me with life's most precious gift. For three years, I'm without child. Oh, Mary, mother of our blessed savior, you above all others knew the joy of motherhood. Pity me! Give me a child. One baby! And Mother, if it wouldn't be asking too much more, my husband wants a son." The lean girl's sad eyes burned in her pinched face. She rose slowly, crossed herself, and then left the chapel.

A man took her place with another candle. "Blessed Mary, my back was hurt when a wagonload of supplies fell on me. I have been unable to work. My wife died of fever. There is no one but me to care for my children. Make me well, or they will all starve."

A young woman now knelt in the place that he had left. "Holy Mother, these horrible sores all over me. Why am I afflicted? How shall I ever get a husband? How many candles must I light?" She started to sob and then rose hastily and hurried from the chapel.

A short woman ambled up to the spot that the young girl had just vacated. With shaking hands, she struggled to ignite a small taper. Successful at last, she thrust it beside the others burning there. "Holy Lady, I am back, for I have been cursed again. Ten babes it is now. My strength is gone. There is not enough food. My last baby lies in his basket screaming, one month old already." The plumb woman struggled to her knees, and tears ran down her broad cheeks. "Oh, Holy Lady, intercede for me. See that I am blessed with no more children. It's a poor miserable life that we lead, and another mouth to feed might mean starvation for all of us. I am not so young anymore. My man is getting old. If he were to die, then what would happen to all our children? I place myself in your hands, my Lady. Have pity on me!

Boris felt a surge of pity for all of them. *The Lord's ways are his own, and it's not for me to question them.* However, he added a prayer of his own, that each of theirs might be answered. *These peasants are close to fetishism. Their religion is a mixture of the heathen and Orthodox. God and the Saints vie with nature's spirits for supremacy.* He shook his head and then reflected on the busy day ahead of him.

The majority of the new entrants to the monastery were peasants with little or no education. *The task before me is to acquaint them with the alphabet so they might read and, if possible, learn to write their names. Many of them will never progress beyond these goals.* He sighed, rose, and left the chapel.

A cold blast of wind whipped his robes, and he hastened his pace to reach the schoolroom.

Nikolai sat before the open window of the hospital, staring at the howling winter storm outside. *It would have been better if I died out there . . . what have I gained? I'm a cripple.* He laughed bitterly. *Name? Wealth? Prestige? What good are they to me now?* "Why? Why in damnation?" he swore aloud, smashing his fist against the windowsill with anger.

I might learn to live without my arm, but I can never learn to live with the loss of Katie. Beautiful Katie! I could send for her, and she would come. Oh yes, she would come. She could never bear to see even a little bird in pain. But I'll never do it. If only we had been married, it would be different now. We would be tied. We might have had *to rearrange the bonds, but we would have had a base and perhaps even a child on the way. Damn the wretched hand of fate! The only thing that I ever asked for, that I ever wanted, and now, what do my tomorrows hold?* His face froze in a rigid cast.

I have always been uncertain about her. I felt there was someone else, somewhere. I guess I always knew that it would never be. As a whole man, I might have won her, but now? His eyes hardened. *I couldn't stand her pity. Now I can never be sure. I must break our engagement so that she may be free to look elsewhere. Perhaps after the war, if she has found no one else, I can approach her. Only time will give me an answer, it has to be love or nothing. I have to be sure.* "Oh god, I have to be sure," he cried aloud in anguish. Then he sat down at the ward desk to write to Katie.

When he had finished his letter, he walked back to his hospital bed and sat on its edge.

"I hear that you're being discharged tomorrow, Sokoloy," a bandaged-wrapped soldier said. "Where are you going?"

"Home," Nicki replied.

"Home?" the youth of about eighteen sighed. "I wish I had a home to go to tomorrow when I'm released." The lad dangled his only leg over the side of the bed, swinging it restlessly. He was a cheerful boy who had never complained during his entire stay. He rarely spoke about himself, but Nicki had wrung from him the fact that he was an orphan. Survival had been one long struggle for him.

How fortunate I am in comparison, thought Nicki. *I have vast lands, and this missing arm will not handicap me in my administration of them. I have a mother and sister who love me. My mishap will upset them, but they won't lavish an unbearable amount of sympathy and pity on me. I have wealth, a fine house, friends, and someday I will marry. If not Katie, perhaps Tanya, or someone like her. Eventually I will have children and grandchildren. Yes, most are far worse off than me.* He smiled for the first time since his amputation.

"Why don't you come home with me, Pavel?" he asked.

"Me? Come home with you?" he replied in shock. "Now what would I do there? Your joke is in bad taste, Count Sokoloy."

"You would work." Nicki's eyes twinkled good-naturedly. "God knows there is plenty to do."

"And what could I do?" he asked. "You are pitying me now."

"And why would I do that?" Nicki said, with his face returning to its former marble cast. "I, least of all people?"

"I am sorry," the boy apologized. "I forgot for a moment."

"It's all right then, and no more of this pity talk. We're both in the same shape now, and we really are shorthanded on the estate. Most of the men are away at the front, and there will be plenty that you can do."

Reading the sincerity in Nicki's face, the youth turned his head away so that Nicki could not see his tears. The others in the ward had listened to the dialogue and nodded their heads in approval while Pavel Tzankovsky lay back onto his bed.

Katie stood before the giant Christmas tree, rubbing her arms in an attempt to push off the cold. Sonya stood beside her with seven-month-old Leon in her arms. The baby's eyes sparkled at the sight of the beautiful tree before him. He tried wiggling free from the warm blanket wrapped around him. Ivan and Tanya stood beside him with wide smiles.

The village children and their mothers gathered about them in a circle, but there was no trace of happiness shining in their eyes. The small faces were pinched and pale. The war had brought about a serious shortage of food. The peasants were the first to suffer from it. The mothers stood silently. If there was bitterness in their hearts, they hid it for the sake of their children. Anything could be endured if it offered some measure of happiness for their little ones.

This year the gifts consisted of small packets of food, the most precious gift possible. Each child approached and accepted the offered gift with a tired "Thank you," making no effort to smile. The family did not present a Saint Nicholas this year, thinking that it would be inappropriate. So many of the fathers had been killed while others were missing or had been taken prisoner.

The ceremony was brief as they did not wish to expose little Leon to the frigid temperature for long. As Katie handed out the last gift, the others started for the sleigh. Katie saw Maria on the fringe of the group and had a compelling desire to stop and ask her if she had heard from Peter. But the others shouted for her to hurry, so reluctantly, she was forced to depart with a mere smile and wave.

On the ride home, she wondered when she would receive a letter from Nicki.

Perhaps he had written to her for Christmas. It seemed incredible that they had been engaged for fourteen months now, and in all that time, she had seen him only once.

She was thankful when they reached Usadiba Na Holme. After they had removed their coats, Sonya and Ivan took the baby upstairs for his nap. Tanya and Katie pulled two chairs beside the roaring fire in the hearth. The warmth slowly penetrated their frozen flesh. It felt good to relax in such pleasant surroundings.

"Another Christmas almost past, Katie," Tanya remarked wistfully. "I suppose this will be the last one that you will share with us. Next year, at this time, you will probably be with Nicki's family. I am going to miss you so."

"No one can tell about the future," Katie mused. "Anyway, perhaps both our families can get together. I hope that we'll be able to work it out some way, as it just would not be Christmas without all of us together."

Tanya sighed. Both were tired after the exciting morning with the long outing. They sat contentedly staring into the fireplace and watching the bright flames dancing about the burning logs.

"Ms. Katrina," called an old stable hand standing in the doorway, "a rider just came with this letter, and I thought you would want it right away." The old man crossed the room, handed her the letter, and then left.

"It's from Nicki," exclaimed Katie excitedly as she tore the letter open. However, after reading a few lines, she frowned and shook her head in disbelief.

"What's wrong, Katie?" Tanya asked. Katie read the rest of the letter hastily then looked at Tanya with bewilderment in her face. She handed Tanya the letter. Tanya looked at her questioningly, in doubt whether she should read it, but Katie nodded and said, "Please."

Dear Katie,

I hope that it will not be too great a shock to you when I tell you that I wish to break our engagement. I have been doing a lot of thinking lately, and I realize that we rushed into our engagement with a great deal of haste. Marriage is a very serious step, and there should be no confusion or doubt on either side.

I am aware that I pressured you into making an important and serious decision rather quickly. With the meddling influence of the war, many young people find themselves making decisions that they would have deliberated over far longer in a time of peace. With death always looming on the horizon, one is compelled to live quickly.

There is no one else, but I think I would like to be free from any obligations for a while. I think that we were unwise to rush into such a binding commitment. I do not want to hurt you, and that is why it is important for both of us to be sure.

Do not feel that you must answer this letter. I am assuming that you will release me from my former declarations. I am going home on leave to see my mother and sister. I am confused, tired, and uncertain of everything. This war has been much too long. I need some time to find myself again. When all of this is over, I will come back to Usadiba Na Holme. By then, both of us will have had a chance to search ourselves. Until that time, let us remain free to live life as it may come to us.

I wish you the best of the season's greetings and give my warmest affection to all the rest of the family.

With deepest respect,
Nicki

Katie was stunned. "Nicki doesn't want to marry me now," she told Tanya. "How strange! I was so confident of his love that I find it hurts!"

I should not be angry though, she thought to herself. *Who am I to judge when I suffered exactly the same doubts during his last leave? I was so filled with terror that I would have broken with him myself if I had had the courage. Now it is done. I'm not to be his wife, and just when I had finally become resigned to the idea.*

Tanya finished the letter, and her face filled with horror. "With deepest respect? Of all the rotten beasts! How could he do this to you, Katie? Does he have to break everyone's heart? I hate him! He's an absolute monster! How could we ever have been taken in by him?" She wrapped her arms around Katie, and there were tears in her eyes. "Oh, Katie, what will you do now?"

"Nothing," she said with a shrug. "Nothing at all!"

"How can you be so calm?" she asked.

Katie looked thoughtful before saying, "It's better that he has broken our engagement now than to find out later that he doesn't really care for me. What if we had married first and perhaps had a child? Such a revelation would be far more tragic then."

Tanya refused to be consoled. "You mean you forgive him?"

"Of course! Oh, I'll not say it doesn't matter." Katie smiled sadly at her friend. "It does. However, war changes men. The horror of it affects them deeply. I feel terribly humiliated, but it's not the end of the world!"

"What will the others say, Katie?"

Katie grasped Tanya's hand tightly in her own and said, "Suppose we go and find out."

CHAPTER 16

JUNE 1916

Vladimir studied the men in the dilapidated tavern. They had unshaven faces, lice-filled locks, and filthy bodies. *Deserters from the German front . . . They are everywhere these days.* Unconsciously, he reached for a handkerchief in an attempt to avoid their offensive smell.

He brushed past a dirty youth with vermin on his collar. The boy noticed Vladimir's look. He laughed coarsely then spit on the filthy floor.

They make me sick, Vladimir admitted to himself. *Wretched and squalid humans. There's not a decent recruit among them.* He shook his head with dismay. *Oh, my Mother Russia, the cream of our manhood answered your call to duty, but look at what has returned. A pack of slovenly creatures. Loathsome to look upon. Obnoxious to hear. Riffraff! Where are the men who will save this country? How will I ever find the rest of the Peters?*

First the aristocracy, and now this scum to deal with. Where are the Russians of my hopes and dreams? Are they all lying out there dead on the battlefields? Is it possible that only the wicked and cowardly have survived? There has to be a remedy somewhere, he reasoned, weary with frustration, *but it will not be here.*

He shoved through the throng of dirty deserters. It was only when he was outside in the fresh air that he let himself inhale deeply.

* * *

Nicki and Pavel looked out over the landscape stretching before them. When they had returned home from the hospital, Pavel, now with an artificial leg, had begun immediately to direct things. He had an uncanny knowledge of the soil. Pavel's enthusiasm rubbed off on Nicki. For the first time in his life,

Nicki experienced the pleasure of turning over mother earth's black soil and extracting a bountiful harvest.

"Before the war, I had never concerned myself with the workings of this estate," he told Pavel. "When I was young, my father administered this land, and others worked it. After my father's death, I was away at the front. There were very few hands available, only old men and young boys. My mother and sister had trouble directing them efficiently. That's why things were in such an abominable state when we returned. But we have wrought miracles, Pavel," Nicki boasted proudly.

Day by day, new bonds of friendship strengthened those originally formed in their hospital ward. Now staring into the evening sunset with bold eyes, sun-tanned faces, and broad shoulders, they did not pause to think about their missing limbs. Life had proved to be more rewarding than either of them could have previously imagined.

If only Katie were here beside me, Nicki thought. *I would ask for nothing more.*

Janusy Gorecki sat outside their old house, smoking a pipe in the warmth of the summer evening.

His youngest sister, Marian, approached. "Another argument with Father?" she asked.

He nodded. She sat down beside him, and he took her thin hand into his own.

"I'm sorry," she offered sympathetically, and he merely nodded his head and searched her pale face while thinking, *You're too tall. Too thin. Your features appear so sharp in your plain face. However, what you lack in beauty is made up for in your unique capacity to understand the sufferings of others. You've always been my favorite sister. It's unfortunate that you have never had a suitor. They are fools that they can't look past your plain face and see the beauty within.*

Marian laid her head against his shoulder, and he stroked her long wavy locks. *Black as midnight. Soft as silk. Ah, my dear one, will you never get the chance to be a wife and mother?*

"Janusy," she said, breaking into his thoughts. "You mustn't let Father upset you so."

"I know," he sighed. "He really doesn't that much anymore. It's only that I feel hopeless because I can't make him understand how I feel."

"He's too set in his ways," she declared.

"I know. I wish I could do as he wants, Marian. But deep inside me, I feel that it's just not the right thing. At least not now."

"Then you must follow your heart, or you'll never be happy."

"Perhaps someday I really will go to the Holy Land," he ventured.

Marian smiled, her dark eyes lighting with tenderness. "Yes, I think perhaps someday you will."

"If I do," he said, "I'll take you with me."

"I would want to go," she nodded with a smile.

The sun hung low in the sky. Streaks of crimson reached out across the massive curtain of blue, and then slowly the sun sank from sight, leaving behind only brilliant hues.

"It is a beautiful sight," Marian observed.

"Yes. Nature never ceases to astound me," Janusy agreed as he puffed contentedly on his pipe.

Maria Sovinsky studied her father with troubled eyes. *His face has new lines, and there are dark circles under his eyes. It's too hard on him, working such long hours on the miserable food that we have. Father hasn't Peter's stamina. The additional labor is beginning to take its toll. He tires so easily these days. Each month he moves more slowly.*

Maria broke two eggs into a pan with some sunflower-seed oil, laid out some rye bread beside her father's plate, and then spooned out a generous serving of kasha made from buckwheat. Her father ate hungrily.

Maria took up her eggs and sat down across from him. Neither spoke. They each dwelled upon their own thoughts. *Everything around us has changed,* Marie mused. *The children, whose cheeks used to glow like berries in the summertime, are now pale in spite of the scorching sun. Their young bodies have lost their air of robust health. They appear listless. So many of them are fatherless now, and an empty stomach does nothing to comfort their painful loss.* Maria looked across at her father.

"Are you thinking of Peter, child?" her father asked softly.

"Not specifically," she replied with a smile. "However, I'm afraid that he's never far from my thoughts. I wish this war would end so that he could come home to us."

"Yes!" the old man said. "Perhaps it might be soon."

Another interval of silence followed before Maria spoke again. "What are your plans for today, Father?"

"To dig traps. The wolves got one of our cows last night. We can't afford to lose the other. Several of our neighbors lost livestock last week. The wolves are becoming more brazen. There's just not enough food in the wilds anymore. These rogues have become increasingly cunning."

"Try not to exert yourself too much, Father," she cautioned.

The old man smiled. "Don't worry. I shall go slow and easy, especially for you!" He stood up, came to her, bent over, and kissed her tenderly on the forehead. "You're a good girl, Maria," he said. "I'll be home at dinnertime."

She watched him stroll away over the fields with a pick and shovel on his shoulder, and then she shuddered. *Why do I have a premonition that something terrible is about to happen?*

Leon laughed contentedly at his adoring relatives and toddled excitedly from one to the other, pointing his finger at the pile of packages in the middle of his playroom floor. He could not suppress his delight at the commotion around him, but he was too young to realize the significance of this day, his first birthday.

"Come on, Leon, open your packages now," Tanya urged.

Sonya sat him down beside the pile and put one of the gaily wrapped boxes in his hands. She helped him to unfasten the paper and ribbon. Inside the box was a beautiful blue silk suit that Katrina had made for him from one of her dresses. The baby looked at it and then disinterestedly tossed it aside. The next parcel his mother helped him unwrap pleased him more. "That's a soldier doll, Leon," his mother said. "From Aunt Katie."

"Odya dall. Odya dall," he cooed over and over again, contentedly holding the toy in his arms.

Sonya removed the doll from him and helped him to open the next box, which contained a bright red sweater with a matching wool scarf that Tanya had knitted for him. He pushed this box aside also and reached for the soldier doll again.

"No, Leon," Sonya told him. "First you must open all of your presents." She helped him with the next gift.

As the paper fell away, Leon squealed with delight at the sight of a pretty colored ball. He threw it across the room and then stood on his fat little legs and waddled after it.

"That's from your Aunt Tanya, Leon," Sonya told him. "Kiss her and Aunt Katie for the nice gifts."

Obediently, he trotted to his aunts and kissed their cheeks, and then he resumed his pursuit of the ball. Sonya had to catch him and thrust him back among the presents. She helped him to open packages containing a warm woolen coat and a set of building blocks from her and a box of hard-to-come-by little candies from his grandfather. When he had finished with the last present,

Leon looked up questioningly. Ivan told him to wait while he left the room. Then he returned with a frisky little Bolognese puppy.

Leon squealed with delight. "Oggi, oggi!" he cried, while he danced up and down, unable to contain his excitement. The puppy dashed wildly around the room. Leon chased the puppy while the others laughed at the merry antics of the baby and the dog.

"He's so precious," Katie sighed. "I wonder what he'll be when he grows up."

"Stop rushing things so," interjected Sonya with amusement.

"It's never too early to plan," Tanya said seriously. "Perhaps he'll enter the diplomatic service. It's a splendid career, and with the personality that Leon has, he's bound to be a tremendous success."

"Nonsense," interrupted Ivan. "He'll go first to the best university, and then when he's finished, he'll enter the regiment of the guards and be a soldier like his grandfather. I really cannot imagine that you would think of anything else."

The three girls smiled.

"Now, since that's settled, what are your plans for this afternoon?" Ivan asked. "I have to leave later today as I'm going on a three-day trip."

"Where are you going?" Katie asked.

"I'll tell you when I return if everything goes well," he promised. "In the meantime, I must pack. Have you any plans for this morning?"

"We thought we'd take Leon on a picnic. Then later, after he has had his nap, we plan to have his cake," Sonya told him.

"Splendid. He'll enjoy that," Ivan said. He picked up his grandson, tossed him into the air, and kissed him roughly. "I'll see you when you get home, Leon. Perhaps I'll have time to join you for your cake before I leave."

The girls rushed to their rooms, changed their clothes, and then hastened down the stairs to collect some blankets and the picnic hamper before setting out for the stables.

The gardens were beautiful during the summer months. The fragrant smell of the flowers filled the air. When the carriage was ready, the three girls and the baby climbed behind the driver, who set off at a slow but steady pace. Little Leon loved to ride, and his cheeks were flushed from the fresh air and sunshine. They drove until their appetites had reached a keen state, then they called to the driver to halt.

They walked across a plowed field and settled under a clump of drooping trees. It felt pleasant to escape from the direct assault of the blazing sun. They spread several blankets and laid out an ample assortment of picnic food. Little Leon clapped his hands enthusiastically at the proceedings. They ate with relish and settled back to rest in the shade offered by the trailing branches. The baby stood up on his husky little legs and toddled off to pull apart some eye-catching flowers. He cooed contentedly as he dissected one petal after another. He glanced at his mother and aunts. They waved cheerfully to him. They resumed their conversation, and Leon started to explore a little farther.

Several minutes passed before Sonya glanced toward the flowers again. "Leon!" she cried. "He's gone!" A look of panic crossed her face. "I can't see him anywhere."

"He couldn't have gone far," Katie reassured her.

The three girls and the driver leaped to their feet and dashed off in different directions, but it was Katie who found him. He lay at the bottom of a deep hole with his little head twisted to one side of his body. Katie screamed. The others came running. She quickly composed herself and grabbed Sonya firmly before she could look into the pit. "He has fallen in, Sonya," she said shaking with emotion. "Stay back until we can get him out."

"I'll get a rope from the carriage," shouted the driver, who was already racing across the field. He returned immediately.

"Tanya and I will hold this end," Katie told the driver," while you go down and get him. Stay back, Sonya."

The driver slid down the rope into the hole and retrieved the body of the child. Then the two girls struggled until they had pulled him to the surface. Once out of the hole, the driver laid Leon upon the grass gently.

"His neck is broken," the driver said. "He must have died instantly."

The color drained from their faces as they stared in horror at the dead child.

"It's not true," whispered Sonya. "It cannot be true!" And then she threw herself down and pulled the dead infant into her arms. "It's not true,' she screamed. "He's not dead!" She started to sob but soon became hysterical. She began to shake the child. "He's not dead! I know he's not dead!"

Katie and Tanya stood mute, unable to move, but then Tanya also started to scream hysterically. Katie fought to clear her head. *Rational. I must be rational,* she thought. *Go home. Yes, we must go home.* She tried to pry Sonya loose from her baby's lifeless body, but Sonya only clung to her child more desperately.

"Help me," Katie cried to the driver. The man stepped in to aid Katie, and between them, they succeeded in separating the baby from Sonya. The driver carried the dead child to the carriage while the sobbing girls stumbled after him, but once in the carriage, Sonya again clutched the dead baby against her breast. Their ride home seemed to take forever as grief, disbelief, horror, and shock gripped all of them.

Hours later, the driver returned to explain the circumstances to Ivan.

"Wolves have been terrifying this whole area lately. Old man Sovinsky found a hole and decided to enlarge it. He dug the pit then covered it over with slender branches and leaves and then tied a chicken there to attract a wolf. The baby much have seen the fowl and tried to reach it. It was a dreadful accident, and old man Sovinsky says that he is so sorry."

"Sorry!" roared Ivan. "My grandson is dead, and all he can say is that he's sorry. That entire family is a curse on my house." He grabbed up his bags in rage.

"Uncle Ivan, you can't go now," Katie pleaded. "You must stay for the funeral."

"Stay?" he roared again. "See his tiny body smothered in the earth. I'll be damned if I will!" Without a backward glance, he rushed from the house like an enraged bull.

Ivan kicked his horse viciously and spurred him on into a galloping pace. Soon, there before him, working in the fields, stood old man Sovinsky. Blind fury clouded Ivan's mind, and without a second thought, he drew out his pistol and shot the helpless farmer in the head.

The nightmare continued long after the funeral. Sonya refused to eat or sleep, and she grew thinner each passing week.

"There's no justice in life!" she wailed to Katie. "I had nothing! Then at last, I had my father's love and a child. Now in a flash, both of them are gone." She moaned, and Katie put her arms around Sonya.

"It was so short a span of happiness, and now little Leon is dead. Father is a murderer, and I am to blame. No one else!"

"No, no, Sonya," Katie said, cradling her anguished cousin, but words could not penetrate the immensity of Sonya's grief.

Many months passed after the funeral before any form of normality returned to Usadiba Na Holme. Katie wandered from room to room, day after day. The house was so quiet now. Mathilde and little Leon were gone forever. Alex was lost to them. Nicki had deserted her.

Old man Sovinsky now lay buried in one of his well-planted fields. Her Uncle Ivan had not returned after his murder but had proceeded on to Petrograd, where he was now serving in an advisory capacity with the army.

Katie wondered if her uncle would ever be able to return to this house with its memories and curses.

That night in the dark, Katie crept out of her bed and stumbled to the window. Staring at the stars overhead, she searched her soul. "There has been so much suffering. So very much suffering! How much more can we endure? If I repent my wrongs, will this test end?" She knelt and pressed her head against the windowsill. "God, I have forgotten how to pray. Help me," she whispered. "Help all of us!"

DECEMBER 1916

The past six months had dragged by at an incredibly slow pace. Nothing had happened to break the monotony. Katie had wandered about the cold, still house with unending sense of melancholy. In all that time, they had received only one short letter from Ivan, informing them that he was still working for the army in Petrograd.

This special morning, Katie dressed in warm clothing. In spite of the other girls' protests, she had made arrangements to have the giant tree in the village decorated again this year. There were no gifts available to purchase this time, so she had busied herself digging out suitable items from her own possessions. From her childhood treasures, she had retrieved a tiddlywinks game, a croquet set, some dolls, and a number of other items. She had taken the liberty of adding some of Alex's old toys: boats, balls, a teddy bear, and a stuffed horse. She had also wrapped some brightly colored holy pictures. She had some sort of gift for each child on her list.

She had carried the packages to the carriage house the previous evening. Now she tramped through the new-fallen snow to the waiting sleigh, disappointed that neither Tanya or Sonya would join her. She knew that the happy memories of last year when Leon was alive were still too painful for them.

The driver sped rapidly across the smooth white fields. Katie smiled as the cold air stung her cheeks. Today had to be wonderful because it was Christmas. When they arrived at the village square, she was dismayed to find it empty. She stepped from the carriage and wandered toward the enormous Christmas tree. Not one of the children had come. A lump rose in her throat. The reason was obvious, of course. Old man Sovinsky's murder. *They will no longer accept our gifts. We've always been a cruel, selfish, and cowardly family. Now our hands are smeared with blood.*

Katie's eyes searched the distance and she sighed. Tears crept down her cheeks and clung there while the icy temperature froze them into place. She walked around the beautiful tree, but there was no comfort to be drawn from this lonely village square.

Oh, for a strong shoulder to cry on, she thought longingly. *Will there ever be one again?* She knelt in the soft white crystals covering the ground, turned her eyes upward, and a soft prayer trembled on her lips. "Dear God, let this era of misery end. Let the war be finished. Send what is left of our loved ones back to us. Nicki! Uncle Ivan! Alex! We need them so much. We are surrounded by hatred. I feel afraid. When I go to bed at night, I lie in the darkness and tremble. So many are dead. So many more are hungry. I feel guilty for having what the others do not. Yet they no longer want our gifts. Please help us!"

And the lull before the tempest settled upon them, without their knowing the full fury of the storm yet to come.

END OF PART 1

PART 2

REVOLUTION

Outside these walls, the rabble cry.
Retribution! We must die!
Pay for sins of long ago.
Die because they hate us so!

Once we were the strong of heart,
Sad that we have lost that part.
Once we were the brave back then,
Strong and fearless gentlemen.

Why then did we lose our way?
What has caused our fall this day?
It's too late, the people cry!
Lords of all, we now must die.

CHAPTER 17

DECEMBER 1916

Vladimir and his followers leaned closely over the flickering candles. "Grigori Yefimovich Rasputin's power has become too great for even the nobles to ignore," Vladimir told his companions.

"Yes, that grubby degenerate must go," another in the room agreed.

"He's nothing but a common peasant born in the wilds of Siberia," a third man added. "His earliest profession was horse stealing, but that kind of life didn't quench either his animal lust for women or his desire for wealth and power. So he abandoned his wife and three children and set out to wander about the country as a holy man."

"Yeah, some holy man! I actually saw the dirty, ragged beggar when he reached the gates of Petrograd," a fourth added. "Now he has risen to such power that he actually rules the largest country on earth."

Another follower inquired, "How did this come about, Vladimir?"

"There was a fanatical cult of mystics already formed in Petrograd society before his arrival in the capital. Rasputin, with his strange physical appearance and hypnotic eyes, declared himself a holy man and was immediately welcomed as an addition to the group," Vladimir explained. "One of the czarina's friends introduced him into the court circles and eventually to the Royal family. It's Rasputin's strange power over the young heir to the throne of Russia that has cemented his position. The czar, weakened by indecision, and the czarina, by her blind adoration of Rasputin because of his mystical power over her hemophiliac son, are both under his control. As long as the sickly czarevitch lives, Rasputin will continue to have an uncontested influence over the fate of all Russia. He must be disposed of."

"So who is going to assassinate Rasputin?" asked the man nearest to the flickering candles.

"Prince Felix Youssoupov, husband of the czar's niece, Irina, has appointed himself in charge of the plot to murder him," Vladimir answered. "Some of the aristocracy feel that if Rasputin is assassinated, the rulers of Russia might once again grasp the realities of our time . . . that perhaps the Romanov throne can be saved. It's a feeble hope, but they feel if Russia is to survive, Rasputin must be removed!"

"How did you learn of the plot?" one of the men asked Vladimir.

"One of the kitchen helpers overheard the aristocrats planning the assassination,"

Vladimir informed them. "Tonight has been a long-awaited occasion. Nothing must go wrong. Their plan must not fail! Russia must be rid of this oversized parasite. I've made arrangements to join the Yusupov kitchen staff. Each of you already has your assignments."

When the gathering broke up, Vladimir made his way to Prince Youssoupov's place and donned the garb of a servant. His followers secretly took up their posts around the palace to wait.

In the kitchen, Vladimir questioned his friend. "How did Prince Youssoupov manage to get Rasputin to agree to come here?"

"He promised him he would introduce him to his wife, Irina," the kitchen staffer confided. "Rasputin loves beautiful women, especially if they are highborn."

"And did the Princess Irina consent to meet with him?" Vladimir asked.

"The servant laughed. "She's in the Crimea."

"Ah," Vladimir sighed and nodded his head.

When the unsuspecting Rasputin arrived, Prince Felix Youssoupov led him to a cellar room that had been prepared especially for him. A phonograph was playing loudly upstairs.

Vladimir crept to the kitchen door and overheard Prince Youssoupov telling the monk, "My wife is entraining some friends upstairs, but she'll be down as soon as they depart."

Through the door, Vladimir observed the monk nod his head. Then Rasputin grunted and followed the prince down to the basement.

Prince Youssoupov's coconspirators were gathered in a room at the top of the stairs, waiting to help dispose of the evil monk's body once the unpleasant task had been accomplished.

The Prince went below and served the monk some wine laced with cyanide. Then he came upstairs to fetch a plate of tiny cakes. One of the conspirators in the group, who was a doctor, had injected cyanide into each one of the pastries that Prince Felix now took downstairs on a tray to Rasputin.

Rasputin consumed all the cakes, one by one, washing them down with liberal amounts of the poisoned wine. He raised his glass to the prince. "To Princess Irina."

Vladimir waited in the kitchen while the conspirators lingered in the room at the top of the stairs directly opposite from him. He could not help dwelling on the thought that soon Russia would be rid of this man and his sinister influence in court.

Soon, Prince Felix rushed up the stairs to his friends in a state of panic. "It's unbelievable," he sputtered. "He has consumed all the cakes and several bottles of the wine. He's roaring drunk, but the cyanide has had no effect on him." Vladimir glimpsed the prince's white face from his position behind the crack in the door.

"Then you must shoot him," one of the other coconspirators ventured.

Youssoupov descended the stairs again, and then Vladimir heard a shot, followed by a loud crash.

"At last," Vladimir sighed.

The conspirators in the room across from Vladimir rushed down the stairs. "Is he dead?" one of them shouted. Just then, the onlookers gasped in disbelief as the monstrous monk jumped to his feet.

Vladimir cautiously crept down the steps after the others. He heard a scream. Then rushing into the hall, the monk came running past him with foam flowing from his mouth down into his long black beard. Vladimir stepped back into the cover of darkness while Rasputin raced into the courtyard. The other conspirators followed in a state of shock. Finally, one of them raised a gun, took aim, and fired another bullet into the holy man. Still, Rasputin did not stop. The gunman fired a second shot. This time the monk collapsed to the ground. The snow under him slowly turned red.

The conspirators examined him carefully.

"My god, he's still alive!" one of them proclaimed.

"It's impossible," another replied. "He can't be! The man isn't human."

"We can't just leave him here," someone else offered. "Get something to wrap around him."

From somewhere, one of the men produced some heavy linen. The plotters quickly wrapped the wounded Rasputin in the cloth and carried him off into the dark night. Vladimir and his men followed the conspirators. Beside the black flowing river waters, the schemers tied weights to the monk's heavy body and dropped the incredible mystic, still alive, into the freezing Neva. Slowly, his body sank into its icy grave.

Nicholas Romanov, czar of all the Russians, hastened from the battle-torn front to comfort his anguished wife. He looked into the proud, beautiful face that he worshiped with such blind trust and devotion.

"Why did they do it, Nicholas?" she sobbed uncontrollably. "I don't understand it."

He wiped away her tears with his handkerchief. "I don't know, my love. I just don't know!"

"They're so wretched, Nicholas. Those ignorant peasants out there! I'm so afraid of them." She started to sob convulsively again. "They hate us. Perhaps we should give them what they ask for."

"No, dearest, that's not the way," he asserted quite firmly. "My grandfather made that mistake, and as a result, he died in agony from a terrorist bomb. I can never forget the sight of him, torn and bleeding in his huge bed with life slowly ebbing from him. I was only twelve at the time, but I learned a vital lesson. Appeasement is weakness! The people look up to me. I'm not responsible to them but only for them. I shall answer to no one but God!"

"Oh, my dear Nicki, she cried. "I have tried so hard to protect our children from this madness all around us. I felt so sure with Father Grigori." The czarina's voice dropped in tempo. "I felt that God was guiding us through him and that our Father Grigori would show you the way to save our country. Now there's no one. We are doomed."

"Alexandra, my dearest Alix, you mustn't let yourself get in a state like this," he begged. "This tragedy has been a shock, but you must remember your heart."

The czarina rubbed her swollen eyes. "Yes, you are right. I must be brave. There's no one left but us now. Never again will Father Grigori coax our dear son back from death. No longer will his gentle voice sooth Alexis's pain." She sniffed back her tears.

Nicholas shook his head. "Yes. Yes," he echoed sadly. "I have no explanation for the fanatical eyes and hypnotic voice of Rasputin that repeatedly proved to be a miracle for our child. Even the sound of his voice on the telephone was enough to enable our child to sleep peacefully through the night."

"I don't understand why our innocent son has been cursed so." Empress Alexandra Feodrovna raised her grief-filled eyes to her handsome husband. "How will we ever stop the bleeding the next time it starts?"

Nicholas shrugged and patted her awkwardly on the shoulder. "Dearest, we can't bring Father Grigori back." Then he removed his hand and stroked his beard nervously. "We simply must watch over Alexis even more carefully, and you must be careful not to tax your heart. I'm certain that God will provide some way." He put his arms around her, and they stood silently in grief-stricken unity.

Nikolai Sokoloy and Pavel Tzankvsky stood looking out over the snow-covered fields. Winter was the most peaceful time of year, if one could endure the frigid temperature and bury the desire to travel any distance over the frozen wastes. Nikolai preferred spring and the hard work that came with it. He loved the warm rays of sun beating down and penetrating the fibers of his strong body, and he thrilled at seeing the earth come alive.

There is little to do during this cold season, Nikolai thought. *Most of the preparations for spring have already been undertaken. Now all we can do is wait for the winter to pass, but time seems to pass so slowly.* In his idleness, Nikolai's thoughts continually drifted to Katie. *Did I make the right decision? Has she met someone else? The war has to end soon. When it is over, I must settle these questions that are tearing me apart.*

Nikolai and Pavel returned to the house. From the veranda, they saw a rider in the distance. Pavel excused himself while Nikolai waited as the gusts of snow flurries grew closer. A neighbor pulled on his reins and dismounted. Immediately, an old servant seemed to appear from nowhere to take charge of his horse. Nikolai invited his neighbor to enter, and they removed their heavy wrappings before retiring to the library. A blazing fire in the hearth drew some of the chill from their bones.

"Rasputin has been murdered, Nikolai," the old man announced.

"I thought it would come to this," Nikolai replied. "Who did it?"

"Prince Youssoupov."

"So!"

"The news merits nothing more than that?" his neighbor asked.

"It was inevitable," Nikolai stated simply. "Rasputin was a scourge, so it meets with my approval."

"Nikolai, it must be obvious to you that there are many factions in our midst these days," he said cautiously. "Danger and intrigue surround us. Yet you haven't told anyone where your sympathies lie."

"Politics is a dangerous game," Nikolai stated quietly.

"Yes, but these are dangerous times," the old man reminded him. "Actually, I have been sent to seek your help. There are some who want you to join their cause."

"I have no tolerance for the loudmouth rabble," he declared passionately.

"No, Nikolai, these are not fanatics but men like yourself, well born and intelligent, who have glimpsed the handwriting on the wall."

"Speak plain, Kotov."

"The czar is a weak man. He hasn't the strength for compromise. He lacks an understanding of what is happening around him. He refuses to see the changes that are moving forward in Russia. He will not consider anything that's not agreeable to him. Time after time, he has gone too far. He has simply used our lawfully elected body, the Duma, as a tool. Whenever it has opposed him, he has dissolved it. The intellectuals have turned against us and stirred up the illiterate masses. Chaos is threatening us, Nikolai. We must organize now to prepare for the inevitable. Are you with us?"

"I am Russian." Nicki smiled. "Need you ask?"

MARCH 1917

Czar Nicholas Romanov of Russian paced the floor nervously. Anxiety lay naked upon his sensitive features. "Stupid peasants! How dare they do this to me?"

His elderly minister stood before him with a pleading expression on his face. "They are hungry, Nicholas. They want food. You have gone too far. Listen to their demands!" He rubbed his hands together absentmindedly. "Listen, while there's still time. At least grant them a few compromises."

"Are you suggesting that I let a pack of ignorant factory workers dictate what I should do?" he shouted angrily. "Never. Not while I am czar."

"You have no choice but to listen to the strikers," his minister begged. "This nation is racked with discontentment and unrest. The war has drained us of so many men. Those who have remained behind have had to work long and hard with their bellies crying with hunger."

"We have lost loved ones too," Nicholas declared. "What do they expect in wartime?" The czar paced back and forth with even greater agitation. "As for hardships, do they think their betters suffer no deprivations?"

The czar waved his hand in a sign of dismissal and turned his back on his frustrated minister. "I will squash this cancer before it extends its tendrils any further."

Ivan Kozakov watched from an open second-story window while the sullen troops below refused to obey their officers' orders to fire into the seething crowd. Defiant shouts echoed from the street below.

"The Duma refuses to dissolve!"

"Down with the leeches and bloodsuckers!"

"Russia for the Russians. Send the German bitch home!"

Ivan was alarmed. He had never seen such an angry mob. He watched as some of the soldiers stepped from their ranks and joined the rioting rebels. One young soldier turned and fired a rifle bullet at his superior. The officer's face registered shock as he reached down and felt the warm blood staining his uniform. Then the officer withdrew his own pistol and fired directly at the youth's head. The young soldier fell to the ground. His angry companions were no longer doubtful of their loyalties. A volley of shots sprayed the spot where the wounded officer stood. The military group joined the factory workers to form a united front against their mutual enemy—the aristocracy.

Vladimir and two of his followers trailed some distance behind the group of revolutionaries on horseback, keeping to the trees and bushes so they would not be spotted. His network of intelligence let few important events slip past. His curiosity was aroused by the act that he was witnessing. Several men had dug up Rasputin's coffin from where it had been buried since it had been retrieved from the Neva. They forced the lid off the coffin and then removed his body. The plotters wrapped Rasputin's enormous corpse in a canvas wrapping and carried it to a wagon.

The conspirators led them on a long and tiring journey before they stopped the wagon and removed the holy man's body. Unaware that they were being watched, the men prepared to destroy the monk's body. They attempted to set fire to his remains, but the cadaver would not ignite. One of the conspirators ran to their wagon and returned with some gasoline. Hurriedly they poured the fluid over the corpse. This time the hair and beard caught fire, but after a few seconds, the flame fizzled down to a thin trail of smoke.

One of Vladimir's men whispered to him. "First they couldn't kill him, and now his damn corpse won't burn."

Another shook his head. "He must have a hide of iron!"

"Shh!" Vladimir hissed at them. "We must not be discovered."

The conspirators were unable to cremate the body. Angrily, they begin to hack at the corpse, chopping it into small pieces. When they had finished, they carried the mutilated remains to an old well shaft and dropped them in. Next, they heaved huge rocks on top of the carcass until it was completely hidden. Then the men departed with haste.

"Rasputin will never be made a martyr now," Vladimir whispered. "Nor will his final resting place become a holy shrine."

"The revolution in Petrograd has been accepted by most of Russia," Maria stated. "Our czar, Nicholas II, was forced to abdicate from his throne on March

15, 1917. A provisional government has been set up with Prince Lvov and Alexander Kerensky as the heads. Now the Provisional Government has issued its first decree. All of Russia is devouring its contents as eagerly as we are."

Her neighbor, Dmitri Gogol, sat across the wooden table in Maria Sovinsky's hut. "I heard," he said, "there's to be a general amnesty granted to all political, religious, and military prisoners."

"It sounds wonderful," Maria agreed. "There shouldn't be any difficulty about Peter returning home now. It also says that all social and religious distinctions will be abolished, but I really wonder about that one," Maria mused. "I doubt that a mere proclamation can erase a lifetime pattern. I doubt the Kozakovs of this world will be willing to clasp hands in brotherhood with us Sovinskys."

Dmitri shrugged. "Perhaps not in our generation," he ventured. "Time will tell. What else does it say?"

"It says there'll be freedom of speech, press, union, and strikes, and they'll be summoning a constituent assembly. That the militia will be of the people rather than the police. And, Dmitri," she added excitedly, "the soldiers who took part in the revolution will remain in Petrograd. They won't be sent back to the front or punished in any way."

Dmitri nodded with approval. "What else?"

"The proclamation states that elections will be based on universal suffrage. And listen to this, Dmitri," she cried, "the soldiers will have the same rights as civilians when they aren't in active service."

"That's good, but what does it say about us, Maria? The farmers?" Dmitri asked.

"That's it," Maria said. "There's nothing more"

"So nothing's really changed. The Ivan Kozakovs will continue to own most of the countryside."

"So it appears, Dmitri," she said, shaking her head sadly. "It looks that way."

"It doesn't look good, Nikolai," his neighbor Katov stated. "Lvov has decided to continue the war in spite of the Socialist's clamor for peace. He's already issued orders for a new offensive. The army of Soviets are issuing orders contrary to those given by the official officers so that the whole army's ready to collapse. The soldiers at the front are telling their officers to go to hell, and they're making friends with the enemy. The war is over as far as they are concerned. They're coming home by the thousands. Those remaining at the front defy the orders issued to them."

"I agree that it's a terrible situation, Kotov. It seems that Lvov is out of touch with the masses."

"Not only that," Kotov added, "the bourgeoisie distrust this administration as well. And all the while, the peasants are screaming for our land, Nikolai. So far, thank God, the administration has not attacked private property, but it's probably just a matter of time. If the war could be ended and the men brought home, the peasants might be satisfied and forget about demanding our land."

"Fate's ironic," Nikolai commented. "All these years, the people have wanted a just government. Now at last, when a new government is trying to establish universal equality that will give them direct voting and secret balloting, the people accuse their leaders of allying with those they hate. All we can do is hope for the best and prepare for the worst."

Peter stood on the crowded railroad platform, watching the trains go by. Not one had stopped in the past two days. Every car that passed was packed to capacity. Men were piled on the roofs, hanging from the sides, riding underneath the sooty cars and engine, or clinging tightly to the ladders.

"How will I ever get to Petrograd?" he asked.

Vladimir had sent him a letter imploring him to come immediately. Peter read the message again.

> The Provisional Government will fall, Peter. It is not giving the people what they want. Their cry is for "peace, bread, and land." Most of them care nothing about equality and suffrage rights. They want food in their stomachs and the return of their loved ones. Can we blame them?
>
> We must make our preparations now. Our time is drawing near. Come quickly, Peter. We need many hearts and hands for our cause. There is no longer any benefit in keeping up a senseless pretense. The war will end soon. There is more important work here, Peter. We need you.
>
> Devotedly yours,
> Vladimir

Peter glanced up again. There was no train in sight. *I'll get something to eat. Then I'll return.*

He strolled down the main pavement of the small town and turned off into a smaller walkway. It was deserted and quiet until a scream startled him.

He rushed to the house from which the cry had come and pushed open the unlocked door. A stout middle-aged woman lay on the floor with a thin stream of blood trickling through her graying hair. Her face was pale. It took him a while before she was composed enough to speak.

"He took my money and everything he could carry," she cried.

"Who?" Peter asked.

"How should I know," she screamed at him hysterically. Then she started to cry.

"I'll call the police," Peter volunteered.

"What good will that do?" the fat woman sobbed. "There's not enough of them. Half of them have been killed. The other half are not worth their salt. They are as crooked as the soldiers. The whole world's gone bad. It's not a safe place to live anymore."

"You had better take it easy," Peer cautioned. He removed a towel from a rack, dipped it into some cold water, wrung it out, and crossed the room to lay it on the woman's injured head. "You're not hurt badly. It's just a superficial scalp wound. Lie down and rest for a while."

"Might as well," she agreed. "There's not much else I can do. There's worthless deserters running home, leaving the way open for the Germans to come and murder us in our beds. It's terrible, I tell you. Robbers and thieves everywhere. I think you better leave now. I don't trust any of your kind."

"Talk about gratitude," Peter admonished. He shrugged and left. *It's the same everywhere. Deserters pillaging as they please . . . a lack of policemen to control them.* He muttered to himself, "It'll take harsh measures to ever get this country to a state of decency again."

He ate a meager meal in a small café and purchased a loaf of bread on his way back to the railroad station. He heard a whistle blast in the distance and ran toward the track. The train stopped, but there was no space on it. Then one of the car doors slid open a bit, and a body was hurled out through the opening.

Peter managed to force his way into the packed boxcar before the door slid shut. Blackness engulfed him. He felt the loaf of bread torn from his grasp. A protest rose to his lips, but he smothered it. Instead, he asked, "How long have you been traveling?"

"Two days," answered a gruff voice.

How in God's name have they stood it, he wondered as a combination of unwashed bodies, excrement, and rotting flesh assailed his nostrils.

"I'm going to be sick," he gasped to those closest to him. He gagged, and the sound set the others off into a fit laughter.

"You'll get used to it," one of them assured him.

Then other voices came out of the blackness.

"In a couple of hours, you'll have crappy pants just like the rest of us."

"Yoo-hoo, the potty's over there!"

"Damn you, shut up and leave him alone," another voice ordered.

"Listen, you've got no sense of humor? You want that we should go crazy in here?"

"Go to hell!"

"We're already in hell."

A soft, mellow voice cut in. "I wish I had a nice big piece of juicy meat and all that goes with it."

"What are you trying to do? Start a riot? Why do you have to keep harping on food all the time?"

"Because I'm hungry," the anonymous voice stated simply.

"Who isn't?" someone said.

The train gave a lurch as it started up. The men swayed with the movement, but there was not enough room for them to lose their balance.

"Be quiet," someone said. "I'm going to try and get some sleep. It's hard enough to be hungry, stand for forty-eight hours in exhaustion, but listening to your crap is the limit."

"Good night, love!" someone called sarcastically. "What station would you like us to call out for you?"

Another burst of laughter ran through the crowd.

Time passed. Peter's stomach growled in protest. The calves of his legs knotted in pain. He tried halfheartedly to scratch his verminous body, but he could not get his arm free. He felt a trickle of urine run down his leg. *Hell?* he asked himself and agreed with the voice in the dark. *Yes, this must be what hell is like. An endless ride of misery.* His clothes stuck to his perspiring body. The moisture seemed to stir his lice into a feverish pitch. *I am so tired,* he thought. *So very tired.* Eventually he fell asleep. A sudden jolt woke him. *What is it? Where are we? How much time has passed?* He didn't know. He felt a pain in his head! Then more time passing and turning wheels.

"Surely we must almost be there," he assured himself aloud, but no one replied. The train kept moving.

After what seemed like a stretch of eternity, the wheels stopped. Someone outside shoved the car door open. The bright daylight stabbed at his eyes like swords of lightning.

"Welcome home, soldiers!" greeted the freight man.

There were tears in their eyes as the soldiers forced their stiff limbs to move. They climbed out of the stationary boxcar to fall upon the dusty ground.

"We thank you, God!" one shouted.

"Did you honestly think we'd see daylight again?" another added.

Peter picked up some of the dust and let it sift through his fingers. A flash of homesickness gripped him, but he shook it off. *I can't go home. Not yet. I must find Vladimir.* "Good-bye, comrades," he called.

"Good-bye, old man. Hope to see you again sometime."

Their parting comments played on Peter's ears as he walked away from his traveling companions.

"Never thought such a terrible place could look so beautiful."

"Let's do the town!"

"Wonder where the women are around here."

"All I want is a bath."

"I'll take a bed first, and then I'm going to sleep for a week."

"It's food for me," said the soft, mellow voice. "I'm starved."

"I'll take some of each," another added.

"A man after my own heart!"

"You old dog. Something of each, eh?"

"You know where you can go," someone bantered back.

"After you, my love."

Easy, friendly, idle chatter. Peter smiled.

When he had gotten out of ear range, his face became grim. Serious work lay ahead of him.

CHAPTER 18

JULY 1917

Peter stopped at the edge of the pavement while a small religious procession wound its way through the noisy, crowded streets of Petrograd. The sun scorched the tiny band of worshipers, but they were indifferent to its rays. None of the observers removed their hats or made the sign of the cross.

Vladimir is right, Peter reflected. *Already the church is losing its grasp. He said the church was merely an escape for those with heavy hearts. With a lighter load, already they are drifting away—their religious feelings changing with their fortunes.*

When the holy group had passed, Peter checked the number written on the card in his hand against the one on a small door. He pushed his way in. The basement was dark and musty. A voice warned him. "Stop. Identify yourself."

"My name's Peter Sovinsky! I've been sent by a friend. All power to the Soviets!"

With the password given, someone struck a match and held it close to his face. "Go ahead," the voice said.

Peter entered a crowded room at the rear of the basement. Two candles burned. It was impossible to distinguish any of the faces. *A wise precaution*, he thought as he lit a cigarette and waited. Other men drifted into the smoked-filled room. Then someone shut the door. A hush fell over the packed chamber.

A man climbed on a table in the center of the room. "We all know why we are here. Each of us questions the regime that now calls itself the government of the people yet still doesn't give the people what really belongs to them. There has been no difference since the czar's abdication. The landowners still have their wealth, while we, the common men, have nothing. The war goes on. Each day hundreds more die for the rich. Our government tells us that we are obligated to our allies, but our allies have not fulfilled their obligations to us."

Murmurs of protest ran through the room, and the speaker paused for a few seconds. "Wake up, citizens of Russia, before it is too late. If you want something in life, you must grab it! Our program is simple. We want peace with Germany. Immediate peace! Not next year or the year after, but now! Peace and the return of our men to their loved ones. They call us radicals for that? Well then, we are radicals! What else do we want? Equal distribution of Russia to all Russians. Are you with me?"

Shouts and cheers filled the room, but Peter sat quietly. At the end of the meeting, a door at the other side of the room was opened. One at a time, the occupants drifted out to merge with the flow outside. Peter followed the others. His mind was racing, his loyalties uncertain. *What do I believe? What do I really want, and to what should my life be dedicated? Vladimir will be hurt by my deception. I should not have attended this Bolshevik meeting without his knowledge. I need to confront Vladimir and let him know of my doubts. He is one of the few people I really trust in these times.*

Vladimir sensed that something was wrong the instant that Peter walked through the door.

"I've just attended a secret meeting of the Bolsheviks," he blurted, his face tense and clouded.

The former professor sighed. "I was afraid that it might come to this, Peter. I have seen how the smell of land blinds you. The vague promise of a plot of dirt extinguishes all sense of intellect and rationale."

"This, I assume, is a polite way of calling me a stupid farmer!"

"Don't talk nonsense, Peter. Don't you think that we want the same things? But you can't change the world in a day. There's a right way and a wrong one. We're on the right road, Peter, and we'll get there. I'm not against bloodshed if it is necessary, but I decry wholesale slaughter. And that is what these Bolsheviks will have. You can't just take over the world and parcel it out. What happens to the old idea of worth? Would you have the peasants take the place of the nobles? If so, then what have you gained by taking land from a selfish count and giving it to an ignorant, hotheaded farmer? Think, my friend!"

"Oh, I am thinking," Peter said. "And I'm perfectly willing to risk the ignorant peasants in place of our aristocratic nobles."

"Ah, but we want a country that we can be proud of, Peter. Peace is the best way if there is a choice. The Bolsheviks advocate violence and will bathe our land in blood. They will destroy the old regime all right, but the good will tumble down along with the bad. We need the intellectuals and knowledgeable men to teach the new uneducated workers. A society merely reversed, with the low on high and the high toppled down or even exterminated, isn't going to work. Is this what you want, Peter?

"It could be no worse than our present society," Peter insisted.

"We Mensheviks must adhere to the middle road, Peter. The Bolsheviks are as much against what we want as the aristocrats. They cry out that all men are equal. That when they have achieved power, every man will have the same. But all men are not equal, Peter! We have different skills and talents. We can't be satisfied with the same rewards. If every man is given the same, what incentive is there for him to strive for his maximum achievement? It is personal drive and competition that pushes men ahead. There has to be that ladder to climb."

Driven by the passion of his words, Vladimir started to pace back and forth across the floor, continuing his plea. "Do you think when the Bolshevik leaders have seized control of the masses that it will be any different? They'll hold the reins, and there will not be centuries of culture to temper their control. Our present leaders will be destroyed in a savage bloodbath. Chaos will follow. It will be twenty years or more, Peter, before we will be able to educate our people if Russia is to survive. Under the Bolsheviks, every peasant and factory worker will want to be his own boss. How will they be controlled?"

"Perhaps you underestimate the masses."

"No," Vladimir said, shaking his head. "The Bolsheviks offer only terror. Once the whip is in their hands, do you think they will throw it down? Never! The Bolshevik cancer will spread to town after town until all of Russia has been infected. Then to our neighbors. It will never stop. Lenin's goal is world conquest. Do not let them play you against your own people, Peter. In the confusion that must follow, they will grab the power before the people of either side know what is happening. There are good men among the aristocracy, Peter. Fine men! It is only the undesirables that we want to weed out. No man should be disqualified by his birth, high or lowborn. Every man has a right to be judged for what he is and what he can do. That is our goal, Peter. Justice! Freedom for men like you to rise because you are intelligent and capable and not just because you're a peasant. You must make your own decision. If you feel you must join them, then I can't stop you, but I beg you not to ever lose your sense of decency. Always judge each man and his acts individually, by what he is, and not by an accident of birth."

"I'll try to do that, Vladimir," Peter promised. "But for the rest, I don't have your patience. Time is important to me. I have met none of your virtuous nobles. I've seen only torture, rape, and murder from their hands. I'm filled with anger and a lust for vengeance. I don't have your intellectual detachment. I have suffered too much beneath their yoke. I want land for myself rather than my grandsons. The Bolsheviks offer it! The rest of what you say may be true, so I will travel my route with caution. Can we part as friends?"

"I love you like a son, Peter," Vladimir said with a sad smile. "Perhaps that is why my hopes have been so high." He laid his hand on Peter's shoulder. "Take care! I'll not forget you. I hope we'll never find ourselves in opposition to each other. Good luck, dear friend!"

Peter took Vladimir's hand and then pulled away. "You know how I feel about you, Vladimir, but you're an intellectual. I'm merely a peasant. We may take different roads now, but perhaps someday, if fate is kind, our roads will join together."

The little man did not speak but merely shook his head. Peter hurriedly took his leave.

Nikolai Sokoloy and his neighbor Kotov stared at each other, bristling with anger in Nikolai's study.

"I'm telling you, Nicki, we know for certain that Pavel is a member of the Bolshevik Party."

"Even if that's true, Kotov," Nikolai said, "what do you expect me to do about it?"

"Threaten to discharge him if he refuses to quit."

"Every man has a right to his own beliefs," Nikolai insisted quietly.

"A noble sentiment, but obviously, you must be aware his beliefs are in direct opposition to yours."

"I think no less of him for that."

"Then you're a fool. Some night you'll wake up with a knife at your throat."

"I doubt that."

"Very well. Don't say that I didn't warn you. Here we are fighting to keep our heritage while you employ one of those who are trying to take it away."

"Pavel is not merely an employee," Nikolai explained, "he's a friend."

"That remains to be seen," Kotov asserted. "However, to change the subject, it looks as if our chances of getting out of the war tactfully are better now since America entered the war two months ago. We're not so urgently needed anymore."

"That's true," Nikolai agreed. "More pressure to end the war is being brought each day!"

"Well, all we can hope for is the best, Nikolai. I have warned you about Pavel, so I feel my duty is done. Now I must get back to my own estates."

Ivan pushed through the masses marching in the streets. They were a firm and determined group. Everywhere he heard the same sentiments boldly expressed.

"End the war!"

"Send our men home!"

"To hell with the Allies!"

The troops warned the mob before them. "Stand back! Go home!"

A stout old woman beside Ivan hissed. "Not until my man and boy can go with me. We're tired of this war. End it!"

Ivan clenched his hands angrily, turned, and started to walk away when a stone hit him on the back of his neck. He whirled about in fury.

"Who did that?" he shouted in fury.

He was answered with jeers and recriminations.

"Aristocratic fancy man!"

"Bloodsucker!

"Get out of here."

For safety, Ivan drew back into a doorway, watching the scene before him. The troops shouted at the mob in a threatening roar, warning them to disperse.

The people refused. The soldiers, loyal to the Provisional Government, fired into the crowd. Ivan saw the old woman fall, clutching at her chest. The boy fell on top of her. Soon her body was buried under many more. Screams ripped through the air. The smell of blood mingled with that of gunpowder.

"You sons of bitching dogs of Satan," someone shouted.

Men, women, and children dropped before the rapid onslaught of death. Bullets ricocheted about the door in which Ivan stood. He tried to open the door but found it locked. Having no alternative, he threw himself on the ground and trusted his life to chance. Finally, the shooting stopped. Ivan rose and studied the piles of wasted humanity before him—a sea of bloodied corpses. He clutched his chest from the pain that he felt within.

Katie read Ivan's letter aloud to Sonya and Tanya.

> My three beautiful girls,
>
> This has been one of the most startling and historic weeks of my life. After three terrible days, the Bolshevik uprising has been successfully quashed, and the communists seem to have lost favor for the present at least. Our victory, though, was not without price, for hundreds of men, women, and children have been wounded and killed.
>
> These events were startling enough to force Prince Lvov, head of the Provisional Government, to resign. The Socialist Alexander Kerensky has been made prime minister, and he is reorganizing

the government. He will have his hands full, I am afraid. Various revolutionists are deep in plots all around him, and the Allies have turned their backs on his problems.

Kerensky has made General Kornilov the commander in chief of the armed forces. The general agreed to take the position only on his own terms, which means a complete return to military discipline. He demands capital punishment of deserters and full authority for his officers. The general wants no government interference in military matters. Kornilov claims military discipline must be restored. I cannot help but agree with him. I pray for the success of his program. Yet I feel that it is doomed before it begins.

The army is a mass of confusion. All of us know that the Soviets are the real power. Yet they dare not declare it for fear the conservatives will protest and take action against them. Already the Soviet council of the soldiers and workers has issued an edict of their own.

In each military detachment, a committee of soldiers has been chosen. They obey only the Soviet's political decisions. If the Soviet's orders are in opposition to the lawfully elected Duma's, then the former are recognized and carried out. You can imagine the inefficiency of our forces. These so-called soldiers' committees now control all weapons. Officers are no longer allowed to carry them, evidently being considered bourgeois persons since they fail to fall under the classification of either soldiers or workers. God help us all, my children.

I think of you often, but I find it hard to take a pen in my hand these days. I feel, though, that I must assure you of my safety and give you first hand news of the events that are taking place here. I hope that all of you still have adequate comforts. Even here in the city, things are becoming scarcer each day.

I am now attached as a civilian advisor to the Personnel Department of the Officer's Roll. The records are being very carefully studied these days. I wonder where it will all end.

All my love, dear children,
Ivan

Katie looked up from the letter. "I have the strangest feeling that we may never see him again."

CHAPTER 19

AUGUST 1917

The steady sound of the wheels droned on as the train sped across the vast expanse of Russia. Nicholas Romanov, the former czar of Russia, wrinkled his brow in torment. He had abdicated, and then everything had happened too fast. Now they were racing toward an unknown destination.

He had desperately sought to maintain the Romanov dynasty by urging his brother, the grand duke Michael, to ascend the throne in place of his frail son, the czarevitch.

"Nicky, my love." The sound of his wife's voice jarred his thoughts. "What are you thinking?" she asked, drawing attention to herself. He looked at his wife and then tenderly cast his eyes on the sleeping child whose head lay pressed against her chest.

"Poor fragile Alexis. He looks too pale," Nicholas replied. "All this excitement and tension so close to his recent illness has exhausted him. His breathing seems so labored."

"I know," she said. "But your mind was on something else."

"Yes, I was just thinking that Alexis is not strong enough to do what would have been demanded of him after my abdication, but my brother Michael might have saved the throne to pass on to his heirs. Fool! He refused to take it without the approval of the constituent assembly. Can you imagine such folly?" Nicholas asked angrily. "Now for the first time in three centuries, Russia is without a czar."

"You look so worried. Will everything be all right?"

"Of course, everything will be fine," he said, running his hand through his beard as he tried to assure her and himself.

"If only we had fled the country," she sighed while wiping the perspiration from her forehead.

"It would have meant Alexis's death, my dearest. He was too ill to move. Better imprisonment for us than losing him."

"I know, Nicky. Still I think we should have sent the girls out of Russia. At least they would be safe now."

"No use in dwelling on what we might have done, Alix. It's too late for that," Nicholas said, trying to hide his concern. *She doesn't look well. She has worn herself out attending the boy during his last bad spell before this crisis.*

He turned his eye to his four daughters, who were quietly talking among themselves. *Anastasia is so young, pretty, and good-natured and almost always in fine spirits. Tatiana is tall and quiet with her mother's courage and a comfort to us all in the dark hours. Maria is the melancholy one, plump as a child, sharp featured now, and constantly lamenting because a suitable husband has not been found for her. It is Maria that needs me the most as her depression seems to increase daily. And Olga is my favorite—her childhood beauty has faded somewhat, but nothing can dull her lovable quick-witted spirit. If only I had followed through with some of the marriage plans that we discussed at various times, but no, she would not leave her family or her Russia! I should not have indulged her protests. We will all become exiles now.* He shuddered, suddenly feeling cold. A guard entered their coach.

"Are you permitted to tell us our destination?" Nicholas inquired.

"Siberia," the guard grunted.

"Oh no," the czarina gasped.

"What happens when we arrive?" Nicholas asked the man.

"How should I know?" The guard shrugged.

It was twelve days before the royal family reached their destination. They were interned quickly and quietly at Tobolsk. Nicholas and his family were allowed to accept food brought to them by the nuns, and they were granted the privilege of worshiping in the church. Their days passed uneventfully while they waited, uncertain as to what the future would bring.

Peter studied the serious, dark-haired girl before him in the Bolshevik office. She finally looked up from the papers that she had been studying. "We've done well, Comrade Sovinsky," she announced. "Twenty-five new recruits! Fifteen of them appear to be the usual rawboned peasants, but the other ten seem to be of a high caliber and quite dedicated to our cause. We can certainly use them. Of course, we'll have to investigate their records. At this point, we can't afford to take chances. All in all, though, we have done well. I'm very pleased."

"Mmm-hmm!"

"Comrade Sovinsky, I find your attitude extremely irritating at times," she reproved. "You seem to take no pleasure in our accomplishments and fail to express any excitement when we reach our goals. If you hadn't already proven your worth many times over, I would suggest that you be expelled from the party!"

Peter grinned. "I know you would."

"You find that amusing?"

"Comrade Nadia, I see now why they call you Hatchet Face."

"Do they indeed!" she bristled. "A pleasant title! How well I can imagine that they might, for men as a whole have not yet accepted the role women will play in this new order."

Peter, still amused, smiled. "What do you say to continuing this discussion over a glass of wine in my apartment? I'm starved. I still have not learned to function efficiently on an empty stomach. Care to share my humble offerings?"

"I suppose we can finish the business at hand in your apartment just as well," Nadia conceded. She gathered up the papers from her desk and shoved them into a folder. She locked the office securely before going out onto the street with Peter to walk the four blocks to his room.

When they arrived, Peter put a loaf of coarse black bread and a small bottle of wine on the table. "There's little food available these days, Nadia, as you know. What can be bought is rather poor and unappetizing."

"We shouldn't complain," she reproved.

"You're right," Peter said as he broke off a large hunk of the bread and set it before his coworker. He poured some wine into two small glasses and held his out at arm's length. "I propose a toast. To us, Nadia!"

"Yes, and to our most worthy cause!"

Peter raised an eyebrow and smiled. "Always to the cause, eh, comrade?"

She eyed Peter warily. "I don't understand you, Comrade Sovinsky. Somehow your words always sound full of ridicule. Do you find our work amusing?"

"Not our work," Peter told her.

"Then it is me that you find amusing, Comrade Sovin—"

"Please," he broke in, "after only a month's acquaintance, do you think it might be possible for us to be a little less formal? My name is Peter. And yes, you are amusing. I have never seen you act like a woman. You know there is more to life than just the cause."

"Comrade Sovin—er, Peter, right now we have a mission. I can't be bothered with the senseless trifles that you're probably referring to," she admonished.

"That seems obvious," he stated.

They ate the simple fare in silence, and then Peter stood up and cleared the tiny table.

"I guess we had better check these lists without further delay, comrade—er, Peter," Nadia said.

"All right, but damn it, can you drop the *comrade*? It's beginning to wear on my nerves."

The girl looked up in surprise. "If I live to be a hundred, I'll never understand you."

"I can believe that," he said. "Now let me see if I know any of these new recruits. Oh yes, this Baranova served with me in Poland. He's an excellent man. Also, Skobikoba and Suba are good men. I don't know any of these others except Yakut. He is a son of a . . . Well, he is out as far as I'm concerned."

"What's wrong with him?"

"For one thing, he's a coward, always ran from a fight. Secondly, he is a work shirker. We can do without his kind. Eliminate him!"

She drew a line though his name on her list. "I'll check these other names through the regular channels," she said stifling a yawn. "It's been a hard day. I'm glad we're through."

"Mmm, me too," he added. "Now how about another glass of wine?"

"That sounds good."

He refilled their glasses, and as they sat quietly sipping the wine, Peter studied her face. *It's broad like so many others from peasant stock but prettier than most. She has a generous mouth but seldom smiles. Her deep brown eyes and long black lashes could be captivating, but her hair is pulled back so severely in a bun, and her baggy dress conceals her femininity.* Peter shook his head in disapproval.

"In what way am I displeasing you now, Peter?" she asked.

He walked over to her. "Stand up, and I will show you," he said.

She stood up hesitantly. He pulled the pins from her bun, loosening torrents of long dark waves about her face. Then he fumbled with the top buttons of her dress until he had it opened at the neck. The curves of her large, well-rounded breasts swelled toward the opening.

"Now smile," he demanded.

She did.

"Now you look like a woman instead of a machine," he announced.

"And how does that help our cause, comrade?"

"It doesn't, but it's a lot easier on my eyes," he retorted. "You know, Nadia, women like you frighten me a little. It makes me stop and think what the devil kind of breed we're developing here with women that no longer look or act like women. I don't know if I am going to like this new world of equality that we are establishing. I prefer women to be women."

"Delicate, fragile simpletons! Bah!

"You're wrong, Nadia. I know many women who are physically strong and intelligent. Yet they are still feminine."

"I don't see the purpose of this discussion, Peter. Let's change the subject."

"What the hell are you so scared of?" he queried. "Being a woman is not that bad."

"That's easy for you to say because you are a man! But I can do as much as you for this country of ours, and I refuse to do it from in front of a stove!"

"Nadia, neither I nor anyone else is trying to put you behind a stove," Peter said smiling. "Shall we call it a truce?"

"Certainly," she said, returning his smile. "Shall we proceed to the next step?"

"Meaning?"

"You want to go to bed with me, I assume."

Peter choked on his wine.

"Wasn't that what all this woman talk was about? I assume you were leading up to that."

"To tell you the truth," he said, "the idea never even entered my head."

"Then it's my turn to wonder what breed of men that we are developing. There's something radically wrong with a man who doesn't think of sex," she accused.

Peter laughed. "You think I want to seduce you?"

"But of course," she said. "And there's no sense in wasting time since I am perfectly willing."

"Why should you be?"

"Because you are a very attractive man, and I am a woman. What could be more simple than that?"

"I thought you were the cold, indifferent type."

"Why? Because I do not douse myself with perfumes and utter trivialities?"

Peter let his eyes wander over her body. It had been a long time since he had had a woman. She did not stir any sweeping tides in him, but she was attractive. "Hell, why not?" he said with a smile, accepting her offer.

Wordlessly, the dark-eyed girl slipped out of her dress and quickly stripped off her undergarments. "What are you waiting for?" she asked. "Your butler?"

Peter grinned foolishly. "You're not very modest!" he said.

"And why should I be?" she asked. "I have a nice body, no?"

"Yes, but it's just that a female usually puts up some sort of protest before yielding her favors."

"Elimination of that nonsense will be one of the first changes in the new order. Why should sexual hunger not be satisfied as naturally as those of food and thirst?"

"Why not indeed?" he mocked.

"You stall. Am I robbing you of your virtue?"

Peter laughed and doused his cigarette in his wine glass. He pulled off his well-worn boots and quickly tore at the buttons on his shirt while the young Bolshevik girl sat impatiently on the edge of his bed, swinging her shapely legs back and forth.

Afterward, Peter lay exhausted and panting in a cold sweat. "God, you're a tigress!"

"I just take some getting used to," she whispered sweetly. "Good night, Peter Sovinsky."

"Good night, Nadia."

It was only a matter of minutes before her breathing became regular and even. Peter lay beside her sleeplessly, angry and discontented. His body was exhausted, yet he still ached with longing. "What is the matter with me?" he groaned. Then Katie's face danced before his eyes. "Damn little witch," he muttered. "No other woman will ever do. I'll never get you out of my system."

He turned over and pressed his yearning body hard against the mattress. *My day will come, Katie, and when it does . . .* His anguished moan filled the quiet room.

NOVEMBER 1917

"All power to the Soviets" was Lenin's cry, and the people echoed it throughout the land. "Give us land, peace, and bread." The old regime was despised. The people were sick of the pathetic reforms that the new one offered. They wanted immediate comfort from their hardships.

The soldiers cursed the useless loss of their comrades' lives, their insufficient arms, the indifference of their commanding officers to their plight, and the unconcerned attitude of the Allies. Meanwhile, women and children starved. The masses could stomach the misery no longer. They were resolved to end the war. Chaos ran rampart through the rank and file of the military, and through desertion and mutiny, soldiers continued to escape from their unbearable existence.

On the twenty-ninth of October, the revolutionists began aggressive action to take control of Petrograd. Trotsky signed orders from the government to the

Sestroretsk Factory for the delivery of five thousand rifles to the Bolsheviks. By the fourth of November, the Bolsheviks began to show their strength in the neighborhoods, and the beginning of a new era was in sight.

Peter fought his way through the mobs gathered in the narrow streets until he was stopped.

"Are you one of us, comrade?"

"Here's my card," Peter replied.

"You may pass, but be careful. Our patrol ends two streets up, but we hope to take more territory tonight after dark."

"I suggest that you drink a little less from your water bottle there, or you'll not be in shape to do anything."

The dirty rebel grinned a toothless smile. "Comrade, you've a sense of humor." He laughed and took another swig from his grimy bottle.

Peter cursed angrily.

"What'd you say, comrade?"

"Nothing," Peter spat in contempt, narrowly missing the guard's muddy shoes before he walked on.

He made a hasty survey of the territory securely in their hands at that moment before returning to the temporary Bolshevik headquarters.

"How are things going, Comrade Sovinsky?"

"Fairly well, but they'd be excellent if we could stop the liquor supply."

"God knows we've tried," his companion sighed. "Those damn whites slip them the bottles. 'Here's something to keep you warm, worthy comrade,' they tell them. Since they're ignorant louts, they accept with gratitude. Sometimes I think that it would be easier to run a children's school."

Peter grunted his agreement. "Anything new?"

"Yes, Kerensky sent out orders to arrest all the Bolshevik leaders, and our newspapers have been banned."

"He's a little late."

"True, but it's a hell of an inconvenience. A lot of us have had to go into temporary hiding."

"Well, we should have things in hand before the week is out. Any more chores?"

"Yes, we have a contemptible character trapped in our territory. We would like to talk to him briefly before our citizens dispose of him. Go and inform him that we would appreciate a few moments of his valuable time."

Peter nodded and left.

A circle of black smoke swirled about Ivan's face as he puffed nervously on his huge, evil-smelling cigar. "It's impossible. How could such conditions come to pass?" He stared out the window at the crowd below and shook his enormous head in bewilderment. A Bolshevik stopped at every fourth house to tape up a huge poster. Within minutes, a crowd would surge around each one to devour its contents.

Shouts filled the streets below, and Ivan realized from what he heard what the poster announced. "The Provisional Government has fallen. Three cheers! Our soldiers will be coming home!" the people cried out.

"Give old Kerensky the axe."

"Hurray for the Reds!"

"Today's the day, comrade."

Ivan threw down his cigar and stamped the burning embers beneath his foot. He turned to his companion. "I'm going down to read it, Karl. Keep trying to establish contact with the Winter Palace, and let me know if any recent news arrives from any other sector of the city."

With that, Ivan descended into the street below to be knocked and jostled by the delirious crowd. With great effort, he made his way to the proclamation on the pole. It made four promises to the people.

1. Immediate opening of peace negotiations
2. Partitions of large estates
3. Control of the factories by the workers
4. Creation of a Soviet government

He bit his lip and fury blazed in his yes. "You'll have a tough time getting my estate, you rebel bastards!" he spat contemptuously, and then the thought struck him. *My girls! They're alone during this earth-shattering time with no one to protect them. I have to get home.* Suddenly, he was elbowing his way through the cheering multitudes and back across the street.

"What did it say?" questioned Karl upon his return.

"Futile promises as usual. The Soviets are going to give them factories, land, and peace. Bah! Any news?"

"None that's good. One of our runners has returned. There'll be no reinforcements. Kerensky tried to call in troops from the front, but the railway employees refused to transport them. To make matters worse, the Petrograd garrison has joined the Bolsheviks. I'm afraid Kerensky's regime is over. The Provisional Government no longer has an armed defense."

"What about the Cossacks?"

"Smart devils, they're refusing to take sides. They'll be safe in the end by claiming neutrality now."

The buzzing of a radio transmitter interrupted their conversation. "It's the line to the Winter Palace," exclaimed Karl excitedly. "Come in! Come in!"

"I must be brief," quoted the strange voice. "The Bolsheviks are storming the palace and meeting with little resistance. I'm afraid that the government is now in Lenin's hands." The transmitter buzzed with static for a few seconds longer and then became silent.

"I wonder," mused Ivan, "what his great appeal is?"

"Destruction of a czarist past," Karl answered. "They mean to carry us along on the tide too. It's not a comfortable feeling."

"No, it's not. There's nothing more that I can do here, Karl. I'm going to try and get home to my girls."

"Good luck, Ivan!"

A new government was formed in 1918 with Vladimir Ilyich Ulyanov, more commonly known as Nicolai Lenin, at its head, the president of a cabinet called the Council of People's Commissar. Trotsky was appointed to serve him as commissar of foreign affairs, and a relatively unknown party member took charge of minor nationalities. His name was Iosif Vissarionovich Dzhugashvil, or Joseph Stalin.

Peter's friend Vladimir, now one of the Menshevik leaders, read the first acts pledged by the new government. "Immediate negotiation for peace without annexations or indemnities. Ha, it would be a fine thing," Vladimir spat, "if they could really accomplish that. However, Germany is not going to give up territory for nothing when she might have it all in the end. Peace will cost us! And it'll be a high price."

He cleared his throat and looked at his men. Then he read the next act. "Abolishment of private ownership of the estates with no compensation to land owners. Land will be shared equally by all laborers." He stopped, and the group saw that his mind had drifted. *This is what you wanted, Peter. Out of all this confusion, I hope that some of us will realize their dreams.*

He dropped his shoulders wearily. "That's it, men!"

"What do you think, Vladimir?" one of them asked.

"It sounds good, but it'll be hell in the end," he prophesied. "This country is in the worst economic crisis ever. The army is totally disorganized. Agriculture and industry have hit rock bottom. Transportation is nonexistent. We're not likely to get loans from our allies after deserting them, nor will our enemies take pity on us. With putting untrained workers in charge of factories and uneducated farmers in charge of the estates, I see starvation hanging over Russia like an ominous cloud."

The men shuffled their feet nervously. The noise of the street fighting reached their ears, and they were reluctant to leave the safety of Vladimir's room.

"Yes, it'll be hell," Vladimir repeated.

Uncertainty burned in the men's eyes, and they lowered them before Vladimir's gaze.

As news of the Bolsheviks' victory spread across the country, panic followed in its wake. Plagues of cholera crept up from the south. Friend fought friend in the city streets. Chaos reigned everywhere. The Communist Party was small but fiercely devoted. Nowhere in this torn nation was there anyone honest or competent enough to stand against its dedicated march.

Ivan tried for days to escape the confines of Petrograd. Every step was a challenge. Fighting continued from building to building with rifle fire everywhere. Armored vehicles patrolled the streets, frequently changing sides. A woman and small child descended the stairs and joined him in the narrow doorway. "Who are you?" she challenged. When he failed to respond, she spit at his feet. "Bloody aristocrat!"

At that moment, an armored vehicle rumbled down the middle of the street and fired into the crowd. A bullet ricocheted off the building and hit the tiny girl in the woman's arms. "Oh my god!" the woman screamed.

Ivan examined the child. "She's dead," he said gently.

"No! Oh no!" she cried. "Filthy monsters! Red beasts!" And the loyal Red supporter of a moment before suddenly charged the Bolshevik vehicle, carrying her baby's body. They could not stop in time, and the huge wheels rolled over her. Ivan turned away from the sight of the smashed bodies. Sick at heart, he pushed himself on until he reached the city limits. *I will be home soon. Sonya, Katie, and Tanya need me. It must be frightening for them to be alone during these nightmarish times.*

"The password," an ugly-looking brute challenged him.

"I, ah, I forgot it," he stammered.

"Likely story," the Bolshevik spat. "Lets me see your papers." Ivan reached into his pants. "Someone has picked my pocket," he exclaimed, feigning surprise. "A slimy white, no doubt!"

The ruffian raised his rifle.

"You're not going to shoot me?" Ivan asked in startled disbelief.

The leering guard laughed out loud, and Ivan saw death in his eyes. *I have to escape. There is no one at home to protect my girls.* He turned and broke into a fast run, but the rifle barked behind him, and the bullet ripped into his back.

CHAPTER 20

NOVEMBER 1917

"We can't delude ourselves that this single victory is a total triumph. Problems definitely lie ahead," Peter told the crowd. "This is just the beginning. If we're to survive, we must keep our promise to end the war quickly. We must suppress the counterrevolutions that have sprung up in the south, and we must solve the economic crisis that faces us."

The men around him listened intently to his words. "We must unify our army," Peter continued. "Infiltrate all the ranks, remembering that most intellectuals and middle-class citizens distrust us. We must win them over to our Bolshevik ranks. Preferable through friendship, but if that fails, we'll use force!"

"You're right, Sovinsky. We're with you," someone in the audience shouted.

"Yes, we're with you!" another voice seconded.

Peter grinned. "This is a new regime, men. At last we have abolished private ownership of land. Banks have been nationalized, and private capital has been confiscated for the masses."

"Is that proper, citizen?" one man asked, shaking his head, a look of doubt upon his face.

"It's an absolute necessity, comrade, if we are to survive," Peter replied. "The aristocrats could buy our men off. Many of our followers would be happy to accept a bribe, and we know many of the aristocrats would not be above offering one."

"You're right there, comrade."

"I'm glad you see it," Peter continued. "Our workers now control industry. We have swept away the stock markets and their previous right of inheritance. Railways and mines are now the property of the state. It's a whole new era for us."

Peter accepted a glass of water that was thrust into his hand. He took a few swallows and continued. "Look what we have accomplished. We have new courts in which any man can be his own lawyer. A president and six of our own kind will judge each case. Civil marriage and divorce have replaced the outmoded religious ceremonies. Strikes have been outlawed. What do you say, men? Our future looks bright!"

"You said it," a youth shouted.

"We each have our job to do," Peter added. "With Moscow and Petrograd firmly in control, we must extend our authority to the provinces. You have your orders. Gather your belongings tonight. I expect to leave in the morning. We must lend our so-called betters a helping hand."

The men laughed. Then Peter spoke grimly. "This is what we have waited a lifetime for. We're going home to take what should have been ours all along!"

"My god, man, don't argue," Pavel pleaded urgently. "There isn't time!"

"I can't run like a frightened dog with its tail between its legs," hissed Nikolai.

"If you don't, you'll not run at all," Pavel warned. "You've no choice. If they catch you, they'll tear you apart."

"You haven't hurt me," reminded Nikolai gently.

"I'm your friend. The others are not."

"True," Nikolai granted. "You know, it's strange, Pavel, but Kotov once predicted that you would slit my throat some dark night. Instead, you are saving my life. Why?"

"I owe you a lot, Nicki. You're responsible for what I've become since the war. Not many would have taken on a one-legged man," Pavel reminded him.

"You forget that we have a lot in common."

"Yes, but we've a lot of differences too."

"What made you join the Reds, Pavel?"

"It goes back a long way, Nicki, long before I ever met you."

"Then why save me now? You know I'll fight against everything you believe in."

"We're even there, and perhaps the next time we meet, I won't be able to save you or vice versa, but right now I'm repaying a debt. Let it go at that."

Spotting the torchlights in the distance, Nikolai regretfully followed his friend through the trees. As the Bolsheviks approached his hunting grounds, they set fire to the tall beautiful timbers.

"Hundreds of years going up in smoke," moaned Nikolai. "What a tragic waste."

"Not so much of one as a human life," Pavel told him. "Hurry, Nicki, I've a horse about a mile down the road, but you'll never reach him if you stop to watch the destruction. Your tracks are an obvious trail. They'll lead those men directly to you in this snow."

"The two men quickened their steps in the slush underfoot. Nikolai was suddenly startled by loud, frightened bellows that poured forth into the empty night. "My God, they're killing the dumb, innocent cattle now."

"Forget it," Pavel barked. "They'll probably destroy everything that made you who you were. There's nothing that you can do about it."

"Savages," swore Nikolai. Then the night grew quieter and he asked. "What are they up to now, Pavel?"

"They're probably plundering your house. When they're through, they'll burn it, and that will be the end of everything you own. No more estate! No more anything. You'll be just citizen Nikolai Sokoloy, and you can count yourself lucky if you're still alive, for they'll be looking for you soon."

"I'll live, and that's a promise," Nikolai vowed bitterly. Pavel pointed in the direction of the waiting saddled horse, and Nikolai jogged quickly over the last stretch of the journey.

Boris lifted his bearded face to the noisy intruders. "What is it that you want, gentlemen?"

Laughter greeted his question. "Imagine," squeaked one, "him, calling us gentlemen."

"Shut up, you fools," their commander roared and turned back to Boris. "I'm here to give you notice that all the wealth of the Russian Orthodox Church is being confiscated by the state without compensation."

"In other words, church dog," squeaked the same character. "Get out."

Boris chose his words carefully. "I know that you are simply following orders, gentlemen, but this proclamation does not apply to us. Our order is not part of the Orthodox Church. We are a simple band of monks without wealth or possessions or the aspiration to acquire them. We ask simply to be left as we are."

"It's against orders," the commander snapped. "Besides, who do you think you're fooling? These acres are the richest in the area. The people will till them now. Your order will have to disband. Scatter yourselves. You must return to the earthly life that you pursued before taking your vows. Religion will be stamped out in this country and all its advocates with it."

"Surely you don't believe that?" Boris asked.

"Religion is the opiate of the people," the commander replied. "They'll awake now that they're free."

The following morning, the black-robed monks were driven from the sheltered monastery that they had known as home since taking their vows.

Sonya and Tanya huddled in their rooms behind locked doors. Katrina stood before her bedroom window, staring out at the glaring torchlights in the distance. They glowed more brilliantly as they came closer. An icy chill traveled down her spine. She trembled. *Should I run? No, if I run, they would be sure to find me. There's no place that I can run to.*

I could hide. But they'll surely ransack the house, and they would discover me. To be caught like a frightened rabbit in some obscure nook would be humiliating. I've really no choice but to face them and hold my head high.

Tiny hammers pounded in her skull, and her stomach hurt. She shivered. Her teeth chattered while she fought down a wave of nausea. *What will they do? They shouldn't hurt me as I have done nothing to them. Yet they're so angry. Will anything matter except that I am one of the despised lot?* She pressed her forehead against the windowpane in an effort to soothe her throbbing pain. The torches danced forward.

Having made the decision to face the angry mob, Katrina walked shakily to her dresser and wiped the sweat from her face. She started to comb her hair and then stopped to peer at the face that looked back at her from the mirror. *I look so frightened.* She bit her lips until some of the natural color flowed back into them. She could not stop their trembling though, so she busied herself with straightening her dress and picking off a few specks of lint that clung to it.

She returned to the window. The babble of the voices outside brought on another seizure of fear. She regretted her recent heroic decision to face them, but it was too late to change her mind. She could see them now. She started toward the stairs to face them.

Before she got halfway down the grand stairway, the front door crashed open, and the hostile mob surged into the great hallway of Usadiba Na Holme. She swallowed anxiously and drew herself up to her full height, forcing herself to face the crowd of men below her, while she clung desperately to the banister for support. *I must not panic,* she told herself as her eyes swept over the unruly crowd. All at once, her heart missed a beat, for Peter Sovinsky stepped out in front of all the others.

The same childhood ringlets fell upon his forehead, but there was a devastating hardness in his deeply tanned face now. Above his right eye was a small jagged scar. "It seems, countess," he said with a sardonic grin, "that our positions in life have suddenly reversed." He raised an eyebrow in obvious amusement at her plight.

Katie's anger overcame her fright. The situation was bad enough without having to suffer his mockery. "So it seems," she said fighting to keep her trembling voice steady. "What do you plan to do about it?"

"Need you ask, fair lady?" he retorted with merriment dancing in his eyes, and the men about him broke out into coarse laughter and shouted vulgarities.

Her cheeks burned with humiliation. "Are you going to murder me?" she asked, biting her lower lip to stay its quivering.

"Ah, that would be such a tragic waste, pretty lady," he retorted cynically. "It is far more practical for us to find the best possible use for any property that we confiscate."

His men broke out into fresh gales of laughter.

Katie's knees shook beneath her gown. Tears crept into her eyes, but she fought to maintain a dignified composure.

"Come down here, countess," Peter demanded at last in a quiet voice.

Stubbornly, Katie stood her ground upon the staircase.

"All right then, my proud thoroughbred," he said. "This lowly cultivator of the soil will ascend to your height." He turned to some of his followers, issued a series of commands, and then added, "Make yourselves at home, men. Enjoy the offerings of our beautiful and gracious hostess. Usadiba Na Holme is yours!"

Then in several bounds, he was up the stairs. He swung Katie over one of his broad shoulders. The men below howled with pleasure. In humiliation, Katie pounded her fists upon his back as he swiftly carried her to the top of the stairs. "Let me go," she cried. "Do you hear me, let me go!"

"In time, my pure-blooded filly. In time! I have waited such a long time to share that elegant feather bed of yours that I'm not about to be cheated of the experience. Now which way is it to your room?" he asked.

When she made no reply, he began kicking open one door after another savagely until he came to her room. "This one has to be it," he announced. "It looks like you." He carried her inside and dropped her in the middle of her bed then retraced his steps to the door. He closed it, turned the key in the lock, withdrew it, and then thrust it into one of his pockets. Leaning against the locked door, he studied her boldly.

Katie, mortified, sat where he had thrown her. "What are you going to do?" she asked with a quiver in her voice.

"I'm going to finish what you started three years ago," he told her.

"You wouldn't rape a helpless woman?"

"Let's just say that I'm settling an unfinished score. Your cousin robbed my sister of her honor. Now I'm repaying the debt."

"That's not fair," she protested. "I'm not Alex's sister."

"I know," he said. "But I'm a little too late to rob his sister of her virtue." He laughed at the anger in her eyes.

"You're a shameless beast," she fired at him.

"Perhaps," he agreed. "But I don't plan to spend any sleepless nights over it."

"Surely you can't find pleasure in forcing yourself on a woman," she appealed to him. "There must be many women who would welcome you with opened arms."

"Thank you for the compliment," he said, bowing sarcastically. "However, I find none quite so charming as yourself."

His face then took on a serious cast. "It's payback time, Katie. Vengeance! Your virtue for my sister's. Your uncle's life for my father's when I find him." He walked across the room to the window and looked out, commenting, "It's a long way down from here."

Peter lit a cigarette and settled down in a soft armchair near Katie's bed. Slinging one leg over its arm, he studied her, letting his eyes wander over her slender body. He noted the increased fullness of her breast and hips. "You've grown even more beautiful since the last time I saw you," he said. "Matured to perfection, I would say!" He paused and smiled at her. "Do you prefer to undress yourself?" he asked at last. "Or would you rather that I do it for you?"

"You can't be serious, Peter?" she stated, even though he made no effort to conceal his ardor. When he didn't answer, she shouted at him angrily. "You're a hypocrite, Peter Sovinsky! You claim justification for rape because of vengeance, but the real reason is much more obvious and is written plainly on your face. It's nothing more than lust!"

"Hey, I can't help it if my revenge has certain pleasant aspects," he said sardonically and stood up. "I'm not about to forsake it for that reason."

She was filled with panic. *There is no way for me to get out of this room. It is too high for me to jump out of any of the windows. I would never be able to wrest the key away from Peter, and there is certainly no one to help me. Perhaps I should just let him have his way. It's my fault that this has come to pass. I did lead him on and then humiliated him. I have always been drawn to him since the day we met as children—but no, this is a matter of dignity and self-respect. I can't let him use me this way.*

Peter sat on the edge of her bed. "Katrina?"

She glared at him in icy silence, but her heart was pounding. Angered by her indifference, he reached out and grabbed her and roughly began to tear away her clothing.

"Don't be a fool, Peter," she cried.

"Quiet!" he demanded as she fought unsuccessfully against his systematic stripping away all of her coverings.

Finally, she pulled away from him and pressed her back against the headboard of her bed. With brazen eyes, he admired her naked body, and then he took off his own clothing. Katie felt terrified, and the whole room seemed to be spinning around.

Peter, seeing her panic, waited for it to subside.

"Do you want me to beg, Peter?" she asked with her voice trembling. "Would it do any good if I begged?"

"None," he said. "I've waited too long for you, Katie." His eyes were dark and serious, with the tiny scar above drawn so tight that it stood out in rigid relief. "Save your pride!"

"I'm a virgin, Peter. I don't imagine that would mean anything to you, but it means everything to me."

"My sister was a virgin also," Peter reminded her quietly.

"I'm engaged, Peter. I could never go to Nicki if you—."

"Your Nicki can't be much of a man if he would hold something against you that you couldn't help. However, to be honest," he added, "I don't really give a damn about your noble betrothed. Besides, I've always had an earlier claim on you that goes back to our childhood. And it is more than likely that someone will finish your noble Nicki off, if they haven't already done so."

Katie tried to hold back her tears, but her control was gone. The tears rolled down her cheeks unchecked. "Please, Peter," she whispered. "Please, don't do this to me."

He ignored her words, pulled her into his arms, and then crushed her lips with his. She told herself, *It would be so easy to let him have his way. So easy!* Then with a final gasp born of sheer desperation, she overcame her submissive thoughts. With every ounce of her strength, she fought against his advances. She hammered at him with her fists, scratched, and bit, but her struggles were to no avail.

Afterward, as she moaned in pain, he pulled her into his arms and buried his face in her hair. Full of shame and humiliation, she feigned sleep. In the dark of the night, when he thought that she was asleep, she heard him whisper with the same tenderness that he had given to her as a child. He kissed her again and again softly, repeating her name. "Katie, my beautiful Katie,' he murmured. "Don't hate me!" His voice was husky with emotion. "I've wanted you for so long that my desire became stronger than I. Perhaps, someday you'll understand."

Then when his breathing became deep and even, she knew that he had fallen asleep. She wanted to run, but there were those others outside her door. So she lay stiff and quiet with her body aching and tears flowing down her cheeks. *What will become of me now?* she wondered in despair until sleep and exhaustion finally claimed her.

Hours later when she awoke, Katie reached semiconsciously as always for the bell cord and jangled it for a servant to come and light the fire and bring hot water for her morning bath. A surge of pain tore through her, rousing her to reality immediately. She sat up abruptly.

Peter was gone.

The house was quiet.

She swung her legs over the edge of her bed, breaking out in a cold sweat with the effort. She noted the bruises on her legs but bit her lip and struggled to stand.

She pulled a blanket from the bed and wrapped it around her nakedness before limping to the window. There was no sign of the rebels outside.

She hobbled to her closet and gathered up some clothing, and then she sponged her aching body with the icy water in her basin. She shivered, but moments later, her stiffness seemed to ease. She dressed and looked into her mirror for the first time, gasping at her image. Her lips were cracked and swollen, and there were bruises on her cheeks. She could taste dried blood on her lips but couldn't remember if it was hers or his. Her hair was in complete disarray, so laboriously, she tackled the snarls with a brush. Finally, she stood back and took a deep breath, determined now to see how things were throughout the rest of the manor.

She caught her breath in disbelief at the wholesale destruction that she saw everywhere. The banister heads had been broken off. The carpet had been smeared with ink, wine, and paint. Hesitantly, she descended to the parlor, where her worse suspicions were confirmed. Her grandmother's portraits had been slashed. The beautiful Oriental rug had been torn into pieces and the draperies ripped from the walls. The highly polished tabletops had been gouged with sharp instruments, and stuffing had been ripped from their beautiful furniture.

She checked the ballroom next and found that the chandeliers had been smashed into fragments. All the portraits had been destroyed, and the huge mirrors had served as target practice for the rebels' guns.

In the library, books had been piled in the center of the room and set on fire. Many of them were now merely a heap of charcoal and flecks of gray ash.

Uncle Ivan's beautiful leather furniture had also been slashed. The satin curtains had been ripped into pieces.

As she surveyed the destruction, Katie's anger mounted. "Ignorant savages," she screamed as she continued with her painful tour. The elegant tapestries were ruined, the vases were smashed, and the moldings had been ripped from the wall. Anarchy reigned everywhere.

In the kitchen, she found the glassware and china smashed and the silverware gone. The food had been confiscated. All that remained were tiny trails from broken sacks that had been carted away. A thick layer of flour lay upon the floor and swirled in clouds around her ankles as she walked through it. Ants had already congregated around a spilled bag of sugar.

She stood at the door of the wine cellar and looked down. Empty bottles lay everywhere. What the mob had not drunk or taken away lay smashed. She spotted a solitary bottle that had escaped destruction. She rushed down and carried it triumphantly upstairs, where she opened it and took a long drink. She returned to the entry hall and sat down on the bottom step of the stairs in a state of shock. Bitter resentment flooded over her. *It is so senseless. To possess or steal, I can understand, but this wanton destruction. It is insanity. Why?* She clenched her fists with intense rage.

Peter is responsible, of course. Every treasure of Usadiba Na Holme has been destroyed, and he let it happen. He once told me that someday my material possessions might be taken away. He has destroyed my home and robbed me of my virtue. She tried to muster up the proper amount of hatred, but it would not come.

"Peter," she whispered to the empty hallway. "Peter, my childhood friend of the forest. Peter, the passion of my youth. Peter, hard, angry Peter. What did I do to you to bring this about? Now you have had your revenge on all of us. Still, even after all of this, it's time that I admit, at least to myself, that I love you, Peter. But now you have left without even a bitter good-bye."

She started to cry uncontrollably, but her sobs sounded insignificant in the silence of the huge house. *Oh, Peter, I know if our paths ever cross again, I must scorn you, for now my pride will let me do nothing else. Pride is all that I have left.* Then she was seized suddenly by a pang of guilt. In her self-pity, she had completely forgotten about Sonya and Tanya.

The door to Sonya's room was partly ajar. Cautiously, Katie pushed it open and looked about. It was empty. Panic-stricken, Katie searched the premises but found only a note pinned to Sonya's pillow.

My own dearest Katie,

Our world has collapsed, and perhaps it is for the best. A murderer, a cowardly rapist, and a tramp are not the prototypes to maintain an honorable heritage for Usadiba Na Holme. If little Leon had lived, but then, he did not. With him died any hope of our resurrecting the glory of our past.

My brief role of motherhood was the only fulfilling one in my life. With my baby gone, the only other talent I seem to have is one for arousing the animal hungers in men. Each of us must maintain our existence in some way. I have taken the easiest route for me. Peter Sovinsky's sergeant is a lusty fellow who has become quite smitten with me, and should I tire of him, there will always be others. I know you will understand, Katie, but be gentle when you break the news to Tanya.

I do not expect that I shall ever see any of you again. One does not return after choosing such a path as mine.

I only hope that last night was not too traumatic for you. Try to remember, Katie, that the Peter Sovinskys are no longer dirt beneath our feet. They are the rulers in our new order, and we must learn to live with this fact if we are to survive.

The men are getting ready to pull out. Because of you, Peter Sovinsky has refused to let them burn the manor. At least you and Tanya will have a roof over your heads.

I must close in haste now without the time to write all the things in my heart. I give you my love, Katie, enough to last a lifetime. I hope that your path will be an easier one than mine and that someday we will both find happiness. Tell Tanya and Father good-bye for me.

I shall never forget any of you.

Sonya

"Oh, my dearest Sonya," Katie cried out with anguish to the empty room. She walked around, picking up different items belonging to Sonya, studying them, and then setting them down distractedly. Tears rolled down her cheeks as she took up Sonya's note again. She folded it carefully, put it in the corner of her cousin's top dresser drawer, and left the room.

She walked slowly down the hall, feeling dread and apprehension about Tanya now. She knocked, and when no one answered, she pushed open Tanya's door.

The auburn-haired girl sat naked in the middle of her bed, staring blankly at the far wall. Her hair was tangled, and her eyes were dull and vacant.

"Tanya," Katie cried in horror. "What in God's name have they done to you?"

Tanya made no reply.

Gently, Katie eased Tanya's head back on her pillow, pushing the untidy locks away from her face. She brought some water and bathed her friend, horrified as she noted the evidence of the abuses on Tanya's body.

"Filthy scum," she snarled convulsively while chills of abhorrence ran up her spine. She put a nightgown on Tanya then leaned over to kiss her.

Without warning, Tanya seized Katie's throat and squeezed until Katie's senses reeled. Like someone drowning, Katie fought with all of her remaining strength until finally, she broke Tanya's powerful grasp and pulled free. Then Tanya blinked pathetically and suddenly seemed to freeze. The vacant stare returned, and she resumed her absorbed study of the wall opposite her bed. Katie stepped out into the hall and locked Tanya's door securely behind her. Then she bent over and heaved the entire contents of her stomach. The horror and fear of the past few minutes, on top of all that had recently happened, were too much for her. She fainted.

CHAPTER 21

JANUARY 1918

Katie threw off one side of her coverlet, and the icy air bit her like a viperous snake. It was with reluctance that she shed the rest of the blanket, exposing her body to the cutting chill of the frigid room.

When she stood, her empty stomach protested. She went to the closet, extracted her warmest robe, put it on, and tied the cord around her waist. Then hugging her own body, she tried to flame some inner warmth to lessen the outer cold.

She walked to the window and tied to peek out of the frosted pane, but it was crusted with layers of snow and sleet. She could see that the sun was shining, but the seeming beauty and warmth were only an illusion. There was no escape from the reality of the bleak winter world out there.

The last two and a half months had been cruel ones. Every morsel of food scrounged up for her and Tanya had been a major labor, and the quest for it never ended. Remembering the former banquets at Usadibe Na Holme, she laughted bitterly. Now she haunted the woods, searching for berries and roots. She waited, scarcely daring to breathe, dangling lines over holes in the ice, hoping to catch a fish. She had eaten leaves, chewed on bark, but slowly the pounds were slipping from her delicate frame.

Every day was a brutal struggle for survival. As Katie looked toward the empty fireplace, she recalled the logs that had once burned brilliantly there in days gone by. Now, a few branches were a luxury. She tramped through the woods, gathering as many as she could carry. Each day her strength waned a little more. Sometimes the weight of a small limb exhausted her before she could drag it home.

Her head ached this morning. Her stomach churned violently. There was no food in the house. She knew that she would have to go out. But first, she must attend to Tanya. Perhaps today she would give her a bath. She dreaded the ordeal.

Tanya had grown worse over these past few months. The skin barely seemed to cover her bones now. Her color was like that of one long since deceased. She lay inactive like a zombie for days, then suddenly she would emerge from her protective shell and go berserk. Katie dreaded these seizures of madness.

Two weeks ago, Katie had decided to take Tanya outside. She had been peaceful for four days. Katie had bundled her up warmly and pushed her to the stairs. Surprisingly, Tanya descended them under her own power. Katie was relieved and followed closely behind her, but when they reached the open air, Tanya went wild. Katie tried to restrain her, but the girl broke loose and dashed down the outside stairs, slipping, falling, so that her body struck each marble step in turn. At the bottom, she struggled to her feet and raced across the snow, running insanely.

Finally, Tanya collapsed in exhaustion and sobbed wretchedly with her face in the snow. When at last she was still and silent, Katie approached her. Tanya's face and hands were cut from the fall, and there was a huge bruise above her right eye. Katie shuddered as she realized that Tanya could easily have been killed. She decided never to take such a risk again.

Katie now made her way down the hall to her friend's chamber, turned the key in the lock, and looked in cautiously. If she saw Tanya walking about, she would lock the door and come back later. Whenever Tanya was conscious, she was a threat, for her whole body generated violence, and Katie was no match for her wild strength.

Tanya was lying quietly. Katie entered the room armed with clean sheets to change Tanya's bedding. She eased the girl out of her bed and sat Tanya on the floor while she removed her soiled sheets and remade the bed. After this, she stripped off Tanya's dirty clothes and eased her back on to the mattress. Katie was always apprehensive since that first encounter with Tanya's insane fury.

Katie removed her own robe so that she could move around more freely and then got a basin of water. The bath was accomplished without Tanya stirring. She dried the girl, put clean clothes on her, cleaned up the mess, gathered up the soiled clothing, and then left the room, locking the door behind her.

Katie returned to her own room, dressed in warm clothing, and then went below to the kitchen. She filled her stomach with water, before setting out in search of something to ease her hunger pangs. She hoped that her search would prove rewarding today. The air was crisp and stung Katie's face sharply. *I am thankful that I still possess warm clothing. I have Peter to thank for that. He wouldn't let anyone take my personal belongings. Without warm clothing, I would never be able to venture out into these frigid temperatures that now prevail.*

She felt surprised at having something to be thankful for. *Up until now, I have done nothing but curse my fate. I am alone, hungry, and saddled with the tremendous responsibility of Tanya's care. I have not thought beyond these handicaps for a long time, but I realize that I am fortunate to be alive and still have a roof over my head. Others have not survived as well. In most instances, the rabble left nothing behind them but complete destruction. Most of the larger estates have been either burned or confiscated by the state.*

She entered the wooded section where she had first met Peter. *The years have winged by swiftly, and our lives have changed, but this forest remains eternal.* She sighed at the memories that its beauty evoked. "Peter. Peter," she whispered to the wind. "Where are you now? I only hope that your circumstances are better than mine." She shook her head sadly and plunged into the ice-clad timberland.

Katie had walked a long distance when she spotted a flash of red on the snow. It was not the berries that she had anticipated but a splash of blood. *Some hunter must have been fortunate. If only I had the means of getting some fresh meat,* she agonized.

I have tried snares and pits, but my efforts have all been in vain. I would give anything for some of the peasants' salt cabbage and cucumbers that I had once considered so far beneath me.

Katie hitched her coat up; it hung too slack on her thin frame now. She had started to walk again when the fragrance of roasting meat drifted back from the clearing ahead. Flinging caution to the wind, she charged into the opening and observed a huge dirty peasant gnawing on a rabbit leg.

Her stomach turned over demandingly. "Oh ho, come here," he shouted loudly, and she approached without further coaxing.

"I remember you." he said "You're one of them up on the hill. Heard the other one's gone daffy."

"She is suffering from shock," Katie admitted.

He laughed cruelly. "You want some of this?" he asked, pointing at the rabbit on the spit.

"Yes."

"All right, Ms. High-and-mighty, but mind your manners first. Say please."

Katie drew back like she had been struck. He wanted her to beg.

"If no please," he grinned, "then no food."

"Keep it, you filthy beggar," she cried, and she turned and fled into the trees. After she had run a great distance, she flung herself down on the ground in exhaustion. There were tears in her eyes, but it took too much energy to cry.

Mathilde and little Leon are dead. Alex, Uncle Ivan, Nicki, and Sonya are gone from my life. Tanya is mad, perhaps incurably so, and both of us are on the verge of starvation. "Why? Why?" she shouted at the snow-clad trees, and a small voice inside seemed to whisper back to her. "Retribution! Retribution for your sins! Uncle Ivan's brutality and act of murder! Alex's cruelty and rape of innocent Maria! Sonya's wayward behavior! Tanya's self-centered ways!"

But I have done no wrong, she reasoned. *Why must I suffer*? Her conscience jarred her memory, reminding her. *I never tried to help those less fortunate. I rejected a man of worth because he had nothing but honesty and pride to offer. I judged worth by material possessions and external surroundings.* Then from out of the past, Peter's voice seemed to echo in the stillness around her. "Enjoy your fine things, Katie! There may come a day when someone will take them away from you." That day had come!

Katie forced herself to rise from the snow-packed earth. She trudged on, but her quest for food proved futile. Rather than go back empty-handed, she gathered some small branches for fuel and then started the long hike home. When she reached open ground again, she sighed in relief. Her arms ached, but she continued to search the area beneath her. And then a potato! Someone had dropped a potato! The wood clattered to the ground as she grabbed the treasure. It was a big potato, gnarled and somewhat rotten, but beautiful to Katie's eyes. It would feed both her and Tanya tonight. She put it in the pocket of her coat and lifted her eyes upward. "Thank you, Lord, for blessing my repentance," she whispered. She gathered up her wood and trekked on home.

Katie built a fire and put the potato on to cook. The smell tantalized her nostrils and filled her whole body with a feeling of delicious expectation.

She decided to get out of her damp clothes while the potato was cooking. She went upstairs to her room and took off her heavy coat. She rummaged through her closet, searching for her robe until she remembered that she had taken it off in Tanya's room earlier that morning. She ran down the hall swiftly and unlocked the door but could see nothing in the darkness. "Tanya," she called, but the room was silent. Was she in one of her trances? Or was she lying in wait?

Katie stumbled across the room in the dark until she reached the chair. Her robe was still on it. She picked it up and started for the door, but something was wrong. The feeling was too strong to ignore, so she went to the bed and felt the covers. Tanya was not there. Her eyes were growing more accustomed to the dark now, and she looked about wildly. It was by the window that she saw Tanya, hanging limp. All at once, she remembered and frantically reached down, feeling her robe. The cord was gone!

She dashed across the room and struggled to free Tanya's neck from the noose. Her body fell to the floor with a crash. She felt Tanya's pulse. There was none. She laid her ear against Tanya's chest, but there was no sound within. She put her lips on her friend's, but no air pushed past them.

"Tanya is dead, and it's my fault!" she screamed in agony. "My stupid carelessness killed her! So, dear God, you have not stopped trying me after all." There were no tears this time, though, for grief had now become an accepted and expected part of her life.

Katie forced herself to rise after a sleepless night filled with tormented memories. Grief and guilt had ravaged her conscience, but as a machine turns its gears automatically, she wearily washed and dressed.

It was strange how one could continue to perform the ordinary acts of life even under such duress. In spite of finding Tanya's body last night, she had gone down to the kitchen and eaten her treasured potato. It had tasted delicious. Since nothing could be done until daylight, she had undressed and gone to bed.

Perhaps I have become heartless, she thought. *However, Tanya's body must be disposed of in some manner. Ordinarily, in winter, our deceased are stored in tombs until the spring thaw. Then they are buried in the family cemetery. Of course, there can be no funeral. Religious groups had been scattered to the four winds, and there is no one but me to pay any last respects to Tanya.*

I cannot bury Tanya in the ice-coated earth, and it is too dangerous to put her body in the family mortuary. The rabble might return at any time and defile her corpse. Thousands of Russian soldiers are fleeing the war zones daily. Those still alive are filled with fury. Their wrath often extends even to the dead. Tanya's remains must be kept safe. I will bury her in the cellar.

Hours later, she returned to her friend's room. All the violence and unhappiness had been erased by death, and Tanya's pale face seemed innocent and free of pain at last. The light from the window shone on her reddish hair, giving it a cast of gold interwoven with flames of fire. She looked so beautiful.

Katie struggled to lift Tanya up on the bed, and then she washed her rigid body before dressing her in a plain white dress. Katie combed Tanya's hair, letting the soft waves fall about the girl's still white face, and then she wrapped several blankets about the corpse and dragged her to the top of the stairway.

Step-by-step, she lowered Tanya's body. Sweat from the exertion rolled down her sides. When she reached the main hallway, she was forced to sit on the lower step to catch her breath. She looked at Tanya's face, and a lump came into her throat. She lifted the girl into her arms and laid her pale cheek against Tanya's cold ashen face. She felt torn apart with sorrow.

Katie whispered to the empty house. "She's gone too. So many dead! Now you have only me. What's my fate? Who could have thought that our family would come to this, old house?"

Once again she resumed the burden of dragging Tanya's lifeless body. She had so little strength that it seemed hours before she reached the dark, musty cellar. She laid Tanya gently to one side, and since she had no shovel, she began to dig with a stick. She tore dirt from the floor a bit at a time, starting with a small hole that inch by inch grew bigger. *The grave will have to be a shallow one. I do not have the strength to make it deep.* She reached up and wiped the sweat from her forehead. She choked from the dust in the air and felt sick again. She stood up and walked over to one corner of the cellar and retched convulsively. Nothing came of her efforts because her stomach was empty.

She had no idea how long it had taken her to dig the grave, but at last she was satisfied. She studied Tanya's face one more time then kissed her friend's cold lips. She wrapped the blankets more securely and rolled Tanya into the shallow hole. She pushed the soft earth back over Tanya's body. When she was through, she stood and crossed herself. She tried to think of some of the words that priests might say at funerals, but her mind was numb. She could only whisper, "Good-bye, Tanya, sweet friend of my childhood. We had so many happy days together and shared such wonderful memories. The road ahead will be lonely without you. May God bless you and take you into his fold, and may you find eternal peace at last."

She returned to the kitchen and retrieved the bottle of wine that she had salvaged on the day when most of the manor had been destroyed. She had saved part of it. Now bitter tasting, the fluid slid down her dry and dusty throat, burning its way into her empty stomach. She felt light-headed, but the welcoming numbness seemed a salvation to her tired body and brain. She took another swallow of the powerful vintage, and a delicious warmth crept through her. She heard a distant banging in her ears. It went on and on. "Stop it," she shouted. "Go away." But the banging continued, and she fought to clear her senses. *What was it? The door? Of course! Someone was banging on the door. But who could it be?* She tried to stand up, but her legs folded beneath her.

What do they want? I expect no one. It must be trouble. I'll ignore it. She closed her eyes, and after a while, the knocking ceased. Relief flooded through her at the silence, and she fell asleep.

It was dark when she awoke. Slowly, the fog of unconsciousness slipped away. She jerked forward with a start. She stood up shakily and hurried to the front hall. It was black. She opened the door and looked out, but no one was in sight. *Who could it have been,* she mused? As she started to shut the huge front door, a flash of white caught her eyes. It was a piece of paper.

She snatched it up eagerly and saw there was writing on it. *Who could it be from?* She had no candle by which to read the message, and she trembled with impatience and frustration. She would have to make a fire before she would have enough light by which to read the message.

When the flames flickered brightly enough, the bold familiar handwriting seemed to leap out at her. Moisture crept into her red-rimmed eyes. It was from Nicki. Her hands trembled as she tore open the envelope. She withdrew the letter and read it with her heart pounding.

> My dearest darling,
>
> How long it has been since I have said those words to you, Katie. Time and events have winged by so swiftly that I find myself at a loss for words. Where to begin? First I must beg forgiveness for my cruel and abrupt behavior in the past. I was wounded in the war. To save my life, it was necessary for them to amputate my arm. Afterward, I was filled with remorse and self-pity. Please forgive me for any pain that I might have caused you because of this.
>
> Since the revolution, I have tried in vain to reach you. The revolutionists have cut off your section of the country completely, and it has been impossible to get word to you. Now I am assured by one of my men that he is certain that he can reach you.
>
> I loathe that my first message to you must be one that brings sorrow, but there can be no avoiding it. I am sorry to inform you of your uncle's death. At the beginning of the uprising, he tried to slip out of Petrograd in order to reach all of you. A Bolshevik shot him in the back. He suffered no great pain as he died immediately. For this much, we can be thankful.

All of you at Usdiba Na Holme are in danger. It is no longer safe for you to remain there. I have made arrangements for you to join me. Someone will contact you the night after you receive this message. All of you must be ready to leave with him. He will come sometime after dark. Bring only what is absolutely essential.

You have probably heard about the formation of the Extraordinary Commission for the Suppression of Counterrevolution, more commonly known as the Cheka or Secret Police. All of your names have been placed on their list of undesirables. You will be pulled in for questioning soon. I do not know how you have escaped their attention thus far. If something does go wrong, and they should lay their hands on you, you must disclaim all knowledge of me. This is essential for your safety. Destroy this note as soon as you have read it.

The Reds' reign has become one of terror. Their goal is to eliminate the bourgeois class and to exterminate all those who oppose their corrupt system. Mercy or justice is completely unknown to them.

In the early days of the revolution when the national constitutional assembly declared the Soviet regime illegal, the Bolsheviks dissolved the assembly by force. Now they dare not stop using force, for to retreat or relent would mean destruction of their party. All those in their way are destroyed. The Red plague continues to sweep down over town after town, grasping control of railways, mines, and humanity itself. God help us all!

You must prepare immediately for departure. I can tell you all of the war news when you are here with me, but that will be only after I have told you the longing in my heart. I love you, Katie. Never has my desire been dimmed for a solitary moment. Now I wait only until you are here by my side. I long so to have you for my wife if you still care for me, but these matters will be decided upon later. Hasten to me, Katie. Each day will be an eternity until I see your face again.

I am forever yours,
Nicki

Katie laid the letter in her lap and felt a lump in her throat. She trembled and sighed. "My wonderful Nicki, why did such a terrible thing have to happen to you? You who were so big, strong, and beautiful," She put her hands over her face and clenched her teeth tightly together. She tried to swallow, but the pain was too strong for her to bear. "Nicki. Nicki. My darling Nicki!"

He still loves me and wants to marry me, but Uncle Ivan is dead! Can no one dear to me survive? My strong, domineering Uncle Ivan felled by a bullet in the back. She laid her head down on the ripped cushion of the armchair. She felt so tired, as if her head were too heavy for her shoulders. She rested a moment before forcing herself back to Nicki's message. She was in danger of arrest, and she had to leave her home.

Nausea struck her again. Her stomach fluttered wildly and seemed to be churning violently. She bolted from the room and vomited the wine that she had consumed earlier. The stench revolted her, and she fought to keep from retching again. When her stomach had settled, she returned to the fireplace and picked up the letter again.

She looked at it sadly and shook her head. "Oh, Nicki. My dearest! If only your letter had reached me several months ago, things might have been different! We might have had a future together. Now it is too late for us."

She left the warmth of the library and climbed the steps to her cold bedroom. *I need some sleep. Tomorrow I'll have to leave here, but I have no idea of where I'll go or how I'll survive. It's a temptation to stay. To stay and go to Nicki, who would take care of me and protect me. I can't do that, though, as I care too much to use him that way. He loves me and wants to marry me. If I loved him in return, perhaps it would be different, but I don't, and I have no right to deceive him. He has suffered enough already.*

"Oh, dearest Nicki, I can't come to you," she whispered hoarsely to the silent walls. "Not when I know now for a certainty that I'm going to bear another man's child."

CHAPTER 22

MARCH 1918

Nikolai Sokoloy paced angrily across the library. "Damn fools!" he uttered savagely. "They couldn't handle the job that they undertook, so they sacrificed Mother Russia and her people without a second thought. Imbeciles. Stupid half-wits!"

"Calm down, Nikolai. The Treaty of Brest-Litovsk has been signed. We are obligated to abide by its terms," Nikolai's aged companion prodded gently.

"Damn!" Nikolai shouted. "How can you take things so calmly? The conditions are disastrous. No man wanted peace more than I, but peace on these terms is a humiliation."

"With every good comes some evil, Nikolai. We have to be thankful for the pluses that it brings and forget the unpleasant part. Now that we're finally at peace with Germany, we can concentrate on freeing our own people from the Bolshevik yoke."

"I'll not be soothed so easily, Markus. Two and a half million Russian soldiers lost their lives, and I gave an arm! For what? For nothing!" Nikolai bowed his head to hide the anguish in his eyes. "God, there's no justice on this earth!"

"We'll be avenged, Nikolai. The Germans will be beaten, but we can no longer afford the luxury of throwing away lives to defeat them. There's too much at stake here at home."

"It's a wonder we have anything left of our homeland," spat Nikolai. "One-fourth of all our prewar European territory is gone. Just like that! What for, Markus? What for? A few months more, and we'd have beaten them."

"No, son. They would have penetrated our barriers, and we would have lost all. Believe me. It's better this way."

"How? We have given away Lithuania, Estonia, Latvia, and most of Poland. Part of Finland. White Russia and the Ukraine. We have ceded Transcaucasia to the Turks, and we have restored Kars and Batum," Nikolai contended. "On top of that, we have lined the Turks' pockets with three hundred million gold rubles when we are on the edge of bankruptcy ourselves."

The older man patted the younger one's shoulder in sympathy and said softly, "We must accept the inevitable, Nikolai, and work that much harder to free what is left of Russia."

Nikolai sighed. "Yes, the underground will have twice as much work to do now. With the war over, the Reds will clamp down with even more force."

"We have our work laid out," Markus agreed.

The two men sat down and studied the various papers lying on the table before them. When they were through, with the facts safely committed to memory, the two underground leaders of the White forces lit a match and burned the records in an iron ashtray. Nikolai then opened the window and let the charred remains blow away into the night. Markus poured two small glasses of wine.

"Why do you suppose the Reds moved the capital from Petrograd to Moscow?" Nikolai asked thoughtfully.

"Who knows what motives lie behind the Bolsheviks' actions? Maybe it is just a matter of convenience. Perhaps they want a better climate, or maybe they just want to show us that they can change anything and that tradition means nothing to them."

"I think the Bolsheviks have bitten off more than they can chew," Nikolai said. "There will be many who will refuse to accept the Germans' peace. Sooner or later, there will be trouble."

"That remains to be seen. By the way, Nikolai, did you ever get word to your betrothed?"

Nikolai's eyes clouded and he shook his head. "No, she was gone. So were the other two girls. No trace could be found of them. It was rumored in the area that one of them had gone mad. The house had not been vacated long. There were signs of recent occupancy, but where they went or why, I don't know. I will continue to search, though, and if she is still alive, I'll find her."

In the city, Katie shivered in the corner of a dark alley where she crouched with fear. The hooligan in front of her had forced his victim to undress. He laughed at the little fat man's discomfort.

"You'll pay for this," the small man whined.

"Don't count on it, fatso. Now toss those clothes over here."

"Please," the frightened man begged. "I can't go home naked."

"I wouldn't bet on that, fat stuff," the sadistic robber laughed. "You'll go home either naked or dead. The choice is yours."

"I'll freeze in this weather," the victim pleaded.

"In March? You're crazy. At most, you'll shiver a few pounds of that blubber off."

The little man began to cry. The hooligan shoved him so that he fell in the melting slush. Then the robber fled from the alley with the man's clothes. The little man stood up and looked around, and then, still sobbing, he fled down the opposite end of the alley.

I should feel sorry for him, Katie thought, *but he's too well fed, and that's a crime when most of humanity now looks like rattling skeletons.* She rose and quietly left the dark alley.

She knew it was dangerous to wander in the streets after dark, but she had no choice. *I have no place of shelter. No friends to whom I can appeal. I dare not apply for work because I would be spotted instantly as a bourgeois and turned over to the dreaded Cheka. I am hungry. So very hungry.*

There are others in the streets like myself. Many are young and beautiful girls, refugees separated from their families, not knowing which way to turn. Some have turned to prostitution, and they walk the streets, filthy and humiliated, accosting the men they see, desperately trying to stay alive. I feel an intense sympathy for them. They are my sisters in misfortune. Perhaps in desperation, I might also have been driven to join them, but my physical appearance makes that life an impossibility now.

Because her frame was thin and almost absent of flesh, the curve of her stomach appeared more pronounced than normal. *What am I going to do? I know it will be a miracle if my child survives, but I'll never stop praying for such a wonder. I want my baby to live. I want to have Peter's child regardless of what other horrors the future might hold.*

Ahead, she spotted a jumper stopping one of the streetwalkers to confiscate her night's earnings. These men were vicious creatures. They draped their bodies in sheets and walked about on silts. With phosphorus glowing faces, they frightened their victims into immobility and quickly robbed them.

Katie ducked up another alley to avoid them and stopped to rest in the dark, cold night. *What a pathetic world I live in now. I wonder what my child's life will be like if he or she is fortunate enough to survive? There will be no luxuries for my baby. But perhaps that will be a blessing. My child will never grow up judging life by mere materialistic standards like I did. My baby will be like his father or Maria—hardworking, strong, serious, and full of pride and dignity. If my baby lives, he will have to fight for survival.*

Katie suddenly felt an overpowering urge to pray and hastened to the large church on the next block, but the door was locked. She longed to kneel in front of the door, but she was afraid to call attention to herself. *Religion is taboo now. The troubled masses can no longer find comfort in the house of God. Instead, each of us has to search within ourselves to find what peace we can.*

The cities are foul and corrupt. My fellow humans have become snarling and despicable. I long to go back to the area of my childhood. I long to see Usadiba Na Holme again. Perhaps it will be safer now with spring coming. Maybe I can find refuge somewhere. I must make the journey before my child is born. It is a long trip. I have no money to take a train, so I will have to walk. I can only hope that some people along the way will take pity on me and give me the few crusts of food necessary to maintain my life. I can't bring myself to beg or steal.

JULY 16, 1917

Provovich, the former driver at Usadiba Na Holme, mused on the strange twists and turns of fate. *I was never unhappy with my position at Ivan Kozakov's estate. I loved caring for the horses, and the master always treated me with respect. But the revolution came. I couldn't very well side with the aristocracy. I am a peasant, and the Bolsheviks are fighting for my rights, so I exchanged my uniform in the czar's army for one in theirs. Now I find myself in this remote place called Yekaterinburg, the capital of the Urals, listening to two of my exalted Bolshevik leaders. Commandant Yakov Yurovsky is pacing back and forth nervously talking to Comrade Grigory Nikulin.*

"Our leaders were worried that the monarchists would try to rescue the royal family from Tobolsk in Siberia. It was too close to the sea, too near Asia, and there were too many in the area with sympathies toward the czar and his family. That's why they moved the czar, his family, and loyal retainers here to Yekaterinburg and quartered them in Engineer Ipatiev's house."

"I know that already," Nikulin replied. "We painted the windows white and erected a high wooden fence around the house. It is heavily guarded at all times by our soldiers bearing rifles and machine guns. But this is not enough?"

"We have our orders," Yurovsky reproved him. "Where is the truck, Grigory? We can't proceed with the assassinations until we have the truck."

Comrade Grigory Nikulin shrugged his shoulders. "It should have been here long ago. Always there's such incompetence."

"That's an understatement," Yurovsky growled.

"You did get the final word from Moscow?" Nikulin asked.

"Yes, in a coded telegram from Lenin himself," Yurovsky replied.

"No chance that he'll change his mind?" his underling asked him.

"No possibility! The damn Czechs who are allies with the Whites are getting too close to Yekaterinburg, and the White forces are not far behind. Our great honorable leader would never risk letting the aristocrats escape. Remember the Romanovs hanged his older brother."

"But Lenin's brother tried to assassinate Nicholas's father for God's sake."

"It makes no difference," Yurovsky asserted. "The sins of the father are passed on. Likewise the hatreds."

"But the children," Nikulin prodded. "Why the young ones?"

"The czarevitch and his sisters could become living banners. No way those in Moscow will let that happen," Yurovsky announced. "Lenin plans to exterminate all the Romanovs. Every last one of them."

"Yeah, well, a couple of our Latvian sharpshooters backed out at the last minute," Nikulin related. "Told me they were soldiers. No way were they going to shoot young girls."

"Ah, moralistic pantywaists. I hate their kind," Yurovsky grumbled. He turned to Provovich. "Is the room ready?"

"Yes, it's in the cellar. All the furniture has been removed to avoid ricochets from the bullets. It has beautiful checkered wallpaper, and there's a heavy railing installed over the only window."

"Good," Yurovsky said. "Soon Russia will be rid of Nicholas the Bloody!"

"Amen," Nikulin echoed. "I think I hear the truck."

"About time," Yurovsky said. "As soon as we get the family down there, have the driver run his engine to muffle the sound of the shots."

"What time is it?" asked Nikulin.

"Already after midnight," the commandant snapped with annoyance.

Commandant Yakov Yurovsky entered Ipatiev House to wake the occupants.

"Citizen Nicholas Alexsandrovich Romanov, there's extreme unrest in the town. Enemy forces are close to the area. There have been wild, erratic gunshots around the city. We fear for your safety and must move you to a cellar room until morning. Please get dressed immediately."

As the residents of Ipatiev House dressed, Yurovsky kept looking at his watch. He returned to the cellar to check on his assassination squad. Besides himself and Gregory Nikulin, there were two Cheka agents and seven Latvians from the Bolshevik army. All of them were sharpshooters. Each one had a handgun and had been assigned their target. "Shoot for the heart," he told the men. Eleven gunmen for eleven victims. "It shouldn't take more than a minute or two," he told his soldiers. "However, we better have rifles and bayonets ready as backups."

Yurovsky was furious that the royal family took forty minutes to wash and dress. Finally, he led his captives down the stairs of Ipatiev House, out into the courtyard, and through a second door that led down an inner staircase to the downstairs quarters where the corner room had been prepared for them. In a storeroom next to it, the detachment of soldiers waited.

Yurovsky and Nikulin led the way and were followed by Nicholas carrying his son. Then came the Czarina Alix; the four grand duchesses; Dr. Evgeny Botlin; the czarina's lady-in-waiting, Anna Stefanovna Demidova; Nicholas's lackey, Trupp; and their cook, Kharitonov. One of the grand duchesses carried a small dog in her arms.

The czar and czarevitch wore army field shirts and forage caps. The czarina and her four daughters wore dresses but not wraps.

Upon entering the cellar room, Yurovsky told them, "You must line up against that far wall."

"For what reason?" Nicholas inquired.

"Moscow wants a picture," Yurovsky told them. "They want to confirm that you are safe." He began to direct their placement. "Please, you stand there, and you here. That's it, in a row. He lined up the czar and his family in front and then had the servants line up in a second row behind them.

"What, no chairs?" the czarina asked in amazement. "May we not sit?"

Yurovsky ground his teeth.

"My wife and son are both having problems with their legs," Nicholas explained. "The soldiers upstairs would not let us bring the czarina's wheelchair down."

"In that case . . . ," Yurovsky commented and left the room, going next door to the storeroom. He laughed cruelly and told the soldiers to bring in two chairs. "Seems," he told the detachment waiting there, "that the German bitch and her son want to die in chairs. Let's oblige them."

Provovich and another soldier brought in two chairs and placed them close to the far wall. Two of the grand duchesses had carried pillows downstairs. They now placed them upon the seats for their mother and brother.

Outside, the motor of a truck roared loudly in the heretofore quiet of the night.

Yurovsky stepped forward slightly, took out a paper, and began to read. "Nicholas Alexandrovich, your relatives have tried to save you. They have not succeeded, and we are forced to shoot you."

Not hearing him well, Nicholas ventured, "What?"

Yurovsky answered by withdrawing his gun and firing at the czar.

"You know not what you do," Nicholas said as he fell.

With the first shot, all the other assassins stepped to the door of the cellar room and started firing in three rows. The second and third rows fired over the shoulders of those in front so that those in the first row suffered severe powder burns. Nicholas and Alexandra fell immediately. Then chaotic shooting ensued as the rest of the victims raced around the approximately one-hundred-foot square room.

The sharpshooters continued to fire.

"My God," one of the soldiers cried. "The bullets are bouncing right off them."

"They are ricocheting around the room like hail," another wailed in disbelief. "God must be protecting them."

"The boy, three of the girls, the maid, and the doctor are all still alive," someone else yelled with confusion.

Lady-in-waiting Demidova shielded herself with a pillow as the gunmen emptied one bullet after another into it.

The assassins were hysterical now.

"The room is so smoke filled that we can't see a thing," a soldier in the back row yelled.

Alexis and the maid were now lying on the floor, but the two youngest duchesses were pressed up against the wall, squatting and covering their heads with their arms.

"Damn," Yurovsky roared. "Stop firing and finish off those still alive with your bayonets.

The killers flooded into the room, stabbing in a frenzy.

"The bayonets won't go in," one soldier wailed.

"Too dull," another shouted.

"Jackasses," Nikulin roared. "Why didn't you sharpen them? You're a bunch of incompetents."

"Yeah, well those who didn't want to kill the girls were right," another said. "We are cursed."

"Shut up and do your job," Yurovsky roared, his control disintegrating.

One soldier was trying to finish off the maid, but she grabbed his bayonet with both hands, and as it sliced her palms to ribbons, she began screaming.

"Use your rifle butts," Yurovsky yelled.

The soldiers complied until at last all eleven victims lay on the floor with blood gushing from them. There were splashes of blood on the walls, puddles of blood on the floor, but the heir to the throne was still alive and moaning. Yurovsky walked over and shot him three times at point-blank range.

"Check their pulses," the Commandant called out.

"Okay," Nikulin directed. "Some of you," he said, pointing at Provovich and the Latvians, "get some sheets from upstairs to carry them out. We don't want to drip blood through all the rooms."

Outside, the truck motor continued to roar, filling the otherwise quiet night.

As the soldiers attempted to lay one of the daughters on a sheet, she cried out and covered her face with her arm. The other daughters now moved on the floor.

The detachment was gripped with horror.

"It's the devil's work we've tried to do here tonight," muttered one of the soldiers.

"Enough of that talk," Yurovsky ordered.

One of the frightened soldiers grabbed a bayonet from another soldier and tried stabbing all those still alive, but the point would not penetrate any of the grand duchesses. Only the tiny dog locked in one of the grand duchesses' arms seemed vulnerable to death.

When at last they felt confident that all the victims were dead, the murderers carried the bodies out to the truck, which still had its motor running. When the corpses were placed in the truck, there was a movement among the victims again. The assassins dared not fire bullets outside the house, so the dull bayonets and rifle butts were brought into play again.

"Let's get them out of here," the commandant ordered. "It's almost dawn."

As the truck pulled away, one of the soldiers left behind returned to the cell of carnage, and with some of the blood, he wrote upon the wall in German.

THIS NIGHT BELSHAZZAR WAS MURDERED BY HIS FELLOWS.

JULY 17, 1917

Sergei Ivanovich Lyukhanov was the Ipatiev House driver, but tonight he had been ordered to take a truck from the Soviet garage by the Cheka. Lyukhanov was a short middle-aged man with a hooked nose. He did not witness the execution since from three o'clock in the morning, he had been sitting in the cab of his truck with the motor running, waiting.

Finally, Provovich and the other men emerged from Ipatiev House, carrying out the bodies of those assassinated. Lyukhanov was a good party member, but he went pale when he saw the royal children. "I thought it was just the czar and czarina who were to be disposed of," he stated. "But the children? And even the servants?"

"Don't worry about it, old man," Upper Isetsk Commissar Ermakov laughed. "The same rotten blood flows in all the Romanovs. Children or adults. It makes no difference."

Lyukhanov turned to Yurovsky. "What's the matter with him?" he asked pointing to Ermakov.

"He's drunk," Yurovsky snapped. "Almost the whole bloody bunch is drunk. Unreliable fools! That's what they are. Commissar Ermakov was to be in charge of disposing of the bodies, but I can't trust him to do the job in his state. I'll have to come along too."

Driver Lyukhanov shrugged, trying to appear indifferent, but he felt nauseated at the carnage that he saw before him. Yurovsky ordered Ermakov into the back of the truck. "He's so drunk," he told Lyukhanov, "that he'll probably pass out on the way. Provovich, you had better get in and keep an eye on him." Yurovsky climbed inside the cab beside the driver. "Let's go," he ordered.

Sergei Ivanovich Lyukhanov started his truck down Ascension Avenue then turned down Main Street. He drove past the city limits by the racetrack and headed down the road toward Koptyaki. A vehicle with members of the Red Guard followed closely behind him.

They traveled without incident until they reached the area of Railway Booth Number184, where the road crossed the mining factory railway line. There, the truck's engine overheated and broke down in a marshy area. All of them climbed out of the truck and were joined by the Red Guards who had been following behind.

"Damn our luck," Yurovsky scowled. "Ermakov, you come with me, and let's see if we can locate those mine shafts that are supposed to be around here while they get this truck operating again."

As soon as Yurovsky and Ermakov disappeared into the woods, some moans escaped from beneath the tarpaulin in the back of Lyukhanov's truck. The driver pretended that he didn't hear them and walked toward the railway booth, motioning Provovich to accompany him. They woke the watch woman to ask for water for the boiling truck. She started to grumble, but the driver Lyukhanov stopped her sharply. "You're here sleeping like a lord while we've been breaking our backs all night."

From the corner of their eyes, the driver and Provovich saw the figures of the Red Guard surround the truck and ease two bodies out of the back. They dragged them off into the dense forest nearby.

Lyukhanov distracted the watch woman by shouting, "We'll forgive you this first time. But don't go complaining in the future." He borrowed some buckets from the woman and began to pump water for his overheated vehicle while continuing to engage the woman in a running conversation. Afterward, when walking back to the truck, he turned to Provovich and explained. "You know, I also have a son named Alexei."

By then, the Red Guards had returned to the truck from the forest. Lyukhanov sent them to collect planks at the watch booth, which they then carried to the swampy ground and laid down so the truck could gather enough traction to resume their journey.

Provovich pondered on what had just transpired. *The Whites are about to take this area. When they discover the royal deaths, they will hang all the officers. If these soldiers have saved some of them, it will go better for them. But I've seen nothing. I know nothing.*

Yurovsky and Ermakov returned, and they all resumed their drive toward a forest area known as Four Brothers, named after four tall pine trees that had once existed there. "There are a lot of old mines filled with water in this vicinity," Yurovsky explained to the driver. "We can dispose of the bodies by dumping them there."

When they finally reached a camp area, twenty-five members of the Executive Committee Soviet were waiting. Some were on horseback. Others had droshkies. Most were drunk.

"What?" several shouted. "Dead already? We were promised the thrill of executing them and told that we could have our sport with the grand duchesses first."

"Get those bodies on the droshkies," Yurovsky ordered with fury. He turned to their leader. "Any problems on the way here?"

"Yes, we encountered a mob of peasants on the road from Koptyaki," he replied. "However, Vaganon here shouted, 'Get back there. Turn around. And don't look back!' He cursed and drove the terrified peasants back to their village." The leader pointed out a man dressed in a sailor suit who stepped forward with his hand extended.

"Name's Vaganon. I'm with the Cheka."

"Pleased to meet you," Yurovsky acknowledged.

One of the crew ventured, "If we're going to burn these clothes, we'd better strip them off the bodies."

"Wait until we get to the burial site," Yurovsky barked. "Load them on the droshkies."

"All the corpses won't fit," one of the soldiers complained.

"Some of these carts are falling apart," another shouted.

Yurovsky cursed again. "It's getting light already, and nothing's prepared yet. Where are the shovels?" he roared.

"Someone forgot them," one of the crew replied.

"Imbeciles!" Yurovsky yelled. "Go find those mineshafts," he ordered some others.

In the areas near the mine shafts, Yurovsky ordered the bodies from the carts. "Get the clothes off the bodies and burn them." The work crew built bonfires and started to strip the corpses. It was then that they discovered a belt of pearls around the czarina's waist and corsets of diamonds covering three of the grand duchesses.

"That's why the bloody bullets bounced off them back there," Ermakov exclaimed.

"Right, now get these men out of here, Ermakov," Yurovsky ordered. "Just keep several sentries and five guards to help us. Disperse the rest of them back to wait on the road."

Ermakov looked confused but complied with Yurovsky's demand. "Move out and wait on the road," he ordered the crew.

When they had departed, Ermakov turned to Yurovsky with questioning eyes. "You think they would steal some of the diamonds?"

"They probably already have," Yurovsky answered. "But are you still too drunk to notice our real problems?"

"What do you mean?" Ermakov asked.

"Count the bodies, you idiot!" the commandant demanded.

Ermakov did as he was ordered and turned white. "Jesus Christ, there are only nine," he declared, sobering up instantly.

"That's right, my friend."

"Who's missing?" he asked.

"The boy and one of the grand duchesses."

"What happened to them?" Eremakov queried in a panic. "Perhaps they got left in the truck."

"No," Yurovsky said, shaking his head.

"Well, we've got to find them," Ermakov said. "It'll be our asses."

"That's right," Yurovsky agreed. "But there's no time to search for the missing corpses. The Whites are all around us and will enter the town anytime now. We've got to get rid of what we have here."

"We're supposed to take a picture of the bodies for Moscow." Ermakov ventured.

"Oh sure," Yurovsky said, looking at him in disgust. "Show them that we only have nine corpses. Are you crazy?"

Ermakov was trembling now. "This was supposed to be my detail. I've messed it up badly. What'll we do?" he asked in desperation.

"Hopefully, they will never find out, but to cover our hides, we'd better have a story."

"What kind of a story?" Ermakov asked.

The commandant just glared at him.

"Well," Ermakov asserted, "we can say that we burned the two missing bodies."

"What about their bones?" Yurovsky asked. "And if we burned two bodies, why didn't we burn the rest?"

Ermakov looked ill now. He didn't say anything for several minutes. Then his face lit up. "It was so cold while we were waiting for the clothes to burn that we doused two of the bodies with gasoline and threw them on the fire to keep warm. They burnt to ashes, and if there were any small bones, the wolves and wild dogs must have carried them off."

"A pathetic tale," Yurovsky said sarcastically, "but since I can't come up with a better one, it will have to do."

Their small crew finished burning the clothing, and Yurovsky gathered up the jewels.

They lowered the bodies down into a pit partially filled with water then threw in fresh branches and burned wood to cover them before lobbing in a couple of grenades in an attempt to collapse the mine shaft. They next brought up horses and trampled the area with their hooves to erase the deep ruts made by the carts in the wet earth. In a state of exhaustion, they returned to the road where Ermakov had gathered the soldiers and work crew together.

Yurovsky stepped forward to speak to them. "You must all be sworn to secrecy about today's events. Moscow will announce that the czar has been executed to prevent his rescue by the White forces closing in upon us, but they'll tell the people that the rest of the royal family has been evacuated to a place of safety. If the truth is discovered, all of us could be executed by the White forces if we are captured. Our enemy must never discover their bodies."

Each of the men stepped forward and took a vow of secrecy.

On the return home, Yurovsky told the driver, Lyukhanov. "Keep the truck an extra day. We'll have to get it cleaned up."

"I understand," the driver said.

JULY 18, 1917

Next morning, when Ermakov and Provovich visited the bazaar, they heard from several merchants where and how the bodies had been hidden. Once again in panic, Ermakov rushed to Yurovsky.

"And how did the whole town find out?" he roared at his partner with fury.

"I think some of the crew might have gotten drunk," Ermakov ventured. "Or perhaps the peasants observed us in the forest. Hell," he exploded, "I don't know!"

"Well, this is great news right when the Czechs are closing in around us," Yurovsky snapped.

"What'll we do?" Ermakov inquired, his composure in shambles.

"We'll have to move the bodies," he said. "We have no alternative. We can't let the corpses be discovered." He started to bark orders to Ermakov and Provovich.

"We can't move them until it's dark. Get Lyukhanov with the truck again for the bodies. Get several extra trucks, and gather a large supply of kerosene and sulfuric acid.

"Right," Ermakov replied, jotting down all his instructions.

"Tell the people in the area that there are Czechs hiding in the woods, so we must cordon off the district for military maneuvers. That will cover us for any rifle fire or exploding grenades."

After dark, Provovich returned with the other conspirators to the mineshaft. By the light of torches, they lowered the sailor, Vaganon, down into the mine shaft, where icy water reached up to his chest. They then lowered ropes, which he tied around the bodies so they could raise them. The royal remains were then pulled out, put on the carts, and transported to Lyukhanov's truck once again.

They drove, looking for another mine site, but failed to find one. With dawn approaching, they finally stopped and dug a common grave. They didn't have enough time to burn the bodies as they had planned, so the faces of the royal family were smashed with rifle butts. Then their faces and bodies were doused with sulfuric acid before they lowered them into the grave. Dirt and lime were shoveled in on top of them. Boards were put on top of the bodies, and then they drove the truck over the area repeatedly until there was no trace of the grave.

"Those bastard Whites will never find this burial site," Yurovsky commented smugly as they departed.

Lyukhanov and Provovich returned the truck to the Soviet motor pool on July 19, 1917. In spite of their attempts to clean the vehicle, the pool superintendent complained. "This truck is filthy and looks like it has traces of dried blood."

CHAPTER 23

JULY 1918

Katie's head felt as if it were baking beneath the July sun. She wished that she had a hat to ward off the scorching rays. Dust swirled from beneath her feet as she trudged along the dirty narrow road. In the distance, she could see the spire of a village church reaching majestically above the rest of the tiny hamlet.

She knew she had to find food here, or she would not be able to continue her homeward journey. She stared down at her body and noted how the skin had tightened at her wrists and joints. Her fingertips had turned blue. The stiltlike limbs on which she struggled were nearly unable to hold her body, now so swollen with child.

She felt so weary that she wondered if life was really worth the struggle. Death seemed to be stalking the land like a ruthless avenger. It seemed the Bolsheviks' machine of terror, together with starvation and plagues, had combined forces to erase Russian mankind from the earth. No one was safe, for if one was fortunate enough to escape the first two, then the germs of the last lay waiting in trains, carriages, hotels, theaters, and public baths. It was impossible to guard against the dreaded pestilence. The summer heat intensified the dangers of contamination. Sanitation had disappeared, and with it, the last hope for any control of the raging fatal epidemics.

Katie drew back as a dog approached her. His bones protruded pathetically beneath the tight skin stretched over him. It was the same with animals everywhere. Their owners were facing starvation themselves, yet they were unable to bring themselves to destroy their pets, so they turned them loose into a hungry world where they either died of starvation or became savage beasts of prey.

The dog stared at her, crouched, whined, and then to Katie's relief, slunk away.

She entered the tiny village. Not knowing where to go, she stopped to rest on the doorstep of a small cottage. She winced at the wretched faces that passed before her. Starvation had made them expressionless. On the other side of the street, she watched an old woman and a dog struggling for the privilege of raiding a filthy garbage can. She was relieved to see that the woman won.

Another woman approached Katie with her hands outstretched. Katie cringed at the eyes that seemed to bore into her. The peasant woman was obviously in the final stage of starvation. Her face was so grotesquely bloated that it obliterated her features. Bleeding gums appeared between her thickened white lips that were blistered and swollen. Her hands were puffed from the water in her tissues, with the surface cracked from chilblains. Her knees appeared bent from the weight of her bloated belly pressing so heavily upon them.

Katie turned away from her pleading eyes. "I'm sorry," she said softly. "Truly I am, but I have nothing either."

The woman studied Katie's pale face, nodded in sympathy, and then slowly limped away.

Katie staggered on for a while. Then gathering the last of her courage, she knocked at the door before which she found herself. An old man opened it.

"Please, I won't ask you for food," she said, "but may I have a cup of water and come in to get out of the sun for a few minutes?"

"Of course, my child," he said. "I have a few lumps of fat that I was just going to cook. I would be glad to have you join me."

Katie's mouth watered in anticipation. She smiled her gratitude as she sat down upon a kitchen chair to rest. A hand mirror lay on the table before her. Idly, she picked it up. The image before her looked like a stranger. The pallor of her face was like a yellow lemon. Her hair was bleached colorless from the endless hours of walking under the summer sun. Her eyes were dull, and her lips were white.

The old man handed her a glass of water. She held the cool liquid inside her dry mouth for a while. He proceeded to set the table and then took his precious treasure from the stove.

"It's not right for me to take your food," she told him as she noted the slices of black bread and cheese that he put before her as well as the fat.

"Hush, young lady, I'm an old man. I haven't much longer to go on this earth. There's a new life at stake here. How have you managed to survive so far?"

"I picked fruit off trees, gleaned fields after dark, picked berries and nuts in the woods, raided garbage heaps. I sneaked in barns and milked cows and goats. Sometimes I was able to work for a little food. Sometimes people would take pity on me and give me food. I did whatever was necessary to survive."

"Ah, young lady, you have my prayers and best wishes."

Katie was deeply touched. "Thank you."

"You're welcome," he said. "Times are bad. This is a wicked world. I'm glad that I haven't much longer in it." He reached up and rubbed his eyes. Katie saw that his lids were rimmed with pus. His withered skin was yellow too, while his chest heaved laboriously.

"Are you all right?" Katie asked.

"My dear, who can look good in such times as these?" He sighed and then smiled. "This is a land of ghosts that we live in. Besides starvation, we have pneumonia in the winter. Plagues of cholera, typhus, and diphtheria in the summer. How much more can our scurvied and anemic bodies stand?" Suddenly he seemed to doze off for a moment.

Katie ate the food that he had put before her.

Then the old man woke up and demanded abruptly. "Tell me what you've seen? What you have noted during your travels."

"Nothing good," she said. "There are starving people everywhere. In the cities. Camped in the swamps. On the open roads. I've seen them eating horses and stalking wild dogs. I've seen them clawing at one another for tiny scraps." Katie closed her eyes, recalling the horrors.

"Such misery! And did you know, my child, that the royal family has been murdered?"

"I heard a rumor," she said. "It's really true then?"

"Yes, they were murdered on July 16. The Bolshevik swine were afraid they would be rescued by the White troops. Filthy killers," he spat. "They tried to hide it from the world, but we people know why the royal family was taken away."

Katie lowered her head. "May they rest in peace." After a moment's pause, she added, "Will this horror never end?"

"Not while the Bolsheviks rule, but aid will come soon."

"From whom?" she asked desperately.

"We'll have to wait and see about that," he sighed. "But now you must rest. Wait until tomorrow before you continue your journey."

"Perhaps I will," she agreed. "But I must not stop any longer. My child is due in a month, and I still have so far to travel to reach home."

AUGUST 1918

Boris cupped his dark brown hand over his black eyes to shade them from the intense rays of the noonday sun. In the distance, he could see a figure approaching. The traveler weaved from one side of the road to the other. Something was wrong. He burst into a run toward the staggering form, but she collapsed before he could reach her.

He lifted the girl's face out of the dusty road and wiped the grime away with the hem of his robe. Her face was familiar, but he had to think for a moment before he recalled where he had seen her before. It had been at his grandmother's funeral.

Katie was flushed with fever and so wasted away that her fragile frame appeared skeleton-like except for the bulge of her child. Boris picked up her motionless form from the dusty road and started back to his cave. Two other monks rushed forth to meet him and relieved him of his burden. They shot a questioning glance at him. He replied grimly, "Typhus."

Their faces paled, but they carried the feverish girl into the recess of their cave. Quickly the three of them set to work, boiling water, bathing her, fixing a makeshift bed roll, and then disposing of her soiled garments. When at last Katie lay clean and comfortable, the other two monks returned to their duties while Boris took up a vigilant watch over the wan form that hovered so close to death.

Katie lay very still. Boris put his hand on her forehead. The heat seemed to singe his palm. Her fever was climbing, so he dipped some cloths in cool water and laid them on her forehead. She stirred slightly, opened her eyes, but then returned to sleep. Boris tucked the covers about her, but she was sweating so profusely that he added still another blanket.

When she opened her eyes again, a frown of pain and worry crossed them. "You're here from the dead," she screamed. "I remember you. You take lives. You're the one that came for the countess!" Her voice rose hysterically, and she started to shriek. "You took little Leon and Uncle Ivan too. Go away! Go away, evil demon! I know you've come for my child, but you'll not get my baby. Do you hear! Go away!"

"Very well, little one," Boris said softly. He tiptoed out of her sight until she had once again lapsed into unconsciousness.

Her night was hectic. She tossed and turned, alternating between deep sleep and frightening nightmares. She reached out her arms to imaginary loved ones and begged them to come and comfort her.

Tears rolled down her pallid face. She lapsed again into a temporary spell of quiet, only for it to be followed by another violent outburst. Boris continued to put more wet cloths upon her brow.

"My head hurts," she snapped peevishly. "Don't do that. Please, stop it."

"Where else are you hurting?" Boris asked.

"My legs and my back. I can't seem to think very well. It seems like a cloud keeps closing up over me. It makes my head pound until I think it'll split open." She turned her innocent face to him. "Can't you do something, Father?" she pleaded.

Boris rubbed a mixture of herbs on her aching limbs and back. Katie then noticed that her stomach was covered with tiny red splotches. "I have the measles," she said. "Imagine that!" She laughed deliriously and then closed her eyes and went to sleep.

Days passed with Katie lying close to death, alternating between violent spells of mania and passive states of delirium. Finally, she emerged from her nightmare world.

Katie sat beneath a big tree with a warm blanket tucked around her legs. She had been conscious for a week now and was slowly regaining her strength. "I can't imagine what would have happened to me, Boris, if you hadn't found me."

"Someone else would have cared for you."

"I don't think so," she said. "I'm not as optimistic about the human race as I once was."

Boris smiled tenderly at her. "You will be again, Katrina."

"I hope so," Katie said, smiling at the formal sound of her given name. She studied the solemn black-eyed monk before her. Without him, she wouldn't have survived the last few weeks. He had stood over her day and night, caring for her tirelessly. "How did you come to settle in this cave, Boris?"

"It was the first shelter that we found after the Bolsheviks drove us from the monastery," he replied. "Two of my brothers and I chose to stay near our home, while the others went on looking for other places of refuge."

Katie shook her head grimly. "Why did they close the churches?"

"You might call it their private war on religion," he replied. "They can't let the people remain resigned to their pathetic lot. The church holds out hope of miracles, and miracles are contrary to modern realities and the true scientific attitude. By confiscating property and scattering the priesthood, they feel they will suppress religion throughout the country. But they cannot repress God or man's need to believe in a divine power greater than himself. For this reason alone, they will fail in the end. God is always supreme."

"But it's so unjust and terrible for you, Boris."

"It's terrible for everyone these days, Katrina. And we don't do so badly here. We grow what we can in whatever little plots of land we can find. Many of the people have remained loyal and give us whatever they can spare. We're the fortunate ones, Katrina. Many of my brothers have already been jailed, exiled, or executed. I feel that as long as I am alive and free, I can be of service to my fellow man."

"I don't see how you can remain so optimistic, Boris," she stated. "I've seen people using the Bible for cigarette paper."

"That's true. And I have seen them tear down crosses and cut them up for firewood. I have seen them use our holy statues for target practice, but all of this is the times, Katrina. It will pass."

"But how can the church survive with its doors closed? With its shrines lying in ruin?"

Boris smiled. "Churches and shrines are only symbols for something infinitely more powerful."

"I'm terribly confused," Katie said. "What caused the church to collapse?"

"There are many reasons. First, the aristocracy supported the church. Their monasteries and lands remained free of government taxation. Many priests grew wealthy and fat from the ample donations given to them by the rich. The church was shielded by the government and extracted dues from each parish. Yet it also demanded food and labor." Boris sighed. "Unfortunately, no service was given free. Payment was required for baptisms, benedictions, marriages, and funerals. Too many of the clergy lacked moral and intellectual education and passed into their professions merely by an accident of birth. The church, in many cases, was too far above its populace."

"It sounds so hopeless," Katie said frowning.

"Yes," he continued. "So many of the peasants are still obsessed with fetishism. I think Russian orthodoxy became doomed at this point in time because it emphasized form and external show rather than substance. So many of our peasants are ignorant. They scarcely know their Bible. Many of the clergy are equally ignorant. Too many of the illiterate expected miracles."

Katie looked perplexed. "So many failures?"

"Yes. Ignorance, greed, and sin," Boris said, nodding his head. "That's the cause of our religious downfall. That's why our churches have been desecrated. Its symbols spat upon. That's why our leaders have been bayoneted and their sacraments cursed."

"And how will it all end?" Katie asked.

"As it always does. In time, man will realize the error of his ways and will return to his redeemer to ask for forgiveness. There is a God, and he will not be denied. People will eventually realize that his hand guides everything in the universe. He guides the birth, life, and death of every crawling insect, every bird in the air, and every animal and human creature that walks upon the face of this vast earth. And he balances their powers so delicately that all exist at the same time, in the same place, breathing the same air."

Katie smiled.

Boris shrugged his shoulders and continued. "Who else could cause the turning of the earth and direct its travels through the heavens or regulate the infinite movement of each star and comet and the countless unknown worlds out there? Can they say there is no God, Katrina? The workings of the universe are so complete and wondrous, that we, mere men, can never hope to understand the pattern. We can only have faith."

"I feel so content here, Boris. For the first time I can remember in so very long, I dare to close my eyes and sleep without being afraid of what the morning will bring. You're so good to me."

Boris shook his head. "No, it's with God that you've found peace. I am but his servant." The young monk took her hand. "Life is often only what we make it."

Suddenly, Katie winced and closed her eyes tightly against the bright afternoon sun.

"What is it, Katrina," he asked anxiously. "Has the fever returned?"

No," she smiled shyly at his concern. "But I believe my time has come."

He frowned and asked, "Do you want me to get a midwife from the village?"

"No," she said, shaking her head. "I would rather put my trust in the hands of the Lord. Will you deliver my child, Boris?"

"It'll not be the first one," he assured her with a comforting smile. "I attended medical school for a while before I decided to become a monk. I'll get everything ready and then call my brothers from their farming plots."

Katie watched him disappear toward the spring and then braced herself for the pains.

The night seemed very long, and it was dawn before she released the child from her womb. Its angry cry filled the dark recess of the enormous cave. Katie reached up and wiped the heavy sweat from her brow and let her torn and weakened body relax in complete exhaustion. *It's over. I can sleep at last.*

It was afternoon before she awoke, and as consciousness crept over her, she cried out. "My baby! Boris, is my baby all right?"

He stood over her, smiling broadly. "And why wouldn't he be?"

"He? It's a boy?"

"Now what else would your firstborn be?" he teased.

Katie laughed with pleasure. "Please bring him to me."

The young celibate carried the infant and placed him in Katie's arms. Happiness radiated from her pale face. "Oh, he's so beautiful," she whispered.

She studied the tiny face crowned by black curls. One curl hung on his forehead. Katie closed her eyes in the pain of remembrance. He was so much Peter's son. A flood of pure joy swept through her.

"There's some good news to celebrate on this day of the birth of your son, Katrina," Boris informed her. "British and French forces have landed at Archangel. Before long, our country should be free of the Bolsheviks."

To Boris, Katie and her son looked like a painting of the Virgin Mother and her Sacred Infant. He was lost in admiration when Katie disturbed his thoughts. "Are the British going to help us, Boris?"

"No, it seems, after all, that their presence is just an unofficial blockade. Nothing more.'

"Oh, Boris, that certainly crushes our hopes," she moaned.

"At least some of them, Katrina. However, the Japanese are trying to establish themselves in Siberia, and counterrevolutions have sprung up in the south, southwest, and the far east. What they'll accomplish is yet to be seen. We can only remain hopeful. Each day more atrocities are committed. Terror continues to reach new heights. We can only hope that the Bolsheviks will be defeated by at least one of these powers."

"When I go to sleep at night, Boris, I still hear the shrieks of women, the sound of breaking glass, machine gun fire, and soldiers' drunken laughter. What a terrible time to raise an innocent child."

"I'm afraid that it will get worse before it gets better," Boris remarked gravely.

Katie's baby boy lay on a blanket close beside her while she munched on a piece of black bread.

"Little Ivan looks very much like his father," Boris commented solemnly.

"How could you know that?" Katie asked, a faint flush creeping over her pale face.

"Because you are so pleased with him," he said. "He doesn't look like anyone whom I knew in your family, therefore, he must take after his father. Do you love him very much?"

"Little Ivan?"

"No, little Ivan's father?"

Katie face clouded. "Yes, but I don't feel like talking about it."

Boris shrugged. "I understand.'

Katie stared at him, then after a while, she blurted out. "I'm not married, you know."

Seeing her discomfort, he said, "Well, I'm not, either," he said, laughing softly.

The tension immediately eased from her thin frame. "Are there no sinners in your eyes, Boris?"

"All of us are only human, Katrina."

"If only all of us could be like you!"

"What a boring world that would be," he said. "Besides, I'm not so pure and holy as you would like to think me, Katrina," he said, lowering his eyes before her gaze.

Katie stared at the stern cast of his face. Boris stroked his beard in distraction.

"I think that you must be tired of me by now, Boris," she stated. "After all, I have been here six weeks, and Ivan is a month old already."

"Foolish girl," he smiled. "Does the earth tire of the sun? Don't talk such nonsense." Then abruptly, without further comment, he stood and stalked off to the fields to finish his chores.

Someone was shaking her roughly. Katie jerked her eyes open.

"Get up and get dressed quickly, Katrina," Boris demanded. "We have word that someone has informed the Cheka of your whereabouts. You are no longer safe here."

Katie leaped to her feet and began to dress quickly. "Where can I go?" she asked.

"There is an old crypt under the monastery that few people know about," he informed her. "It's filled with the skeletons of former monks peacefully resting in their coffins. It is not exactly a pleasant place but reasonably safe and only a few hours from here."

"I'll get the baby," she said.

"He's gone," Boris said. Katie's face expressed immediate alarm. "Don't worry, he's safe," he assured her. "It would be too cold and damp for him in the crypt, so Yuri took him to the cottage of one of our patrons, where he will be taken care of for several days. We will come and get you and take you to the baby when it is safe."

"I can't just go off and leave him," she insisted frantically.

"You have no choice, Katrina. If you're apprehended, you'll be imprisoned or be put to death. What will happen to your child then?"

Katie's eyes filled with tears.

"It's only for a couple of days," he reassured her gently. "If the baby is found here, they will know that you are close by. They will not think to look in a peasant's hut.

"They know the people hate your kind and would never take you in. The woman who is caring for your child does not know to whom he belongs. There is no other way."

"Promise me, Boris, that one of you will check on him every day."

"It's a promise," he said. The other two monks nodded their heads.

Boris and Katrina started out before dawn. They walked very rapidly, scarcely speaking during their long journey. They reached their destination before noon.

Boris's face contorted in grief at the sight of the monastic grounds. The fields, once so orderly and neat, were now overgrown and wild. The unpaved streets were thick with weeds. Many of the cells had been burned to the ground, and the windows and doors of the chapel had been boarded tightly to prevent entry.

Boris led her to an old building quite some distance from the well. Inside, he proceeded down to a subbasement where he quickly located a trapdoor, and then he led Katie into the tomb below. It was damp, cold, and very dark.

"I have some candles and food here. It will not be pleasant, but there is no choice. Now we had better get some water from the well."

They went up the stairs, and Boris studied the area carefully before he allowed her to venture out into the warm sunshine. They drew ample water for several days and stored it in jars below. Then Boris decided that it would be fairly safe to spend a few hours in the woods beyond before he started back to his cave. He took her hand in his and led her to a secluded spot. There, they ate their lunch that he had brought and settled back to relax. They watched a tiny column of ants marching about, engrossed in their numerous tasks.

"I wonder if they're ever plagued with endless grief like men," Katie mused.

"Probably. They're God's creatures, too," Boris replied.

She wrinkled up her nose while Boris's black eyes searched her face intently.

Noting this, she said, laying her hand upon his cheek, "Sometimes, Boris, it's better to talk about things rather than keeping them buried inside."

"No, Katrina," he sighed sadly. "Not when one has taken a vow such as mine."

"You are ashamed of loving me?"

"You know then?" he asked, his dark face flushing.

She didn't reply.

"What you must think of me," he said. "Aren't you shocked?"

"You're a monk, Boris, but your vows do not make you any less a man."

Katie could see his intense pain.

"How could this happen to me, Katrina?" he asked. "All this longing after so many years?"

"Do you remember, Boris, how I once told you that you were good for me? In turn, you told me that it was God that was good for me and that you were but his messenger. I accepted that as you helped me to find peace and restore my will to live again. You were my link to salvation. Perhaps, in return, I am yours."

"I don't understand, Katrina."

"You've become too wrapped up in your dedicated life, Boris. To be a servant of God, you must be a servant of man. But to be a servant of man, you must understand his pain and anguish, his joy and sorrow. By loving me, you've crossed back over the bridge to temporal life."

He pulled her gently into is arms, buried his bearded face in her soft hair, and began to kiss it lightly. Then he raised her face, and she could see tears running down his cheeks. "Thank you, my Katrina. It had to be you to show me the way. You are right of course. Too often, I've been impatient with men's imperfections. You have made me feel human again."

He stood and pulled her to her feet. She kissed his cheek and lay her head against his pounding chest.

"Have faith, Boris. Everything will be all right."

"Yes," he said as he kissed her forehead tenderly. "I believe you," he said softly. "Now, reluctant as I am to leave you, I must get you to safety." He took her hand, and they started back in the direction of the monastic grounds.

Their conversation was disturbed by noise in the underbrush. They paused momentarily, trying to determine from what direction the rustling was coming.

"What is it, Boris?" Katie asked.

"There is someone following us," he said.

Then a shout. "A priest. Look, a priest has come back! Let's get him."

Without warning, a bullet crashed through the dense thickets. Boris clutched his side. Katie's face filled with alarm, but he pushed her forward. "We must get out of here, Katrina, or they will catch us."

He forced his pace to match hers as they continued on for some distance until Katie refused to go any further. "I will not move another step until you let me see your wound," she insisted.

Boris sank to the ground and took his hands from the gaping hole in his side. Katie gasped in horror. "Oh no! Take off our robe quickly, Boris."

He motioned her to silence. "Katrina, listen to me. You can't help me now. You must escape."

"I'm not going to leave you."

"Who are we to decree our fate, Katrina?" he asked. "The bullet is lodged in my intestines. Whether you stay or go will make no difference, for I am going to die. If you stay, they will find you. How can that help me? And what will happen to your baby?" His words came more slowly now. "God's ways are not always known to us."

Tears rolled down Katie's pale cheeks as she held his body in her arms. "If it hadn't been for me, this wouldn't have happened," she sobbed.

"It was meant to be, my dear Katrina," he explained philosophically. "My death is for a purpose. What that purpose is, I don't know, but someday you will. I must die so you may live, and you must live so that your son will live."

"No, Boris."

"It may be that the Lord has ordained little Ivan to accomplish a great task someday. It's all been decided above. We have no choice but to abide by that decision," Boris said with his voice growing weaker. "Go now, Katrina, and have faith! Never turn your back on God, no matter how great the temptation or how great the pain. Trust him. Do not forsake him, and he will never forsake you." Boris coughed weakly, and then he closed his eyes. Suddenly, his heaving chest was still.

Tears ran down Katie's cheeks as she laid his head down gently on the grass. She stood up, fighting the convulsions in her chest. She must be quiet so that they would not find her. She tried to control her sobs as she burst into a run and hurried toward the ancient crypt of Boris's brothers.

CHAPTER 24

The long hours of darkness combined with the stench of decay in the crypt had taken their toll on Katie's nerves. At the scudding sound of rats near her, she stamped her feet and shouted at them in an attempt to keep them at bay. She then hastily made the sign of the cross. Catching herself in the act, she smiled, recalling how their servant girl Anna would cross herself when she yawned to keep the evil spirits out. *These past few days, my own behavior has become something akin to fetishism.*

She had no idea as to the passage of time. It seemed like weeks, but she still had food left, so it could not have been more than a few days. At first she kept a candle constantly burning, but finally, with only one candle left, it was a luxury that she could no longer afford.

She bit into a piece of black bread, recalling the disdain that she had once felt for peasant food when she had dined on herring and caviar. She pulled the thin blanket that Boris had left more tightly around her body in an effort to shut out the damp coldness of the crypt.

To distract herself from her present misery, she dug out memories from the past. *The beautiful gardens at Usadiba Na Holme. Fireworks on summer nights. Orchestras in the gardens, and my dream of a grand debut in Petrograd wearing beautiful jewelry and attending a glittering fairy-tale ball. Ah, but my past has vanished. The peasants are the lords and masters now.*

A shiver ran up her spine at the creaks echoing round her in this dank tomb. She felt pressed to light her last candle. It illuminated the coffins surrounding her along with the few treasures that Boris and his brothers had managed to hide. The most beautiful one was an icon of the Sacred Mother cast in gold. There were bottles of wine too, this being one cellar that the Bolshevik hordes had not yet found. She was tempted to open one. *But no. I must keep my mind alert.*

With nothing better to do, she walked around and peered at the names on the coffins. *I wonder if the monks still alive will ever be able to return here again to this monastery to rake hay and gather their harvest, to pick wild mushrooms and berries on their hills, or pray in the deserted chapel above.*

She blew out her precious candle. Once again the rats began their excursions around her feet. "Get away from me, you vile creatures!" she cried. *I dare not leave this crypt. If I miss the monk coming for me, I might forever lose the knowledge of where my child is hidden.* "I feel like I'm going insane," she whispered into the surrounding darkness.

Her heart pounded when at last she heard the sound of footsteps overhead. Was it one of the monks returning? Or was it an agent of the Cheka? She trembled with the uncertainty. She rubbed the cold sweat from her forehead as the trapdoor creaked open.

"Are you there, Katrina?"

A hoarse sob of relief tore loose from her lips at the familiar voice. "Oh yes, Yuri! Yes! I thought you'd never get here." She hastily lit her candle while the elderly monk descended.

"I'm afraid that I have some evil tidings, little one."

"I know already, Yuri," she said softly. "I was with Boris when he died."

The old man sighed painfully and crossed himself. "God rest his soul. We buried him close by so he would be near the monastery. Someday we will dig up his remains and bury them in our graveyard, but it is too dangerous now."

"Amen!" Katie whispered.

"I wasn't able to come sooner," Yuri explained. "Since Boris's death, they have kept us under close observation. It was only by one of the peasants exchanging places with me that I was able to slip away to come here tonight, so we must hurry. There's very little time. At the other side of the woods are two horses. They'll take us to your child."

"Thank God!" she breathed as they climbed from the crypt.

Outside, they mounted the horses quickly. She followed closely behind Yuri. The animals' muffled steps sounded excessively loud to Katie's overwrought nerves. She was so tired. Between her eerie surroundings and her fear of missing Yuri, she had found sleep in the crypt almost impossible. Now, at every turn, she expected to be apprehended. She could not guess how long they had traveled.

She looked around now, and the familiarity of the landscape astounded her. She realized that she was close to home. Her pulse hammered excitedly, and she could hardly breathe. "Where are you taking me, Yuri?" she called. He didn't hear her, but at the sight of Usadiba Na Holme in the distance, she lost the need for an answer.

Yuri pulled to a halt before the Sovinsky cottage, and Katie felt numb. The old monk helped her dismount and then led the horses to the rear of the cottage where they would be out of sight. Then he returned and knocked on the door.

"Come in," someone called.

As the door opened, the sight of a roaring fire met Katie's eyes. Maria was sitting before it, feeding little Ivan a bottle of milk. Yuri shut the door hastily. The two women stared at each other in stunned silence.

Maria spoke first, and her voice was soft and gentle. "I should have known that he was yours, Katrina, but I never guessed. Not even with the name Ivan."

Katie drew closer to her infant, and Maria held the baby out to her. Katie took her child and pressed him tightly against her chest. Tears ran down her cheeks.

"Have you any place to go, Katrina?"

"No, she hasn't," Yuri replied. "And the police are looking for her."

"Then you must stay here, Katrina," she insisted. "Yuri, you'd better go and return the horses before they are missed. Don't worry, Katrina. They will never think of looking for you here."

"God bless you, my child," Yuri whispered. "Farewell, Katrina, and may peace be yours." The monk blessed each of them before disappearing into the darkness.

Neither of the women spoke until the thundering hoof beats had faded away, and then Katie asked. "Why should you want to protect me, Maria?"

"The moment that I saw this child, I knew that only my brother could have fathered him. I felt that it was an act of fate that brought him to my arms. Isn't it natural that I should want to protect his mother too?"

"It's not the way you think, Maria."

"Katrina, the night that the soldiers stormed the manor, I waited with fear and uncertainty, not knowing what was happening. Peter came to see me before he left. His face was hard and somber, and I could feel the tenseness in his body as he kissed me good-bye. I asked him if he had hurt you. There was pain in his eyes and his voice as he told me, 'In my attempt to humiliate her, Maria, I merely humiliated myself.'"

Katie turned away and stared into the dancing flames. Her eyes were moist, and she did not want Maria to see her tears.

"Do you hate him, Katrina?" Maria asked. "His only real crime was in loving you too much."

"I know," she said, turning to Maria. "I could never hate him, Maria. I think you know that."

The dark-haired girl smiled. "Yes, but it's sad that you could never swallow your pride enough to tell him so."

"You're right," she acknowledged. "Have you seen him recently, Maria?"

"Only once since that time. He sent a messenger for me, and I went to his camp. He looked very handsome in his Bolshevik uniform. He has developed an authoritative air that commands respect, but there's an unpleasant hardness in him too. He's a good soldier, Katie, but I know that he's longing for the time when he can return to the soil."

"Does he really believe in the Reds' doctrine, Maria?"

"Wholeheartedly, Katrina. He sees the new order as the fulfillment of his dreams."

Katie shook her head. "And what do you feel, Maria?"

"That this new order is no better than the old order."

Katie sighed. "Do you think that it's strange that I'm the mother of Peter's child?"

"I think it's wonderful, Katrina, and so will Peter."

"Oh, Maria," she cried in alarm, "you must promise that you'll never tell him."

"I can't do that, Katrina," she said. "He has a right to know."

"But then my humiliation would be complete. It's unlikely that our paths will ever cross again. Please, Maria, you must promise me."

"I promise, Katrina," Maria said, "but it is with great reluctance."

The baby started to cry as Katie hugged the dark-haired girl. "I don't know what I'd do without you," she said. "And please, you must call me Katie."

"Well, I suggest for a start that you let me take little Ivan before you crush him and then get some sleep."

OCTOBER 1918

One lazy autumn day drifted into another until the month of September had passed. Katie and Maria harvested the small plot that Maria had planted the previous spring. They worked diligently in the crisp, cool air and shared the care of the bubbling dark-haired infant. As time passed, Katie's and Maria's friendship deepened, and after the child lay asleep at night, they would talk for hours.

"I remember when I scorned the idea of living in a thatched-roofed hut," Katie informed Maria. "And I scorned the idea of working out in the fields. Strangely, I have come to love it. I like the warmth of the sun beating down upon me and the smell of the good clean earth. I am so happy here."

Katie was cautious at all times to protect Maria. She never ventured out without binding her golden hair with a handkerchief, and thus far, no one had made any inquiries about her. It was Maria who went to the village whenever the necessity arose. Now the days were growing colder, and the fields lay covered with frost. Winter was rapidly approaching, and it was comforting to know that there would be even fewer people traveling about as the weather grew harsher.

Late one afternoon, Maria returned from a trip to the village looking quite disturbed. "Is something wrong?" Katie asked as Maria removed her wraps. "You look upset."

"Yes," she said. "The party has decided that I have harvested more than I can use. Of course, they don't know about you and little Ivan, so they have ordered me to turn over my surplus. An agent is coming tomorrow."

"That's not fair, Maria. You half killed yourself raising that food. They've no right to take it from you."

"Right? Who has rights these days, Katie? Our new masters are as harsh and ruthless as the old. And we the people are their most ardent supporters. Our villages are now divided into four groups: the rich, the middle, the poor, and the poorer. Now the poor have the power to check on the rich and seize their grain and cattle. This is communism—a people divided! No longer do we stand united against our common enemy, the aristocracy! Instead, we spy on one another so that everyone has come to fear his neighbor. Our own people are the supporters of our Bolshevik tyrants."

"What are you going to do?"

"Hide what I can. You and Ivan must go into the woods early tomorrow. Bundle him warmly, for it is chilly. Don't come back until after dark."

"You're taking a chance."

"I must. My conscience won't allow me to support such terror. These men have decided to exterminate all those who oppose them. They're no better than those before them. Torture, rape, and murder. All the same atrocities again."

"Peter is one of them."

"You don't need to remind me of that, Katie, but at least Peter still has some decency. I keep praying that he will see the light. However, I can't accept their ways just because my brother chooses to follow them. I would give my life for my brother, but not for his beliefs."

"Will they pay you for the food?"

"With what?"

"I'll leave at dawn," Katie said. "Now let me help you hide some of the food."

The soldiers of the White Army sat around the campfire and sang with strong voices. Though their clothes were ragged and they had few weapons, their spirits were high. Nikolai Sokoloy felt a surge of pride at being a part of this brave army. They had survived incredible hardships and had cleared the Bolshevik forces out of the North Caucasian and Don areas. Others like themselves were fighting in Samara, Omsk, and Siberia. The Bolshevik forces controlled only the central part of European Russia now.

"Well, Sokoloy, what's the good word tonight?" someone called out to him.

"Southern Russia seems to be ours," he responded cheerfully. "The Ukraine is still under the Germans and Austrians, while the Southern Ural regions and Siberia are either under the Czechs' thumb or local rule. Our esteemed allies occupy the extreme north and east. It seems to me that the Reds are desperately fighting for their lives."

One young soldier shook his head. "I don't know how they maintain their army. How can anyone of Russian blood follow the Bolsheviks in their foul schemes?"

"Some of the old-timers are afraid, son," one of the soldiers replied. "They've worked hard all their lives. They can't find the courage to abandon what they have devoted so many years to. Others have their families endangered by the Cheka, so they stick through fear even though they know if they're apprehended by us, they will be shot as traitors. And other peasants are merely eager followers. The Bolsheviks have picked the choicest of their young men. They've given them excellent wages and the best rations. They've made a few of the most zealous ones officers. So the Reds are confident of their troops' loyalty to the new order."

The boy spat in the dirt. "Scum."

Nikolai smiled. "Well, at least we know that the Communists can never get Russia on her feet again," he said. "Their leaders are great talkers and writers, but they have no technical knowledge. The damn fools are killing off all the experts. The ruble has fallen, and inflation has set in. The railroads are in terrible condition. The Communists are reduced to confiscating the peasants' food for redistribution without giving any compensation. So the farmers have become bitter and confused. Many of them are coming over to our side. In some areas, the Bolsheviks have reestablished the ousted landlords. The people grow more resentful. In many districts, they have refused to accept the German peace. Some even want to secede from Russia and form their own state. How can the Bolsheviks possibly win a victory under such adverse conditions?"

The men broke into cheers.

JANUARY 1919

Peter Sovinsky gave his men their orders for the day before their dismissal. He then reported to his superior officer.

"Aha, Sovinsky! Come in. I wanted to talk to you."

"Yes, sir."

"You're a loyal man, and I need a good ear. Things are going badly. The Cheka has taken the law into their own hands. Today, in flat defiance of Lenin's reprieve, the police commission in Petersburg executed the grand dukes. It smells, Sovinsky."

"As long as the czar's uncles lived," Peter pointed out, "they were a threat to us."

"Mmm, there's no disputing that, but since when do individuals have the right to overturn the judgment of the people's chosen government?"

"They don't," Peter agreed. "I'm afraid there may be repercussions."

"I can barely sleep nights. I thought when the armistice was signed last November that our troubles would lessen. Instead, what do we have? The French and the British are in Archangel, the Japs are in Siberia, as well as Admiral Koltchak. The French and Greeks are prodding the Romanians in the south." The officer coughed loudly before continuing. "General Denikin is in the Crimea, loaded with British war materials and supported by the French fleet. There's rebellion in the Ukraine, and the peasants are being undermined all around us. Everyone's goal is Moscow. I have ulcers." The officer then laid his head back against his chair.

"I grant that there are obstacles, sir, but they'll be overcome. I seriously doubt that the English and French will stick their necks in too far. They're sick of war. All we have to do is show them that there's no doubt of our victory, and they'll put their tails between their legs and run for home."

"Show them that we are bound to be victorious? And how do you propose we can do that?"

"The people are on our side," Peter reminded him.

"Like hell they are," he snapped. "The peasants are only for themselves. They are an ignorant pack of savages and can't be trusted. Their refusal to cooperate with us is causing famine in the towns. They refuse to give up their grain, and due to our many labor troubles, the factories are producing nothing we can give them in exchange. What should we do about that, Sovinsky?'

Peter frowned. "Even though these people are for themselves, the party is the people, so in the end, it's all the same. They want peace and security. When they're assured of it, they won't be so frightened. There will always be some scum who will take advantage of the inefficiency of the times, but those caught plundering and abusing must be dealt with harshly, or we'll never win the trust of our common man."

"You've got more confidence than I, Sovinsky," he sighed. "I'm a sick man. Sick of the odds. Sick of those that send us out to die while they slowly take over the land. It's too bad, Sovinsky, that you're not a religious man, or you could pray for us."

Peter smiled. "It there was a God, I think he would have turned his back on me a long time ago."

Peter opened the door of his office and was startled to see a man waiting there.

"You're Peter Sovinsky?

"Yes," he replied.

"I have a message from Vladimir," he stated as he handed Peter a tattered, grimy note. Peter immediately opened it.

> To Peter, whom I love as a son,
>
> It is a sad world when one man cannot think differently from another. This is not the Russia that we dreamed about, Peter. This is not a proud, majestic land held in awe by the world but rather a nation in ruin with a force of ruthless devils ruling over a mass of ignorant and bewildered people.
>
> We have destroyed ourselves with civil strife and war. Our former allies have blockaded us, and we have earned the hostility of the outside world. The future holds nothing but famine and decay. I can no longer fight for my Russia, Peter, and there is no one to take my place. This is not the free world that we envisioned but a police state, where fear has replaced the hopelessness of old. I send you my warmest farewell and hope that you will live long enough to see this country emerge from this barbaric chaos.
>
> My love and my hopes lie with you, Peter.
>
> Vladimir

"Where is he?" Peter demanded of the messenger.

"Dead! Executed by the Cheka," he said. "Vladimir hated them you know."

Peter clutched his stomach and found it hard to swallow. He could not speak for several minutes. Then he said in a harsh voice, "Let me pay you for your trouble."

The man raised his hand in protest. "I loved the man," the messenger told him. His last wish was that you should receive this letter. Now that I've delivered it, my conscience is at rest."

"Did he die quickly?" Peter forced himself to ask.

"From the bullets? Yes. Before then, though, he didn't have it so easy. You know their methods."

"Yes," Peter said. "I know their methods."

"Well, so long, Sovinsky. It's strange that the old man should have had such high hopes for you when you're one of them."

After the stranger had left, the impact of the message hit Peter even harder. *Vladimir is dead! My small, thin friend will never speak again. The passionate eyes and voice will stir no new followers.* Pain clutched Peter's heart as he realized the depth of his love for the little professor. Images of Vladimir in the crowded cafeterias, on grassy lawns, and in small hotel rooms rose up before him. Tears fell from his eyes as he remembered their parting. *"The smell of land blinds you who spring from the soil."*

Vladimir had been right. Here I am a soldier instead of a farmer. It has all gone wrong. You, my friend, told me, "You cannot change the world in a day." But the Bolsheviks had tried it, nevertheless. You cautioned me. "I decry wholesale slaughter, and that is what the Bolsheviks want."

Peter cried aloud and smashed his fist into his other hand. "And now even you, my little friend, who loved his country like no other, even you they have murdered! You warned me. 'You cannot take the world and parcel it out. Why take land from a selfish noble and give to an ignorant farmer? You are simply reversing high to low and low to high. Why destroy the good with the bad?'"

And that's just what we've done, Peter thought bitterly. *We have slaughtered our countrymen who had the training and experience to run this nation, and in doing so, we have destroyed ourselves. Now we have such a small number with expert knowledge, and they must direct so many,*

Vladimir, you proclaimed, "Judge a man by who he is, not by whom he was born . . . Peace is best if there is a choice."

You were right, my friend, and now you are dead. How many of the peasants are happier now? What has really come of it all? What has become of Katie? Of Maria? Is my sister happier now? No, she couldn't be. How could she understand men such as these who murdered you? And I? What have I become? An avenger bent on savage destruction. He ground his teeth together. *I am no better than an Ivan Kozakov.*

You warned me, "Never lose your sense of decency." Vladimir's words hammered painfully in his ears. He felt confused and no longer sure of what he believed in. *I had wanted land for my people, but it has all gone wrong. Why has a secret police organization like the Cheka been developed? Is it necessary to drive fear into men's hearts and righteousness from their minds? Maria would pray, but I don't believe in God. No God would allow such wholesale suffering. There is no one to turn to. No one now to dispel my confusion.*

Peter stepped outside into the cold, snow-covered world, but even the bleak sky overhead seem to mirror the gloom and depression in his heart. He knew that it was time to decide where he really belonged.

CHAPTER 25

Katie sat beside Maria's bed, anxiously watching her feverish face. Maria had been caught in a blizzard returning from the village and had lost her way. The hours of wandering in the icy chill before she found their cottage had brought on this fever. Her condition seemed to be growing worse. Her friend slept fitfully between hacking fits of coughing. Katie did what she could for the fever, but then, out of despair, she sent a neighbor for the monk Yuri.

Katie wandered over to her baby's bed and checked that he still slept soundly. She put another log on the fire then returned to Maria's side. It seemed so unnatural for strong, healthy Maria to be sick. Maria coughed again, and Katie took her hand reassuringly. The peasant girl opened her eyes and smiled weakly. "I'm so glad that you're here, Katie."

"You're going to be all right," she said, smiling tenderly. "It just takes time, Maria. I've sent for Yuri."

At that instant, they heard a soft tap on the door, and Katie rushed across the room to open it. The elderly monk shook off layers of snow before he entered the tiny hut. He removed his wet outer garments and then rushed to Maria's side to examine her thoroughly. "Pneumonia," he announced gravely.

Katie caught her breath. "Will she be all right?"

"If the fever breaks shortly," he said. "All we can do is keep her warm, wait, and pray."

He dropped to his knees, and his low muttering tones filled the quiet cottage. Katie was relieved to have him here. Her apprehension eased, and she felt a glimmer of hope. Katie was so afraid for Maria. It seemed that sooner or later, everyone that she came to love was destroyed.

The rest of the night, Yuri and Katie took turns watching over their feverish patient. At dawn, Yuri woke Katie with the news. "The fever has broken, and the crisis is past. She'll be all right. All she needs now is rest and loving care. I will watch over her and your child while you get caught up on your sleep.

Gratefully, Katie accepted Yuri's offer to stay. Maria and Katie both slept through the rest of the day.

They were disturbed after dark by a loud pounding on the door. Fearfully, Katie lifted the latch and looked across the threshold into the bitterly cold night. A tall young soldier in a Red Army uniform stood there. The color drained from Katie's face, and she drew back from the doorway in fright.

"I have a message for Maria Sovinsky from her brother," the soldier announced.

"Oh, come in," Katie cried immediately.

The Bolshevik youth entered the cottage, and Katie shut the door against the wintry blast outside.

Maria looked up and smiled at the frozen soldier. "Will you have something hot to eat?" she asked.

"Gladly," he replied with an eager smile.

Katie immediately busied herself with the task of preparing food for him but kept an eye on the unexpected intruder.

"Your brother wishes you to return with me," the soldier told Maria. "We'll be moving out soon, and he longs to see you before the distance becomes too great to travel."

"I'll get ready at once," Maria announced, trying to sit up.

Katie tore across the room and pushed Maria back into her bed. "Are you crazy?" she shouted. "Do you want to kill yourself?"

"I must go," Maria pleaded. "I might never have another chance to see him. Who knows what the future holds?"

"You'll never see him if you try to travel in your condition in this weather," Katie warned.

"She's right, Maria," Yuri added. "You can't expect a return to good health without a long convalescence."

"If I don't go," Maria reasoned painfully, "he'll be so worried that he might try to come to me."

"Your going is out of the question, Maria," Katie insisted.

Maria frowned, and then a crafty look stole into her eyes. "I'll stay here on only one condition,' she said.

"And what's that?" Katie asked.

"That you go in my place to reassure him that I'm all right," Maria told her.

"Never," she said quickly, sucking in her breath. "It's impossible. I have to take care of you and little Ivan."

"Yuri will take care of us," Maria said.

"I can't chance it, Maria."

"You'll be safe, Katie. You'll have an armed escort." She turned to the young soldier. "You'll see that no harm comes to my friend, won't you, comrade?"

"Her safety is guaranteed," he promised.

"Please, Katie," she begged. "Please."

Katie's heart pounded. *This is a chance to see Peter.* She was torn with indecision. She wanted to go. Yet she was afraid. *I might never have another chance, and I owe it to little Ivan.* At last she nodded and then straightened her shoulders with determination.

She set a bowl of hot porridge and some bread before the soldier and then hastened to prepare for the journey. She kissed her sleeping infant, embraced Maria warmly, and lastly, she kissed Yuri's weather-beaten palms. "God bless all of you," she said.

"God give you a safe journey, Katrina," Yuri said.

"Give Peter my love, Katie," Maria instructed.

"I will, dearest! You just hurry and get well. Good-bye, Yuri, and bless you for your kindness," Katie murmured, embracing him.

She blew a last kiss to her friends before following the soldier out into the frozen night. The young Bolshevik helped her to mount. Then the horses started a fast trot into the surrounding darkness.

The weather was fierce, with wind tearing at their clothing and icy pellets lashing their faces. The moon sank behind some clouds, making visibility poor. The journey was long and tiring.

Katie heaved a sigh of relief when they reached their destination at last. The camp consisted of a central cluster of huts, with only a few smaller ones isolated some distance from the main body. The only soldiers in evidence were the posted sentries. Snow was falling heavily, and sleet stabbed at Katie's eyes. Her escort helped her to dismount and then gave the weary horses to a guard. He took her arm to guide her across the slippery clearing. Knocking on one of the doors, he identified himself. Instantly, the door was flung open.

"Maria, come in and defrost yourself," Peter exclaimed.

The sound of his voice thrilled Katie's saddle-worn body. Gratefully, she stepped into the warmth of the tiny room. Her escort withdrew and shut the door. Katie's hooded cloak hid her identity as Peter unsuspectingly swung her up off the floor into his arms.

"It's been such a long time, sister mine," he whispered.

As he released her from his enthusiastic embrace, the hood fell away from Katie's face, and the firelight caught the clusters of snowflakes nestled in her golden hair. There was a moment of silence, and then Peter's dark face drained of color. A look of grim determination appeared, and his voice was gruff and angry. "Where's Maria?" he demanded.

"She's ill, Peter," Katie explained. "She could not travel at this time. She begged me to come in her place to reassure you that she will be all right soon."

Concern replaced his anger. "What's wrong with her?"

"Pneumonia, but the worse is over. However, she must remain in bed and rest for a while. One of the monks is caring for her while I am away."

"It seems, then, that I owe you a debt of gratitude," he apologized.

Katie felt embarrassed and looked down at the floor, unable to think of anything to say.

"Forgive me for being so stupid," Peter said. "You must be very cold and tired. Strip off your wet things before the fire here. You'll find some blankets on my bed. I'll go and get some hot food while you warm yourself." He put on his overcoat and fur cap and stepped out in the midst of the howling storm.

Katie pulled several coarse army blankets off his bed and spread one of them on the floor before the fire. Slowly, she stripped off her wet clothing and wrapped herself in one of the blankets. The fire was warm and comforting after the exhausting ride. The leaping flames hypnotized Katie, and their soothing warmth lulled her into a state of complete relaxation. She was startled when the door opened and surprised that Peter had returned so quickly. He pushed the door shut with his booted foot and placed the covered tray before her.

"You had better drink the broth right away before it gets cold," he told her. She took his advice and began to sip it appreciatively while he stood over her and watched.

"Why don't you take off your wet coat and talk to me?" she said, trying to dispel his apparent discomfort.

He needed no further coaxing. He removed his hat and coat and hung them on a hook. Brushing the thick snowflakes from his damp hair, he sat down beside her on the blanket. He watched her intently as she savored the warm broth and ate the small chicken leg and munched on the thick black bread. Her cheeks were flushed from her recent ride. Neither spoke. When she had finished eating, he placed the empty tray on his table and joined her again on the blanket before the hearth. Uncertain of what to say, Katie stared into the fire. She could feel his eyes upon her, and her flush deepened. His voice was low and tense when he finally said, "Katie, look at me."

Timidly, she moved her eyes from the fire and let them rest on Peter's dark face. Katie could see a vein in his throat throbbing steadily, and his dark eyes were moist with barely controlled emotion. "Do you hate me for what I did to you?"

Katie lowered her eyes and relied softly. "No," she said turning away from him. The movement caused the blanket to slip from her shoulders, exposing her soft white back. She hastily snatched it up again and turned back to him, stretching her shapely legs out toward the warmth of the fire.

Peter lit a cigarette and inhaled deeply. "Why did you really come here, Katie?"

"I told you, because Maria asked me to."

"Is that the only reason? Or did you come with some premeditated thoughts of vengeance in your pretty little head?"

"Really, Peter. You're absurd." She grinned. "How could I wreak vengeance on you when you're surrounded on all sides by an army?" Deliberately, she lowered her blanket so the swell of her breasts were visible, and then she smiled at him.

Peter clenched his fists. "Damn!" All the same old passions and longings rose to hammer in his veins, and because he was helpless to hide them, he felt angry. "You should have learned by now not to trifle with me, Katrina Kazakinova!" he stated.

"Should I have, Peter?"

He inhaled on his cigarette then angrily exhaled the smoke. *Always she plays with me. She knows how to provoke me. I'll never be free of her. She will always creates this ache in me. This never-ending torment.* "Katie," he demanded, "look at me."

The only sound in the room was the roar of the draft amidst the crackling blaze of the fire. Katie turned her face to his. Sweat rolled down from Peter's brow, and he reached up and shoved the damp locks off his forehead. The gesture caught at her heart.

Beads of moisture stood out on his skin. His intense gaze burned into her like a branding iron.

"Why do you think I should be frightened of you, Peter Sovinsky?" she asked.

"For obvious reasons. The last time we met, I took what I wanted. Now you are using your wiles to taunt me again. You are counting on me not being a heel twice in succession, but do you think that is a safe assumption?"

"I'm not that big a fool, Peter," she said, biting her lip nervously. "Especially since you have never even expressed any regret for your pervious brutality."

"I could say that I'm sorry, but I'm not really sure that I am. In fact, I'm not even as confident as you that you are safe with me now," he said.

Katie laughed. "Stop feeling so uncomfortable, Peter. Maria sent me merely to deliver her love. Do you suppose it would be all right for me to deliver a kiss for her?"

"For Maria, huh" he growled.

Before he could refuse, she pressed her lips softly against his and found them hard and hot.

"Oh, Katie," he moaned, reaching out and pulling her savagely against his body to return her gentle kiss with one of raw passion. Katie felt her head spinning, felt herself being drawn into that same whirlpool that had caught her before, when she was only sixteen. Panic-stricken, she fought against him until she was free of his embrace.

He looked at her in disgust. "Same old Katie! Stir up passion in a man, and when you have driven him to the brink of insanity, you turn and run. You are a coward, Katrina Kazakinova!"

Tears crept into Katie's eyes. "You don't understand, Peter."

"Like hell I don't," he snapped contemptuously. "I understand only too well. Your cousin Sonya was very good at playing this same game, but at least she delivered. You are just plain scared to go to bed with a man. Why don't you admit it?"

Katie's face drained of color. She tried to speak but couldn't. When she found her voice, she tried to keep it steady. "If you feel that way . . ." She was unsuccessful, and her voice quivered pathetically. "You can always rape me again."

"No thanks, Katie," he sighed. "You are out of my reach. The unattainable goddess. For me to force myself on you again would be your triumph, with you emerging the untarnished angel while my hands would be unclean. I would be defeated once again with self-hatred." He closed his eyes in pain.

"If you have so much contempt for me, Peter," she asked, "why do you still want me?"

"The contempt is not for you, Katie, but for myself. All my life, I have been a slave to my passion for you. I thought that if I could have you just once, I could free myself of it. But that night, I only succeeded in enmeshing myself deeper than ever. I have loved you since you were a child. It's my own private curse. There doesn't seem to be much that I can do about it. I thought if I could humiliate you in payment for your humiliation of me because of my poverty that I would have my revenge. However, I only succeeded in further humiliating myself. Vengeance will always elude me. I love you, and I suppose that I always will." He half smiled whimsically. "You see, at least I'm honest. You ought to try honesty sometime, Katie. It's good for the soul. You've grown now, and it's about time that you figure out what you really want from life. There's a sword hanging over all of our heads these days. In these times, anyone's life is apt to end abruptly."

Seeing the distress in her face, Peter's look softened, and he took her hand in his and asked gently. "Do you love this Sokoloy so very much then, Katie?"

Confused at the abrupt change in the direction of his conversation, she searched his face and then sought refuge in the dancing flames of the fireplace again.

"Katie, you're not looking at me," Peter admonished. "Is this Sokoloy the man that you really want?"

Her mouth trembled, and tears crept into her eyes. "Oh, Peter," she said, turning to him, and this time her eyes did not waver before his direct gaze. "You want honesty, and you are right. It is about time that I face up to all my truths. I have been a coward for too many years."

Peter braced himself.

"I'm very fond of Nicki, and I always will be. Before the revolution, he could have given me all the things that I was used to. He would have made a good husband, but I don't love him."

He looked at her for a long time without moving.

The blanket slid from around her as she raised herself to her knees and put her hands on his shoulders. "It's you that I love, Peter. It's always been you, since that day in the woods when we first met. But in my snobbery, I couldn't admit my true feelings, not even to myself, although a hunger for you constantly burned within me all these years." She then pressed her mouth hungrily to his.

He needed no further encouragement. His arms closed around her and crushed her body against his own. His heat singed Katie's flesh, and she felt his desire kindling her own. Her body grew weak as chills of desire ran up her spine.

Peter freed her lips momentarily. "Are we sure that we're grown up enough now, Katie?" he asked.

She laughed softly. "You'll see, Peter. Oh, I do love you so!" She gave herself to his kisses and made no protest when he flung aside the blanket that had covered her. He raised an eyebrow quizzically. "Still afraid, Katie?"

"A little," she said with her mouth trembling. "But I want you too much for it to matter."

He kissed her gently, and they then eased the years of hunger they had accumulated. It was in the early hours of the morning before their bodies finally sought refuge in sleep.

As dawn was breaking, Katie turned her head and saw Peter grinning at her.

"Didn't you sleep well?" she asked him.

"Mmm . . . some, but I can do that anytime. Who knows when I'll get a chance to observe your beautiful face at such close quarters again."

She blushed with pleasure.

"This is a hell of a time to get modest on me," he accused. "Now how about a good-morning kiss?" He pressed his mouth tenderly on hers then buried it in her hair. "I can't really believe it yet. Is the beautiful Katie of my dreams mine at last? You had better reassure me again by telling me how much you love me."

"More than the earth, moon, and stars combined," she whispered.

"I hate the thought of you leaving me today, Katie."

"I know, but . . ." She knew that she should tell him about little Ivan and didn't know why she hesitated. "Besides, I have to make all the arrangements you know," she said at last.

"Arrangements?" he asked. "What arrangements?"

"For our wedding, silly. Would you mind if Yuri rather than an orthodox priest married us?"

"Slow down a minute," he said, frowning. "I didn't mention anything about a wedding!"

"I thought . . . I mean . . . I assumed . . ." Katie's voice broke, and she stared at him in bewilderment.

"Katie, you know that I do not believe in the Church. I never have! For me to go and stand before one of those money-grabbing parasites would be a blasphemous mockery of everything that I believe in," he reproved.

Katie stared at him in disbelief. "You're not serious, Peter?"

"Of course I am."

"Well, even if you don't believe in religious ceremonies, you could go through the ceremony for Maria and me."

"Hey, Katie, I'm the man who believes in honesty. I refuse to be a hypocrite."

Suddenly, Katie wanted to cry, but she didn't dare. "This doesn't make any sense, Peter. I don't know what to say."

"Then why say anything. I'm yours, and you belong to me. It's quite simple. Nothing can change that. We don't need some religious character to tell us that it's okay."

"It's not that simple, Peter."

"Why not? I love you more than anything in the world. What is so complex about that? If you love me the same way, then why should there be any difficulty?

We don't need a third party to tell us that it is all right for us to love each other for the rest of our lives." He stared at her. "But then, perhaps your love is more conditional than mine, Katie."

"Honestly, Peter, you have the capacity for twisting things so."

"Then you don't love me enough to stay with me without the benefit of clergy?"

"Peter, you are being childish."

She wanted to tell Peter about their baby and how he needed a name, but she didn't want to use him as a weapon to get her own way.

"Katie, if you insist on a piece of paper, we'll have a civil ceremony when time permits."

"Oh, Peter, try and understand," she pleaded. "I believe in God. Without his sanction, I'd never feel complete."

"In other words, your religion is more important to you than your love for me?"

"Must I choose?"

"Oh yes, Katie, you must," he said. "I have to be sure. Really sure. I have to have all of you, or it's no good. I have to be first to make up for all the years when I was last."

"You and your stupid pride!"

"My pride is all that I've ever had, Katie."

She buried her face in the pillow to smother her anguish. *I love him so, and after last night, I know more than ever how empty life will be without him. Why am I insisting on marriage? Who bothers with it in times like these? I should let him have his way.* She started to speak, but then she hesitated, for inside of her a quiet voice spoke. "*Never turn your back on God, no matter how great the temptation might be. No matter how great the pain! Trust him. Do not forsake him, and he will never betray you.*" All at once, Boris's presence seemed to fill the tiny room, and Katie lifted her head. Tears were still in her eyes. "You mustn't make me choose, Peter," she pleaded.

"You're wrong, Katie. You do have to choose. If you love me, you must accept me for what I am. I am a Soviet soldier and a godless man. You'll never be able to change that."

Katie's face filled with pain. She knew it was true. If she went to him on his terms, she would be forsaking all that she believed in. Little Ivan would idolize his father and strive to follow in his footsteps. He too would become a godless man. She felt so confused. "Peter, please don't be so stubborn."

"Do you or don't you love me enough to give yourself to me without conditions?"

She reached out her arms in torment. "Peter!"

He stood before her, grim and silent. But that other face intruded before her. Boris's dying words echoed in her ears. "*You must have faith, Katrina.*" And once more, she could feel the life ebbing from his body. He had given his life for her and her child.

Peter knelt and took her hand. "Katie, I love you so!"

She stammered painfully. "I . . . I . . . I . . . just can't forsake God, Peter. If you force me to choose, then there is no choice."

"Well then, that's it." He shrugged and started to dress. The room was cold and silent.

"Peter, it can't make that much difference to you. Why can't we be married?"

"It just wouldn't work, Katie," he said with a sigh. "Perhaps it's for the best. Always it seems that we have been of two different worlds, divided and apart. There seems to be no bridge between them. My love for you remains the same. I want you. I need you. I ask nothing of you but yourself. Once you turned your back on me because I lacked worldly possessions. Now you are turning away from me because I refuse to become a hypocrite. A man must stand for what he believes in, Katie, or he is no longer a man. I don't ask you to adopt my beliefs but merely to accept me for what I am. You can't change me, Katie. I remain Peter Sovinsky. If you ever think that you can accept me on such terms, come to me. I'll always be waiting."

He finished dressing and then knelt down beside her. His serious dark eyes burned into her soul. "I'll never forget last night, and I'll always love you, Katrina Kazakinova." Then without another word, he was gone.

CHAPTER 26

Katie stared at the back of the Red Soldier leading her homeward. It seemed strange not to flee from that uniform of the Red regime, for it represented everything that she had come to hate and fear. Yet it was the uniform that Peter wore.

She had waited all day for Peter to return before finally resigning herself to the fact that his good-bye had been final. Her anguish seemed unbearable. Yet she believed that she understood Peter. He felt that the aristocracy and the church had oppressed him all his life. Now that he was free of their yoke, he would not bend beneath the weight of the old authorities and traditions. Peter wore pride like a badge of honor, and she loved him for that. Yet invisible chains bound her to Boris who had given his life for her and her child. She could not bring herself to raise her child in a godless world.

It had stopped snowing, and the countryside was clean and white from the recent storm, although the stinging from the cold still prevailed and penetrated beneath her wraps.

Katie's horse whinnied softly, and she looked around apprehensively. *He's probably tired,* she thought. *We have ridden for such a long time.*

"Comrade," she called out to her escort, "do you think we might stop and rest awhile?"

"There's a village ahead," the soldier replied. His horse neighed loudly then stopped abruptly and pawed at the ground. The Bolshevik steadied his stallion. "I think that we had better make a fast break for the village," he called. "I see some hostile-looking peasants ahead."

She urged her horse to close in on the lead that the soldier's horse had now taken. The soldier entered a clump of trees ahead. Suddenly, a band of jeering peasants jumped out and surrounded him. The angry farmers yanked the soldier from his horse, and he turned his head to Katie and shouted, "Flee for your life!"

Katie quickly spurred her horse in the opposite direction without waiting to see if anyone was following. She rode hard until she had put a safe distance between herself and the angry mob. Then she circled back, looking for her Bolshevik companion, but could find no trace of him. She was cold and knew that she had to find shelter for the night. She turned toward the direction of the village, hoping that she could find a place to stay.

The sun was setting as she neared the edge of the settlement. Still apprehensive about the hostile peasants, she left her horse temporarily in a grove of trees and proceeded on foot. She tied a cotton peasant kerchief over her yellow hair and cautiously entered the town. She was surprised to find that the village was quite large with a number of shops, but their windows were small, dirty, and almost completely empty of merchandise. It was dark now, but some lamps glowing in the windows of the peasants' huts dimly lit the main street. She breathed a sigh of relief when she spotted a dilapidated hotel.

Entering the two story dwelling, she found the lobby empty. She impatiently shook the brass bell on the counter. Eventually, a huge Tartar woman appeared from behind a pair of faded curtains. "You want a room?" she asked.

"That's right."

"Traveling alone?"

"Yes."

"You'll have to pay in advance."

"All right," Katie agreed.

The dark woman reached under the counter for a dusty ledger and placed it on the counter. "You must sign it and show your papers."

"Of course," Katie replied and reached for the forged documents that Peter had given her for her trip home. Katie pulled out the papers and handed them to the woman, who spread them out over the countertop and studied them seriously. Katie suppressed a smile. She didn't think the woman could even read. She studied the clerk, amused by her airs of importance. She had good skin and teeth and pronounced Oriental eyes. At last, she bobbed her dark head up and down in approval.

"Good," she said at last. "Sign here, and then pay me, and I'll show you a room."

Katie did as she was told, counting out the required amount. The room that the woman led her to was a small dark cubbyhole. She asked the woman if someone could fetch and care for her horse. The woman nodded affirmatively and promised that she would take care of the animal herself. Then she asked, "You want food?"

"Yes, if you have some."

"Soup and bread, that's all, but you must pay in advance."

"Of course," Katie answered, looking at the sign posted and handing her the correct amount of money.

The woman returned shortly with a wooden bowl of watery cabbage soup and two hunks of dark bread. After she had left, Katie locked the door and ate hungrily. Then, without undressing, she crawled beneath the heavy blankets and spent a restless night trying to sleep while hearing frequent footsteps on the creaking stairs.

The following morning, Katie finished the last of her breakfast in a small dining area downstairs. It consisted of the same watery soup and black bread as the night before. She heard a commotion in the street outside. The Tartar woman looked out the window and shook her head.

"What is it?" Katie asked.

"An execution," the woman replied grimly.

Katie joined the heavyset woman at the window. She observed a frail woman being forcibly dragged along the snow-covered street below. The slender captive struggled to free herself from the tight grip of the Bolshevik soldiers on each side.

As the armed escort surrounded her, she cried out, "Mercy." Her bare feet slipped in the thick slush, and she fell to the ground. Her long black hair struck a vivid contrast against the brilliant white snow. Katie felt her chest contract painfully. There was something about the girl that disturbed her frightfully. "What are they going to do to her?" she asked the woman.

"Shoot her."

"But why?" Katie asked.

"For murder."

"How horrible."

"Yes. She used to live in this very hotel. She was a no-good slip of a thing, if you know what I mean. Had a weakness for men, always with one man after another. Yet there was another side of her too, a thoughtful one, kind and sweet in her own way. And you should have seen her with her baby. She was a picture of innocence then."

"Where is her baby now?"

"Dead."

"How terrible," Katie stated.

"Dreadful," the woman agreed. "The baby was a beautiful child, and the mother loved her so. The child had blue eyes and yellow curly hair. In spite of the mother's loose ways, the babe always came first. That's what caused her the trouble. You see, she first came here with a soldier and then left him for another soldier. There were a long string of them after that. Anyway, she finally had this child, although heaven knows who the father was. It was quite a surprise to me to see how she was about the baby. I mean, you wouldn't think she'd be the mothering sort. She was though."

The Tartar women brought Katie another serving of cabbage soup, and when Katie sat down at the table again, the woman continued her tale. "The child and the mother were both beautiful, but in different ways. The mother's hair is black as a crow's feathers, while the babe's was like sunlight. Then she took up with a rough one, mean as Satan he was. He beat her, mistreated her so, still she stayed with him. Jealous he was too. Wouldn't let her look at another man. Then one night, the baby was crying, and she was fixing the child's dinner when he came home drunk. Wanted her to come to bed right then, but she told him that he'd have to wait 'til she fed the babe. The little one kept crying, and the brute got mad. He told her to forget her damn brat, but she paid no mind to him, so he got himself into a terrible rage and picked the child up and dashed her against the wall."

"My god!" Katie gasped.

"A doctor pronounced the child dead. When everyone had gone, she killed the brute. Blew his brains out with his own gun, leaving him as dead as her babe. The soldier was an evil bastard but one of their own, you know, and she was nothing but a trollop. Hadn't a right to have a child, they told her, and her loving that baby so. But then who am I to judge? So they sentenced her to death."

"It seems so unjust," Katie said. "Did she have any relatives?"

"Who knows? No kin that came to call upon her leastways. I think she might have had a sister. I do remember that she used to talk about someone to the baby. Named the child after her I believe. She'd laugh and say, 'You are as golden and good as my beautiful Katie.' That's what she called her little one, 'her precious Katie.'"

Katie's face turned pale. How could she have failed to recognize her? Without a word to the woman, she fled from the room and down the stairs. Even as she reached the street, the roar of gunfire filled her ears, and she realized that she was too late. She rushed toward the village square and found a huge crowd gathered around the tragic scene. "Get out of the way," she screamed at them as she pushed to the front of the spectators.

The soldiers ordered the crowd to disperse, and some of the people began to drift away. Katie now had a clear view of the fragile dark-haired beauty lying there. The blood flowing from her wound stained the snow about her. A scream stuck in Katie's throat as she looked upon the white mask of death covering

Sonya's lovely profile. Katie clenched her fists tightly, trying to smother the sobs building up within her. There was nothing that she could do now. It would be folly to call attention to herself. She had to get back to little Ivan. As she walked away, tears slid down her cheeks, but she made no effort to wipe them away. Sonya's death, like her life, had been tragic. Even in her last moments on earth, she remained unwanted and alone.

As Katie stumbled along the strange street in the early morning light, her lips trembled. She lifted her tear-stained face and whispered, "Darling, beautiful Sonya. I loved you so. But now you are free of torment at last."

JULY 1919

Six months drifted by without any unpleasantness. Maria and Katie's days had been full and rewarding. Each day, little Ivan grew huskier and taller, and though he was not yet a year old, he was already taking his first unsteady steps about the cabin floor. His mischievous face filled Katie's day with sunshine and pride. It was the nights that she dreaded, for with them came her longing for Peter and terrifying nighttimes that filled her with horror. Now, without realizing it, Katie moaned aloud, causing Maria to lift her dark eyes from her mending.

"Is something wrong, Katie?" she asked.

"No, not really," she relied. "I just feel a little depressed today."

"I know the mood, but it will pass." Maria smiled sympathetically and returned to her sewing.

Ah, if I could be like her, thought Katie. *If I could resign myself to take life as it comes without complaint. Surely Maria's life has been filled with as much tragedy as my own, yet she continues to toil hard, smile often, and pray. Maria has the same serene thoughts and gentle ways as Boris. I am fortunate to have her as a friend, and I probably lean too heavily on her strength.*

Her bond to Maria was one of respect. They shared a mutual love for Peter and his son. They understood each other so well that they seldom needed to indulge in long conversations or explanations. Katie rose and replaced the blanket that the baby had kicked off in his sleep.

"What are you sewing?" she asked Maria.

"A dress. It's nothing but a rag, but it doesn't look like we'll be getting any new clothes in the near future. We will have to make do with what we have. Heaven knows, we may soon be going naked," Maria said with a grin.

"How right you are, if something is not done about the factories. Perhaps, though, things will soon be back to normal. Our neighbor told me that he heard in the village that Admiral Kolchok and General Denikin now hold southwestern Russia from Odessa to Ufa, and the Estonians under General Yudenitch are marching on St. Petersburg. If they are victorious . . ."

"Yes, if they are victorious," Maria agreed. "The Bolshevik control is now limited to the area around Moscow. Our neighbor Dmitri Gogol told me today that the Soviet Regime is expected to collapse within the next two weeks."

"That would be so wonderful!" Katie replied.

"Yes, but I worry so for Peter's sake. What will happen to him?"

"Peter will be all right," Katie assured Maria and herself. "It's the big fish they always want. Peter has always managed to take care of himself in the past. I'm sure that he'll continue to do so."

Maria smiled. "You're probably right," she agreed.

But the defeat of Russia came by the sword of the Bolsheviks viciously slashing at her precious internal arteries.

CHAPTER 27

OCTOBER 1919

Tears rolled down Maria's dark cheeks, and her voice cracked with emotion. "I don't want to send you away, Katie! If I didn't love you so, I wouldn't even think of asking you to go, but it is not safe for you here any longer. If they found you, they would kill you."

"Things can't have gotten that bad all at once."

"But they have. Since the British and French withdrew their troops last month, Leon Bronstein and Joseph Stalin have directed the Red Army. They have begun to check the advance of the White Army until they now have complete control of southern Russia. General Yudenitch has been routed, Kolchak has been forced to Siberia, and Denikin has retreated to the Black Sea. Today in the village, I heard a rumor that the British will evacuate Denikin's troops by ship. So the Cheka is breathing down hard on everyone. Your description has been given in this vicinity."

"But why should they want me? I'm not important."

"I don't know why, Katie!" Maria said, twisting her hands in agitation. "I only know that you are in grave danger and must leave here."

"But where can I go?" Katie cried. "They are more apt to find me on the streets than hidden away here."

"Katie, I overheard your presence in this cabin being discussed by some in the village," Maria insisted. "It is no longer a secret."

"It's just that it was bad enough before when I was alone, but now that I have Ivan, I don't know how I will manage to get the food that he needs."

You mustn't consider taking him.

"But, Maria, he is all that I have in this world."

"And that's exactly why you must consider his safety. Suppose they apprehend you? Even if you were later released, think of all the things that could happen to him in the meantime. You will miss him, but at least you can be certain that he is well fed and safe with me. You will know where he is when you want him. And if anything dreadful happens to you, God forbid, you know that he will always be taken care of."

Katie winced. "I know you are right, Maria, but my heart refuses to listen."

"Make it listen!' Maria urged as her arms circled Katie and held her comfortingly. "It is a pretty terrible world that we live in, and we have to consider the young first. They are our only hope for tomorrow."

Katie choked back a sob and raised her head. "I will be so miserable without him."

"Perhaps it will only be for a few weeks. The terror might die down at any time. Maybe this is just a final grand sweep to frighten everyone."

"I really wish that I could believe that," Katie said. "Well, I don't imagine that there is any point in my putting it off. I will go in the morning."

"I think you will be safer in a big city for now."

"You're probably right," Katie said. "I'll miss you, Maria. What will I do without you and Ivan?"

"Or I, you, Katie, but it is better for me to be lonely than to have you apprehended by the Cheka. It is fortunate that you still have those false credentials that Peter gave you. It would be hopeless without them. I will give you what money I have. I won't need any here. There is nothing to buy. The city is the only place where one can purchase anything these days."

FEBRUARY 1920

Katie had been hiding for months in a tiny dank room in a rooming house, where her landlady had been kind enough to buy groceries for her each day. She thought that her landlady recognized her as an aristocrat but still seemed to be sympathetic. Now as she stepped out into the cold, dark street, she pulled her collar tightly about her face. The first snatch of conversation that she heard was from two workers passing by.

"The Allies have abandoned their economic blockade. All their troops have been withdrawn from Russian soil."

"Ah," the other replied. "And I heard that General Denikin and his forces also have been taken off by British and French ships."

Katie sighed. The Bolsheviks' victory meant the defeat of Russia. She tripped over a fallen lamppost and cut her hand on a piece of broken glass. She wiped the blood on her scarf before continuing on.

Nothing had been repaired since the revolution. The lampposts still standing had shattered glass. The sidewalks were broken and jagged. The streets had gaping holes. The drains were cluttered with debris. Everywhere there were scars of the street riots.

At a corner, a man with a weather-beaten face confided to a man in an old torn trench coat. "Admiral Kolchak has been overtaken and made captive in Siberia."

The other shook his head and replied. "The Bolsheviks are the tools of the Germans. They are the ones who delivered Lenin in a sealed box car so that he could force the German peace upon us."

Yes, Katie thought. *It was Lenin who stirred this revolution into the flames of destruction from which none of us have been able to escape.* She crossed the street, hugging the buildings closely as always during her walks. Not many people ventured out after nightfall. Clothes and boots were no longer available. People's old ones had become shabby, threadbare, full of holes, and grossly inadequate against the harsh winter weather that now prevailed. On her walks about the city, she heard that many technicians had been exiled and executed, leaving no one to run the factories.

Two old women stood in a doorway, whispering to each other. Katie moved closer to overhear them.

"More priests have been murdered. Bayoneted by the riffraff.

The other woman crossed herself. "The devil's henchmen they are!"

The wind was sharp and cutting tonight, but it felt good to escape from her room. In front of an empty food shop, a man with a long beard and disheveled hair confided to another. "Villages are refusing to give the Bolsheviks their grain, so the Reds have put torches to their huts and stripped them of all their belongings."

"A good thing in my opinion," the second man said. "They should realize that we here in the city have to eat too. Selfish bastards."

"Well, spring will soon be here," the first replied. "Things will get better then."

Gathering fragments of conversations, Katie sifted through them and tried to make sense of it all. It was like putting a puzzle together. She heard that many hated Lenin. The death toll was climbing all over Russia. Many Russians were being tortured in the Cheka's dungeons.

Completing her walk, the final bit of news that she heard whispered into the night was "General Kolchak has been shot."

Tomorrow, she decided, *I am going to brave the daylight hours.*

Katie's faltering spirits lifted under the cheering light of day. She smiled as she moved along the busy streets. Somehow, things did not appear so bad. The menacing threat of the Cheka had faded, and Katie decided that she would return home. After all, it had been four months now. Her mood was one of exhilaration. Her previous pressing weight of gloom had disappeared. It was a wonderful day. It was on such crisp, cold days as these that she and her horse, Pride, had raced across the countryside, challenging the wind and the world. Sadly, the Bolsheviks had taken all the horses at the manor.

Now without a warm *shuba*, it was a bit uncomfortable. However, she refused to let the chill dampen her spirits. She strolled up one street and down another. No one, except for an occasional beggar, seemed to notice her amidst the crowded throng.

Suddenly, a hand reached out and clutched her shoulder. She recoiled in terror. She turned quickly to see her captor and caught her breath in relief when she saw it was only a blind beggar. He was tall and scrawny, with flesh that pulled almost to the breaking point over his sharp protruding bones. He had yellowish skin and a dirty buff-colored beard that hung to his chest. As he coughed, his body shook with agonizing tremors. "Please, anything," he begged. "I'm starving."

The voice sounded familiar, but then most beggars sounded alike. Katie reached into her purse. *Tomorrow I am going home. I might as well share what I have left with this poor creature.* She looked up, and the sightless watery eyes repelled her. The beggar turned his face as he reached up to scratch his nose, and a shudder of horror crept through Katie. High on the beggar's right cheek was an ugly red scar about two inches long in the shape of an *R*. Her first impulse was to run, but she fought for control of her emotions.

"Can't you hear me?" he whined impatiently. "Please . . ."

"Alex?" she whispered, trembling.

The beggar startled and started to draw away.

"Don't you recognize my voice? It's me . . . Katie."

"My cousin?"

"Yes."

"You're wanted by them!"

"Who of our class isn't?" she answered.

"That's true! Where are you staying?"

"Come, I'll take you there. We can have dinner together."

He smacked his lips greedily. "I am hungry," he admitted.

She took one hand while he clasped his cane with the other. She led him through the crowd, trying to suppress her disgust at his smell.

In the safety of her room, she prepared the scant rations that she had left, and he ate voraciously. After they had eaten, she asked, gently, "How did you lose your sight, Alex?

"I had an illness with a high fever. I don't know what it was," he said. "Being a deserter, I was afraid to seek medical care. I was afraid I'd be arrested and shot. When the fever was gone, so was most of my sight. All I can see now is shadowy images. It is like I am walking through a never-ending fog. However, with my cane, I manage to get around.

"Oh, Alex, how terrible for you," Katie gasped. "How have you survived?"

"It hasn't been easy," he admitted. "In fact, it's been pretty terrible, but I don't really want to talk about it."

"I understand."

"Where's Father now?" he asked.

"Dead. He was shot by a Bolshevik guard during the street riots," she told him.

He was quiet for a moment and then said, "I think I'm glad that he's gone." He paused. "And Sonya?"

"She's dead too. She was shot before a Bolshevik firing squad," Katie replied and explained the circumstances.

His face clouded briefly. "I'm sorry about that. She was the only one of my family that I ever really loved. I had always hoped that I'd meet her again someday." He shook his head, and then he spoke again. "And Tanya?"

"Dead too. She had a nervous breakdown after the Bolsheviks raided Usadiba Na Holme and later hanged herself."

"Yes, I suppose that's what Tanya would have done. Never Sonya. She loved life too dearly. And our home?"

"It's still standing, though it's in the process of decay and has been emptied of all its furnishings."

"Perhaps, then, there is still hope. My only dream all this time has been to return there someday and become the master. Now that Father is dead, I am the rightful heir and lord. It's really mine at last."

"Have you forgotten the Reds, Alex?"

"They'll have to restore some of us to power in the end. They can't murder all of us," he reasoned.

"Well, they are making an awfully good try at it."

He grinned malevolently. "But obviously, I'm not going to prove to be a threat to them now, so only time will tell! And so we are the only survivors, eh?"

"I'm afraid so, Alex."

He mulled over what he had just learned and then rose abruptly. I think I had better get back to my own miserable hole in the wall now," he announced. "Not seeing, I can tolerate its wretchedness."

"Oh, please stay here, Alex. I am going home in the morning, and I'll take you with me."

"I see." He scowled fiercely for a moment. "I need to go back and get my things then."

"Of course. I'll come with you and help."

"No!" he shouted angrily.

"All right, if that's the way you feel. Can you find your way?"

"I've managed quite well up until now, thank you," he snapped. And with that, he left, slamming the door behind him.

Katie felt angry at his ungracious manner. She brooded for a while and then shrugged her shoulders. *After all, what else can I expect from Alex?* She began to gather her belongings and prepare for the journey home.

CHAPTER 28

Fists smashed against the door. A loud voice thundered. "Open up!"

"Who is it?" Katie inquired, trying to suppress her sudden fear. Before she could slip the bolt, the door crashed in, knocking her to the floor.

"Katrina Kazakinova?" demanded the man standing over her.

"Oh my god," she muttered as the two secret policemen seized her by the wrists and pulled her to a standing position.

Before she could catch her breath, one of the men shouted, "We are the Cheka, and you are to come with us." The men dragged her into the hallway. It was then that she saw his evil face. Stunned, she cried out. "Why did you betray me?'

He replied with a shrill laugh. "You said you were going home. I am not about to share Usadiba Na Holme with you. It's mine and mine alone. You always had everything. My father loved you best, but now I am going to have what is rightfully mine."

"You treacherous Judas!" she screamed.

His wicked laughter rose in pitch as the Cheka officers jerked her down the corridor with his words ringing after her. "Do you think I care what happens to you? You're a small enough sacrifice to pay for the only thing that I ever really wanted."

Katrina was driven in a police van to Cheka headquarters. Inside, she was pushed into an interrogation room where a stout officer sat in a chair behind a huge desk.

"Sit down," he said, pointing to a stool in the center of the room.

Katrina climbed upon it. Without warning, a bright light shone into her eyes so that she could not see the man before her.

"Name," he began menacingly.

"Katrina Kazakinova."

"Family?"

"The Kozakovs."

"A poor relation, eh?"

Katrina's cheeks flamed crimson, but she said nothing.

"Your uncle's name?"

"Ivan Kozakov."

"Your cousin's name?"

"Which one?" she asked.

"The male."

"Aleksander Ivanovick Kozakov"

"Oh yes, quite a gallery of portraits among your relatives," he sneered. "A pack of cowards, deserters, whores, and murderers."

Katrina gritted her teeth and gave no reply. *It is obvious that he is trying to humiliate me.*

"And what do you know of Nikolai Sokoloy?"

"He is a good friend of our family."

"A friend of the family?"

"That is what I said."

"I know what you said!" he shouted angrily. "Now tell us the truth."

Katrina sighed. "I am telling the truth."

"He is your lover!" her interrogator accused.

"No, that's not true."

"Liar!" He shouted at the top of his voice.

Katrina winced and looked down at the floor.

"Where is he now?"

"I don't know," she said, turning to look about her. The only other presence in the room was a guard with a gun standing in the doorway.

"Liar!" he repeated. "When did you see him last?'

"Before he went to the front."

"You had better tell us the truth," he thundered. "We know that he sent for you."

"That's not true," Katrina insisted. Nicki had sent for her after the revolution, but it would be dangerous to confess this. She felt panic rising in her. "I have not seen him for many years."

"Is that your story?"

"It's the truth."

"You don't seem to know what the truth is," he roared. "He's an officer and one of the leaders in the White Army, and we know that he has been in contact with you. Where is he now? Answer!"

"I don't know! I don't know!" she cried out.

"Very well. We'll give you a chance to reconsider. Guard, take her away."

The guard pushed Katrina into a tiny cell. She stumbled and groped her way to the narrow cot attached to the wall. She sat staring into the inky blackness until she lost all track of time. She let her thoughts drift. *It is Nicki that they want. I am so glad that I really don't know where he is.*

The first two days, she tried to keep track of the time by the flashes of light when her food was shoved through the narrow slit in the door, but then, her stomach churned with hunger pains, and she realized that she was no longer receiving three meals a day.

It is this silence that disturbs me the most. Indisputable quiet. Hour after hour, no one comes near me. This cell is so small and barren except for the hard cot attached to the wall and a slop jar. The stench was unbearable at first, but now I have become more accustomed to its smell.

The air is suffocating, and time seems to pass so slowly. I am light-headed with a dreamlike sense of unreality about everything. As the hours drag on, I feel utterly abandoned.

Her heart raced whenever she heard a noise. She got up and walked around the tiny cell. She tried to clear her throat, but a thick lump lodged there stubbornly, making it difficult to breathe. Tears trickled down her cheeks. She reached up and rubbed her burning eyes. Feeling limp, she sat back down on her cot. A dull throb in her head began to pound, and she shut her eyes, trying to erase the pain. *I will wake up at any moment now and find that this is all a terrifying nightmare. It will all go away.*

But it did not go away. She ran her fingers through her matted hair. *I refuse to think what I must look like.* A spasm of coughing seized her, temporarily rendering her helpless. When it had passed, she returned to her thoughts. *If only there were something that I could do.* Anger periodically flooded though her at thoughts of her betrayal. *Dwelling on Alex's treachery cannot help me now.*

She turned her thoughts to her loved ones and tried to picture what they might be doing now. *I am fortunate to have so many beautiful memories. So many loved ones. If only there were some way of letting those outside know of my plight.*

She knelt on the cold floor of her cell and started to pray, seeking peace. Just then, the heavy bolt on her cell door was shoved back and swung outward.

Katrina shut her eyes, blinded by the unaccustomed light. The guard motioned for her to follow him. She shuffled after him down a series of corridors until they came once more to the interrogation room.

Again the questions began.

"What is your name?" the Cheka official demanded.

"Katrina Kazakinova," she answered.

"What is your uncle's name?"

Katrina felt that she was trapped in a nightmare. The Cheka officer would not believe anything that she told him. She tried to understand the significance of his inquiries. *They are not really interested in me. It is Nicki that they want. Why won't they believe that I really, truly do not know anything about him now?*

After several days of repeated questioning, they moved her to a new call. This one had a glaring lightbulb that burned constantly. Having become acclimated to the dark, her new surroundings were painful at first. Her life now became an endless series of rigid acts. She was awakened early in the morning to wash, was given food, and then within minutes, the guard returned to confiscate what she had not managed to bolt down.

Sometimes the slop jar was taken away, and she had to wait hours before the guard would answer her call to bring it back. No one spoke to her.

She was allowed to sleep only at certain times. Someone indicated when she was to go to bed but allowed her to lie only on her back. The glaring bulb overhead made it difficult to sleep. If she turned over, the guard woke her with a sharp blow from his gun butt and forced her to resume the same fixed sleeping position directly under the blinding light. Her new cell became as unbearable as the old. The incessant light became as miserable as the constant darkness. The rigid routine preyed on her nerves as much as the isolation of her previous cell.

She plied the guards with questions when they ventured into her cell. "How long are you going to keep me here?"

When they refused to answer, she shouted at them. "Talk to me!" They paid no attention to her hysterics.

Katie cried, prayed, and formulated wild schemes to escape. Some days they failed to feed her. Some nights they refused to let her sleep. Slowly, fatigue, hunger, and depression took their toll, and she lost all track of time. She chewed her fingernails, stared around apprehensively, always anticipating some new danger. She would hear noises that did not really exist. She stamped her swollen feet, rubbed her arms aimlessly, and looked about the empty cell. Nothing ever changed. Only the continuing silence filled her hours.

How can I maintain my sanity? I must! she vowed.

She had no idea how much time had passed when they sent for her again. She was taken to the same interrogation room as before, but this time there was no stool to sit upon. The same Cheka officer sat smiling behind his desk.

"We hope that you will be a little more cooperative this time, Katrina Kazakinova." Katie said nothing.

"Now isn't it true that your family worked young children in the fields until they fell in exhaustion and begged for death as a mercy?"

"That's not true! At least the way that you put it," she replied, forcing herself to remain calm. "Children did work in the fields, but we didn't work them to death."

"Are you certain?"

Katie bit her tongue when she realized that she was not really certain about what happened to the children of the peasants. She know that they had been exploited, but she had always turned her back on the unpleasantness of it.

"Well?"

Katie shrugged. "I am not sure what happened to them. I had nothing to do with the field hands, but I think you must be mistaken," she replied.

"Do you now? That's interesting," he said. And with that, the bright lights were turned on. Katie lowered her eyes before the blinding glare.

"Didn't your uncle murder an old man who had done nothing but faithfully toil for him all his life?"

"It was a misunderstanding."

"Answer yes or no."

Katie sighed. "Yes."

"Yes, of course." Her interrogator laughed coarsely. "And didn't your family flog their workers?"

Katie thought of Peter. "Maybe some of our overseers did, but these are not my crimes," she shouted.

"Did you try to stop them?"

"I didn't even know about them."

"Don't lie to us!" he bellowed, pointing his finger at her.

"I'm not!"

The questions went on hour after hour. Perspiration poured from her body, and she grew light-headed and confused. They accused her of every crime the aristocracy ever committed. Her denials served to bring forth fresh accusations. She grew increasingly exhausted. Her legs ached unbearably, and she longed desperately to sit down.

But the questions did not end. They proclaimed her guilty. Guilty! Guilty! Finally, she could stand it no longer. "Stop it," she screamed. The continual hours of standing added to her weakened and hungry state made her body sway unsteadily.

"Where is Nikkolai Sokolay?" *So they are back to that again. They continually sandwich that in between ridiculous accusations and vile insults. I am forever thankful that I am ignorant of that knowledge.*

Her answers took on the monotony of a photograph record. "I do not know," she repeated over and over. Then the room began to swim around crazily. Suddenly, everything began to grow dark. She felt herself falling. Then the blackness came.

When she awoke, she was back in the lighted cell. She waited in terror for them to send for her again. When finally a key turned in her cell door, her heart pounded. Panic-stricken, she slowly followed the uniformed soldier back to the same little interrogation room. Everything was the same as before, even to the same smiling officer.

"Katrina Kazakinova, won't you be seated?" he said as he waved her to a chair next to his desk. "Would you care for some tea?"

Katie stared at him in confusion. "Oh yes," she blurted out. "That would be fine."

He motioned to a guard to bring some and then offered her a cigarette.

"No, thank you, I do not smoke," she said.

The guard returned immediately with a pot of steaming tea, two cups, and a plate of tiny pink frosted cakes. Katie stared at them hungrily as he poured the tea into the cups.

"Won't you have some cake?" the officer asked.

Eagerly, Katie reached for one of the sweets. She chewed the iced cake slowly, enjoying every morsel of it, but within moments, she felt nauseated. It had been a long time since she had eaten such rich food, and her stomach rebelled. She sipped the warm tea and looked at her enemy suspiciously. *Surely they are planning something.*

"There's no sense in our being antagonistic, countess," the officer remarked, smiling and leaning back comfortably in his chair. "We can just as well be friends, can we not? So just relax and make yourself comfortable. You have been through quite an ordeal. Let us hope that it has ended now, especially since it was all so unnecessary. You are an intelligent person and know that this hostility has not been beneficial to either of us. There are certain questions that we have to have an answer to, so let us get them over with, and then things will be much more pleasant in the future.

This is a new method, Katie realized. She smiled sweetly.

"I will be very glad to assist you in any way that I can, but I do not know where Nicki is, and that is the truth."

Her captor's face grew dark. "I see," he said. "When did you last hear from your young man?"

"He is not my young man, and I have not seen him since the war."

"I'd rather be pleasant to you, young lady."

"I am sorry. I do not know the answers to your questions."

Thus it continued. One time she would be met with tormenting hostility, and the next, with courtesy and friendliness. Finally, they gave up in disgust, and they transferred her to another prison where she was thrust into a damp black cell and forgotten.

The dungeon was dark, damp, and full of rats. Sometimes she would be left for days without food. Slowly her strength ebbed away, and the rats became bolder. All she could do was scream and stamp her feet in a desperate effort to keep them at a distance.

"What do you think the purpose of all this is?" she asked her rodent companions. "There has to be one. Why should any person be forced to bear so much suffering?

"I am tired! So tired of it all that it hurts. Hurts and hurts and hurts," she cried out passionately. An uncontrollable spasm of grief caught hold of her. She strained to see something in the darkness. Anything!

Peter! The thought of Peter will comfort me. He loves me. Perhaps it is not too late for us.

Who are you trying to fool? barked back the other part of herself. *He is gone! Dead for all the good it will do you. Like Nicki and all the others! You are alone! You are going to die here, and no one will even know or care.* Tears rolled down Katie's cheeks. *I am so tired. So tired, hungry, and lonely.*

She had lost her sense of time since she had been thrust into this putrid dungeon. At times no sound disturbed the eerie silence in her raven tomb. At other times, she was disturbed by the rapid scuttling sounds of the rats that seem to reverberate off the wall.

She mused often now on Alex's betrayal and could still hear his laughter as the Cheka dragged her down the corridor of the rooming house. *Poor, pathetic, foolish Alex. There was no way that he could know that home to me now is Maria's cottage and baby Ivan. The mansion is a pile of ruin. Alex is incapable of change though. Time has only fashioned him into a more selfish and treacherous being. If only I had not brought him home with me that night. My pity has cost me deeply. Now I shall probably never see my child again.* "Damn you, Alex!" she screamed. "Damn your self-serving cowardice."

The darken days dragged on. Her head seemed to grow heavier and her depression deeper. Left with nothing to fill the hours, she reflected on her past and explained her life to the rodents who had become quite friendly with her now.

"What have I accomplished? I lived in contentment and luxury most of my life. I rejected Peter because of his poverty. I destroyed Tanya's happiness when I became engaged to Nicki. I turned my head away from seeing all the abuses of the peasants. So this must be retribution. I was too happy, but the contented mortal has no need to move mountains. It is misfortune that spurs one to achievement, anguish that propels us into the realm of the gods, but I have no strength left. I just don't want to go on."

With frantic determination, she tore what remained of her underskirt into long strips and braided them together. When she had finished, she tied one end of the crudely made rope around her neck and then walked slowly to the cell door. There was a large metal handle on it. She fumbled in the darkness until she found it and then drew the strip up over it. She pulled the strand down the other side and knotted it tightly in place.

When next they come to feed me, it will be over. When they open the heavy iron door outward, the weight will pull the cord tightly around my neck. Then all my pain will be ended. I just have to wait. "Please hurry, guard!" she whispered. "There is nothing left. Nothing."

But what f Maria's friendship and little Ivan? No, Maria will care for my child. No one has the right to expect me to struggle anymore. She closed her eyes, but the image of little Ivan would not go away. Suddenly, she knew that she didn't really want to die. *What does it matter if I'm alone now? If I ever get out of this prison, there is still the sun, rain, wind, and snow. There is my child, and there is Maria.* A new strength rose within her just as she heard footsteps outside her cell.

Footsteps!

Cold panic seized her. Frantically, she tried to undo the knot encircling her throat, but her fingers were numb, and the knot remained fast. Then the key turned, and as the door opened, the pressure around her throat grew tight. *It was all for nothing. It was too late.* Her petticoat rope grew so taut that she could not breathe. She tried to cry out but could expel no sound. Then the feeble rope broke, and she fell to the dungeon floor.

Time flowed once again.

Then noise! Gunfire! Shouting! *Someone is coming. Someone is storming this wretched jail. Will they come down here? Will they free me?* Desperately, she tried to crawl to the door, but her body was too weak. She tried to call out, but her voice was too faint. *They will never find me! I will die in this dark cell.*

After a while, Katie heard voices on the stairs. Keys! The sound of keys. Someone was opening cells. She waited, and at last her own cell door swung open.

Strong arms seized her, and she was slung over someone's shoulder. It was too dark to see her liberators, but it did not matter. *I am going to live. I am going to be free. I am going to see my son and Maria again. I am going to see the sky again.* The blood rushed to her head, and she smiled. "Someone will take care of me now," she murmured as she lost consciousness.

APRIL 1920

Janusy Gorecki paced the floor, speaking as he had so many times before to the old man standing there. "I must do this, Father."

"You have done enough, Janusy. All through this war, I prayed and waited. At last, you've come home safe to me. Now you tell me that you are going to fight again. How much have they the right to ask?"

"I know how you feel, Father," Janusy said softly, "but I have to defend our country."

"No!" the old man shouted. "It's the French who incited Poland to declare this war. They are afraid of the Bolsheviks and want to cripple them without the personal loss of their own lives and fortune. Go to the Holy Land, son. Go while you still have the breath of life."

Janusy's anger rose. *Always the same pressures are brought to bear upon me.* "I am a Pole."

"Marian, speak to your brother," the old man demanded. "Give him his life!"

"I'm with Janusy, Father. Poland is our country."

"Two the same," he said, shaking his head. "What can a father do?"

Janusy lit his pipe and puffed nervously to calm his raging feelings. He pushed his black hair back from his forehead and studied the old man. Then he sighed. "Perhaps you are right, Father. Perhaps this is not our war. Nevertheless, I must fight it. Many of my best friends are Russians. We can't let the Bolsheviks' influence infiltrate into Poland. Being Jewish, you must realize the danger. The Bolsheviks are godless men, Father. They would destroy us. Not all Jews are free to escape to the Holy Land. This threat to Poland has to be removed."

"And after this war?" his father asked.

"I will go to the Holy Land as you wish," Janusy agreed. "And I will take Marian with me and find a husband for her in the land of our forefathers."

"You will promise me this, my son?"

"I promise," Janusy said.

"Then hurry and finish your war, Janusy Gorecki."

CHAPTER 29

APRIL 1920

Katie opened her eyes and looked around the room. A stout woman sat by an open hearth, stirring something in a huge iron pot. The aroma tantalized Katie's nostrils, and her stomach turned over hungrily. She coughed to attract attention. The huge woman turned to look at her. "So you have finally come to life. Well, he'll be happy."

"Where am I?"

Before Katie had a chance to say anything else, the woman was beside her with a bowl of soup. "Stop staring and open your mouth," she demanded. ""You're a bit improved since they first brought you here. Never saw such a dirty one." Katie blushed, recalling her previous sordid condition.

"Now eat," the woman demanded as she shoved spoonfuls of hot broth into Katie's mouth. "You're in a boarding house. It's a cover for the underground, but we try to keep it authentic looking."

"Was it the underground that freed me?"

"That's right. Now be quiet until you have eaten."

Katie finished the soup and then stretched in the huge feather bed. What luxury.

"Just rest now," the stout woman ordered. "Won't none of them be back until tonight."

"All right, but just one more question. How long have I been here?"

"Two days."

Katie stared in amazement. "I can't believe that I was that tired."

Katie woke from her deep slumber at the sound of the familiar voice. Could it really be him?

She opened her eyes and saw him staring at her. "Nicki. Oh, my darling Nicki!" she cried and threw her arms around his neck. "Is it really true, Nicki? I am not dreaming, am I?" She pulled away and looked into his green eyes while her own filled with tears.

"If you are dreaming, Katie, then I am, too," he said, brushing his lips against her forehead.

Katie laughed happily. "How did you ever find me?"

"It was not easy, love, but that's a long story. I want to hear about you. Why didn't you come when I sent for you?"

"That's a long story too, Nicki, but just let me look at you for a while. You've grown even more handsome."

He smiled as Katie studied him. Time had done nothing to dim his good looks. His ruddy cheeks glowed. His chestnut-colored hair curled tightly from the warmth of the overheated room. His eyes danced with familiar good humor. The empty sleeve was the only difference, and a look of pain crossed Katie's face when she saw it.

"Don't feel bad, Katie. I've been used to it for a long time," he said.

She smiled and took his hand within her own, but then a frown crossed her brow. "Oh, Nicki, it was so terrible! They thought that I knew where you were and hammered at me for the longest time."

"Poor sweetheart. I know what you must have gone through, but you can be sure that they will not hurt you now. You are safe. All you have to do is rest and get well."

Katie sighed. "I feel so wonderful already."

"You're still pretty weak, Katie. Getting well is going to take a long time."

She snuggled her shoulders into the pillows. "I'm not in a hurry. Will you stay with me?"

"As much as possible, kitten. I am pretty busy these days. There are so many to get out of the country. It has become increasingly difficult since Poland declared war."

"How did that happen? I want to hear all the news. It has been so long since I have heard anything."

"There really isn't any good news, Katie," he said. "The French stirred the Poles up, and they have let us have it with both barrels. Our own General Wrangel has taken on Denikin's task of continuing the fight against the Bolsheviks. The Poles were almost driven back from Warsaw, but they quickly recovered with French assistance and supplies. They have recently made advances into Russia, and we, in our divided devastation, aren't equipped to combat them successfully."

"My poor Russia! How much more can she bear?"

"I don't know, but let's not talk about such unpleasant things now. It has been so long since I have seen you. Five whole years, Katie."

"Five years! Almost a lifetime. Yet we are not strangers. Isn't that a wonderful thing, Nicki?"

"Time could never dull my heart, love."

Katie blushed and searched his face. *He still loves me.* "Nicki, there's something I must tell you. I have a son now."

Nicki swallowed and then wet his lips. After a moment, he raised his eyebrows. "Do you know where he is?"

"I left him with a woman called Maria Sovinsky near my home. I can give you all the necessary instructions," she said.

"Then I guess we had better start searching for him."

Tears crept into her eyes. "Thank you, Nicki!"

"Is this why you didn't come to me before?"

"How could I, Nicki, when I was carrying another man's child?"

MAY 1920

The war-battered country cottage was small, but though it was only May, already roses were climbing up its walls. As soon as Katie was well enough to travel, Nicki had sent her here to convalesce. It was in a dry section of the country where the air was warm. Nicki had come to see her twice, but he brought no word of her child. *Had Maria moved? Will I ever find Ivan? My arms ache to hold him again. He is twenty-one months old now, and I have missed most of his infancy.*

At the sound of the knock, she flew to the door and threw it open. There they stood, Nicki and her child. She threw her arms around little Ivan and smothered him with kisses. He lifted his dark solemn eyes to hers. "Are you my mother?"

"Yes, my darling. Come in. Come in, both of you."

Katie spent the rest of the day hovering over her long-absent son. It was only when the child was asleep that she turned to Nicki. "I'm afraid that I've neglected you badly today," she said.

"I'm not crushed." His eyes danced mischievously. "I would like to tell you the latest war news, though, while I'm here."

"Of course."

"The Poles have occupied the capital in the Ukraine. However, the Bolsheviks claim they will drive them out of Kiev before the week is out."

"I don't know what to say."

"Let's not dwell on it. I only have a few hours left. It will be some time before I will be able to get back here. There are several pressing missions that I must attend to."

"I worry so over you, Nicki. Do you have to continue your work?"

"No one knows the answer to that better than you do."

Katie laid her head back against the couch. "Yes, I know. You must save others, as you saved me."

He sat down beside her. "It's so good to see you, Katie. You are like medicine to me." He reached over and pressed his lips gently on hers. She returned his kiss, smiling warmly.

"Thank you for everything, Nicki. My life. My child. Had Maria moved?"

"Yes, but we found her through a monk called Yuri."

Katie smiled. "I remember him well."

Maria Sovinsky unfolded the letter and read its contents hastily.

> My dearest sister,
>
> Forgive my long silence as I was in the front line of battle for some time, and now I am lying in a hospital bed. I did not want to alarm you, so I waited until my news was better. I was wounded in a skirmish with the Poles. At first it was feared that amputation of my left leg would be necessary. Fortunately, my limb has been saved. All I will have as a reminder of the wound is a scar on my thigh.
>
> This brings me to the purpose of my letter. I long so to see you again. I wonder if you could come and stay close to the hospital until my release. I applied for a medical discharge from the army, and it has already been approved. As a reward for my services, I have been granted the land adjacent to that which we already own. Our future looks bright.
>
> I am so tired of blood, war, and pain. I long to return to the land, feel the sun tanning my skin and the soil between my fingers again.
>
> I will await your reply anxiously.
>
> Love from your brother,
> Peter

Maria lifted her eyes from the letter and frowned. *I have looked forward to this reunion for so long, but now there are unpleasant factors that might mar it. I will have to tell Peter about Alex Kozakov's return to Usadiba Na Holme. I did not recognize the blind man at first until I saw the scar that proclaimed his identity. For some reason, the Bolsheviks had granted him immunity and the possession of Usadiba Na Holme. No lands. No income. Just a decaying house. He became its blind lord for a while, but alone without any source of income, surrounded on all sides by those who hate him, with starvation staring him in the face, he has been forced to return to his previous haunts, wherever they might have been. His fate seems like poetic justice. The majestic old manor still stands atop its hill, empty and slowly rotting from neglect.*

My most pressing thoughts, though, are of Katie and her child. I can't refuse to answer Peter's questions, and he will ask about Katie. I will have to tell him about her capture by the Cheka and her rescue by Nikolai Sokoloy. Katie is with Sokoloy now, and he loves her with an intensity equal to Peter's own. Nothing could be more disturbing to Peter.

And the child, what of him? The problem returns to plague me often these days. I had no choice but to surrender him to Sokoloy that day. Though I had misgivings, I could not refuse to send little Ivan back to his mother after hearing about her ordeal in the hands of the Cheka. How I miss that little boy, though. Does Peter have the right to know about his son? Can the knowledge do him any good? The chances are that he will never see the boy. Her head ached. *There is no sense in my dwelling on the negative. I am not going to let anything spoil my joy in seeing Peter again. I think I will not mention the child as Katie wished, and I will just let the future take care of itself.*

CHAPTER 30

MAY 1920

Janusy Gorecki staggered, fighting to keep his weary body moving and his eyelids open. The moon had long since disappeared, leaving the night as black as his despair. He had welcomed this patrol behind the enemy lines. He needed a dangerous mission to numb his grief. The letter from his father's old friend had been a shock to him, with the words permanently burned into his memory,

> A gentile destroyed by bad investments in the war sought to lay the blame for his own misjudgment at someone else's feet. As in times past, Jews are always an acceptable scapegoat, so with a group of his friends, he marched into our ghetto to harass those who had prospered. From what started with verbal accusations, a riot soon ensued. In the turmoil, someone set fire to your home. Your father was dragged from the blazing building, but your sister, Marian, was asleep at the time and perished in the fire. We thought at first that your father might live, but his spirit had been drained. His dying words were for you, and I wrote them down.
>
> "Ask Janusy if he thinks that he can still be a Pole. Ask him if he thinks that his children can grow up to be loved, honored, and respected in this country that he chooses to call his own. If Marian's death and my own help to open his eyes, then God's will is known. Janusy, may you be showered with God's blessings always."

Janusy shook his head savagely. He had been wandering about for thirty-six hours. A skirmish with the enemy had surprised his patrol. He had put down his rifle to crawl to a wounded comrade. Gunfire then scattered all those surviving. He cursed when he was not able to get back to his rifle, leaving him only with his officer's pistol. Failing to find any of his comrades, he dodged Russian soldiers, continuing his elusive search for the retreating Polish army. Suddenly, a voice broke into his train of thought. He froze at the sound of the Russian words and held his breath.

"Step forward and identify yourself," barked the Russian voice. Instinctively, Janusy's hand flew to his holster. The Russian shone a light upon him. Janusy's shot echoed in the silent night.

The soldier fell clutching his chest, groaned, and then lay still. Janusy approached him cautiously. The fallen flashlight illuminated the young Russian's face. He lay in a pool of blood soaking through his overcoat. Blood splashed on Janusy's boots as he leaned over to take the soldier's pulse. Dead! Janusy picked up the fallen light, snapped it off, and put it in his pocket.

I am tired of death. Tired of war. Tired of life itself. When this war is over, I will fulfill my father's dream and migrate to the Holy Land. Perhaps I will find the peace there that eludes me here in Europe.

Up ahead he saw a small cottage. *I hope it is empty.* Exhausted, he turned his feet toward the little hut. *I have to find a place to sleep.*

Janusy kicked open the cottage door and then waited a moment. Hearing no sound, he started to enter the dark dwelling, but a feminine voice halted his progress.

"Stay where you are. You make a perfect target in that doorway. Throw your gun forward over here in my direction, and then raise your arms. One false move, and it will be your last."

Janusy hurled his gun toward the voice while straining to see the figure in the blackness. Without the moon's light, the cottage was darker than outside. He raised his arms. The hair on his neck bristled and the tension became unbearable. "Look, I mean you no harm," he explained. "I'm just a soldier lost from his comrades. I only came in here to sleep."

"A likely story," the soft voice said.

"But it's the truth!" Janusy protested while thinking, *How ironic it would be if I have gone through two wars only to be felled in the end by a woman's bullet.* "I mean it," he insisted. "I only want to sleep for a while. Then I will go away." As his eyes became accustomed to the darkness, he saw the form of his adversary in a distant corner. He also saw a cot on the opposite side of the room.

He took a step forward, and her voice warned him. "Stay where you are, or I'll shoot."

"I'll have to take that chance then," Janusy declared. "I can't stay awake any longer." He made his way to the cot and collapsed upon it. Instantly, he was asleep.

At each sound, Maria Sovinsky turned to look at the sleeping soldier. It was almost midday, and still he slumbered on. At first she was tempted to run away, but she feared what might be lurking outside in the darkness more than this solitary Pole. As the day crept on, she grew more relaxed. The man did not look particularly savage, and what's more, she now had his gun.

After studying him for hours, she knew every feature of the man's form. He was long, lean, and muscular, with a strong masculine face covered with a heavy growth of beard. His hair was black but straight rather than curly like her own. The sound of his deep breathing filled the room, and he moaned often.

Toward evening, he gave an abrupt sigh and opened his eyes. He was startled at the sight of her and sat up immediately. Maria tensely leveled his pistol at him. "Stay where you are," she demanded.

"All right," he said, smiling firmly. "I'm not going to argue with you."

Maria stood uncertain before the rugged-looking Pole. She did not know what to do next.

"Very clever," he remarked. "A prisoner of my own gun." Then sensing her agitation, he relaxed and grinned with open amusement. "Well, now that you have me, what are you going to do with me?"

"Just stay where you are, and there will be no problem." Maria said.

"That might do temporarily," he said. "But you can't keep me sitting here forever. You had better decide on your course of action because eventually, you will either get sleepy or it will get dark. Then you will be in trouble."

"That may be, but I am not sleepy now," she said, pressing her finger against the trigger.

"Don't get nervous. The gun might go off accidentally," he cautioned.

"Don't pressure me then."

"All right! Do you mind if I have a cigarette? They are in my shirt pocket."

"Go ahead, but don't try anything."

"Wouldn't think of it," Janusy promised, reaching into the pocket of his shirt and extracting a cigarette. He lit it, leaned back on the cot, and studied the girl before him. A long spell of silence passed. At last, Janusy asked, "Do you mind if I stretch my legs? They feel rather numb."

"All right, but stay on that side of the room."

He nodded and complied with her wishes. Maria's arm now drooped somewhat from the weight of the gun. Janusy observed this and raised his eyebrows questioningly. "You are weakening, fair maiden." She jerked her arm rigid again. He burst into an amused laugh. "Come on now," he said. "You know that you don't really want to shoot me."

"That's true, but I will if you leave me no alternative."

He stood up and started to approach her.

"Stay back," she warned.

He smiled and continued to draw closer.

She hesitated then withdrew a step and then another. "Stay where you are, or I will shoot," she warned.

He stopped and raised an eyebrow. "Then go ahead. It really wouldn't make much difference," he said.

Startled at his words, confusion registered in her face. Arrogantly, he drew closer, and she retreated until her back was against the wall. He reached her, gently removed the gun from her hand, and placed it in his holster. Then grasping her wrists, he pinned her against the wall. "You are so beautiful."

Immediately, he felt desire rise and spread through his body. "It has been such a long time since I have had a woman," he said, leaning down to press his lips against hers. Hungrily, he tried to draw out some response to the passion now flowing though him, but Maria pulled away.

Her face drained of color but reflected no fear. Her dark luminous eyes bore into his. "Are you going to hurt me?" she asked softly.

Confusion washed over Janusy. "And if I tried, would you resist?"

Her voice was quiet and steady. "Yes, but you are stronger than I am."

He scrutinized her face and felt angry to find it so calm. He grabbed her again and forced his mouth roughly upon hers. Her lips felt soft and warm, and his desire grew more intense. He tried to evoke some feeling in her, but her body remained cool and unresponsive. Flushed with frustration, he withdrew his lips but continued to hold her wrists tightly.

"Don't you realize what I intend to do?" he demanded. "Aren't you afraid?"

"I have been raped before," she said, a look of pain crossing her face.

Shame washed over Janusy, yet he could not bring himself to let go "And if I ravished you, would you despise me?" he questioned.

"You would despise yourself," she replied gently.

He bit his lip. "Why do you think so?"

Her eyes smiled, and she tilted her head a little to one side. "One cannot give in to passions that inflict violence on others without inflicting pain and guilt upon one's self."

"The guilt would be but momentary," he assured her.

"For some, perhaps, but not for you," she said. Her voice was tender, and it sent a warm shiver up Janusy's spine. "The pain and torment burning within you can't be erased by adding more shame and humiliation."

"You win, dark lady," Janusy sighed. "If you screamed, scratched, bit, or kicked, it would have made no impression, but I can't take this kind of treatment." He released her wrists and stepped back. Then with a scowl, he removed the gun from his holster and held it out to her. "You had better keep this in case I get out of line again. If I do, use it."

Maria shook her head. "I won't need it."

"Pretty damn sure of yourself, aren't you, pretty lady?"

She shook her head. "No, only of you," she confided. "Are you hungry?"

"Starved."

"Then I had better fix us some dinner," she said. Without another word, she proceeded to prepare a meal from the simple stores stocked in the little cottage.

"I'll go out and get some wood," he offered. A short time later, he returned with an armful of logs. After the meal, Janusy watched Maria move about the cabin, washing and putting away the dishes. "You know," he said. "I don't even know your name."

"Maria."

"Do you live here?" he asked.

"No, but it's a long story as to how I came to be here."

"I would like to hear it," he said. "Come and sit by the fire with me while you tell it."

Maria complied. "My wounded brother sent for me to come and keep him company while he was convalescing in a hospital. When I arrived, your army had broken through the lines. The hospital was not in any immediate danger, but they had begun to evacuate their patients to other hospitals. When I found that my brother had been moved, I insisted on going to him. They tried to convince me not to go," she said, "but I was afraid of missing connections with him."

She looked into his face as she explained. "Our separation has been a long one, and I was overly anxious to see him. Finally, they gave me a soldier as a guide. You can probably figure out the rest. Your forces made a sudden sweep, and I found myself trapped in this no-man's-land. My guide quartered me here while he went to feel out our situation. He never returned. I was here all day yesterday, but I heard nothing but firing in the distance. You know the rest."

"I think I might have killed your guide, Maria."

She looked crestfallen. "He was so young."

"Fortunes of war." He shrugged his shoulders. "But you are a brave girl, Maria."

"I have no other choice," she replied.

"Most women would have panicked in your situation," Janusy remarked. He got up and put another log on the dying fire. New flames sprang to life.

Maria smiled. "You know, I do not know your name."

Janusy's body stiffened, and a dark shadow flashed across his face briefly. "It is Janusy Gorecki."

Maria raised an eyebrow thoughtfully. "Is that a Polish name?"

A tight knot formed in Janusy's stomach. His body tensed, and his eyes blazed with subdued anger. "Yes, but I am also Jewish."

"You sound so defensive about it," Maria said, her eyes softly caressing him.

Janusy exhaled, and he felt some of the tension ease from him. *Why did I fear rejection by this girl? She has the same soft, tender ways as my sister, Marian.* He smiled, and a warm glow crept through him.

"Your name sounds familiar to me, Janusy, Maria said thoughtfully. "Did you, by any chance, once save my brother from some Germans when he was trapped under a tree?"

"What is your brother's name?" he asked.

"Peter Sovinsky."

A flash of recognition crossed Janusy's face. "Of course! I should have seen your resemblance to him. How badly is Peter hurt?"

"They feared that they might have to amputate his leg, but he is going to be all right now."

"I'm glad. Did he ever get over that girl?" he asked. "The one who married someone else?"

"She didn't marry after all, but she is gone now. I am afraid that he will never get over her completely."

"I'm sorry about that. He loved her very much."

"He still does, but let's not talk about that."

Janusy shrugged his broad shoulders. "What do you want to talk about, Maria?"

"You. I knew that there was a reason why I couldn't hurt you. Just imagine if I had killed the man who had saved my brother's life!"

Janusy grinned. "You know that you could never hurt anyone, Maria."

Maria lowered her eyes. This tall dark Pole stirred mysterious emotions in her. "Tell me about yourself, Janusy," she urged.

"What do you want to know?"

Her voice was a mere whisper. "Everything," she said.

And Janusy found that he could talk so easily. He told Maria of his family's murder, the pain tearing at him, and described his dreams for the future. This miraculous girl listened to him with glowing eyes and encouraged him with gentle words to continue. And when his flow of words had ceased, he took her lovely face in his hands, and her name escaped his lips like a primitive cry. "Maria!"

Her smile was tender, and in her face, Janusy saw strength and courage. She was the blinding light of the morning sun that washed away the dark hours of the night. He reached forth like a drowning man to clutch at this vision of hope and life.

And in the warmth of his embrace, Maria found the purpose of her life. A tall quiet stranger had come out of the darkness and in a few short hours had dispelled her fears and captured her heart. She gave herself to him without reservation. In return, she felt her love draw out his anger, hurt, and pain.

Just before dawn, Janusy woke her gently. "I must get you to safety now, Maria. It will be easier before the light is full. When this war is over, I will come back for you, and we will go together to the land of my father's dreams."

Maria nodded her head sleepily. The idea of going to a distant land did not seem strange to her. Nothing would be insurmountable at his side. She had known him but a few short hours, but she had waited a lifetime for him.

"I will wait for you," she promised.

CHAPTER 31

NOVEMBER 1920

Nicki's eyes lingered on Katie's face before falling on the dark-haired boy sitting quietly at her feet. *The child is too serious*, Nicki thought. *His eyes reflect such a solemn disquiet, and a slight smile is the nearest that he ever comes to laughter.* Ivan halfheartedly played with a set of wooden soldiers that Nicki had bought him, but his eyes constantly returned to rest on his mother's face.

"I can scarcely believe that Ivan is already over two years old. These past seven months since you returned him have just flown," Katie remarked.

Nicki smiled. "Happy times always pass swiftly."

"Yes, but the months before seemed like years."

"Try not to dwell on the bad times, Katie," he said. "Look to the future."

"That looks dark too."

"Then you've heard the news of the treaty signed at Riga?" he asked.

"Only that it is not to our territorial advantage."

"That is stating it mildly," he acknowledged. "Several million White Russians and Ukrainians have been taken under Polish rule."

"There seems to be no end to Russia's wounds, Nicki. And what happened to General Wrangel?"

"He is suffering the same destiny as General Denikin. After destroying crops and food over large tracts of our land, he is being forced to retreat into the Crimea and will soon be backed against the sea by the Reds. There he will have to depend upon the mercy of foreign powers to the West for his salvation and hope that they will evacuate his forces to Constantinople."

"Then what, Nicki?"

"Russia's doom! Since the war with Poland has ended, the Bolsheviks have gathered all of their forces and thrown them at us. In two weeks, one week, or perhaps even a couple of days, the civil war will be over, and we will have lost, Katie."

She lowered her eyes to avoid seeing the pain in his. "And what does the future hold, Nicki?"

"God alone knows. All of Russia lies in a state of ruin. She is financially wasted. Morally shattered. There is nothing left but chaos and devastation. That is what I need to talk to you about, Katie," he said with his face locked in grim determination.

"Very well, but I had better get Ivan off to bed first. Pick up your toys, darling, and tell Uncle Nicki good night."

The child gathered up his wooden soldiers methodically and placed them neatly in a box. Standing on tiptoe, he put his arms around his mother's neck and kissed her on the cheek. She kissed him tenderly in return. He then solemnly stretched out his hand to Nicki, who took it within his own large palm. "Good night, Uncle Nicki."

"Good night, Ivan. Sleep well."

Katie took Ivan's hand, and the child followed her from the room.

On her return, Katie apologized. "I'm sorry that I took so long. I always read Ivan a bedtime story." She smiled at Nicki. "Now what is it that you wanted to talk to me about, Nicki? It has been ages since we've had a decent conversation. You are always so pressed for time."

"Not tonight though," he said. He crossed the room, took her hand, and led her to the davenport. He studied her pale face while her blue eyes searched his intently.

"You have something on your mind," she said. "I know that look! You had it on your face the night of the ball when you kissed me for the first time. Do you remember that night?"

"How can I ever forget it? I could not convince you that night that I was serious about you. I wonder if I can convince you now. The night of the ball at Usadiba Na Holme, you were a million miles away, lost in the glamour of the night. Now you are lost in the wonder of your child."

"Why, Nicki, you sound jealous!"

"I am a little. Can you really blame me?"

"Honestly! You know that no one can ever take your place. You've been a part of me from the day that we met. We have shared so many happy times. Do you remember the day that we went on the strawberry hunt with Tanya?' Her face clouded momentarily at the memory of Tanya's fate. Nicki took her hand comfortingly.

"I remember." he said. "I remember every hour that we ever shared, but that's all in the past. Memories are not enough any longer, Katie. I want more than that. I want a future. One with you at my side. Will you give it to me, darling, or is it too late?" His eyes searched her face.

Katie stood up and walked to the window. Avoiding his gaze, she stared out into the frozen night as she spoke. "Years ago, I told you that I was confused and needed time to grow up. Since then, an eternity of time has passed. Yet I find that I am still confused. There has been so much trauma in my life that I no longer know what is right and what is wrong."

"I find that hard to believe."

She laughed nervously and turned to face him. "Why should you? What is the use of planning and aspiring when horror is always waiting around the corner? To give your heart means only that it will be broken. Chances are there is nothing but pain and suffering ahead and the probability that more of one's loved ones will be snatched away. No, Nicki, I don't want to look ahead. I want to live each day for itself. I want nothing more than that."

"But a person can't live like that indefinitely, Katie. The war will end any day now, and with it ends our safety. We will have to flee like common criminals to any country that will take us in and be thankful for the privilege of living on foreign soil."

"Is that what you plan on doing, Nicki? Fleeing?"

"There's no other choice. To stay means a life of continual running and hiding. What kind of life is that? Capture is inevitable, and after that, death. We are entitled to more than that. I have my work cut out for me this coming month, but then I plan to depart. I have already made the arrangements."

"Where will you go?"

"To China first. To America eventually. The United States is a land of opportunity and promise. A man can reap what he sows there."

"You plan to forget Russia?"

"No man ever forgets his native land, Katie. Russia will always be a part of me, but I must be able to be a complete man. I want to work, build, create, and it is no longer possible here, so I will have to go where it is possible."

"Then you have already made your plans?"

"Not entirely. I want you to come with me, Katie. I have booked passage for the three of us on a whaling boat leaving Vladivostok next month."

"I can't leave Russia!"

Nicki shook his head. "You have no other choice, Katie," he explained. "You have been a guest of the Cheka. Stay here, and you will be the same again. Only next time there will be no underground to free you. You will stay until you rot. And what of Ivan? You may not be able to find someone to care for him next time. He will just be left. To what fate, Katie? It is about time that you started being sensible. You don't have to marry me. You can decide about that later, but you do have to get out of Russia. In a few months, such a feat will be impossible."

"I don't like to be told what I have to do, Nicki." Katie bristled angrily "I have managed on my own for a long time now."

"And look where it got you," he pointed out. "Stop being childish."

"I'll do what I please," Katie retorted. "I have no intention of leaving my country." With that, she got up and stalked off to her room.

Nicki knocked on her bedroom door. "Katie!" When she did not answer, his voice rose in volume. "I have to talk to you. We can't let things go like this." He opened her door, entered, shut it, and stood awkwardly with his back against it.

Katie's golden hair hung loosely around her shoulders. The simplicity of her nightgown made her look like a child. "I'm sorry," she said.

He shrugged awkwardly and then strode across the room and pulled her tightly to him. "Katie," he murmured. She looked up, and he pressed his lips softly on her forehead. He tilted her chin upward, and she saw the pain in his green eyes.

"I love you so much, Katie. And I have waited so long." His voice was husky. When she made no reply, he tightened his embrace and pressed his mouth hard upon hers. Without being conscious of it, her body stiffened, and Nicki turned her loose in anger. "Poor, dear Nicki!" he mocked. "I must not hurt his feelings. I owe him so much." He clenched his fist. "Damn you, Katie. Damn you for all these years that you have kept my heart captive without ever telling me that you loved someone else."

"You don't understand, Nicki . . ."

"You don't understand, Nicki," he said, mocking her. "I understand perfectly, Katie. I got the crumbs for faithful servitude while he got it all with no strings attached. I should not have been such a gentleman. Perhaps I should have just taken what I wanted." He shoved her down on the bed and held her forcefully. "Maybe that is where I made my mistake."

"You don't have to treat me this way, Nicki," Katie said with her voice trembling. "I'll not deny you anything."

He studied her grief-stricken face, and humiliation replaced his rage. He laughed scornfully. "I am quite a man!" Then he buried his face against her chest, and she gently ran her fingers through his hair.

"You are quite a man, Nicki," she said. "Everything that any woman could ever dream about. That is why I have never been able to understand myself. I wish we could control our hearts. Tanya loved you, but she was forced to watch you longing for me, while I, in turn, have made a complete mess of my life. There seems to be nothing that I can do about it."

"Why isn't there?" Nicki asked, rolling over on his side and searching her face. "Why can't you let some of my love rub off on you? Perhaps I might even be able to help you forget him." His voice was soft and assured.

"It's not that easy, Nicki," she sighed and closed her eyes. "Circumstances have built a wall around me."

"Then I'll break it down," he said forcefully. His eyes were grave. "But you must promise to be truthful with me."

"I promise."

"Do you still love him?

"Love who?"

"Ivan's father? Nicki asked. "Do you still love Peter Sovinsky?"

Katie eyes widened and her lips trembled. "How could you know that he is Ivan's father?"

"My god, Katie, one look at Ivan leaves little doubt of it."

"I was never aware that you even knew of Peter's existence."

"A man is always aware of his rivals, Katie," Nicki explained. "It was not very difficult to figure out. When we were young and rode through the fields, your eyes always lingered on Sovinsky too long. I was irritated. I could see the obvious attraction. He was tall, strong, and handsome and proud. Still I was confident that his class removed him as any serious competition. Marriage to him was out of the question. I knew that you would never give up your social position and physical comforts, and I had wealth, a name, and everything else that you could ever want. Nothing but a brief love affair could have ever come of your attraction to Sovinsky, and I felt you were too prim and proper for that." He paused. "Were it not for the revolution, I feel certain that I would have won you."

"But we had the revolution, Nicki."

"Yes, and he won you. Not right away, I'm sure. You were too proud and preoccupied with your social status to succumb immediately."

"I was a snob."

He smiled. "And now you don't have to be ashamed of loving him. He has proven himself an intelligent and courageous officer who rose from the bottom of the ranks to a position of respect."

"You don't have to sell him to me, Nicki," she said with tears creeping into her eyes. "I know his positive values, but he's against all the things that I believe in."

"So you denied him your love as you did me?"

"Yes, and he doesn't even know about our child."

"Yet you still love him?"

"I don't know," Katie said, covering her eyes with her hands. "I'm not sure of anything anymore."

"Poor little Katie," he said, as he reached out and stroked her hair gently.

How ironic, Katie thought. *In his time of need, he is consoling me again. Always it has been he who gives and I who takes. Friendship. Devotion. Admiration all these years. He has saved my life. Nursed me back to health. Restored my child to me. He has saved the lives of others. Served this country that we both love so well. And now he has nothing. Not even me. I have retained the shallowness of my youth in spite of all that has happened. Dear, handsome Nicki.*

She closed her eyes and thought of Peter. *I have my memories, and I have Peter's child, but Nicki has nothing.*

"Nicki . . ." she reached up and pulled his face down to hers. His kiss was gentle this time, and she did not freeze. He had loved her for so long.

In the morning, she felt a sense of peace. Nicki's love was a haven in this confused and hate-filled world. *If I marry him, perhaps I can find the happiness that has eluded me for so long.*

Nicki studied her face with tender eyes, and his voice was soft. "You will come with me, Katie?"

"I don't know yet, Nicki," she said. "I need time to think. Just let me love you for these few weeks that we have now."

"I suppose that's the most that I can hope for. I'll go ahead with the arrangements and send someone back with the papers for you and Ivan to travel with. We will meet on the boat five weeks from today."

DECEMBER 1920

Vladivostok was one of the few ports that were ice free during the bitter arctic months. Japanese troops now occupied the city, but they gave no harassment to the fishing and whaling boats plying their trade.

Nicki stood on the deck, staring into the choppy water slapping at the sides of the old whaling schooner. Foaming crests of large waves crashed loudly as they broke around him. His observations were shattered when the captain roared.

"Draw the gangplank!"

Nicki's impatience mounted to terror. *Where is she?* He strained his eyes toward the city, seeking some sign. Frantically, he searched the shoreline again. Then finally, he realized that she was not coming.

The crew raised the gangplank, and slowly the whaling boat sailed out to sea. Pain tore through Nicki, and he clutched the ship's rail until the knuckles of his hand turned white. *I have waited so long. Now all hope is gone.* With a supreme effort, he swallowed hard while continuing to search the slowly disappearing Vladivostok shore.

"Katie," he whispered in anguish to the wind sweeping over the sea, but the golden-haired girl of his youth did not answer. He swallowed hard again in painful resignation. *It was never meant to be.* And so turning away from the vanishing coastline, he walked to the forward deck. There he stared stonily ahead, for it was in that direction that his future lay.

CHAPTER 32

DECEMBER 1920

Holding little Ivan's hand, Katie stood some distance from the Vladivostok docks, staring at the small whaling boat anchored in the harbor. She felt as if her heart were tearing in half.

Nicki's friend had accompanied her and Ivan on the long train trip across the Soviet Union, bringing them safely to Vladivostok. On the journey, her thoughts continually returned to the memory of Nicki's kind gentleness. *Oh, Nicki. I felt so very safe in your embrace. I know you'll always love and protect Ivan and me. Why can't I let myself have this happiness? After all the misery that I have endured, I deserve it.*

Upon arriving in Vladivostok, Nicki's friend bade them good-bye and departed upon some mission of his own.

Now her chest felt tight. Her small son looked up at her, questioning. "Are we going on the boat, Mother?"

It seemed as if clamps were bolted to her feet. *Memories pound upon me . . . the blood of Boris, Sonya, and Uncle Ivan have been spilled and absorbed into the soil of this great, sprawling giant that I love. Russia. Every fiber of my being is Russian. How can I transplant myself and my Russian son somewhere else? The ghosts of all my loved ones wander across this land, calling to me. The roots of the birch and pine forest hold me to this ground.*

She shivered and reached down to pull Ivan's hat lower on his forehead and button the top of his coat. "God, it's cold."

Then the small whaling boat in the harbor began to move out to sea. Agony gripped her, and she cried out, "Nicki!" But the boat soon disappeared, swallowed up beyond the horizon.

Have I made a mistake? Have I foolishly given up love and security for an insane patriotic notion? Well, it is too late now. I will never be able to find Nicki again out there in that great foreign world beyond the horizon.

Ivan tugged at her coat anxiously. "Mother, the boat is gone."

"I know, my love," she said, bending to kiss his cheek. "We are going to stay here after all."

"I miss Uncle Nicki," he said in his serious voice.

"I know, and I miss him too, Ivan. Oh, so very much!"

In this isolated corner of southeastern Russia, Katie felt relatively safe. The peasants were not particularly friendly to her, but no one had turned her over to the Cheka yet.

Katie and Ivan wandered about, searching for a place to stay. She found that one Siberian village was pretty much like another. They tended to be small clusters of dwellings built close together, separated only by narrow dirt streets. Now, in the midst of winter, the streets were hardened with layers of ice, one frozen on top of another.

The living quarters here differed from the thatched huts near Usadiba Na Holme. They were built of wood and often had triple layers of windows to protect the inhabitants from the severe arctic chill.

Katie finally chose a village located on the edge of a great lake that was surrounded on all sides by dense forests. As they walked the snow-packed streets one morning, an old man presented Ivan with a small hand-carved horse. Deeply touched, Katie questioned him and found that he lived alone. His cabin was on the edge of the lake some distance from the village. She convinced him to take them in as boarders.

Nicki had left Katie a fair sum of money for her needs. With her small hoard of cash, she managed to extract bargains from the local peasants who were only too eager to sell a little of their illegally cached surplus.

Stenin, her landlord, was small and stooped from years of bending labor. His face was a mass of wrinkles, but his toothless gums radiated a perpetual smile. He was too old to work now, so he spent his days whittling wood into fascinating works of craftsmanship. His long life of toil meant nothing under the new regime. His food allotment was barely able to sustain him. Yet he never complained.

The child and the old man became friends instantly. Soon, Katie too was included in their circle of friendship.

The peasants no longer had any admiration for the Bolshevik government. They had been anxious to take over their masters' lands. However, when it came time for them to surrender part of their harvest to their unknown city cousins, they rebelled inwardly. They dared not rebel overtly. The Bolshevik collective agents rendered harsh punishment upon anyone holding back surplus crops.

One day, outside their cottage, Katie turned to her landlord. "Stenin, is this strip of land next to the cabin yours?"

"Yes," the old man replied.

"Why is no one farming it?"

"I'm too old, Katie," he said. "And it's so far from the village that no one else is really interested in it."

"Then I shall plant it when the spring comes," she declared. "I should be able to raise enough food to sustain the three of us through the next winter. My money is running out, and we must do something to survive."

"Then you'll be staying awhile," Stenin stated with his toothless smile.

"We have nowhere else to go," she said. "At home, the Cheka lies in wait like a beast of prey."

"And here the air is clean and clear," he pronounced proudly.

"But also cold," she added with a laugh. "Very, very cold."

FEBRUARY 1921

During the cruel Siberian winter months, Katie had devoted herself to Ivan and his education. *There will be little time for him when spring arrives. I must do all the planting myself since Stenin is so old. I am fortunate, though, to have him help me with Ivan's care.*

Katie took long walks whenever the harsh climate permitted it. She always kept to the wooded sections, shying away from the village, fearful that a new Soviet agent might appear and report her to the Cheka.

Today, Ivan had pleaded to stay behind with Stenin. Katie left the two of them together in the warmth of the tiny kitchen.

The sun was shining, and her spirits lifted until suddenly, a wave of nausea hit her. Her stomach churned violently.

She gagged and began to vomit. She continued to retch long after her stomach was empty. She kicked snow over her waste and then leaned exhaustedly against a birch tree. When she regained her strength, she began to walk again. She shivered, and her eyes filled with moisture. *God, it's cold in spite of the sun.*

There is no sense in deluding myself any longer. I am going to have Nicki's child. Nicki's child, and Nicki is gone. Gone forever over the sea to America. "God, why this?" she asked the silent woods. Her lips trembled. Tears froze on her pale cheeks.

"Nicki! Nicki!" she murmured to the wind. She shrugged her frail shoulders in a gesture of hopelessness. "You would be so happy about this child if you knew. But you will never know. You will never see our baby!" She put her hands over her face and wept softly.

She stopped and encircled one of the majestic birches with her arms, laying her face against the icy bark. "All right, Boris. You believed that everything had a purpose," she called out. "Why now this child?"

It seemed as if his voice came out of her from deep inside. "Pray, Katie. All will be revealed."

She fell to her knees and waited. She expected a booming voice to come out of the surrounding wilderness, but nothing happened. She stood up, lifted her arm to the naked branch above, then it came to her in a sweeping revelation.

Nikolai and Peter! Both strong and courageous. Both ready to die for what they believed in. The backbone of my Russia. They are the two halves of the great nation, but this great nation has now been divided. Nicki is now lost to Russia. But is it not fitting that the firstborn child of each should be raised together as brothers? Siblings joined together by the common blood flowing in their veins. United by the love of the same mother.

It is so simple. I'll never lose either Nicki or Peter for I have a part of each of them forever. I and their children can unite this new generation. Unite it so that this torn and bleeding Russia will emerge from her chaos to once again be powerful and heroic. She felt a surge of joy flow through her.

JULY 1921

The sweat dripped from Peter's body as he stood up straight to survey his fields of golden wheat. They were beautiful. He had labored since dawn. Now the sun was directly overhead. His neck was burned, and his body ached with fatigue. He decided to seek refuge in the shade.

He walked to the edge of his fields and sat down under the branches of a large tree. He opened his lunch and began to eat a heel of heavy black bread. He closed his eyes momentarily to rest them from the glare of the sun.

He opened them again when he heard something in the midst of the tall grain. Suddenly, he saw a hoard of the *bezprizorni* children rushing toward him, a pack of lost homeless orphans from the war years. Starvation had made predatory beasts of them. They swept across the land like packs of vicious wolves. They robbed, murdered, and destroyed everything in their path. The peasants viewed them with a mixture of pity and terror.

Peter barely staggered to his feet before they were upon him. He thrashed at them, and his fierce struggle arrested their attack momentarily. They drew back and eyed him warily. Their half-naked bodies were filthy and covered with festering sores. They bared their rotten fangs and snarled at him.

Peter moved his hand toward his lunch. Instantly the pack stirred. With a quick movement, he flung the food into their midst. The hoard sprang into action, snarling and tearing at each other, fighting like savage beasts to get a crumb. Amongst the mass of tangled hair and intertwined bodies emerged hacking tubercular coughs mixed with savage, primitive screams.

After a battle, the group drew apart and turned back toward him. Seeing that his hands were empty and there was no more food in sight, one of the older children grunted an indistinct order. Following their leader, the others ambled off behind him.

Peter wiped the sweat from his brow. He gave a sigh of relief. Others had not been so fortunate as he.

He scanned the area before starting back to the field in which he had been working. He almost stumbled over the child lying there so quietly. The boy was helpless. Too feeble to move. His large blue eyes reflected a mixture of fright and distrust. Peter knelt beside the child and touched his shoulder gently. The child pulled away in terror.

"There, there, boy! I am not going to hurt you," he said softly.

The boy whimpered like a puppy in pain. Peter sought to reassure him with gentle words and then reached down and tried to pick him up. The boy tried to crawl away, but Peter grasped him firmly by the ankle.

As they sat drinking tea, Peter's neighbor Dmitri shook his head. "What a horrible experience! What were they like?"

"Contaminated creatures from which human instincts seemed to have completely vanished," Peter lamented. "Children reduced to mere skeletons—the ultimate ravages of our time."

"God, I'm glad that my Cecila didn't meet up with them," Dmitri sighed. "Were they sickly?"

"A doctor's handbook," Peter recounted. "In their faces, you could see the yellow of jaundice, the whiteness of anemia, and the pink flush of cholera and typhus. Pink eyes peered out of puffy faces attached to swollen lacerated bodies bobbing above rickety legs. These pathetic children are the ultimate living proof of man's will to survive."

"Well, some peasants have formed hunting parties to exterminate these packs," Dmitri said.

"I know. The government has tried to round them up and put them in camps, but they have had little success. The *bezprizorni* are cunning and craftily elude their traps."

"Hopefully, they will eventually die off," Dmitri stated.

"But heaven help those in their path until such a time," Peter replied.

"Well, now that you've got this one, what in God's name are you going to do with him?" asked Dmitiri.

"Keep him, what else?" Peter answered.

"Are you crazy?" implored his neighbor.

"Of course not. I haven't labored over him all these days for nothing."

"You are crazy!" Dmitri exclaimed.

"Now, now, Dmitri. Calm down."

"But he's as wild as a lion."

"Lions can be tamed."

"It seems all we want is trouble these days. We don't have enough, but you've got to ask for more. Ha!"

"But look at him, Dmitri."

The child did look angelic. His face had been scrubbed and seemed to shine as he lay sleeping. His pleasing facial features were topped by a crown of golden curls. His dark lashes contrasted vividly against his pale cheeks. "You can't deny that he's a handsome child," Peter proclaimed proudly.

"He looks all right, sure. All you need now is a cage to hold him. Tell me, what on earth do you want him for?" Dmitri asked.

"I'm going to adopt him. Make him my son," Peter told him.

Dmitri threw up his hands in horror. "You want a son? Then why don't you marry my Cecila and have one of your own?"

Peter's face flushed, and he turned away from Dmitri's penetrating gaze. Cecila had grown into a beautiful girl. Though young, she already had the body of a grown woman. He had considered the idea. Cecila was a wonderful cook, an excellent housekeeper, and she had worshiped Peter since she was a child. He could do worse. Yet something always kept him from committing himself. Now he felt embarrassed at Dmitri's direct question.

"You don't like my Cecila?" Dmitri asked.

"You know that's not it, Dmitri. I'm just not ready to get married," Peter said.

"You ever going to get ready? You're not sixteen, eh? You're a pretty big man!"

After Dmitri left, Peter went and stood over the boy again. *How could I tell Dmitri or anyone else what I feel for this boy? He could have been my own son.*

If Katie and I had married that summer when I first declared my love for her, we might have had a child about six years old. He might have had the same blond hair, fair skin, and sky blue eyes like my Katie. It is such a coincidence.

I've been so lonely since Maria married Janusy at the end of the war and immigrated to the Holy Land. Their letters come regularly, and I am content to know that they are happy in their adopted country, but letters are no substitute for Maria's presence, and she probably will never be coming home again. And Katie! If only I could forget her, but she continues to haunt me. Maria said she went away with Sokoloy. They are probably married now. The thought served to prick him anew, and a look of pain crossed his face.

The boy woke and reached out his hand. Timidly, he laid it on Peter's arm.

Startled, Peter looked down. Then a warm smile stretched across his face. Such a tiny gesture. Yet a fierce glow crept through Peter. *This was a start.*

Peter's voice filled with emotion when he spoke. "My name is Peter Sovinsky. What is your name?"

"Name?" the boy asked.

"Yes, your name," Peter said as he touched the child's chest.

"Name Vladimir."

Peter's breath caught in his throat. *It is too much of a coincidence! Could it be possible?*

The boy waited expectantly. His face was tense and uncertain. Peter gained control of himself and spoke softly. "My name is Peter Sovinsky. Your name is Vladimir Sovinsky now. Do you understand?"

The boy lay quiet for a long time and seemed to be digesting the words. Then a smile spread across his face, and tears escaped to fall on his pale cheeks. Peter reached out and took him within his arms, and the boy wrapped his own frail arms around Peter's neck and clung tightly. Somewhere from the past, an emotion came to life again. The ragged waif hung on to this strange man in a desperate effort to return from the animalistic world in which he had lived for so long. Peter felt the fierce pounding of the boy's heart. In that moment, a bond was formed.

CHAPTER 33

AUGUST 1921

Katie walked over the sterile fields, languishing beneath the scorching sun. Shriveled crops lay parched on the heat-cracked earth. A surrealistic yellow world stretched in all directions with a blazing yellow sky hanging over this dull-sulfured landscape. Never before had such an unusual drought hit this part of the country.

"My poor Russia," Katie sighed, wandering across her burned-up field. "Everything has failed you. How long can we, your people, survive under such conditions?"

She walked, searching the ground for anything that might be eatable. All the cattle in the area had long since been slaughtered. Then the people had turned to horses, dogs, and cats. She had been squeamish at first, but hunger eventually cured her nausea. Now meat of any kind was a delicacy. Spotting no roots, she stripped the remains of bark from a sagging tree. *I'll brew a soup or tea from it. All the grass has long since been eaten. There is nothing left.*

Reluctantly, she returned to her cottage. Stenin sat in front of the little house. Katie knew that he couldn't last much longer. It was an effort for him to speak, and his voice was feeble and cracked. "Find anything?"

"Only a little tree bark," she answered. "What are we going to do, Stenin?"

"There are some chewing leather. Others use clay to stop their stomach pains."

"But that is only warding off hunger, Stenin. It can't prevent starvation."

"I heard tell some have been robbing the graveyard."

"Why that's cannibalism," Katie gasped.

"Times are bad," he said simply.

"Bad times! Yes, and they never end. We are drained, Stenin. Finished. This famine will eliminate us from the face of the earth. How much can human beings take? How often can we be smitten and stagger back to our feet, only to be felled again? We have had seven years of war, and seventeen million men, women, and children have died." Wearily, she sat down beside him.

"It'll be better next year, Katie."

"How can it be? Most of our horses were destroyed during the war. Those left have been eaten. Our railroads have been damaged. Our money is worthless. The farmers have been cheated so badly that they refuse to grow more than what they need for their own use. No plows have been made. Only guns. Oh, Stenin!" She broke down in tears.

The old man wrapped his arms about Katie. She pointed to the wasted landscape. "There was nothing in this land but what we could pull out of the earth with our own sweat. Now even the earth refuses to yield. We've been reduced to eating the soil itself and every form of filth on it. Whole villages of men have sat down in their homes to die. God! Now it seems there is but one last choice—to dig in the graveyards or perish!"

"There are goods in other countries, Katie. Maybe they will help us."

"How can it reach us, Stenin? There are no transportation lines open. And why should anyone help us. They spent millions of dollars in military operations against the Bolsheviks. Why would they contribute to us now? It would only strengthen what they want to destroy."

"You are overwrought, child."

"Oh, I suppose you are right. Perhaps I will go out and look again."

"Do you feel strong enough?"

"We do what we must," she said.

The labor pains came upon Katie quickly. She sat down a moment to rest. *I'll never be able to make it back to the cottage to bear my baby.* She was seized with panic. *I felt this same terror when I found myself alone with Tanya. When Ivan was born, Boris was with me. Now there is no one.* She stood up and started to walk, but the force of the pains doubled her over in agony. *The baby is ready to be born. I have no choice but to deliver it myself.*

I feel like an animal . . . forced to deliver in the wild. She found a hollow gully and glanced about for something that she could used to sever her umbilical cord. There was nothing close by but a sharp stone. She picked it up and then lay down to await her child's coming. The birth was swift. Afterward, she hacked through the connecting tissue and tied the newborn's umbilical cord into a knot. She pulled the baby up into her arms, and then blackness swept over her.

It was night when she awoke. The infant was crying. She wrapped her skirt around the baby and put it to her breast, praying that she would have milk. It was a long time before she could gather enough strength to get to her feet and start for home.

Stenin and Ivan were waiting for her. Their faces clouded in alarm.

"Mother, are you all right?" Ivan asked anxiously.

"Yes, son."

Stenin stretched out his gnarled hands for the infant. "What is it?" he asked.

Dismay filled Katie's face. "I don't even know," she admitted. Anxiously, she laid the baby down on her cot and unwrapped the skirt covering it. "It's a boy! Ivan, you have a little brother," she shouted joyously.

Ivan studied the baby critically. "He's so small, Mother," he said, shaking his head.

"Yes, he is," she agreed.

The infant was tiny, but a heavy crop of chestnut hair was atop his pinched face. Katie felt a flush of pride. He was a handsome child.

"He'll fill out all right," offered Stenin comfortingly.

"Let us hope so, Stenin. I am going to call him Nikolai."

"Can I hold him, Mother?" Ivan pleaded, his small white face filled with desperate longing to share in this exciting event.

Katie put the baby in her three-year-old son's arms, and the sight of the curly dark hair against the chestnut locks made her eyes brim with tears. Her heart pounded, and she slid weakly to her knees beside her sons. "Everything is going to be all right," she told Ivan.

NOVEMBER 1921

"I can't believe that you really mean to try this. You will never make it, Katie. Already the blizzards are upon us. Such a trip is madness," Stenin insisted.

"Little Nicki is already three months old," she pointed out. "To stay here means certain starvation. We have slaughtered all the wild birds and animals in the area. Torn everything possible from the ground. Nuts and berries from trees and bushes. Even their bark and leaves. We have even eaten the seeds for next year's planting. There is nothing left here but the endless bodies in the graveyard. Perhaps we will meet death on our journey, but at least we will be on our way home."

"Ah, Katie! Why?"

"I want my sons to see the places of my childhood and the countryside that their fathers loved."

"But they are too young to understand the meaning of such things."

"Stenin, I feel that if I do not go now, I will never make it."

"Supposing that you do survive the journey, Katie? What will happen when you get there? Do you have friends? A place to go? Will you be safe from the Cheka?"

"I doubt the Cheka has any interest in me now that Nicki is gone. They would scarcely expect me to return home. They probably think I have already fled the country. Besides, the purge has died down, and I'm just as apt to be found here as there. As for a place to go, I have none, but I will find one, just as I did here.

Stenin sighed. "Such a homing instinct must be in your blood."

Katie smiled whimsically. "I suppose it is," she agreed. "Will you come with us?"

"No, child. I could never survive such a long trip. So many miles. This land is in my bones, as much as the other is in yours."

"But you will starve here."

"Perhaps, but I am an old man. Besides, it is rumored that the Americans have organized relief. Maybe it will come soon."

"I'll finish packing then. I plan to leave in the morning."

"I will miss you and the little ones, but I'll pray that you will have a safe journey."

Katie pulled on the sleeve of the tall strapping officer in charge of loading the train. "Please, sir, could you help us?" The soldier startled at the unexpected voice and turned to look at the slim woman standing there. She was holding an infant in one arm and clinging to a small boy with her other hand.

"What appears to be the trouble?" he asked.

"I don't know what to do," she explained. "Someone has stolen my papers, and I am completely helpless."

The frightened look on the young woman's face softened the hard-crusted war veteran's armor. "Perhaps you had better tell me about it."

"I don't know where to begin," she explained. Katie's teeth chattered, and a series of chills gripped her.

Alarmed at her weakened state, the soldier grabbed her arm. "You had better come inside the station where it is warm."

Manufacturing the proper amount of tears, Katie poured out her fabricated story. "My husband was a commissioner in the provinces. He didn't ask to be sent there, but he felt an obligation to go where he was needed. He poured his heart into his job. You don't know what he suffered. The peasants wouldn't give up their grain. He just couldn't make them understand that the people in the cities were starving. Then the drought came . . ." Katie stopped her tale and released a new flood of tears.

"There, there . . ." comforted the big soldier awkwardly.

Katie sniffed and choked for several moments before continuing. "When the crops failed, the peasants turned vicious. When my husband made his rounds, they stoned him. You can't imagine what it was like. Then one day, a mob caught and tied him and proceeded to—" She stopped as if the memory was too horrible.

She had witnessed such a scene and had been plagued by guilt since. Fearing to call attention to herself, she had made no effort to help the man. Katie's face turned pale, and she trembled violently. She could only whisper the words. "They buried him alive!"

The soldier felt rage boiling within but suppressed his emotion. He had seen more than his share of horror during the war, but it still went on. This beautiful woman and her two small children pulled at his heartstrings.

"I made reservations to go home to my parents," Katie continued with her carefully woven tale, "but at the last stop, when I got off the train to get some fresh air, someone snatched my bag and ran. The authorities would not let me back on the train. They said that they would have to check but that it would take time. Lots of time! I didn't want to stay in that wretched little station, so I started out on foot."

"That was rather fool-hardy in this weather," admonished the soldier.

"I know that now," she admitted.

The soldier cleared his throat in embarrassment as the innocent-looking eyes continued to search his face. "I guess I can put you on this train," he said. "It only goes fifty miles, but perhaps you can get your papers straightened out at the next check point. At least there are better facilities there."

"How can I ever thank you?"

The officer flushed at her display of gratitude. "Don't mention it," he growled. He took her outside and installed her in a warm boxcar. Soon the train wheels began to turn in slow motion. As they gathered speed, Katie smiled to herself. "Well, my little ones. We are starting our journey with a trail of deceit. But even if I must become a great actress en route, I will do whatever it takes. We are going home! We are going home!"

And the wheels seemed to take up the chant. *We are going home! We are going home!*

MAY 1922

Katie stood in the midst of the tumbled ruins of the monastery. Vegetation ran wild over the once neat and orderly paths. The beautifully cultivated gardens were now a jungle of malignant tares. The tangled mass of overgrowth almost covered the rotting monastery walls. The wall around the sacred well had crumbled. It was obvious that the monks had not been permitted to return.

With a heavy heart, Katie left the monastic grounds and made her way to the nearest hamlet. It was risky to ask for information, but she approached an elderly woman. "Please, can you tell me if any of the monks are still living in this area?'

The old woman studied her before her sharp voice expressed her uncertainty. "Why do you want to know?"

"I am searching for a friend who promised to baptize my baby."

The woman looked around cautiously before speaking. "Some still live in the caves. It is against the law to harbor them."

"Would you know where the one called Yuri lives?"

"I would. He lives with two of his brothers close by."

"Could you tell me how to get there?"

"I can," she replied, giving Katie the directions.

The day was warm for the month of May. It was dusk before they reached the cave. The sun seemed to be hanging tiredly in the sky, reluctant to sink below the horizon. Katie's eyes searched the dark interior of the cave, but she could see nothing.

"Yuri?" she called.

Yuri stopped his activity at the sound of the familiar voice. "Who's there?" he called back.

"Katrina Kazakinova."

Yuri caught his breath and rushed to stand speechless before the thin girl at the mouth of the cave.

"Aren't you going to invite us in" she asked, smiling.

"Forgive me, my child," he said. "You gave me such a shock."

After dinner, Katie wrapped blankets around the children and put them to sleep close beside the fire. She then related all the adventures that had taken place since she had last seen Yuri. He shook his head in amazement. "It is a miracle that you have survived, child. How did you get here?"

"I begged rides whenever I could. I rode trains, wagons, sleds, and walked when there was no other way. It has taken me six months to cross this continent," she told him.

"Thank God that you made it. But you and the children are nothing but shadows. We are going to have to nurse you back to health again."

She laughed contentedly. "And you, Yuri? How has life been for you? Your clothes are threadbare."

"Yes, and our food is bad, but we are no worse off than millions of others. We make a little money by selling candles. The old ones are still loyal to their religion. The Bolsheviks have emptied and desecrated our churches, but the grandmothers keep our faith alive. Someday we will rise again."

"I can't understand why the Communists fear you so. They have all the power."

"They know a religious man can never be a good Communist. Religion would confuse and weaken their followers. We appeal to our people to resist these tyrants, so they must eliminate our religion if they are to survive. They tried to crush us at first with extreme brutality, but that did not work. So now they are trying to eliminate us by reducing us to extreme poverty and starvation. But we continue to cling to life."

"Maybe they will give up eventually."

"No, Katie. The persecution continues, but it is quieter now. They have stopped all religious works from being published. They have bombarded the public with propaganda against us. They shout that science disproves religion. Children of priests are denied higher education. Heavier taxes are levied upon us even though all our valuables were seized long ago. They are fighting us with every means available, but we are fighting back. Someday we will win. Someday the churches in Russia will open again, and that will be proclamation enough to the whole world that man's love for God will always triumph."

"I believe you, Yuri. Let us pray that we will live to see that day," Katie said.

CHAPTER 34

JUNE 1922

The small boy swung his slender shoulders, imitating the bold stride of the big man walking in front of him. Peter turned to look at the boy, noting the worship shining in his pale blue eyes. "You're turning out to be quite a farmer, Vladimir," Peter said with a gentle smile.

The boy beamed happily. His small face flushed at the compliment. "I want to be a good one, just like you."

Peter smiled again. The change that had taken place since he had found the boy eleven months ago was miraculous. He had been amply rewarded for the grueling hours that he had spent educating this child back to the ways of civilization. He took the boy's hand, and the two of them walked side by side. "Now that today's lessons are over, we had better get back to work."

"I guess we'd better," Vladimir grinned. "These crops are not going to grow by themselves."

The odor of Cecila's cooking tantalized Peter's nostrils long before he reached the Gogols' cottage. He remembered how good it was to have a woman in the house. In answer to his call, Dmitri swung the door open. And Peter saw Cecila laboring over the blazing hearth.

"Hungry, Peter?" she called.

"Starved," he admitted. "I have saved my appetite all day so that you could satisfy it."

She laughed happily. "I'll have dinner ready in a few minutes. Did you get Vladimir fed?"

"Yes."

"Don't you worry about leaving him alone?" Cecila asked.

"No," Peter replied. "He was alone a good part of his life and is used to it."

"What will he do while you are gone?" Cecila inquired.

"I left him with his lessons. He has so much to catch up on."

"He's an apt pupil," she remarked.

"That he is," Peter said, and he grinned with pride.

"Even I have to admit to it," added Dmitri grudgingly. "Whoever would have thought it?"

"Peter foresaw it," Cecila said teasingly. "He's absolutely psychic."

"Don't talk nonsense, Cecila," Peter admonished.

"Better be nice to me, Peter," she laughed. "Especially if you want dinner tonight."

Peter smiled and turned to Dmitri. "Who else is coming tonight?"

"Six men from the next village."

Cecila dished up three bowls of cabbage soup and served them with side dishes of salted cucumbers. In the center of the table, she set a plate of thick slices of black rye bread.

The men ate ravenously and then pushed their dishes aside and leisurely lit up cigarettes. Inhaling deeply, they sighed with contentment. Peter watched Cecila while she ate, and a pleasant silence descended upon the room. After she had finished her dinner, Cecila cleared the dishes off the table and then retired to a corner where she took up some mending. A short time later, the men from the next village arrived to join Peter and Dmitri around the huge wooden table.

A burly fellow was the first to speak out. "How goes it with this village?" he asked huskily.

"I think conditions are pretty much the same everywhere, Simon," Peter answered.

"Stinks in other words, eh?

"Ah, it's not that bad," injected Dmitri. "At least we get money for our surplus grain now."

"True," Simon agreed reluctantly.

"But, Dmitri, the money really hasn't much purchasing power," Peter reminded him. "Grain prices are fixed, and there are very few goods for sale. With this inflation, you need an excessive amount of cash to purchase even those few items that are available."

"What went wrong, Sovinsky?" a small man with a quiet voice asked. "We were so sure that we were right when we fought this revolution. It hasn't turned out like we expected though."

"Things seldom do," Peter said with a frown. "We have made so many mistakes, Felix. The first was letting hatred rule our heads. The murder of our professionals was a tragedy. It will take more than a decade to make up for that error."

"He's right," injected another. "But that's not the major reason for our troubles."

"No," amended Peter. "We lacked foresight. We failed to see that when our theory was put into practice, it would stifle motivation. When all men receive the same rewards, no one strains to give his maximum effort. The incentive is not there."

The men sat silent for a few moments, and then Dmitri spoke. "We're been working under a handicap from the beginning. People everywhere are filled with so much hostility."

"Can we blame them?" asked Peter. "Their bellies are caving in from hunger. The city folk have had to flee to the country in search of food. The factories have no leaders, so the workers are leaving. We promised the people the same possessions as the elite, and we failed to make good on our vows. The people have little more than before, and hunger and poverty still prevail."

"We were not wise enough to temper those at the top," Peter admitted. "The Cheka has been a vengeful sword slaying friend and foe alike. They'd rather eliminate a hundred innocent than let a single guilty person escape. Russia has become a landscape of graves. Enough of our people's blood has been spilled to fill a river. Our dream of a better world has been crushed beneath an avalanche of fear and destruction."

The quiet man drummed his fingers nervously on the table. Another man spoke for the first time. "At least we no longer have free-loaders and parasites. Our labor force is working everyone from sixteen to sixty. Those that don't work don't eat."

"Yes," agreed Dmitri, "but we are producing less."

"But at least we are raising our own food rather than someone else's," the man countered.

"But our government is distributing it," injected Simon. "This isn't the freedom that we fought for."

Peter raised his hand. "Comrades, let's not dwell only on our failures. Lenin has proposed that we be given the freedom to dispose of our surplus through private transactions. Reintroducing this policy of partial capitalism is at least a step forward. It will help our sagging economy. Industry will be able to reorganize, and production should soar. There will be goods to buy. This should improve the morale of our countrymen."

Dmitri grunted. "I wouldn't mind owning some new farming tools."

"Aye, and you're not the only one, Gogol."

"We all have our hopes for the future," Peter said. "If we could only end the famine! Five million people are already dead, and thirty-three million more are said to be in the process of starving."

"What a hell of a time to live!" Simon spat.

The quiet man spoke hesitantly. "America has offered to distribute food to our stricken. Their relief could be our salvation."

"Yes," Peter agreed. "It's a humane offer, especially since they despise our form of government. It's more than England or any of the other countries have offered. Still, charity hurts! We can be thankful, though, that our crops will multiply this year. By next year, we should be on our feet again."

One of the peasants who had remained silent now spoke. "I question this new economic policy. We fought to abolish capitalism. Now you say that it is necessary to bring it back. That doesn't make sense."

"It is a compromise," explained Peter. "The idea of pure communism has failed. The government is restoring small plants to private control now, with the hope that a competitive spirit will raise production."

"They hope?" one man questioned.

"They hope!" Peter echoed. "We no longer have trained professionals. We are a mass of ignorant peasants struggling to overcome the hatred of the whole world. We have made mistakes. We will make more. But we are learning."

"The lessons come hard," Dmitri injected.

"Yes, and painfully," Peter added. "It is fortunate that we have strong backs."

A heavyset farmer with cracked hands shook his head. "What have we really accomplished, Peter? Was our fight worth it?"

"I think so. Our people are still threadbare and hungry, but our children are going to school for the first time. We all have our own land that we can work as we please. Though we are short of doctors and teachers, the humble have as much chance as the rich and powerful to obtain their services. We have broken down the barriers! Our new regime is only a crude framework, but we can build from it. Someday we will be the first in everything. Perhaps not in our generation. But someday! For now, we must concentrate on educating our people and eliminating the reign of terror that is holding them down. If we can join our masses together in brotherhood, then we will not have failed!"

Simon blew out a cloud of smoke then pounded his fist on the table. "You have said a mouthful, Sovinsky! Better that we all stop bellyaching and pitch in to help. I am sending my boy to that new school next week!"

The air was brisk, and Peter enjoyed the walk home. His stomach was full of good food. His sprits had risen from the evening's stimulating talk. He pushed his hands into his pockets and whistled a cheerful tune as he ambled along.

It was not until Peter reached his cottage that his spirits sagged. It was dark. The small hut looked desolate. *It is strange how different things look at night.*

This morning I stood before this cottage with a feeling of pride at all I have accomplished since my return home. I threw all my energy into improving it. I tore off the thatched roof and replaced it with one of sturdy wood. I fashioned a huge center beam running across the ceiling inside that gives the main room a spacious look. In back on the left, I added a large bedroom and furnished it quite elaborately. My most precious possession is a huge hand-carved four-poster bed that I purchased with a portion of my army savings.

When I adopted Vladimir, I added another small room on the right side of my cottage. I purchased a chest to hold Vladimir's scant belongings. I could never bring myself to part with the cots that I, Father, and Maria used for so many years, so I placed all of them in the new room. I hope Maria and Janusy might come for a visit someday, although with the distance involved, I know that it is not likely. I am proud of my house and land. It is what I wanted all my life. Yet tonight, standing before it, I feel lonely.

He entered the cottage, lit a candle, and then quietly tiptoed into the boy's room and looked down upon him sleeping. He pulled the covers over the slumbering child and smiled. He was contented that he had Vladimir.

He entered his bedroom and sat on the edge of his bed, dreading the sleepless hours that he knew lay before him. He undressed, blew out the candle, and crawled beneath the covers. As always, a thousand thoughts seemed to crowd into his head. Memories flashed by of happy times, tragic times, ordinary times, and always they ended with the same face before him. Katie! He stretched out in an effort to relieve the tension mounting within him. Then with resignation, he rolled over on his stomach and pressed his throbbing body against the hard mattress. *Always my nights are bad. Always the same longings return. Will my desire for you, Katie, never end? Why can't I feel this way about another woman?*

He pounded his fists savagely against the pillows. "Katie, Katie!" he moaned. "I need you so." His body was rigid like steel. "All I ever really wanted was you."

Tears came into his eyes. "The tragedy is that I could have had you, but I sent you away because of my arrogance. I was such a fool! You loved your God and wanted him to sanction our love. But no, I wouldn't share you. I recall my words to you. 'I am a Soviet soldier and a godless man. It is not likely that you will ever change me.' But you have changed me, Katie. I realize that now." He sat up in bed, trembling with emotion.

"Everything good has come from my love for you. This home! Vladimir, whom I first wanted because he reminded me of you."

He climbed out of his bed and started to pace the room. *My values were wrong. I held a false set of beliefs. I didn't foresee the violence and injustice that emerged as end products.*

I tried to deny you your religion, Katie, while embracing my own. Communism. I denied you your God while embracing my own. Lenin. I wanted to rid Russia of the tyrannical Ivans and the cruel Alexes, but the Cheka stepped in to replace them. It was my Bolsheviks who murdered my friend Vladimir and almost killed you, my beautiful, innocent Katie.

I have the land that I always wanted, but it is a hollow victory. Too many people have suffered and died. Vladimir told me that every man has a right to be judged on his own merits, but I refused to listen to him. I was too obsessed with the importance of my own ideas.

Stubborn pride and selfish disdain have been my crimes. They have cost me dearly. I wonder if it is possible for me at this late date to put on a robe of humility like one of your beloved monks, Katie. I see where peace lies. If only I can reach it . . .

AUGUST 1922

"We really can't stay any longer, Yuri," Katie insisted. "We've been here three months already. We can no longer impose upon your generosity since the children and I have regained our health."

"You know you will always be welcomed here, my child," the monk replied.

"I know that, Yuri, but it's neither fitting, nor proper for us to continue taking food from your mouths. The time has come for us to venture out into the world again and find a place for ourselves. Little Nicki is a year old already."

"It isn't safe," he replied. "Where will you go?"

"We can't hide forever, Yuri," she explained. "We'll find a place, but I want to go home first."

"Usadiba Na Holme is empty and falling apart. You cannot live there, Katrina."

"I know that also," she said. "It would not be safe anyway, but I just long to see it again."

"Your mind is made up?" Yuri asked.

"I'm afraid that it is."

Yuri shrugged his shoulders and gave a loud sigh of resignation.

CHAPTER 35

AUGUST 1922

The enormous barn was jammed with peasants and the smell of unwashed bodies. Party members from all over the district had trekked here to hear the hysterical words now pouring forth from the huge beefy-faced leader.

"There can be no co-existence with the capitalistic swine. Our fight here has been victorious thus far. We can't stop now, or all that we have fought for will be lost. We must continue to stretch out our arms until we enfold the entire world. We are but the roots of a gigantic tree just beginning to grow. We must reach to bring all our brothers under our branches."

"By what means do you plan to accomplish this, comrade?" Peter asked.

"By any means necessary! Our victory isn't complete until the whole universe has been conquered. We have many methods of persuasion."

"Shouldn't we just be satisfied with throwing off our own shackles?" Peter demanded. "Perhaps the rest of the world is content to stay as they are. Why should we force our system on them?"

"I find your words most disturbing, comrade. It is our duty to free those less fortunate. We are a chosen people. We must dedicate ourselves to this task!"

Someone in the audience shouted, "But that will mean more war. We fought to end war."

The party official's voice dripped venom. "Cowards do not belong in this party, comrade."

"It seems to me," ventured Peter, "that you think we are on an endless conveyor belt. If we stop or take a step back, we are lost. This is not a rational outlook, comrade. You want to spread Communism like a malignancy. The Christian and Islamic religions claimed coexistence was impossible, but after two thousand years, both are still here."

"What is your point?" bristled the red-faced official.

"That it doesn't necessarily follow that the rest of the world is trying to eat us up. They will leave us alone if we leave them alone."

"Do you really believe that?" the man asked in an outraged voice.

"I want to," Peter said. "I am tired of fighting. Tired of hating."

The man's face was dripping with sweat. Dmitri put a restraining hand upon Peter's arm. "Don't go too far, Peter," he cautioned in a whisper. "It will do you no good to argue with someone like him. Let it drop."

Peter shut his mouth but brooded during the rest of the obese man's speech. *Communism has brought some good things to my people, but something went wrong. The party has become too powerful. Now it is a violent and ruthless dictator. Merciless. Unrelenting. Destructive to any obstacle in its path. Marxism sounded beautiful, logical, and just, but the classless society that we struggled so hard to obtain has formed a new hierarchy consisting of party officials, party members, workers, and the bourgeoisie. The ruling proletariat still does not exist. We peasants merely exchanged a landlord for a commissar. For every success the party has had, we have also chalked up two failures.*

* * *

Katie stood staring at the pathetic shell of Usadiba Na Holme. The windows were smashed. Peeling paint hung loose on its decaying walls. Parts of it were burned to the ground while the remaining walls stood charred. The roof sagged drastically. The once beautiful Usadiba Na Holme was nothing but a crumbling ruin.

"It's awfully old and ugly, Mother," whispered little Ivan.

A shiver traveled across the base of Katie's spine. The young were not dulled in their perceptions by rose-colored glasses. "Yes, it looks that way now, son, and gloom hangs over it like a black mourning veil, but once it was so very beautiful. There were crystal chandeliers, beautiful paintings, and fine tapestries on the walls and magnificent rugs on the floors. There were grand balls where ladies wore lovely gowns and jewels while musicians played stirring music to which everyone danced."

"I never saw anything like that, Mother," Ivan said with his eyes widening.

"I know," she replied. "And I don't suppose that you ever will," she sighed. "In that dark ruin, I can still see my huge roaring uncle whom you were named for. He was powerful, domineering, and had an atrocious temper, but I still loved him. I remember his laughing face as he swung me up in his enormous arms." She turned to look at little Ivan standing beside her. "You have the same strong will and stubborn nature as your granduncle."

She turned to look at baby Nicki slumbering in her arms and smiled gently. The past was so far away. Yet that house up there on the hill bridged it solidly to the present. Mathilde's face rose before her. *Poor, unhappy woman always snarling, nagging, and seeing life merely as a burden to be borne with dignity. And Alex! His soul is bared for my scrutiny. He was a coward, a rapist, a bully, and he betrayed me. Yet his love for Sonya redeems him somewhat in my eyes.*

The rustle of the wind in the trees sounded like a human wail, and she recalled poor, demented Tanya's last days. Katie shuddered and could not control her tears. *I loved Tanya so. She was guilty of no wrong. Her only real weakness was her passion for Nicki.*

"Mama, why are you crying?" demanded her four-year-old.

"Because, Ivan, I feel a great sadness. Most of the people that I loved lived in that house, and now they are all dead."

With a wisdom beyond his years, the child remained silent.

For Katie, memories continued to unfold. *I can still hear the music that they played on the night of the ball. See beautiful, daring Sonya dancing before my eyes, only to be replaced instantly by the vision of her massive mane of raven hair spread out on the crimson-stained snow.* The image of little Leon at the bottom of the wolf pit rose next to torment her.

And Nicki! He belongs to this house too, dancing and laughing, captivating all of us. He is gone now, but his is the only link that has not been totally severed. She looked down again at his child and felt a sudden surge of tenderness. *Something positive has survived!*

There was one more place that she had to see. She put little Nicki against her shoulder, and clasping her other son's hand tightly, she trudged on again wearily through the darkness. Soon, Katie stood before the Sovinsky hut, which had now been greatly expanded. Tingling shivers of nostalgia ran up her spine as she recalled the ecstatic hours that she had spent inside this dwelling. They were such happy days. Full of peace and contentment. "I wonder who lives here now," she whispered into the darkness.

Yuri had told her of Maria's love, marriage, and migration to a new land. She had been happy about Maria's newfound joy, but at the same time, she was filled with a painful sense of loss. *My dear Maria, I shall probably never see you again. I shall always miss you so.*

As she stood before the cottage, the longing to see it again was too powerful for her to resist. There were no lights, so she knew that the occupants must be asleep. *What would they do if she woke them now? Surely they would think that she was insane,* a lone *woman with two small children, disturbing them at such an hour.* But since she had come this far, she could not bring herself to turn away. With the baby in her arms, she dragged little Ivan, now exhausted, to the front door and knocked softly.

No one answered.

Katie waited and then rapped again more loudly. Everything remained silent. Perhaps no one was at home. She started to move away but then turned back and reached for the doorknob. Opening the door, she peered into the darkened interior. Then she stepped inside and stumbled across the room to the cupboard where she located a candle and match.

The flickering flame flooded the room with a dim illumination, and Katie caught her breath. Very little change had been made. The cots were gone, but the rest of the furniture stood in the same place. A wide beam had been added to the ceiling overhead. A feeling of giddiness crept over her. *I once scorned Peter's offer to live in this hut. Yet later with Maria, I spent some of the most wonderful days of my life within these walls.* Then she whispered, "How wonderful it feels to be here again."

Taking the candle in her hand, she crept to the new bedroom and peered in. The huge bed had not been slept in that night. She sighed with relief and then crossed from the rear of the room to the side and opened the other unfamiliar door. She could hear the low regular breathing of someone sleeping in there.

She tiptoed in softly and stood over the child sleeping on one of the cots. The other two were empty. She shook the boy gently. He opened his eyes, and though surprised, no fear registered in them. "Where is your mother, little boy?" Katie asked him.

"I have none," he said.

"And your father?"

"He had to go to a meeting."

"Will he be back soon?"

The boy shook his head. "No, not for a while because he went far away tonight."

Katie felt relieved. "Do you think he would mind if we visited here for a few hours? You see, I used to live here once."

"No, I don't think he would mind," Vladimir said, staring at Katie.

"Good, then I will put my children here to sleep for a while," Katie said. She left the room, returned with her two sons, and tucked them in. Within minutes, the tired children were asleep. As Katie turned, she saw the confusion in the other child's face. "What's your name, little one?" she asked.

"Vladimir."

"I see. I hope that I have not disturbed you too much. You had better get under the blankets where it is warm," she said. She smiled, pushing the covers up under the boy's chin, and then she stooped and kissed him softly on his cheek.

Katie went back to the main room and set about building a fire in the hearth, which she sat close to once it had burst into flame. *It feels so good to be here again. It seems as if Maria's presence still lingers in this room.* Katie passed a contented hour sitting before the roaring fire before removing the kettle from the cupboard and filling it with water. After she had hung it over the fire, she returned to the cupboard to fetch the teapot.

Peter was surprised to see a light in his cottage at this time of night. He quickened his pace to cover the remaining distance to the hut, fearing that perhaps something was wrong with Vladimir.

He shoved the door open impatiently, and at the sudden noise, Katie whirled around. The teapot crashed to the floor. Peter gripped the doorknob, and his knees trembled violently.

Katie's hand flew to her mouth. Each stood staring speechlessly at the other. Recovering from his shock, Peter closed the door and leaned against it.

Katie found her voice first. "I've broken your teapot," she whispered in confusion. "I'll clean it up right away."

All at once, Peter burst into laughter. Katie viewed him with alarm. Her dismayed look immediately sobered him, and his laughter trailed off into silence. Though his voice was harsh, his eyes shone with amusement. "Forget the damn teapot, Katrina Kazakinova," he said.

And then he was across the room, and his lips found hers like a starving animal. Katie was instantly caught in his blazing passion. She fought for a few seconds to get her breath, but suddenly it did not matter. She let herself sink to a bottomless abyss.

His lips covered her eyes, ears, neck, and returned to her mouth hungrily. "Katie, Katie," he whispered. His intense desire purged her and ripped aside the final veneer of civilization. Neither spoke except to whisper the other's name with longing. Unable to bear the torture any longer, Peter lifted her up into his arms and carried her into his bedroom.

"I bought this majestic bed for you, Katie," he announced. "It has no rivals when it comes to beauty, and, countess, it has the most superb feather mattress!" With that, he dumped her unceremoniously upon his bed. Grinning good-naturedly, he crossed the room to shut the bedroom door and then began to disrobe. "I have waited so long for you, Katie!"

Katie awoke several hours later, a candle was burning. Peter sat up in bed, smoking. His eyes devoured her so hungrily that Katie led.

"Peter," she whispered.

"Don't talk, Katie," he said, bending down to kiss her tenderly.

"It has been so long, Peter."

"A lifetime," he said. "Where have you been?" And through the quiet hours of the night, Katie poured out her travels in distance, time, and pain. And he in turn told her of his own struggles, disillusionments, and the story of how he had found Vladimir.

"It has all been so terrible, Peter."

"I know," he agreed. "These past few years, all of Russia has been caught up in a storm that swelled the gentle streams of our lives into a frenzied deluge—gushing, surging, and changing everything in its path."

"You have become a philosopher, Peter."

"Perhaps," he grinned. "I've learned, though, that violence constantly boils beneath all of us. When the upheaval finally burst, everything was swept away. We have all had to learn to swim with the currents of this raging river or be drawn beneath."

"And the tide stayeth for no man," Katie quoted softly.

"For no man, Katie," Peter agreed. "The war and this revolution have all been part of this destructive turbulent tide, but I think the current is slackening. The frenzied waters are receding. Eventually, the river will return to its normal course."

"For how long, Peter?"

"That I don't know, Katie," he replied. "But there are always some of us who survive."

"Some of us who survive," she repeated. "And who go on living and loving."

"And the loving is the most important part."

"Well, on that subject," she laughed with an impish gleam in her eyes, "I wish to inform you that I was correct in my thinking at age sixteen."

"In what way?"

"It is infinitely sweeter making love in a feather bed!"

"You shameless hussy," he laughed, hitting her with his pillow. "You have lost all sense of modesty."

"I confess that it's true," she declared, throwing her arms passionately around his neck, and once again they made love.

"I shall never get enough of you, Countess Katrina Kazakinova."

"I should hope not, Peter Sovinsky," she said, trying to suppress her mirth. "It would be absolutely shocking for me to have to go shopping around for a new lover at my advanced age."

"Hussy," he quipped again, pulling her back into his arms.

"But now we must be serious, Peter," she said, drawing back from him. "I have not told you the most important thing of all. I have two children."

She searched his face, but no trace of emotion crossed it.

"Then we have three children, Katie," he said. A surge of joy rushed through her at his quiet words.

"You don't mind?"

He smiled at her. "Nothing matters now that you are mine."

Katie reached out and grasped his hand. "Come, you must see them."

They rose and dressed hastily. Katie led him to the room where the children slumbered. She led him first to little Nikolai and put the candle close to his face. The sleeping cherub opened his eyes and burst into a contented smile. "Mama!"

Katie turned to study Peter's face. One eyebrow was raised thoughtfully as he scrutinized the baby's face.

"What do you think of him?" she asked anxiously.

"Truthfully, there can be no question of his parentage," he stated.

"Does it matter so much, Peter?" Katie asked with alarm.

"I would be a liar if I said I didn't mind at all," he answered. "But surprisingly, I do not mind as much as I thought I might. After all, he is half yours. As for Sokoloy, the problem was always that I was so jealous of him because of you. Sometimes when you were riding with him, I felt my heart would break. He had good looks, breeding, wealth, position, a title, and all the social graces that I lacked. I was filled with rage because there was no way that I could ever compete with him." He sighed and held his head off to one side while studying the child.

"Yet I never felt anything personal against Sokoloy himself. He was superior to your uncle and cousins because he was a man of honor. He fought with courage against the Germans. Then when our civil war erupted, he again fought with dignity for what he believed in, just as I did. Had circumstances been different, we might have been friends. I think if Sokoloy's son grows up to be even half the man his father is, then I will be proud to have him bear my name." Peter bent down and kissed the child gently.

"And Katie," he added, standing erect again. "He will bear my name. We will be married by this friend of yours called Yuri."

"Oh, Peter," Katie whispered softly and reached up and kissed his forehead. "I love you so."

...ne here and see Ivan," whispered Kate, and she laid the candle ...ldest son.

... frowned at the sound of that hated name, but when he stooped to see ...nbering child, he caught his breath.

What do you think of him, Peter?" she asked. "There can be no question ...his parentage either, can there?"

A softness crept into Peter's eyes. "When, Katie?"

"The night of your raid on the manor."

"But you never told me!"

"No, I didn't want it to influence any decision that you made about us."

"But it wasn't right of you not to tell me, Katie!"

"I know," she agreed. "But it doesn't matter now, Peter. The past is gone. We cannot change it. For what it is worth, Nicki was equally willing to raise your son and give Ivan his name."

"Then at least I can repay that debt of honor," he said. "I have been such a fool. I was so corroded by a false philosophy. I've so much to make up for." He reached down and stroked the dark-haired boy's face, and the child opened his solemn brown eyes. "Hello, son! It is good to have you home," he said.

Ivan sat up and looked questioningly at his mother.

"Yes, dear," she said. "This is your father."

Ivan put out his small hand, and Peter grasped it firmly.

"It seems we now have three fine sons, Katie," Peter assessed. "I think we should try for a daughter next."

"Well yes," she said, "considering that fine feather bed in there, I don't think we should let it go to waste."

Peter started laughing and then shouted to Vladimir. "Wake up, sleepyhead. I want you to meet the rest of your family."

Vladimir sat up in confusion.

"Come here, son," Peter called out with rapture in his voice. "I want you to meet your new mother, Katie, and these are your brothers, Ivan and Nicki!"

Vladimir stepped timidly across the room, looked into Katie's face, and then shyly lowered his eyes. She laughed softly and stooped down to kiss him lightly on the top of his head. "Love us, Vladimir, as we are going to love you."

"Look," Peter said, pointing toward the window, "the sun is rising. Shall we go out and see it?"

With baby Nicki in his arms, Peter led the way while Katie followed with the other two children. Standing together in the earliest hour of the dawn, Peter put his arm around Kate's waist and drew her close. Vladimir clung tightly to Katie with one hand and grasped little Ivan's hand with the other.

As they stood silhouetted against the vanishing night, a profusion of colo spread across the sky with streaks of red, orange, pink, and yellow blende majestically together.

"It's like a brilliant painting," Katie whispered. "A luminous blazing aurora of promise."

"Yes," Peter said. "Our sunrise assures us eternally that beauty will always be reborn and that the first blush of morning with its radiating light always erases the black shadows of the nocturnal hours."

"Yes," Katie echoed. "It's the birth of a new day in which men may reach out with hope to one another in brotherhood and love."

"Or at least in the hope of a hope of brotherhood and love," Peter amended.

As the sun slowly climbed into the heavens, it sent out its strong crimson rays of light, and the nebulous shades of darkness began to fade.

ON ANY PARTICULAR DAY

Your people have suffered under you, Mother Russia . . .
muzhiks in the fields under the Czars,
monks driven into caves during the red resurrection,
and modern-day men in factories.
There has been wailing in the wheat lands,
crime and punishment in Siberia,
an icy house of the dead in the Gulags.
Still your masses etch their pain
in poetry, art, and literature.
The haunting melody of the Volga boatman
soothes their hearts when the Baltic winds bear down
and blizzards blast the landscape.
Hands reach out with hope,
but the great bear slaps out his tyrannical paw.
Truth is torn to fragments,
and the cosmic clouds of Chernobyl
once again blind their vision.

Ruth Wildes Schuler

CPSIA information can be obtained
at www.ICGtesting.com
Printed in the USA
LVHW08s0138100818
586431LV00001B/14/P